Perfec...
Ordin...y
People

Perfectly Ordinary People

nick alexander

LAKE UNION
PUBLISHING

Text copyright © 2022 by Nick Alexander
All rights reserved.

No part of this book may be reproduced, or stored in a retrieval system, or transmitted in any form or by any means, electronic, mechanical, photocopying, recording, or otherwise, without express written permission of the publisher.

Published by Lake Union Publishing, Seattle

www.apub.com

Amazon, the Amazon logo, and Lake Union Publishing are trademarks of Amazon.com, Inc., or its affiliates.

ISBN-13: 9781542032476
ISBN-10: 1542032474

Cover design by @blacksheep-uk.com

Cover illustration by Jelly London

Printed in the United States of America

For Ethel and Pierra; for Pierre and Jo.
For anyone who ever needed courage
to love against the odds.
And for those whose dreams of love were cut short.
May we never forget them.

Prologue.

Tall Tale #1: Living With Wolves.

Did I ever tell you the story about the man who replaced his guard dogs with wolves?

He was a rustic young farmer with a huge moustache – we'll call him Moustache to make things easier – living out in a remote village called La Vieille-Loye at the western edge of Alsace, right in the middle of a forest. He'd been struggling for years with the local wolves that continually visited, killing his sheep anytime they fancied a snack.

Some nights, in summer, he could lose ten or even twenty sheep in a single night, and that made him incredibly sad, because not only were his sheep his livelihood, but he loved them, giving them names and treating them like pets. The wolves didn't always seem to kill because they were genuinely hungry, either. He knew this because sometimes they would kill twenty sheep and only eat three of them. So it seemed to him that they were killing just for fun.

When Moustache spoke to the other farmers, they advised him to get some Pyrenean Mountain Dogs – in French they call them *patou*. These are huge dogs with shaggy white fur, and what the farmers do is to raise them with the sheep from the moment they're born. That way these dogs end up thinking they are sheep as well and, because they think the sheep they live with are their mothers and brothers and sisters, they'll do anything they can to protect them, even laying down their own lives.

So that's what this farmer did. He bought three baby *patou* dogs and he raised them to think they were sheep. And for years afterwards he didn't lose a single animal, because the *patou* would scare off any marauding wolves.

But one day, when he was in his thirties, he went down to his field and found that a massacre had taken place overnight. Not only had the wolves killed ten of his sheep, but they'd killed all three guard dogs as well. Why had they killed them? Well, the dogs believed they were sheep, and so I think the wolves just thought the same thing.

Now Moustache loved those dogs even more than he loved his sheep, so this made him very, very angry.

He thought about replacing them but worried that any new dogs would also be killed by the wolves.

After a few days thinking about the problem, he came up with what he thought was a better idea. Instead of dogs, he would raise wolves to think they were sheep. The only problem was getting hold of wolf cubs, but he asked around until someone told him about a wolf breeder in the South of France.

That was a very long way from where Moustache lived, but he decided to go and get them anyway. It took him two days and about ten trains to get there, and two days and ten different trains to get back.

But finally home with the three baby wolves he'd bought – they were still tiny and fluffy and cute – he put them in with the sheep. And he was in luck, because one of the sheep, who'd just given birth, fed the wolves, letting them suckle alongside her lambs.

When these wolves grew up, his plan worked perfectly, because the wolves were convinced that they too were sheep. And whenever any wolves tried to attack his flock, the wolf-sheep would defend the real sheep and chase the wild wolves away.

This worked well for years, but then one day, at the beginning of the Second World War, the Germans invaded Alsace, and everywhere they went they robbed and killed and plundered.

Eventually some very bad soldiers happened upon the remote village where our farmer lived. Luckily he was out at the market that day, because otherwise the soldiers would no doubt have killed him. Instead they started killing the sheep, initially because they thought they might want to eat them, but then because, just like the wolves, they decided that killing was fun.

When the wolf-sheep heard all the commotion they came bounding over the hill, and when they saw what was happening to their brethren – because wolves are very intelligent, you know – they ran so fast across the fields that the Germans didn't even have time to shoot them. They leapt at them and with single bites ripped out their throats, killing them as easily as sheep.

By the time the farmer got home, everything was calm again. There were three dead sheep lying at one end of the field but he was surprised to see that they hadn't been killed by wolves but had been shot. His wolf-sheep looked fatter than usual, and rather sad, as if they were maybe grieving the deaths of the three sheep, one of which was the ewe that had suckled them when they were cubs.

But it was only at the end of summer when he happened to cross the field in exactly the right spot that he was able to work out what had happened during his absence at the market that day. Because he found something strange in that field: three German soldiers' helmets, and three German rifles.

But that's *all* he ever found. There were no arms, no legs, no swastikas, no uniforms, no boots . . . Turns out that his trusty wolf-sheep had not only killed those German soldiers, but they'd eaten every last crumb!

Ruth. Part One.

My grandfather Chris told us a lot of rather gruesome stories that my parents didn't entirely approve of, and he always began them with the phrase, 'Did I ever tell you about . . . ?'

There weren't that many different tales, so I can only remember about ten of them, but when we were little and we saw him, he would sit us down and tell us a story without fail. We never tired of hearing them, either – especially the scary ones. In fact it would be true to say that the repetition made our excitement, our anticipation, even greater. Our eyes would widen at the first mention of the wolves and our mouths would drop as we awaited to learn the fates – awful fates we already knew – of those evil German soldiers.

My grandparents had divorced before I was born, though in a rather bizarre fashion they'd continued to live in the same building. It was all, apparently, quite amicable.

Grandpa had rented a bedsit upstairs while Grandma Genny remained in the marital home, which, for financial reasons, she shared with her cousin, a woman we referred to as 'Aunty' Ethel.

We didn't see a great deal of either of them, and I never really knew why that was. With them living over in Vauxhall while we were back home in Walthamstow, getting together more frequently would hardly have been a logistical nightmare, but that's just how things were.

We would see them once before Christmas, when they would drop by to deliver our gifts, and once before each of our birthdays for the same reason. And because things had never been any different, we never really questioned it.

In the seventies, Grandma Genny moved away and Grandpa Chris reclaimed the original, larger apartment.

As I say, we'd never seen a great deal of either of them, but once Genny was an epic forty-five-minute train journey away in Brighton, she all but vanished from our lives. Oh, she'd come up to London once or twice a year and have lunch with Dad, and if my brother and I weren't at school or with Mum or out on a play date – basically if Dad was having to look after us – then he'd take us along. But there was always a weird feeling that something wasn't quite right. The conversations he had with his mother were shockingly bland: how was her Billy doing? Did he have a lot of work on? How were we doing at school? If you've ever had to have lunch with a stranger, you know the kind of mundane conversation I'm talking about.

Looking back on it, I think one of the reasons things seemed stilted was that Dad never reciprocated by asking Grandma Genny about herself, merely answering in the most efficient way possible so it felt more like an awkward interview than lunch between mother and son.

But she was lovely to Jake and me – don't get me wrong. She always brought sweets or a toy, or some clothes, and she always gave us a lipsticky kiss and sat us on her lap for a cuddle. So I liked her. It's just that we saw so little of her that I never felt entirely at ease. We saw so little of them both.

My mother's family, on the other hand, were omnipresent. Being Irish Catholic and with her mother and brothers living less than a mile away, they completely filled any family-shaped void we might have had. On any given day we'd receive drop-in visits from at least two of Mum's three brothers – usually around meal-times – and as for Grandma Siobhan, who everyone referred to as Mavaughn, Dad used to joke that she spent so much time at ours she should pay rent. Her husband, Mum's father, had died when Mavaughn was in her thirties, so I suppose she had her own husband-shaped void to fill.

Overall, we were a happy family, and I consider my childhood quite gilded, especially when compared with the horror stories told by some of my friends. Dad was a mellow, happy-go-lucky sort of chap, and Mum a warm, generous homemaker who liked to hug everyone constantly, and that included her kids. I got on well with both my parents and for the most part with big brother Jake as well. In a way, I think that thanks to Grandma Siobhan and my three uncles (plus wives), and their numerous children – our cousins – there was so much coming and going through our house that it was hard to concentrate long enough to develop any kind of grudge. Mum always complained that the place was 'like Connolly Station', but with a special half-smile that revealed just how much she loved it that way.

We weren't rich, but we never lacked for anything, and our house was full of noise, and fun, and love.

My point in telling you this is to say that if things had been different, if we'd had needs that hadn't been met, whether material, spiritual or emotional, then we might have made more effort to get to know our paternal grandparents, or at least to question why they were so distant . . . And knowing what I know now, that's almost certainly something that would have enriched all of our lives. But I didn't feel I had any unmet needs – none of us did. And so that distance remained essentially unnoticed, their absence barely felt.

Jake and I did well at school. Jake was – is – the geeky one. He excelled at physics and science and geometry: in a nutshell, the subjects that made my brain bleed. He ended up studying computer science and now works as a network engineer, whatever that might be. Occasionally he'll try to explain it to me but something weird happens every time, and I can sense my mind glazing over just the way it used to during geometry lessons in that awful hot classroom way back when.

I, on the other hand, am the arty-farty one – that's what Jake says. He actually introduces me that way, as in, 'Do come over here and meet my arty-farty sister.' He doesn't mean it in a bad way though. I've always been aware that he's proud of my arty-fartyness.

Even as a child, I was into drawing and photography and poetry, though I shan't be inflicting any of my poems on you.

Mum pushed me towards the arts quite heavily, exorcising her own unrealised ambitions, I suspect, by enrolling me in dance classes and theatre workshops, buying me paints, a weaving loom and a sewing machine. But I thrived on it all and, as I say, we both ended up doing pretty well: Jake in Birmingham learning to be a network engineer and me at Exeter studying English lit. To everyone's relief, we both found jobs after college without any problems at all.

Throughout uni I told friends that I wanted to be a writer, but if I'm honest it was more the concept that appealed rather than the actual work involved. I'd picture myself working from home in my pyjamas, sipping cups of tea and sucking thoughtfully on a pencil, and that seemed like a great way to make a living. The only problem was that I had no actual desire to *write*. Specifically, my concentration isn't great, so the idea of sitting down to work on a single project for months on end has always given me the heebie-jeebies. So at some point in my twenties, I stopped mentioning my illusive-yet-imminent novel and gave up on ever publishing a book. Until now, that is. Let's see how I do with this little non-fiction project.

After college I got a job in journalism, working for a local rag, which seemed to suit my butterfly nature much better, and then in the nineties I went to a PR company, before ending up in the job I do today.

I'm an acquisitions editor for a minor London publisher you won't have heard of (we're called Impressionable – see?) and that basically means I get to read manuscripts all day while, you guessed it, wearing my pyjamas, drinking tea and thoughtfully sucking on a pencil.

My friends seem to think I've got the world's cushiest job, but that's merely because they fail to realise just how dreadful most of the dross on the slush pile is. The things I have to plough my way through . . . There are no words to describe just how bad most of it is.

As you have probably guessed, Jake and I have very differ-ent personalities. He's a practical, methodical, rather reasonable sort of chap, while I tend towards vague, flighty and emotional. Jake, for instance, had precisely three girlfriends during college, one for each year he was there, while I was single for two years – a period I used to refer to as the Great Desert Crossing – followed by three passionate, overlapping affairs with otherwise involved men. The overlapping bit was complicated while the otherwise involved aspect surprisingly wasn't. After these came a brief three-day love affair with a pretty holidaymaker from Tokyo called Sakura. Of the four, I'd have to admit that the one I loved the most was, without a doubt, Saky. But the sex thing . . . was . . . Look, I don't want to go into details, so let's just say I tried it and it wasn't for me. Whereas sex with men . . . Well . . . Never had any problems there.

In a nutshell, my love-life was as dramatic and amorphic as Jake's was methodical and geometric, which raises the question of how two people who share that much DNA can be so radically different. Because as everyone constantly reminds us, we *look* like identical twins.

What kept me sane throughout these crazy shenanigans was my friendship with touchstone Gina. Gina defines herself as flexisexual, which means that she alternates between guys (mainly) and girls (occasionally). She doesn't, like, care about gender, yeah? She only, like, cares about the person who's, like, inside. Obvs.

And before your mind goes there, there's never been a hint of romance between us. If I'd been able to be with a woman, it would have been Saky, and it would have lasted for eternity. But the sex thing just wasn't possible, and as I can't imagine living without sex, that, pretty much, was that.

If I need a drinking buddy, Gina's a drinking buddy, and if I want to go dancing then she's up for it. If I'm sad and need someone to listen to my moaning then she's the most sympathetic ear I could hope for, and if I need to shop for clothes then she's just about to go shopping herself. The list of Gina's strong points just goes on and on.

So other than her tiny, admittedly annoying tendency to insert the words *like* and *obvs* at random points in every sentence, she's, obvs, like, a perfect friend.

Christmas at our place tended to be wonderful. During my teenage years I rebelled from time to time by insisting on spending Christmas at a friend's house but it was never a patch on our Christmases because, though there might have been better-dressed participants or a video game to play, though there were sometimes more gifts – and I remember one, in particular, where the pile of gifts was so high, so *obscene*, that the sight of them all ploughing their way through them made me feel physically sick – they simply weren't as much fun as Christmas back home.

The major reason for this was that at our place the drinking started before lunch, which meant that the present opening was *drunken* present opening, and charades meant *drunken* charades . . . And when you combined alcohol with the fact that Christmas rarely involved less than fifteen participants, and when you threw into the mix the genes from the Irish side of our family that make us the happiest drunks on Earth, what you got was a level of fun and mayhem that was just about impossible to beat.

Christmas at our house was, without exception, 'good craic' and that lasted right through until 1994, the year when everything went wrong.

Why was '94 different? Well, to start with, Jake and I threw some random elements into the mix by inviting guests – Jake bringing new girlfriend Abby along and me, Gina. Gina's family were spending Christmas on Bondi Beach and being a redhead who peels at the sight of a low-energy lightbulb, the only thing that Gina hates more than Australian men (ex-boyfriend, don't ask) is sunshine. It seemed the perfect occasion for her to discover the craziness of a Solomas Christmas.

But the main thing that changed that year, the tiny element with unimagined destructive power, was a board game called Scruples.

The day got off to a promising start, Uncle Tom arriving early with a five-litre keg of Guinness and a bottle of Bushmills, and Uncle Harry with a litre of Bombay Sapphire and a six-pack of tonic water. Lucky Uncle Eirla was holidaying in Thailand, so he avoided all the drama.

Mavaughn was on fine form, wafting around in a black velvet dress and dispensing a stream of constant, unwanted advice while simultaneously sipping at her Baileys.

Newbie guests Gina and Abby were a bit wide-eyed at it all, but that threw them together in a way that a boring sit-down meal never could have, so that within an hour they'd become tipsy new best friends.

The temperature was incredibly mild that year, and the sun even shone a little, which removed the only issue that ever caused any kind of conflict in our house – the requirement to smoke out back.

So yes, everything was panning out just fine.

Christmas dinner came next, and that was a success too. Sure, the turkey was burnt and the sprouts overcooked, but these were such standard features of Christmas dinner that they merely made everyone laugh. And though I could tell Abby was a bit shocked by Harry's rude jokes, and though I suspected Gina couldn't understand a single word Mavaughn said, everyone got on just fine.

And then we played Scruples.

Now if you've never played Scruples, a brief explanation is required.

As far as I recall, cards are dealt, and the first person to get rid of theirs is declared winner. Each card features a moral dilemma such as, 'You are offered five thousand pounds to pose naked for a magazine. Do you accept?'

The person holding the question card chooses an answer card from a pile, and if it says 'Yes' for example, then they must address the question to the person they think is most likely to agree, in this example the person most likely to say, 'Yes, for five grand I'd pose naked.' If the reply corresponds with the answer they're holding, or if the respondent fails to convince the majority that they honestly wouldn't pose naked, then the cardholder wins. I think that's how it works, anyway.

The point is that it's an awful game that inevitably leads to some poor soul arguing with his entire (in our case drunken) family that 'No, he would NOT steal a ten-pound note left in the check-out zone' while said family shouts for blood by insisting that YES, he knows damned well that he would, and they all know it too.

For half an hour we resisted the temptation to fall out. Tom declared he wouldn't sleep with the best man's girlfriend, *even if she was the most beautiful woman he'd ever seen*, and for the sake of family unity, we pretended to believe him.

Gina said that yes, she would go hungry for a week to save a starving chimpanzee, and everyone voted that they believed her. Totally true, that one, by the way. That girl would die to save a worm.

But then Uncle Tom asked my father the following question and it was like pulling the pin from a grenade: *Your teenage daughter is dating a young man of another race or religion. Do you try to break them up?*

Gina caused the first ripple by saying, 'How do they know she'd be dating, like, a man, anyway? She might be dating, like, a woman.' This caused Mum and Dad to shoot worried frowns in my direction.

The answer on Tom's card – though we didn't yet know it – was a 'No', so in directing the question at my father, he was giving him the benefit of the doubt.

But Dad surprised everyone by saying, 'Yes, I'd possibly try to break them up,' which initially, because we thought he was bluffing, made us laugh.

But when Dad began to argue, quite convincingly, that certain religions and races 'just weren't compatible' the debate started to get heated. In particular Cousin Jim, who was dating a black girl back then (not present), began to get pretty arsey.

Mavaughn kept reminding everyone that it was 'just a game' but what she'd failed to see was that by that point it no longer was.

Finally Jim, fuelled by three beers, half a bottle of wine and a couple of whiskeys, tackled Dad directly. 'Aisha's black,' he said. 'And her dad's a Rastafarian, too. So are you saying that you don't approve? Are you saying that she wouldn't have been welcome if I'd brought her because she's the wrong colour?'

'Of course not!' Dad replied. 'I've got nothing against blacks at all. How could you even think such a thing?'

A sigh of relief went around the table and Mavaughn refilled the three nearest glasses with whiskey without really caring who they belonged to. It was her way of demonstrating we'd moved on.

But then Dad continued. 'It's not so much race that's the problem, in my opinion. The problem these days is *religion*.'

Now he was drunk, I'll give him that. He was actually red-in-the-face drunk. So I think that everyone, with the possible exception of his devoutly Catholic mother-in-law, would have been able to swallow that single slip up and move on. If only he had let us do so.

But then he continued, looking, for some reason at me, saying, 'Suppose he was Muslim! Suppose your imaginary boyfriend was a Muslim who wanted you to wear a burka or whatever.'

'Oh, for fuck's sake, Dad,' I said. 'Could you be any more clichéd?'

Dad was looking embarrassed and panicky by this point, but he's never been good at quitting while he's ahead. His efforts to extricate himself generally have the effect of digging a little deeper, and never more so than when drunk.

He looked around the room and saw that everyone was staring at him. Even Mavaughn was gritting her teeth.

'Or Jewish,' Dad said then, which presumably was supposed to make things better. 'I'm not singling out Muslims in particular. Any of the daft religions will do.'

'Oh, do shut your gob, will you, Billy?' Mum said, which from her was pretty shocking.

'Don't tell me to shut my gob, woman!' Dad snapped back. Then, turning to the rest of us, 'I'm just saying that sometimes their beliefs aren't compatible with ours, that's all.'

'Jewish . . .' Jake repeated flatly. 'So, how would *that* be incompatible Dad? Do tell.'

Now, for most of his teens Jake had been a real lads' lad, playing rugby and telling inappropriate jokes. Since meeting Abby, however, his corrosive sense of humour had become a thing of the past. He was on a mission to prove just how profound his transformation to 'new man' was, and though for the most part I approved of the change, his political correctness could occasionally get on my nerves.

Dad, as so often, was clueless. He shrugged and, having mistakenly interpreted Jake's relaxed tone as a sign that the worst was now over, slumped back in his chair.

'I don't know,' he said. 'Suppose Ruth brought home some Jewish chap who started making a fuss about our sausages. Or refusing to use light switches on a Saturday or whatever.'

'Our sausages?' Jake said.

'Yeah. They don't eat pork, do they? I mean, there's nothing wrong with a bit of pork. If you don't like bacon, you don't like life, that's what I say.'

'You've never seemed to object when people are vegetarian,' Jake said. He was starting to look a bit red in the face. I was worried about where this was heading.

'Well, that's different, isn't it?' Dad said.

'So it's OK to avoid pork if you're veggie, but not because you're Jewish?'

'Yes. Because being veggie's about loving animals, isn't it? It isn't about trying to demonstrate you're some kind of master race because you have divine knowledge about what God thinks everyone should eat.'

'Um, I don't think the Jews were actually the ones to claim they were a master race, Dad,' I pointed out.

'No,' Jake said. 'That's another pretty ignorant statement.'

'Don't,' Abby said, laying her hand on Jake's. 'It's not worth it.'

'And yet,' Dad said, 'there they are, running all the banks and what have you. Running the bloody world. They're all Jews, aren't they? All the millionaires, the billionaires. They may not have said it out loud, but they certainly act like they think they're a master race.'

'Dad, please stop,' I pleaded. 'This is . . .'

'Yes,' Jake said. 'Please do shut the fuck up.'

'What?!' Dad shouted, banging the flat of his hand on the table. 'What did you just say to me, boy?'

'Boy? Did you actually call me "boy"?'

'I did. And I must say, you're sounding pretty infantile to me.'

Jake stood up so fast that his chair fell backwards. 'Fuck this,' he said. 'Come on, Abs, we're leaving.' And before his neighbour could even pick up the chair, both he and Abby were gone.

'Oh, well done!' Mavaughn said, nodding exaggeratedly as she too stood and exited the dining room. 'You've really done us proud this year.'

'What?' Dad asked. 'How is that idiot telling me to shut up my fault? In my own home! Jesus!'

'Oh, let's throw a little blasphemy into the mix!' Mum said, standing and following her mother out into the hallway. 'That always helps.'

Within a minute, about half of the family was gone. Most of them were only out in the back garden lighting up, but the effect of their exodus felt quite brutal.

Those of us who remained sat in ghastly silence. Harry ran a finger around the rim of his glass until it sang.

'Would someone explain to me what just happened?' Dad eventually asked.

'*Abigail*,' Gina said pointedly. 'Abigail's what happened, obvs.'

'Abigail?' Dad repeated. 'Jake's girlfriend?'

'I think Abigail might be a Jewish name,' Uncle Tom said.

'Not sure about the name,' Gina said, 'but Abigail is definitely Jewish. She was just telling me what they did for Hanukkah.'

'Christ,' Dad said. 'I didn't realise. If I'd known, I wouldn't have said anything.'

'But is it true?' I asked. 'That's what's important here. *Do* you disapprove of Jake dating Abby because she's Jewish?'

'Well, I didn't know,' Dad said.

'But now you do know. So do you disapprove? Do you think she believes she's part of a master race?'

'Just say no,' Tom advised him.

'No,' Dad said. 'No, of course not. *Disapprove* would be too strong a word for it. That said, I could hardly say that I'm keen. Look at the effect she's had on Christmas! We've never had arguments like this before, have we?'

'Not keen?' I said. 'Oh wow!'

'Yeah,' Gina said. 'Like, wow.'

'I'm just saying out loud what everyone else is thinking,' Dad said.

'Which is?'

'That if she hadn't been here, everything would have been fine.'

'That's not what everyone's thinking, Dad,' I said. 'What everyone's thinking is that you're a knob.'

'Don't you start as well,' Dad said. 'You're not too old for me to put you over my knee.'

'Um, I actually am too old for that,' I said; then, because anger was rising up within me, I stood. 'Shall we go too, Gina? I'm not that keen on the atmosphere here today.'

16

It took us five minutes to say goodbye to everyone in the smoky backyard, and by the time we stepped out front, Dad was there sitting on the wall.

We loaded our gifts into the trunk of Gina's Fiesta and then, as she climbed in and started the engine, I returned to speak to my father. He looked so forlorn that I felt sorry for him.

'Phone Jake and apologise,' I told him. 'And do it like you mean it.'

'I will,' Dad replied. 'Of course I will.'

'Good,' I said, and I let him give me a hug.

But then he glanced at the waiting car and gave a little nod. 'What she said, your friend, Gina . . . You're not, are you?'

'Not what?' I honestly wasn't following his drift.

'You're not . . . into the ladies . . . are you?' he asked.

'Why?' I asked, starting to bristle all over again. 'Would that be a problem as well?'

Dad shrugged. 'Not, you know, really. Not in a big way. Though I'm not sure your mother would be thrilled, either.'

'Either?' I repeated.

'I only mean it wouldn't be ideal . . .' Dad started.

But the anger was still upon me. I was so disappointed in him, that was the thing. Because in the space of half an hour, he'd shifted from being the tolerant, generous centre of my world – someone I'd always been proud of – to an Islamophobic, anti-Semitic, homophobic old dobber. It was like I'd stepped into some dreadful 1970s sitcom.

'Yeah, you got me. I'm a lesbian,' I muttered. 'And as soon as it's legal, me and Gina are going to get married. Oh and Gina's a Muslim, by the way. She forgot her burka today, that's all. Just in case you were wondering.'

And with that I climbed into the car and slammed the door.

'Why did you say that?' Gina asked. 'Why did you, like, tell him I'm a Muslim?'

'Just drive, will you?' I said. 'Just drive and get me out of here, OK?'

And Gina, being Gina . . . Gina being the perfect friend, she did exactly that.

◆　◆　◆

So, yes . . . Christmas dinner was the start of The Great Falling Out, as we came to call it. Jake and Dad didn't speak for months.

Dad did call Jake to apologise as instructed, it's just that Jake had caller ID and refused to take Dad's call. Faced with Jake's answerphone, Dad left a stuttering, abrupt message which – though I'm sure the lacklustre nature of his apology had more to do with Dad's dislike of voicemail than any reticence to apologise, per se – Jake interpreted as 'absence of remorse'. They were stuck in silly, angry stasis.

Jake and I stayed in touch, and Mum, ever the peacemaker, played go-between so that everyone continued to know slightly more about everyone else's business than they needed or indeed wanted. But none of the news – not Jake cutting the top of his thumb off with a Stanley knife in February, invisibly stitched back on at A&E, nor Dad becoming bedridden with the flu in March, was enough to convince either of them to pick up the phone. In the end, it wasn't until October that they spoke again, and in our family, such discord was unprecedented.

I tried to talk Jake round but he was being stubborn about it all. In addition to providing a perfect opportunity to demonstrate to Abby how PC he was, I felt that the argument had come at the perfect time for him. He was busy with a new job and increasingly involved with Abby's extended family. He was in need, I suspected, of some distance from our rather suffocating clan. So though what Dad had said was totally unacceptable, and though Jake was understandably mortified that Abby had witnessed such a spectacle, I couldn't help but think that the repercussions had been amplified for the simple reason that the resulting 'time out' suited him.

The person who turned out to be the most forgiving about the whole episode was Abby herself. I had dinner in a restaurant in Soho with them both a month after Christmas and Abby explained that she was 'pretty used to low-level anti-Semitism' and that it was 'far more common than people tend to realise'. She had learned to brush such comments aside, she said, because otherwise she'd just be annoyed all the time, and what was the point in that? 'If Jake hadn't made us leave, I probably wouldn't even have remembered it,' she told me, and though that seemed unlikely, it has to be said that she seemed pretty authentic when she said it. She even made a joke about how Dad was right, and not using light switches on Saturdays could get incredibly complicated, which was why she was dating a 'goy' so that he could operate all the electrical items for her instead.

But when, laughing, I turned to face Jake, I saw he was staring intently out of the restaurant window, pretending that this conversation wasn't even happening. When Abby moved the subject on to my job, and Jake snapped back into the room, I understood that the subject had become taboo, even between them. And from that I deduced that Abby, too, had been trying (and failing) to talk Jake down from the ledge he'd got himself stuck upon.

So no contact whatsoever between Dad and Jake from Christmas until October. And I don't think they would have come together even then had it not been for a death in the family. Yes, it actually took a death before they would talk.

Dad wasn't the one to tell Jake; in fact, if I hadn't happened to visit them that Sunday in October, I'm not sure that he would have even told me.

It was a sunny afternoon, and I found Mum stacking the dishwasher while Dad, in the back garden, slept off all the chicken he'd eaten. Tom and Harry had gone to the pub, while their wives had taken the kids to Lloyd Park.

I chatted with Mum for a bit – she told me that Harry was 'still made up despite everything', because he'd won £600 a month before betting on Frank Bruno. 'Such a shallow boy, that one,' she said.

I should have twigged at the 'despite everything', but I must have only been half listening. I told Mum I was going to go out and say 'Hi' to Dad, and she said, 'Go easy on him. He's more upset than he's making out.'

I froze in the doorway and looked back at her in puzzlement. 'Upset about what?' I asked.

'Well, about his mother!' Mum said, her head almost inside the dishwasher. 'I know they weren't close, but your mother's still your mother. You only get one. You'll find that out one day.'

She straightened then and with a flick of her foot followed by a tap with one knee, deftly closed the dishwasher door. Then she looked at me searchingly before saying, 'Oh, Jaysus! Billy didn't tell you, did he?'

Mum explained that Grandma Genny had died. It was lung cancer, she said. She'd been 'battling it for years'. Which though I'd known she smoked 'like a fireman', as we like to say in our family, was also news to me.

Mum crossed the kitchen and caressed my shoulder. 'Are you OK?' she asked. 'Because you look a bit peaky.'

It was undeniable that I was feeling a bit strange, but for a while I couldn't work out why. I think, with hindsight, that I was momentarily submerged by a complex set of emotions that would take a few days to unravel.

In the end I managed to sift through them, and worked out that I was feeling:

a) shocked that Dad hadn't told me my grandmother had died, and

b) guilty that I hadn't even known she was ill, and

c) ashamed that I hadn't spoken to her in a decade, let alone given her any support or care during her illness.

But above all, the thing upsetting me was that:

d) I had definitively missed the boat; I'd lost the chance to get to know her forever, and that seemed incredibly sad, and suddenly quite shockingly incomprehensible.

As I explained before, we had a big, busy, bustling family life, so Genny's absence from our lives had rarely been noticed. But I realised in that moment that I'd had a semi-conscious background plan to get to know her at some point, and the fact that the moment that plan moved into consciousness was the exact moment it became impossible to achieve – because she was gone – left me feeling quite heartbroken.

'The funeral's on Wednesday,' Mum said. 'Will you be able to come? I know your dad would like you to be there.'

And though it seemed unlikely that the man who'd failed to even inform me of her illness wanted me there at all, I managed to not raise an eyebrow. Instead I nodded and accepted the hug she was offering. 'I'll be there,' I said. 'Of course I'll be there. She was my grandmother.'

The funeral took place in Brighton and, though I'd struggle to put my finger on a specific reason, I did find the whole thing pretty strange. Not that I'm an expert on funerals or anything – I'd only ever been to one before that, and that was when I was nine. But everything struck me as inexplicably weird that day – like an uncomfortable dream, or a slightly surrealist play.

Dad must have known it was going to be peculiar, because he told me repeatedly that I didn't need to be there. But every time he said it, Mum would contradict him, sometimes with actual words but more often than not with a complex glance or a raised eyebrow. The only thing Mum believes in more than ritual is family, and as funerals combine both, I knew she expected us to go.

But I wanted to go, anyway. I wanted to see Grandpa Chris and Aunty Ethel and anyone else who might turn up.

I couldn't make up for the lost years – I knew that – but I could, I hoped, at least get a glimpse of who my grandmother had been by studying her friendships.

Most of my family drove down to Brighton, each in their own petrol-powered bubble, but partly because I don't have a car and mainly because I really like trains, that's how I chose to travel. Eirla offered me a lift in his massive BMW, but the idea of watching the countryside slip silently past seemed so much more attractive than a car full of shouting kids that I resisted. When I saw how frazzled they all looked on arrival, I was glad of the choice I'd made.

The venue was surprisingly pretty. I couldn't remember much from my friend's mother's funeral when I was nine, but I did remember that it had taken place in a horrible modern building. Woodvale's grassy grounds and church-like architecture came as a bit of a relief.

It was a biggish gathering in the end, thanks largely to the multitudinous nature of Mum's side of the family. Uncles Tom, Harry and Eirla were present with wives Tracey, Suzie and Pippa. All seven of their offspring, from six years old to twenty-three, came too, all beautifully turned out in sombre suits and black dresses.

Mavaughn had wanted to join us but, other than Mum and Dad's wedding, no one could remember a single occasion when she might have spent any time with Grandma Genny. As the main reason she wanted to attend was because she had an Irish expectation of what a funeral entailed, and because Dad explained to her that this would be a mopey English kind of a funeral with very little alcohol and no dancing whatsoever, she quickly decided to drop out.

Jake and Abby came, in essence because I lied to Jake, telling him that Dad wanted us all there. I was pretty scared that one was going to backfire on me, but in the end it was the lie that brought them together, so I was left feeling rather proud of myself.

As for Dad's side of the family – or rather Grandma Genny's side – only six people turned up. Her cousin, 'Aunt' Ethel, wore a shockingly inappropriate floral dress which she later explained had been Genny's favourite (so wearing it was a sort of tribute). Grandpa Chris (the deceased's ex-husband, and Dad's father) came with a friend called Igor who, when he managed to stop crying for long enough to speak, sounded Polish. There was an elderly, old-school gay guy called Tony wearing jeans and a billowy, black satin shirt, and his partner, Glen. Glen looked sober and sophisticated, while Tony seemed to be channelling Elton and Liberace simultaneously, so they made an unlikely couple. But in a way it pleased me that they were there. It gave a hint that living in Brighton had brought a little diversity to my grandmother's life. A bit of diversity that, it crossed my mind, wouldn't have done my father any harm to experience more frequently.

Finally there was a youngish woman who'd worked for Genny in some business she'd owned and who, judging from her copious tears, had very much enjoyed the experience.

The service was short and non-religious, which was what Grandma Genny had wanted. If I'm honest, it's the sort of funeral

I would have requested for myself, but ultimately I found it a bit sad. I mean, evidently it was sad – it was a funeral. But a bit more celebration of life and a little less weeping over death wouldn't have gone amiss. Perhaps it's just the Irish in me, but since that day I tend to think the Mavaughns of this world have the right idea. Music, alcohol and dancing. That's how I want to be sent off.

Anyway, it was over quickly – too quickly really. Grandpa Chris declined to speak – he was too upset – and when Igor tried to replace him, he too broke down. Ethel only said about thirty words but managed to make them moving all the same, saying that Grandma Genny had been the best friend anyone could have and that having a friend like that for life changed everything. I thought of Gina and wished that I'd brought her along, and cried.

And then before I'd realised what was happening, the coffin had vanished, we were out in the sunshine, and everyone was bumming cigarettes off Harry.

When he offered me one I declined and commented that it would feel a bit inappropriate 'considering'.

Tony, to my left, was ostensibly involved in a different conversation with Ethel, but he overheard and spun to face me. 'Oh, take the damned cigarette, hon!' he said. 'Smoking was one of her great pleasures in life. She smoked right up to the end. She'd love to know that everyone was puffing at her funeral.'

Ethel nodded and a tear slipped down her cheek. 'It's true,' she said. 'Even when she had to take the oxygen mask off for a puff.'

And so, partly because of the peer pressure, but also because I fancied one, and no doubt because, despite the cancer and everything, I secretly aspire to Grandma Genny's devil-may-care attitude, that's exactly what I did.

Afterwards we ended up in a local pub but even there the atmosphere seemed strange. The Irish contingent continued to smoke, laugh inappropriately and drink in the pub garden, while Genny's side of the family chatted respectfully at the bar.

Dad flitted back and forth between the two groups as if he couldn't decide where he felt the most at ease, or more precisely, where he felt the least ill at ease, and I quickly gave up on the smokers and squeezed myself in at the edge of the indoor group, hoping to get a word in with Grandpa Chris. But he was – and this was something I'd forgotten until that moment – an incredible raconteur. So though you could sit and listen to his tales – because there was nothing he liked more than an audience – it was almost impossible to engage him in any kind of meaningful conversation.

Jake came in to fetch fresh drinks at one point and I commented on his suit. Generally speaking, Jake had terrible dress sense, so it was a relief to see him wearing something decent. I hoped this was Abby's influence.

'That *is* a nice suit,' Grandpa Chris agreed, rather cheekily opening Jake's jacket by the lapel to take a peek at the label inside.

'Jesus, it's Moss Bros, OK?' Jake said.

'It's still lovely, Jake,' I said. It was deep blue – almost black – with a very subtle purple and burgundy check. It looked like it had been pretty expensive.

'It actually wasn't,' Jake said, when I told him this. Then, 'Abby helped me choose it. We thought it was dark enough for a funeral, but, you know, OK for afterwards as well.'

'I think you're right,' I told him. 'Good choice.'

I turned back to try to speak to Grandpa Chris then, but it was too late because he was already in full flow with his next tall tale.

Interlude.

Tall Tale #2: The Disgruntled Employee.

Did I ever tell you about the place your grandmother worked after the war?

It was the first job she found on arriving in England, out in East London, in a factory. Actually, I say factory, but it was more of a sweatshop.

It was owned by a rich, mean, old Sikh guy called Rashid and there were about fifty women working there who sewed twelve hours a day, six days a week.

But old Rashid was a bit of a bastard, and he used to treat those women like slaves. They weren't allowed to pee more than once each shift – that's once in the morning and once in the evening – and if he thought they were working too slowly he'd take away their chairs and make them stand.

Anyway, your grandmother Genny hated him and almost from day one she desperately wanted to leave. But jobs were few and far between after the war, and what with working six days a week she didn't even have time to look for another job. So for a long time – about a year, it was – she was stuck there, working for Rashid.

Anyway, one day they fell out big-time because old Rashid said she didn't work fast enough, so she decided to leave. She'd saved up a little money by then so she thought she could survive until she found something else.

They'd been sewing men's suits all week. When the soldiers came home from the war, the government gave each of them a suit to wear. It was called 'getting your civvies', and you got a choice of single or double breasted, and pinstripes or Prince of Wales check. That was it. Those were the choices.

Anyway, your grandmother knew she was leaving and decided to get her revenge.

So that final day, from dawn to dusk, she sewed all the arms the wrong way round, so they stuck out backwards, like this. When she finished each piece, she folded it neatly and added it to the pile, and no one could see that anything was wrong. And then at the end of the day she went to Rashid, thanked him profusely for everything, and left.

Apparently old Rashid was so angry when he found out that he collapsed and had to be taken to hospital. But don't worry, he didn't die. Within a week he was back slave-driving your grandmother's replacement.

Ruth. Part One (continued).

Once Grandpa had finished his tale and vanished to the loo, Jake leaned in to speak to me. 'Didn't Dad tell us that same story, only it was Mum who worked there, and the owner was a horrible old Jew called Elijah?'

I rolled my eyes. 'Oh, Jake,' I said. 'Please don't go off on the whole Jewish thing again.'

'Then tell me that you haven't heard it before. And tell me that Dad didn't make it about a horrible old Jew. He had loads of stories about old Jews. And jokes, too. You do remember all the Jewish jokes, don't you?'

The problem was that what Jake said was true. There had been a glut of Jewish jokes over the years. I *had* heard the story before, too. And it had been about our mother, sewing dresses, in a Jewish-owned sweatshop.

'It was dresses, not suits, wasn't it?' I said, trying to sidestep the Jewish thing. 'And didn't he say that she sewed all the buttons on backwards?'

Ethel, who was standing nearby, came to my rescue.

'Actually, he *was* Jewish,' she said. 'And he was an old bastard.'

'It's a true story then?' Jake asked.

Ethel laughed. 'Well, it was me working there, not your grand-mother. And it was during the war, not after. And we were sewing uniforms, not suits. And the reason we fell out was nothing to do with how fast I was working. But you know . . . why let the truth get in the way of a good story?'

'God, it was you!' I said. 'And did you really sew all the arms on backwards?'

'Only on one jacket,' Ethel said. 'And only the last one I did. I wouldn't have dared to ruin any more. I was brave, but I wasn't that brave! Plus, it was uniforms. I would have felt like I was sabotaging the war effort.'

Grandpa Chris returned then, and proceeded to tell everyone the wolf story, which seemed a shame as I'd been hoping to talk to him.

Instead, I tried to ask Ethel how distant a cousin she was to my grandmother, but she merely laughed as if the question was frivolous, and shushed me. 'This is a good one,' she said, nodding in Grandpa Chris's direction.

Jake, who, like me, had heard the story many times before, picked up his drinks and went outside, and when Grandpa finished, I jokingly asked Ethel if she knew whether that one was true as well.

'Bits of it,' she said, then intriguingly, 'It's just how he deals with the past. There are worse ways to do that, believe me.'

Tony and Glen muscled in on our barely initiated conversation at that point, and began to talk about an upcoming party.

Ethel said that she didn't think she'd be able to stomach parties for some time and Tony insisted this was nonsense, and it was what Genny would have wanted.

It was one of those moments in life when, watching from the outside, you can see that two people really aren't listening to one another, and they're totally out of sync, Ethel being utterly serious that this was not the moment to talk about parties, and Tony insisting it would be just the thing to cheer her up.

Because their increasingly heated conversation made me feel uncomfortable and in some way voyeuristic, I slipped outside to join my family.

They were in clusters having varied, more-or-less rowdy conversations about football and kids and holiday destinations, and I drifted between them for half an hour. But ultimately because none of their conversations seemed entirely funeral-appropriate – having nothing whatsoever to do with Genny – they also made me feel uncomfortable, and I wished again that I'd brought Gina along for company.

In the end, I made my goodbyes and phoned for a taxi. I asked the woman driver to take me to the train station, but when I caught a glimpse of the sea, shimmering on the horizon, I changed my destination to Brighton Pier.

There, I climbed out, bought a greasy, sugary doughnut and walked to the far end, where, leaning on the railings, a funfair ride spiralling around above me, I peered down at the grey, swelling sea for a bit before looking out at the horizon and wondering once again why I hadn't come to see my grandmother here while she was alive. At that moment, unexpectedly, she appeared in my mind's eye so vividly that I felt like I was a child again.

So in my head, I apologised to her for having been absent, and in my head, she replied that it was fine, and that it wasn't in any way my fault.

And then she surprised me by asking if I fancied another doughnut, because it had looked rather good, and I couldn't tell where the thought had come from – whether it was a memory or a random phrase generated by my own hunger, or if she really was momentarily there with me.

I told her that I was fine for now, but that if she fancied one herself, she should have one. And that's when I started to cry.

That evening, Dad phoned me.

It was late and I was in my pyjamas, in the process of brushing my teeth before bed.

'I just wanted to check you're OK,' he said. 'I didn't see you leave.'

I swished the toothpaste from my mouth and took the phone through to the bedroom. 'Actually, you did,' I said, perching on the edge of the bed. 'I pecked you on the cheek as I was leaving but you were telling some story about a plumber.'

'Was I?' Dad said.

Because his voice sounded unusually vague, wistful almost, I asked if he was OK.

'Sure,' he said. 'I'm fine. It's not as if we were close.'

But there was a sadness in his voice that gave the lie either to the fact that he was 'fine', or the fact that they weren't close. Or maybe it was a sadness because it was true they weren't close, and that was something he regretted.

'Will you tell me why that was?' I asked. 'Not today, obviously. But sometime in the future, can we chat about it all? About your childhood and Grandma Genny and Grandpa Chris?'

'There's really not much to tell,' Dad said.

'Maybe not. But Grandma Genny's . . . um . . . *passing* . . . has made me think,' I told him. 'About all the things I don't know about them, and you, and your childhood.'

Dad cleared his throat, a sure-fire sign that I was making him uncomfortable, and I was aware that it was not the best of days to be doing so. 'Grandpa Chris seemed on fine form,' I said, to relieve the tension. 'Telling all the same old stories.'

'Yes,' Dad said. 'It's what we do.'

'What do you mean?' I asked.

'Oh, nothing much. It's just . . . you know . . . a family trait.'

'Telling stories?'

'Yes.'

'Did he tell you all those same tales when you were growing up, too? Jake and I recognised some of the ones you used to tell us, albeit with subtle changes.'

31

'Yes,' Dad said. 'Yes, he did.'

'That must have been nice. I know how much we enjoyed them when we were little. Especially the scary ones like the wolf story.'

There was a silence then. It wasn't an uncomfortable silence as such, but it was unexpected.

'Dad?' I prompted.

After a further few seconds he said, 'Yep. Still here, my lovely.'

I waited for him to continue and eventually he did. 'I was just thinking about what you were saying. About the stories. They're a sort of displacement activity, really.'

'A displacement activity?'

'Yes,' Dad said. 'To avoid having to talk about anything real.'

'That did cross my mind,' I said.

'We all do it, you know. It's a Solomas thing.'

'I don't think I do,' I said.

Dad laughed gently. 'Oh, you do,' he said. 'Jake does too. But you're right. I did enjoy them when I was little. All those stories by the fireside . . . But then later they started to frustrate me.'

'Because he used them as a wall?'

'That's exactly it,' Dad said. 'I never thought about it that way before, but yes. He used them like a wall. They both did.'

'You mean Grandma Genny too? I don't remember her telling stories.'

'No, she didn't so much. But she'd urge your grandfather to tell one. "Tell them the one about so-and-so," she'd say. It was the way she turned attention from herself. She liked to remain unnoticed, in the corners. It suited her that he was constantly holding forth.'

'Right,' I said. 'I see.'

'Anyway,' Dad said.

'You do sound sad, Dad,' I commented. 'Not that it's in any way unexpected. But you do. Are you sure you're OK?'

At the end of the phone I could hear that his breathing was becoming ragged. 'I'm all right,' he said, unconvincingly. 'I just need a good night's kip. Your mother's already gone up.'

'Me too,' I replied. 'Goodnight then.'

'I do worry about you, on your own,' Dad said. 'No one to snuggle up to.'

'Don't,' I told him. 'I've got Buggles.'

'You shouldn't sleep with a cat,' Dad said. 'They give you worms. They crawl out of their arses and into yours.'

'Dad!' I said in a mock-plaintive voice. He'd told me this a hundred times, but I'd never believed it to be true. 'Anyway, he hasn't given me worms yet, and I've had him for almost five years.'

'Goodnight to you both, then,' Dad said. 'I, um, love you. You do know that, don't you?'

'Of course I do Dad,' I said. 'I love you too.'

And then just as I was putting the phone down, I heard him say 'I . . .' but it was too late. The phone had hit the base and when I raised it to my ear again all I got was dial tone.

I waited for a moment, hoping he'd call back to say whatever it was. And then I hesitated about whether to phone him myself, my finger hovering above the keypad.

But then Buggles jumped up on to the bed and nuzzled my hand, so, with a shrug, I put the handset down. 'Hello you,' I told him. 'Would you like to hear a story about some wolves?' He didn't seem particularly interested.

I reclined on the bed to stroke him and I thought about how little I'd known my grandmother, or indeed how little I knew my own father. I thought of Grandpa Chris, then, and wondered if getting to know him might be the key to finding more out about them both.

At that point I still hadn't the faintest idea just how much there was to know.

Cassette #1

ML: *OK, so . . . it's the twenty-first of June 1986 and this is Marie Lefebvre, interviewing Genevieve Schmitt for* Gai Pied *magazine.*

GS: Sorry, but before we get started, why are you called that?

Why am I called what?

Gay Foot. [Note from Translator: 'Gai Pied' – literally Gay Foot magazine.]

Oh, sorry, of course. Um, do you know the phrase 'prendre son pied?' [NT: To 'take one's foot'.]

Yes, of course I do. It means to have fun, yes?

Yes. And it also means, um, to have an orgasm, actually.

An orgasm.

Yes. And now I've shocked you, haven't I?

Nothing shocks me, dear. Really, nothing. And of course I knew that too. I just forgot.

OK. Well, good.

So, *Gai Pied.* Is this interview for some sort of racy magazine then? Because I'd hate to disappoint.

No, no, not at all. The name of the magazine is, more . . . Well, it's an honesty thing, I suppose. They dare to write about everything, including sex. I suppose the point is not to have any hang-ups.

Right. OK, well, I'll bear that in mind.

Yes, please don't ever feel you have to censor anything.

No censorship. OK. I can do that.

So shall we get started?

We probably should. But don't you need to switch that thing on first?

This? The recorder? Oh, it's already running. That's why that green light is on.

Oh, OK. Fine. I kind of expected it to be whirring and clicking or something.

It is very quiet. It's brand new. I just bought it. But the thingy is going round. Look.

Oh yes. That's a tiny cassette.

Yes. But each side lasts a full hour. Neat, huh?

I like your hair, by the way. It wasn't that colour when we met before, was it?

No, I was blonde, I think.

Well, I like it. Pink suits you.

Thanks. My partner did it.

But I'm drifting off track, aren't I? You're going to have to be much harsher with me if we're ever going to get this done.

<Laughs> Don't worry. I'll get my whip out if need be.

Well, that might make things a little racier for *Gai Pied*.

You're naughty! So . . . Where do you want to start?

I thought you'd probably have a plan.

Not a plan as such. But I thought maybe you'd simply start by telling me about when you met?

When I met who?

Well, Ethel, of course! When did you meet?

Oh, OK. So, we met when we were both thirteen . . . And I'm sixty-five now, so that would have been . . . Actually, can you work that out? I'm not so good with mental arithmetic – 1933 or '34 I think, but . . .

Well, 1986 now minus your age – sixty-five – must mean that you were born in 1921, right?

Yes. I know that!

Plus thirteen – because you met when you were thirteen – so, that would be 1934. Does that sound about right?

I'm so silly! Of course it was 1934.

And how did you meet?

Quite simply at school. We'd seen each other around for years . . . We were in the same year, though not the same class. So I'm not sure if that counts as an actual first meeting. But that's when we became friends.

And this was all in Mulhouse, in Alsace?

Yes. You know that.

I'm sorry, it's just for the interview. For the tape . . . Sometimes I'll have to ask you things I already know.

Of course.

I don't suppose you remember the actual date for any reason?

No, I'm sorry. But it was summer. It was hot. That much I remember. We were in the playground.

So June or July, maybe? Before the summer break?

Possibly. It was after the Night of the Long Knives, if that helps.

The Night of the Long Knives?

Yes. You know about that, don't you? You must have studied it in school.

I'm sorry, but no, I don't think we did.

It's the night Hitler killed Ernst Röhm. Oh, you don't know about him either? Ernst Röhm was a very high-ranking Nazi. And he and some other high rankers weren't happy about the way the whole Nazi project was going. There was a power struggle going on, I think, between different wings of the party. And on that night – I can't remember the date so you'll have to look it up – Hitler and his SS men murdered them all. [NT: June 30th, 1934.]

And you remember it was afterwards that you met Ethel?

Yes. It was very important. People talked about it. And Röhm was homosexual, so until he was killed, Berlin's homosexuals thought they'd be safe.

Röhm was gay?

'Gay' hadn't been invented yet, dear. People said 'queer', or 'homosexual'. But yes, it was quite widely known.

I'm surprised that one of Hitler's top men could have been gay – that's quite shocking.

Yes. Well, as I say, a lot of German homosexuals imagined they were safe because of Röhm's presence at the top. Berlin was quite frenetic with queer clubs and bars back then. Of course, the Nazis had already burned down the Hirschfeld Institute in '33, so that should have been a bit of a warning. But Hirschfeld was Jewish, so people were able to believe, if they so chose, that the reason for his persecution was his Jewishness. Oh gosh, you don't know who he is either, do you? I can tell by the way you're jotting things down.

I think I've heard of him, but . . .

I'm afraid you may have to look all this up at some other time, because otherwise we'll be doing this for weeks!

I'm sorry. I feel terrible. Just give me a rough sketch.

Please don't feel terrible. I'm surprised, but it's fine. So, in a nutshell, Hirschfeld was a psychologist, or a psychiatrist, or whatever. He was one of the first sexologists, and he set up an institute in Berlin to explore the diversity of sexuality. In the thirties he campaigned quite vocally for homosexuality to be legalised. But the Nazis burned down his institute in '33, which of course made homosexual Berliners nervous. But as Röhm was high up and was known to be gay, many chose to believe they'd be fine. That all changed on the Night of the Long Knives. Röhm was killed and the

Nazis went on a rampage, shutting all the remaining homosexual bars and clubs and arresting people left, right and centre.

So there was a proper gay scene in Berlin, before the war?

Yes, before the Nazis shut it all down it was crazy there. There were clubs for men, and clubs for women and lots that catered for both. Before we left Alsace, I had a friend, Anne-Sophie, and her older sister, Josette – who incidentally I had a bit of a crush on – used to go dancing in Berlin. She had a men's three-piece suit she used to wear, which was the fashion for lesbians, back then. She had a monocle, too! The stories she told were pretty wild.

Right. Thanks. I really should know more about this.

Well, I suppose, in a way, that's why we're here.

Yes, it's why your story will hopefully be so interesting for our readers. So we've established that you and Ethel met in 1934.

Yes. It was summer and we were in the playground. Two older girls tripped Ethel up and when she tried to stand they pushed her back down. So I went over to help her.

She was being bullied?

Yes.

Was that because she was gay? Or for some other reason?

No, it was because she was Jewish. No one could have told she was gay back then. I doubt *she* knew she was gay at that point.

She was being bullied for being Jewish, in France?

Yes.

That surprises me.

<Laughs> That's because we've all been so good at forgetting how anti-Semitic everyone was before the war. Which is, of course, because we're ashamed about it. But no, anti-Semitism wasn't a uniquely German phenomenon by any means. It was common-place in France, and rife in England too. You'll have to look up the Dreyfus Affair or Mosley's blackshirts, but I can assure you, it was

everywhere and it went right up to the top. King Edward was pretty chummy with Hitler, for example.

OK. And you went over to help Ethel get up?

Yes, I helped her to her feet. She was fine. She had a tiny graze on her knee, and she was a bit shaken, but she was basically fine. I was quite tough, so I looked out for her from that point on and we became friends.

You were tough, you say?

Yes. I'm tall for a woman. Or at least, I was, back then. I've lost a few centimetres since, and of course the youngsters are all so tall these days. But back in the day, I was probably the tallest girl in my class and I was sporty too. I was in a junior rowing club on the canal. I was one of the first women rowers they had. So I was pretty strong. The other girls tended not to mess with me. Not even the older ones.

You protected Ethel. That's sweet.

I didn't really protect her. But once people knew she was my friend, I suppose you could say that they left her alone. And Ethel liked that. We both liked that.

So you became friends. You said earlier that Ethel wouldn't have known she was gay at that point. But what about you? Did you know? About yourself, I mean?

Oh, definitely. Some people don't work out their sexual orientation until their forties, but I honestly can't remember ever having not known. I knew I liked girls before I even knew that sex existed. And when I saw Ethel . . . well! She was so pretty, with all this lovely auburn hair. She's lucky that way. My hair's not quite straight, and not quite curly either, so it always looks a mess. But Ethel has the kind of hair that settles naturally into perfect little ringlets. And she has beautiful hazel eyes. Anyway, you get the picture. I liked her a lot.

So did you set about seducing Ethel? You were only thirteen so perhaps 'seduced' isn't the right term. But did you set out to seduce her in the romantic sense of the word? Did you try to make her fall in love with you?

No, it wasn't like that at all. You make me sound like some sort of predator! I thought she was pretty. And I liked her company, and she mine. We were friends, school friends, for years, and just got closer and closer.

She developed a great sense of humour as she got older, which I often think is a bit of a Jewish trait. They have a certain sense of repartee, don't you think? A special sort of quick-fire wit. So Ethel made me laugh a lot, and I do love to laugh. She enjoyed *making* me laugh, too. She was smaller than me – petite – which I liked. My nickname for her was *petit oiseau* – baby bird – and I called her that for decades. I sometimes still do. But for years, like I say, it was all perfectly platonic. She lived in Dornach, the Jewish quarter of Mulhouse, in a flat above the shoe-shop her parents owned. And because the walk to Dornach was nice – you could walk along the canal, you see – she'd come and meet me after rowing practice and I'd walk her home. Then one day when we were about fifteen she said something witty and made me laugh – it was about Hitler, as I recall – and I kissed her. It was just a peck on the cheek, but she didn't flinch – in fact she didn't even stop talking. We walked on for a bit and then she said another funny thing, and then turned and kissed me back. I don't think either of us thought much about what was happening. We were just reacting to how we felt about each other.

Because you were falling in love.

Exactly. We were falling in love. And then a few days later, as we walked past the same spot, beneath a big overhanging tree, she grabbed my arm and kissed me again. That was the first time either of us had kissed someone properly.

You mean with tongues?

<Laughs> No, I mean on the lips. The other kisses had just been pecks on the cheek.

So still no tongues.

Gosh, OK! No – the tongues came later.

This was, what, 1935?

Our first kiss? I'd say '35 or '36. I seem to remember that Hitler had just banned Jews from the military – actually, that might have been what she joked about that day. Her father was very political, so we talked a lot about what was happening. I think she said something about being banned from the military being Hitler's greatest gift to the Jewish people. We didn't know what was coming at all then, so we thought we were being very amusing, as I recall.

So did you take things very slowly? Were you romantic?

Yes, we took things slowly. We were friends, and then we became inseparable friends. There were pecks on the cheeks, and then a few kisses on the lips. We didn't much want to see – or talk to – anyone else. In fact I can honestly say I never met anyone I'd rather talk to. Until I met Ethel my best friend had always been Pierre, the boy who lived next door. I was attracted to women, but I preferred the company of boys, you see.

You were a bit of a tomboy, then?

Yes. And it was the same for Pierre. He didn't much like boys' games. He hated football and that kind of thing. I didn't have brothers or sisters either, so most of my childhood had been spent hanging out with him. His nose was well and truly put out of joint when Ethel appeared on the scene.

Was he in love with you, do you think?

Gosh, no! It was a childhood friendship, that's all. We rode our bikes together, and we threw stones in the canal. We smoked our first cigarettes in his father's shed. But in the end, after sulking for a bit, he decided he liked Ethel as well. So from that point on, the three of us used to go around together. And then eventually, of course, Pierre admitted that he was of a similar persuasion.

Pierre turned out to be gay?

That's right. It's probably why we were friends in the first place. So we went around together as a trio after that. We used each other as a sort of alibi. My father assumed I was sweethearts with Pierre, and his parents hinted at marriage from time to time. And that suited us all.

Did you need to be discreet back then? What was it like being gay in Mulhouse in the thirties?

What was it like?

Yes. I mean, did you have places you could go? Were there gay bars and things?

Not as such. There was a park where the men used to do their wicked deeds. They were always far more direct about that kind of thing than the women. And occasionally, on a sunny day, you'd see couples of women there too, lying on the grass together. There was a café, as well, with a big upstairs room we used. Downstairs it was a regular bar, but on Sundays you could buy a drink and slip upstairs, and there you'd find men kissing men in the corners, and women lounging around on the sofas talking to each other and smoking. Everyone smoked in the thirties. The room was so smoky that it provided a certain level of cover for whatever people wanted to get up to.

But it was only open on Sundays?

Yes. It was called a tea dance, though I'm not sure why, as there was no tea to drink and no one danced much either. We'd go there together, the three of us. And then Pierre would inevitably meet some chap and slip discreetly off to the park.

But you'd just sit and chat?

Yes. We'd sip our drinks very slowly, because we could only ever afford one, and we'd talk to whoever was there. The women mostly kept to themselves, and the men with the men. But because we went around as a threesome, our sofa was often mixed, so I knew quite a few of the boys too. There was a piano in the corner so from time to time there'd be a singalong. Sometimes we'd even dance.

But you didn't get hassled . . . by the police or the authorities or whatever?

No. Homosexuality wasn't illegal. It hadn't been illegal since the French Revolution. So no, we weren't hassled at all, not officially, at any rate.

And unofficially?

Well, there were people who hated homosexuals. That's like hatred of Jews or blacks or gypsies – hatred of people who are different has always existed, and sadly will probably always exist. So there were Catholics who insisted it was a terrible sin, and the men in particular could get quite aggressive about it. I always thought that was probably because they were tempted themselves. But anyway, no, not officially. Because there were no laws outlawing any of it.

I'm surprised by that. I assumed that the police would be harassing you.

Alsace had been German in the late 1800s, as well. So lots of people had family in Germany and many people spoke German as well as Alsatian and French. All the older homosexuals had tales to tell of the nightlife in Berlin. So perhaps that made us feel a little more free about the whole thing too. Which is, of course, ironic.

I had no idea it was so free and easy back then.

<Laughs> I wouldn't say it was free and easy. I wouldn't want you to get the wrong idea. Pierre's parents were Catholic, so they were horrified when they found out. My father did everything he could to keep Ethel and me apart once he began to suspect that this wasn't just a normal friendship. So no, it wasn't *free and easy* at all. But it wasn't illegal either.

Right. So when did things get serious with Ethel?

Well she started to stay over at ours. My father liked her, and her parents didn't seem to mind, because I was a girl. They'd been worried that she didn't have many friends, so . . .

And when she stayed, did she stay in your bed?

Yes. Our flat didn't have a spare room. So she had to stay in my bed. My single bed.

Nice! Did you jump on each other straight away?

Not really. We'd been friends for a few years, as I said. And then we started pecking each other on the cheek. And then on the lips. But I suppose I'd have to admit that once we started sharing a bed things did go a bit faster.

And Pierre? Did he have a boyfriend?

Pierre had a lot of encounters. I don't know you could call them boyfriends.

Sexual encounters?

Yes. And from very early on. He was an 'early bloomer', as we used to say back then. I think he was only fourteen or fifteen when he started hanging out in the park.

But no boyfriend, as such.

No. And I don't think any of his adventures made him very happy. Not until he met Johann much later, in '38.

The year before the war.

Exactly.

When Pierre would have been what, sixteen?

Seventeen, I think.

That's still quite early for a first relationship.

Is it? Perhaps. I just meant that he had a lot of five-minute partners before he met Johann. Tens and tens, at a guess. Perhaps even hundreds.

While you only ever had Ethel.

That's right. So I was a bit shocked by all his shenanigans. Not in a bad way, but . . . Let's say it was something we used to joke about. I used to pull his leg about it.

And you'd go to the tea-dance thing as a threesome, with Pierre.

Yes, like I said, Pierre was our alibi, albeit an unconvincing one. He'd come to the house and take me out and then we'd meet Ethel down by the canal and all go together.

You said he was unconvincing . . .

Well, Pierre wasn't exactly butch, you know? He dressed in the Zazou style, so . . .

Zazou?

Yes. He wore huge oversized suits. They were fashionable back then, but more in Paris than in Mulhouse. They weren't very mainstream. So he was a bit of a dandy. People used to stop and stare sometimes.

And you?

What did I wear?

I'm just trying to imagine you all.

Well, the style for women like us in Paris or Berlin was to wear men's clothes. Suits and shirts and ties and things. But that was all a bit too risqué for Mulhouse. I loved that style, but my father would have had a nervous breakdown if I'd started dressing that way. So I was quite boring really. I wore skirts and blouses and a blue woollen coat I'd been given. The only piece of clothing I had that I really liked was a sailor dress – you know, like the one Shirley Temple used to wear? They were quite the thing back then – I did love my sailor dress. Ethel liked me wearing it too.

And what about Ethel? What was her style?

Ethel had no choice, really. She wore the long dresses her parents chose. For a Jewish family, they were quite relaxed, but her clothes were still pretty traditional. At first we used to try to pin the hem of her dress a bit higher to make it look less frumpy, but it never really hung properly. Later, she started taking her sister's cast-offs and altering them at ours on my mother's sewing machine. She'd take these creations in her handbag and change in the toilets so that none of her parents' friends would spot her dressed that way on the street. It was my mother who taught her how to sew, actually. My own clothes weren't very exciting, but even Mum felt sorry for Ethel. She had a horrible old fur coat she'd inherited from her aunt as well. When it rained it smelled like an old dog. Whenever she couldn't find her coat we used to joke that it had probably died and gone to heaven.

You mentioned that Ethel's father was quite – 'political' is the word I think you used. Does that mean you were more aware than other people around you of what was happening in Germany?

We were perhaps a little more aware than most. Her family had relatives in Germany, so her father knew quite early on that things were going wrong. The Nazis were organising boycotts of Jewish businesses as early as 1933 and Ethel's father would definitely have heard about that. I was a bit young to remember whether it was in the newspapers in France, but I suspect it was. But in 1938, once the *Kristallnacht* happened – when they burned all the Jewish shops – everyone definitely knew what was going on. I can remember talking about it quite a bit with Ethel's cousin, who was visiting at the time.

But Ethel's father wasn't the only reason. By then, by 1938, I was old enough to have my own friends with contacts in Berlin, too. The Nazis had started sending gay men to Dachau – the concentration camp – in '35, so we'd heard terrible tales about that too. It's such a shame no one reacted. People could have got together and sorted Hitler out before he built up that massive army. But they were 'just' homosexuals, after all, so no one cared. And then it was 'just' the Jehovah's Witnesses, and 'just' the Jews and the communists . . . There's a real lesson to be learned there.

But anyway, in France we considered ourselves relatively safe. The French government had built the Maginot Line . . . Yes, I guessed – you don't know what that is either! I do wonder what you learn in school these days. So, the Maginot Line was a series of forts and fortifications all the way down the German border. It was supposed to be impenetrable; that's what everyone said, anyway. The French were very proud of it. They told us we were safe. And for some reason we believed them.

So you weren't scared, even a bit?

I don't know. It's hard to say. These things build so gradually. We were very aware, I'd say, and as the years went by and we heard rumours from homosexual friends and other rumours from Jewish friends, we were more and more aware. At some point that awareness morphed into fear, I suppose, though I'd be hard put to say exactly when that happened. But it wasn't our single subject of conversation, strange as that might seem. Not by any means. People carried on living their lives.

You mentioned Ethel's cousin coming to stay? Can you tell us something about her, because as I recall she ends up being quite important.

Yes. She was important. So, Ethel had a cousin – quite a distant cousin – living in London. Her name was Hannah, and she was a dumpy, rather dull girl from a pretty orthodox Jewish family. Her father had made a killing in the garment trade. Hannah was studying French, so she was sent to stay with Ethel's family for a few months to practise, not that she made much effort. She arrived for Rosh Hashanah – Jewish New Year, in September – and was supposed to stay until December, I think. But after the *Kristallnacht* – that happened in November – her father started sending quite hysterical telegrams ordering her home.

Because he thought that France would be invaded?

I don't know exactly what he thought, but he certainly didn't think it was safe. He had a friend, I believe, who was a diplomat. So he was one of the rare people who believed the rumours and who understood that war was coming. And that's when we all became very aware. Because he considered our town too dangerous for his own daughter.

And did Hannah go home?

Yes, she went back to London almost immediately. They tried to convince Ethel's family to leave as well, but Ethel's father wouldn't consider it. Like most people, he was convinced they'd be just fine. I remember Ethel's father gesturing around his shop and saying, 'Everything we have is here! Where would we go?' And 'What makes you think England is safer than France anyway?' A lot of people assumed that if France fell – which they considered unlikely – that England would fall too. That said, he was open to the idea of his daughters leaving, just until things calmed down. But neither of them wanted to.

Ethel didn't want to leave because of you, I assume?

Yes, I suppose it was because of me. With Hannah staying, we hadn't been able to . . . you know . . . *be intimate* . . . for ages. We hadn't even been able to kiss. So we were pretty happy when Hannah's visit got cut short. But once she'd returned to London, she started writing to Ethel's father, and sometimes to Ethel too, begging them to leave and even offering them accommodation in London. Ethel's sister was engaged to be married so she wouldn't leave either.

So they all stayed put?

Yes. Sadly, they did.

That must have been a scary time.

Well, I was worried about the possibility of war, in an abstract kind of way. We all were. France had lost millions in the First World War, so every family had a horror story to tell about that. But – and this is embarrassing, shameful really, with hindsight, the stupidity of youth – I didn't feel like it really affected *me*, if you can understand that? For starters, I was a girl. So I knew I wouldn't have to do national service, and I wouldn't ever get called up to fight. You see how selfish this sounds? It's horrible, isn't it?

I just think that it's great you can be so honest.

I was young, I suppose. And yes, I was a girl; I wasn't Jewish and I lived in France behind the impenetrable Maginot Line. So I was worried about the poor Jews in Germany, and I was worried about the homosexuals in Berlin, but in a distant kind of way, the way you might worry about people in Chile or the Soviet Union today, you know? Without television and everything, the world felt much bigger in those days. Places seemed further away.

When did that change? When did you first start to feel threatened personally?

Not until 1939. Everyone was talking about all the German troops on the Polish border but even that wasn't what made us realise. What brought it home was when France started mobilising all the men. So suddenly there were all these soldiers marching through the towns with their kit bags. That's when things got real.

Did your family discuss leaving at that point? Actually, did your father get called up?

No, he was just too old to be called up. He had a wooden leg from the first war as well, so he would have been exempt anyway. And yes, there were many discussions about leaving. My parents argued about it constantly.

In September Germany invaded Poland, and Britain and France declared war. France evacuated everyone who lived near the German border – it was a ten-kilometre-wide strip, as I recall. There were thousands of people crossing the town in cars and on motorbikes, with hand carts or on donkeys . . . People travelled any way they could. It was quite shocking to see.

But you weren't evacuated?

No. We were told to stay put. We were outside the ten-kilometre danger zone, or at least, that's what they told us. So we stayed put. But Jewish families were terrified. I'm not sure if they were advised to leave, or whether they made their own minds up, but many of them fled at that point.

And where did all these people go?

The people from the border were sent on trains to south-west France, I believe. And the Jews tended to go wherever they had family. There were people on the move everywhere.

Including Ethel and her family? Did they leave?

No. No, Ethel's family stayed put. But her father did insist that Ethel go to London to stay with Hannah.

So you were separated?

Yes, I was heartbroken. We both were. But even then we still thought it would only be for a few weeks. I can't tell you why we thought that way, but it's what we believed. I often think that our biggest problem – as humans – is our belief that things will stay the same. Our incapacity to imagine just how much, and how quickly, everything can change. People think their rights – their human rights – are set in stone. But all it takes is one bad government and it's all over.

Did you ever consider going with her?

Oh, I begged and begged my father to let me go with her! Not because I was scared so much as because I couldn't bear to be separated. We were very much in love by then. But he'd worked out that our relationship wasn't a normal friendship, I think. And the more I begged, the more he saw that and the more determined he was to keep me at home in Mulhouse. That's probably partly why Ethel's father sent her away, too.

To keep you and Ethel apart.

Yes. Sort of killing two birds with one stone . . . Keeping her safe from the Germans, and from me. My own father called it an

unhealthy obsession. He definitely considered Ethel more dangerous than the Germans.

An obsession?

That's how he used to describe it. 'You need to get over this
unhealthy obsession you have with that girl!'

And you had no desire to disobey? To follow her to London?

No. This was the 1930s, remember. Girls, especially unmarried
girls, didn't disobey their father's wishes. Not even at eighteen.

So what was it like being left behind once Ethel had left?

Well, it was awful, as you can imagine. I was wretched. I
couldn't sleep because I was upset about Ethel and worried about
the Germans . . . I'd fallen out with my father, so we were barely
speaking to each other. My mother had timidly taken my side, so
things were difficult between her and my father as well. I basically
sulked and worked and waited for letters.

Of course. No phone calls!

No. Hannah's father had a telephone, I think, but we didn't.
And even if we'd had one, I'm not sure you could make international calls back then. It was something that never even crossed our
minds in those days. If it was urgent you'd send a telegram. But
otherwise, you'd just post a letter. We wrote to each other every day.
And the letters took a week or so to arrive.

*You mentioned working. I don't think we've covered that yet. What
were you doing?*

I was working in a Jewish bakery. I'd got the job through Leah,
Ethel's friend, who was the owner's daughter. Leah was newly married and her husband hadn't been happy with her working. So her
parents had needed someone to replace her. Under normal circumstances they would probably have chosen someone Jewish, but
most of their Jewish friends had evacuated by then. I used to start
at six a.m., emptying the ovens and stacking the bread in the shop.
Sometimes I had to do deliveries. Leah's father taught me to drive

the van even though I didn't have a driving licence! It was only up and down the street, but it made me feel very grown up. Ethel, in London, was working too, sewing cushions for Hannah's father in some kind of sweatshop. They switched to making uniforms for soldiers quite early on and I remember her saying that she hated that, because the material was so thick. Some days it made her fingers bleed. But anyway, that was my life. Writing letters, waiting for letters, working and sulking. I did a lot of sulking.

Was Pierre still around?

Yes, he was still there but I saw much less of him. He'd met Johann by then and was in what I suppose you could call a cocooning phase. Neither of us wanted to go to the tea dances anymore, me because I was miserable going out without Ethel, and Pierre because he was seeing Johann. We tried it a few times as a threesome but I don't think any of us enjoyed it much. And then the dances stopped anyway, so . . .

Because of the war?

Yes, most of the men had been called up. And no one was in a very go-out-and-have-fun mood. We were all very anxious. People tended to stay at home and listen to the radio.

OK. Tell me about Johann a bit – Pierre's lover – what was he like?

Oh, Johann was gorgeous. Even I could see what the attraction was. He was tall and dark with jet-black hair and huge eyes. He had beautiful long eyelashes, I remember, and one of those 1930s haircuts where it was long on top and short at the back and sides. So when he leaned forwards, his hair used to flop over his eyes, and he'd have to brush it out of the way. He was very shy, and very subtle. But funny too. Yes, Johann was quite lovely.

Were Pierre and Johann called up?

No, they were too young. You had to be twenty, I think, to fight. Pierre took over his father's plumbing business – because his father had been mobilised – and Johann was a postman. Neither of them seemed to suit their jobs, if you know what I mean. Once you'd seen Pierre in one of his Zazou suits, it was hard to believe you were looking at the same person when you bumped into him in plumber's overalls. Johann was the same. He looked like a writer or a poet rather than a postman. But Pierre's father was a plumber, and Johann's father worked at the post office . . . That's how things were in those days. Lots of people did the same jobs as their parents.

And did it feel like the country was at war?

Not really. There were soldiers everywhere, mostly heading towards the border, and people evacuating in the other direction all the time. They evacuated the whole of Strasbourg, you know? I saw an exhibition, and there are photos of empty streets full of the starving cats and dogs people had left behind. But in Mulhouse we carried on as normal, and nothing happened for months – I think it was eight months, from September to May. The Germans were busy building weapons and an army and harassing the Jews, herding them into ghettos and building camps and such. And the longer it went on, the more the French got demoralised. I don't know how to put it really, but there was a feeling that the mobilisation had all been a bit of an overreaction. The men who'd been conscripted got bored. People would say – and it's amazing to say it, but it's true – people would say, 'If they're going to invade, I wish they'd just get on with it.' People either wanted to fight or go home to their families.

This is the period people called the 'phoney war', right?

They did teach you something in school!

I think I saw it on television, but anyway . . . Things stayed that way until May, you say?

Yes, May 1940. When Germany invaded.

So, eight months?

Yes. But it honestly felt like eight years.

And how long did France hold out for? Was that defence system you mentioned any good?

The Maginot Line? <Laughs> No, the Germans just went through Belgium instead. It seems the French hadn't thought of that.

The Belgians fought though, didn't they?

Yes, they started off neutral but had to defend themselves when Germany invaded. But they couldn't stop the whole German army.

How long did it take? From them attacking Belgium to arriving in Mulhouse?

I think it took a month, maybe a month and a half. But you know, I'm not a history teacher. So you'll have to check all of this.

I realise that. I'm just trying to imagine how things were for you, knowing the Germans were close.

Our family were pretty scared, but not everyone was. Lots of families in Alsace had links to Germany and some of them admired Hitler. Lots of people hated the Jews, too. So not everyone was aghast at the idea of the Germans arriving. But we were. My father had lost a leg in the first war. He was under no illusions about the Germans.

But your father still wouldn't let you join Ethel? Actually, were you still getting her letters, despite the war?

Surprisingly, yes. They'd arrive in batches, maybe once a week. I'd sort them by the postmarks and read them in order, over and over again. But yes, the post carried on working quite well. As for joining her in London, nothing had changed. Dad wanted me to forget her. If he got to the post before me, he'd destroy her letters. Plus, we were at war by then. There was a feeling that it was too late to leave. Travel, especially international travel, had become complicated, impossible, perhaps. I don't really know, but that's how things felt. Plus London was evacuating millions of people to the countryside in case of bombing raids so there was a feeling that London wasn't necessarily any safer. And on top of all of that, Ethel was having problems with Hannah's family. She was saying she might have to leave.

What sort of problems?

She messed up, really. It was silly. She told Hannah the truth – about us being in love. I think Hannah had wanted to read the letters I was sending, so Ethel told her. Hannah, who I think just wanted her room back, told her father about it, and he wrote to Ethel's father and then dragged her off to see the rabbi. So that was all a right unholy mess and it wasn't entirely clear whether they were going to send Ethel back to Mulhouse or not. In one of the last letters I received before the invasion, she said that she'd probably have to find a new job, because Hannah's father was being horrible to her, and that she'd either leave Hannah's house and find somewhere else to live so that I could join her, or she'd come home. She promised we'd be together soon. My God, how I treasured that letter, that promise! I read it so many times that the paper fell apart at the folds. I still have it upstairs, actually. Perhaps I'll show it to you later.

I'd like that, if you can find it.

Oh, I can definitely find it. I know exactly where it is. Anyway, what would you like to know next?

OK . . . Why don't you tell me about the day the Germans invaded? That must have been terrifying.

The day they invaded France, or—

No, sorry. I meant the day they invaded your town – Mulhouse. I'm more interested in your personal experiences. Did you know in advance that they were coming, or was it a surprise?

We knew. I couldn't name a specific date when we knew because it wasn't something that happened suddenly. It was more like a slow build-up, like breathlessly watching a car crash in slow motion, you know? The French had been fighting alongside the

Allies, and losing, since May, first along the Belgian border, then in the Ardennes mountains, then Arras . . . There were so many battles fought and lost I can't remember them all. But in June – it was the tenth, I think – the French government declared Paris an 'open city' which meant that basically they weren't going to fight back anymore, though there were battles all the same. But in a couple of days Paris had fallen and from that point we knew we were done for. On the seventeenth we heard that the Germans had arrived in Colmar, which was less than an hour away. And the next morning they reached us in Mulhouse.

Can you explain to me why you didn't leave, even then? I can't quite get my head around the fact that you knew you were about to be invaded, but you stayed put.

I know. It does seem strange with hindsight. I wanted to leave. When they said on the radio that the Germans were in Colmar I screamed and cried until my father slapped me to shut me up. But remember, the government was falling apart. They were declaring cities 'open' and then bits of the army were fighting all the same. They were telling us to stay put even while they were evacuating people on trains – it was utter chaos. Plus, my father was a military man. Following orders was how he functioned. So when the government said to stay put, stay put is what he did. Maybe he hoped they had a secret plan. Pétain had been a hero in the First World War, so people like my father tended to assume he had something up his sleeve, or at the very least that he knew best. And of course, there was nowhere left to run to anyway by then. Paris had fallen, remember. So it seemed obvious that the rest of the country would follow suit.

That must have been incredibly stressful. How did you cope?

I don't know. I'm not sure we had the concept of stress back then, but we were certainly worried out of our minds. I hadn't slept for days. But you had to cling to whatever you could. There were rumours, for example, coming from the towns the Germans had already occupied – rumours saying that they were polite and pleasant to everyone. So if you wanted to cling to something in the midst of all that mayhem, you could try to convince yourself that they were just young men, just people, like us, after all.

I'm trying to imagine the arrival of German soldiers in your town. Can you describe it for me? Were they in tanks or on trucks or on foot? Was there fighting in the streets? How many people died?

<Laughs> They freewheeled into town on pushbikes.

I'm sorry?

The scouts came first – about thirty young soldiers on pushbikes.

And no one challenged them?

No one at all. Mulhouse, like lots of cities, had followed Paris and declared itself an open city. We were under strict orders not to resist. So we stood at the side of the road and watched them cycle past. Some of us cried. I saw a few people wave, which made me cry even more.

People waved?

Yes. As I said, there were people in Alsace who considered themselves more German than French. There were people who were scared, I suppose, and who hoped that trying to look welcoming might make them safer. So yes, some people waved, and the soldiers waved back. They were young and good-looking and smiling. They were happy to have arrived without a fight, I suspect. They rode to the town hall, where the mayor greeted them solemnly. They took down the French flag and put up a swastika. That was the very first thing they did.

And what did you do?

I went back to work. They ordered us to return to our homes and our jobs and we did what we were told. It was mid-morning by then, so I went straight back to the bakery. The Rosenbergs were waiting in the doorway. Mrs Rosenberg asked me over and over again to tell her what had happened. She was trembling, I remember, and Mr Rosenberg eventually sent her upstairs to lie down. That's when the soldiers started coming in.

German soldiers in the Jewish bakery?

Yes. And just as we'd been told, they were polite and friendly – flirty, even. They had French francs and they were hungry. They insisted on paying for their bagels and bread, even when Mr Rosenberg told them it wasn't necessary. And in spite of myself, even I started to think things might be all right. I think we were so scared, deep down, that we were desperate to believe. They were even polite to Mr Rosenberg, so that had to be a good sign, didn't it? Of course it was all part of a plan to avoid any resistance.

More and more troops arrived as the day went by, on trucks and in cars and on foot. They were all starving hungry and by mid-afternoon we'd completely sold out and the till was stuffed full of money. Mr Rosenberg even made a joke about who ever knew a Nazi invasion would be so good for business.

At the end of that first day, Pierre dropped in to buy bread and I gave him a baguette I'd put aside for him. It should give you an idea of just how hard the Germans were trying in those early days if I tell you that there was a soldier outside the shop at the exact moment Pierre came in. I'd just told that soldier we had no bread left, but then served Pierre while he was still watching through the window. I felt bold, as if in my own tiny way, I was resisting, so I was scared. He had a gun slung over his shoulder, after all. He stepped back into the shop, but do you know what he did? He just laughed. He laughed and said, '*Brot gibt es also nur für Liebhaber! Aber vielleicht wirst Du morgen ja mich lieben.*' I think that was it – my German's pretty rusty, as you can imagine. But what it meant was, 'So, there is only bread for lovers! Maybe tomorrow you will love me.'

The next morning we got up and it felt like we'd been moved to Germany overnight. We didn't know it yet, but Hitler had decided to re-annex Alsace. There were already flyers on the lamp posts saying it was forbidden to speak French and a few days later they changed all the street names to German. Actually, and this is a funny story for you: they made the mistake of renaming Rue de Sauvage [NT: Savage Road] Adolf Hitlerstrasse. That really made everyone snigger. It was so appropriate! When the Nazis realised their mistake they renamed it Wildermann Strasse. My father used to secretly refer to it as Sauvage Hitlerstrasse. But having to speak German was a shock. Most of us knew how to speak a bit of German, but we weren't by any means fluent. I remember my mother asking my father if it was too late to leave now, and he said, 'Leave? To go where?'

'Anywhere,' Mum said.

But Dad replied that this was our home. He said that if things went well, if the Germans had learned the lessons of the Great War, then maybe we wouldn't have to leave. And if things went badly – and he thought they would go badly – then someone would have to be there to kick the bastards out. Mum pleaded on our behalves, but Dad said that for better or worse it was our home as well.

The following day, defeated French troops began streaming through the town on their way to German prison camps. They marched through Mulhouse by the thousands – actually I think there were hundreds of thousands – it went on day and night. And all the families who'd sent their men to the front stood at the side of the road calling out the names of those they'd lost contact with, hoping to get news. No one ever knew if they really wanted to know – perhaps someone would tell them their father or brother or son was one of the hundred thousand dead. Or maybe someone would answer to his own name, which meant he was on his way to a prison camp – the Germans had taken almost two million prisoners, I think. So was it better to hear or not? But people stood and called names all the same, and the noise of that marching and calling was awful; it was chilling. When I went to bed at night I'd stuff bits of material in my ears to try to drown out the noise but it always worked its way into my dreams, turning them into nightmares. I had constant nightmares during the war. Everyone did.

About a week after the Germans had arrived Leah's younger sister, Dinah, knocked on our door. It was late at night, well after the curfew, so we were scared to open the door. She'd come to tell us, tearfully, that the Germans were making them leave, and by the next morning when I got to work, they were gone. The whole family had been sent packing – along with thousands of others – over the border to France. The Germans called it 'cleaning out the undesirables' from what they now considered was part of Germany. They'd had to leave in the early hours with whatever they could carry. Many left with food still on the table.

So with the Rosenbergs gone, who ran the bakery?

That first day a soldier asked me if I knew how to bake bread and I lied and said I didn't, so they sent me home. And then two days later a German man called Schumacher knocked on the door and told me to get back to work. I never knew, or dared ask, where he and his wife had popped up from, but from that point on they ran the bakery. The bread they made was horrible, and the locals all joked that it tasted like shoe leather. Oh, you didn't get the joke, did you? Schumacher means shoemaker. So we had a baker called shoemaker who made bread that tasted like shoe leather.

And do you know what became of the Rosenbergs?

I do, I'm afraid. They spent some time moving around in occupied France and then got over the border to what was then Zone Libre. Leah's brother, Joshua, got separated from the others at some point and escaped to America, but her parents, grandmother and sister Dinah were all interned by the Vichy regime and then shipped off to the Sobibor extermination camp, where they died in '43. Leah died earlier on, in Vorbruck-Schirmeck camp in late 1940.

My God, that's horrific. Is there a reason Leah died first?

Yes, it was because she didn't leave at the same time. Her family went when the Germans kicked them out, so they were rounded up later on in France. But Leah didn't believe that the Germans were sending them to France at all. She was convinced that they were all going to be shot at the side of the road, so she and her husband went into hiding.

I'm guessing that by now people's illusions about the polite Germans had begun to fade?

Oh, totally. They only pretended to be friendly for a few days – just long enough to fill the town with troops. I think it was about day four when they started rounding up the Jews and shipping them off, and then after that it was the communists and gypsies and any criminals. People who'd fought in the Great War, and homosexuals, of course. There were so many people the Nazis didn't like.

Were you scared they'd come for you?

Not so much. Unless you were caught working for the resistance or something, women generally slipped under the German radar. Nazism, like most 'isms' of the time, was pretty macho. I just don't think they considered women important enough to spend any time worrying about lesbianism. But I was terrified for my father – he'd been wounded in the First World War, after all – and for Pierre and Johann and all our friends. Everyone I knew was in some kind of danger.

I'm wondering: how did the Germans know who was who?

I'm sorry . . . Who was who? I don't . . . ?

How did they know who was communist and who was gay, for example? How did they know who'd fought in World War One?

Oh, I see. That information came from the local police mostly. The SS had taken all the important jobs in the town hall and the police force almost immediately. So they had access to all the lists.

And the French held those sorts of lists? Of who was communist? Who was gay?

Apparently so. It was a bit of a surprise. None of us realised they'd been keeping all this information, but they had. Sometimes there were no actual lists, but even then it wasn't that difficult to piece one together. The local police knew pretty much everyone's business in those days and some of the more zealous ones were only too happy to help out. A lot of personal vendettas were dealt with that way too. People informed on their neighbours, sometimes even family members, telling the Germans that they were this or that or the other and, most of the time, by morning they'd be gone. Sometimes people even made stuff up, just because they were jealous, so that they could have someone's house or their clothes or their horse or whatever. So in a way, even if you weren't in one of the specific groups the Nazis were targeting, you still felt scared all the time. You never knew when they'd come for you.

But you were still working for the Schumachers. How was that going?

It was awful. I hated them. I hated them for being German and I hated them for having replaced the Rosenbergs. The Rosenbergs had been like family to me.

And how did the Schumachers treat you?

Like a slave. They just barked orders at me all day. It was horrible.

I suppose leaving wasn't an option?

No. There were no jobs. Food was scarce. Everyone was broke and desperate and hungry. Many women turned to prostitution just to stay alive.

Servicing the Germans?

Yes, they were the only ones who could pay. They had money and bread; they had meat and butter. I don't know what the going rate was, but I definitely knew of girls who had sex for cigarettes, for example.

For cigarettes?

Yes. You could trade cigarettes for anything, so people would have sex in exchange for cigarettes. So working in the bakery, even a horrible German-run bakery, was a godsend. I was never hungry, and I used to be able to sneak out bread rolls for my family and for Pierre's family, and for Leah, too.

You knew where Leah was hiding, then?

Yes. She was in a cellar with her husband and newborn baby. It was down by the boathouse where our club had been based. So I'd sneak down there with a roll in my pocket. She was dreadfully skinny and was breastfeeding, so I was worried about her.

Wasn't that dangerous? For you, I mean?

Everything was dangerous. And in a way, when everything is dangerous, you have no choice but to get used to it. But ultimately I lost my job because of it.

That was the worst day ever. So much happened, I'm not sure where to begin. But Mr Schumacher caught me stealing and sacked me – that was the start of it. I was scared the Schumachers would tell the SS that I'd stolen and I'd be arrested as a criminal so I went straight away to tell Leah that I wasn't going to be able to bring her bread anymore. But when I got there she was in a panic, about to leave to go to the police station. Ezrah, her husband, had gone missing, and she was heading out to try to find him. She said, 'Thank God you're here. I'll come by your house when I've found him,' and she thrust baby Menashe into my arms and ran off down the street. I was pretty shocked. She was supposed to be in hiding, and there she was running off in broad daylight. Plus I had no idea what to do with a baby. He was only about a month old.

I went upstairs to ask the family who'd been letting Leah hide there if they could look after the baby, but no one was home. Menashe started to cry and so, thinking my mum would know what to do, I took him back to our house.

When I got there, I was greeted by the sound of weeping – it was so loud I could hear it through the front door. Inside, I found my mother wailing in the lounge. Pierre was there too, which was unusual, a look of panic in his eyes.

The local police had taken Dad away for questioning, they explained. Then Pierre looked me straight in the eye and said, his voice really flat, but somehow full of meaning because of it, 'They've, um, arrested Johann, as well.'

I explained about Leah thrusting the baby on me, and my mother shouted at me for bringing him to the house. It was dangerous, she said, and we had enough problems already.

Eventually Pierre headed off to see what he could find out from his policeman friend Matias, who was, you know . . . one of our group.

You mean he was gay?

Yes. No one in the police force knew that, of course, but yes. He was one of Pierre's conquests, I suspect. So Pierre went off to see if he knew, or could do, anything.

I asked my mother how I could help and she said, 'Get that screaming baby out of here before the Germans come back and take us all!' So I scooped him up again and went off to try to find either Leah, or news of Leah, or even just some baby milk to feed him with.

He cried all the way to town – he literally didn't stop – so I was terrified that he was making me conspicuous. We always tried to be invisible back then, to slip into the shadows, to be plain and boring and discreet. But the German soldiers all just smiled at me as if it was funny, and I realised that in a way the baby, by taking the attention away from me, made me even more invisible than usual.

By the time I got back home, Mum had calmed down a bit. She helped me make a teat out of a rubber glove, and we fed the baby cow's milk, and thank God, he finally shut up.

And then we sat and waited for news of my father, and for Leah to come and claim her baby.

The first person through the door was my father. He arrived just as the sun was setting, and my mother ran across the room into his arms.

He said everything was fine. He told us all to calm down. He said they'd just wanted a chat, 'that was all'.

Mum asked him what they'd wanted to know, and he said, 'Just stuff about the other war.' He said they were perhaps a bit nostalgic. It was typical of him to try to reassure us by joking about it, but I could tell from the tremor in his voice that he was shaken.

He noticed the baby then, so I told him how I'd been to Leah's place and how she'd dumped the baby on me and he said he hoped that she would be back for him because a trainload had gone out at five.

A trainload of Jews?

Yes. I asked him where they'd gone, and I remember he said, 'To wherever they go.' It was all pretty mysterious back then. The rumours were the south-west, he said, but no one knew for sure.

'So what do we do with the baby?' my mother asked him. He was someone else's child, after all, and Jewish, and therefore dangerous. Dad said he'd ask around to see if there were any of Leah's family left. But he said we'd have to keep him until the next day because of the curfew.

When Mum told him that my friend had been taken in too he thought at first that she meant Pierre and got really angry. He was still hoping that I'd come to my senses and get married to Pierre someday. So I explained that no, it was Pierre's friend Johann, and he calmed down.

Dad asked me if I knew why they'd taken Johann and I just shook my head. I remember that felt less like lying than saying I didn't know.

'They're probably just being nosey then,' he said. He was sure that Johann would be fine. They seemed to want to talk to everyone, he said.

And was Johann fine?

No. No, Johann wasn't fine at all. I waited until it was dark and the baby was sleeping and slipped next door to Pierre's house. We weren't supposed to go out after seven p.m., but our gardens joined up and were pretty overgrown. As long as you were quiet there wasn't much chance of getting caught.

His mother told me rather abruptly that he was in his room and went back to her sewing, so I opened his bedroom door and slipped in. He was lying flat on the bed with his head in the pillow, and when I touched his shoulder, he jumped and looked up at me. His eyes were all red from crying.

I asked if he'd found anything out, and he explained what Matias had told him: that Johann was in a cell with all the others. When I asked him what he meant by 'the others', he said, 'Davide, Michel, Princess, Lala . . . all of them. They're all there. They've been rounding them up one by one.' These were all names I recognised from the tea dance. Michel, particularly, I knew really well.

I asked him how they'd got hold of everyone's names, and he said, 'That . . .' but stopped short because I don't think he could think of a bad enough word to describe her. 'That . . . Lala,' he finally said. 'Apparently she's given them a list.'

He started to cry again then, so I hugged him. I asked if he was on the list too – if I was on the list – and he said he didn't know, but he thought it was unlikely and they'd have already come for him if he was on it.

I asked him about Matias, too, but he said she wouldn't dare name a policeman. No one would.

I'm confused. Who wouldn't dare?

Sorry, Lala. Lala was a man, but everyone referred to him as 'she'. He was pretty camp. His real name was Leonhardt, I think.

Right. Of course.

When I asked Pierre what else Matias had said he started to shake. Matias had told him to get out while he could. He'd said to escape over the border into France.

Gosh, was that feasible?

I hadn't known that it was, but apparently Matias knew of someone in a place called La Vieille-Loye – some carpenter chap – who'd been helping people get through the forest and over the demarcation line.

That sounds incredibly dangerous.

That's what I said. And that's when Pierre explained, through sobs, the other thing that Matias had told him: that they were torturing Johann. And that it was only a matter of time before Johann gave them Pierre's name too.

God, did they really do that? Torture people just to get their friends' names?

Yes. They absolutely did. Which is no doubt why Lala had given them a whole list of names in the first place. Apparently no one ever resisted for long. Their interrogation methods were brutal.

Selfishly, I thought about myself then, because Johann definitely knew my name and address, but Pierre said that, no, they weren't interested in women, only the men.

I asked him if he was going to try to get over the border and how – there were Germans everywhere by then – and he said he didn't know. Johann was still at the police station and Pierre was terrified they'd release him and he wouldn't be there to help – he loved that boy so much. But he was also terrified they'd come for him next.

And what did you want to do? Were you tempted to escape as well?

Not at that point. I just went back next door to bed. I was shattered, but I couldn't sleep. I had Leah's baby in my bed, and he was really annoying. He kept kicking me and squirming and crying. He was dirty, so I got up and changed him – Mum had made some nappies out of old towels – and I remember looking to see if he'd been circumcised. I suppose I was already starting to imagine that he might be with us for a while, and I wondered if he was visibly Jewish, which of course might pose an extra problem. But the truth was that I couldn't tell. I wasn't very expert on penises, in fact I'd never seen one up close. My mind was going crazy, wondering where Leah was, and if they'd really shipped her out on the train, and what we'd do with that poor baby if that was the case. I was thinking about poor Johann being tortured and wondering what they were doing to him, and about Pierre maybe leaving, and being tortured himself if he didn't leave . . . And of course there was no one I could talk to about any of it, because I couldn't explain to anyone why Johann had been arrested, nor why Pierre might be in danger. And despite Pierre's reassurances, I was pretty scared for myself. I definitely didn't know for sure that the SS wouldn't start going after women too.

The next morning, on Mother's orders, I went in search of Leah and/or baby formula again, and this time I at least managed to find some baby milk. But there was no sign of Leah, nor of any of her family or friends.

I thought Ethel's parents might have an idea who could take the baby so I walked all the way there, but their shoe-shop was shuttered and no one was home. In fact, every Jewish business was closed and the streets were eerily quiet.

I wondered where they all were and hoped that they'd simply been sent to south-west France, as Leah's family supposedly had.

On the way back I called in to Pierre's house, but there was no one home. I'd half expected Pierre to be out at work, but it was rare that his mother was absent. I wondered if perhaps the whole family had fled, but that made no sense because, of course, Pierre couldn't have told them why he was in danger either. So I was left wondering if he was just at work or whether he'd vanished over the border and his mother was out looking for him or . . . I really didn't know. All sorts of ideas went through my mind, but none of them made much sense.

The following day, the baby had the whole household up at dawn. He wouldn't sleep and he wouldn't take a bottle. He also had diarrhoea, which Mum said was perhaps because of the cow's milk. He screamed until he was bright red.

'He's missing his mum,' my mother told me. She said that there was nothing to be done. 'Eventually, he'll realise she's gone and he'll shut up,' she said. She shocked me with that. I think that was the first time I realised how the war was changing us all – how hardened we were all becoming.

At six I went and knocked on Pierre's door, but still no one was home. Then, just as I was about to leave, his mother appeared, shuffling up the garden path like an old person. She had a black eye and a ripped dress and looked absolutely shocking.

I asked her if she was OK and she shook her head. I asked her what had happened, and she shook it again. And then I asked her where Pierre was, and she said, 'They've got him. But don't go there. Don't try to help.' She said that no one could help him now.

I'll never forget those words, because I was stunned that she'd already abandoned hope. And then she walked to her front door, let herself in and slammed the door in my face.

That is pretty shocking. For a mother to just give up like that, isn't it?

I think she'd tried. I think she'd tried her hardest. And she'd suffered horribly for having done so.

Did she ever tell you what had happened to her?

No. But I can make a pretty good guess. Everyone knew the kinds of things that went on.

Sorry, but could you give us some idea, for the record?

I think she probably went to the police station and caused a stink to try to help her son. And got beaten and very possibly raped for her trouble.

Oh God. That's what I was thinking, but . . . I guess I didn't want to believe it. And Pierre?

Well, I went off in search of Matias. He was the only person I could think of who could help. There was a café I knew the policemen went to for their morning coffee. I thought he'd perhaps be able to tell me where Pierre was, or even better get him released. I hoped he'd have some news about Leah too, or be able to tell me what we should do with the baby.

I didn't dare go inside so I hid opposite in the alleyway between two houses and waited for him to arrive, but he must have been inside already, because the next thing I saw was him coming out with a colleague. I followed them from a distance until they went their separate ways and then, just as Matias was getting on his bicycle, I ran over the street to talk to him. He was furious with me – that was his first reaction. He pushed me into someone's garden, out of sight of the road, behind some bushes. He told me that what I'd done – coming to talk to him – was too dangerous. I asked him about Pierre and he looked like he might cry. He said I had no idea, and he said that they'd got them all and that he was petrified he'd be next.

I asked him if Pierre was OK, and I remember that made him laugh – a horrible, sick kind of laugh. 'None of them are OK,' he said. 'None of us are going to be OK.' And once again he told me that I didn't know what they were like.

I asked about Johann and he said, 'Schirmeck, probably.'

That was the first time I'd ever heard of Schirmeck, so I asked him if it was a prison, and he said that it was much worse than a prison and I remember trying to imagine what that could mean. I asked him about Michel then – because I really liked Michel – and he closed his eyes and shook his head and said, 'Gone.'

I thought at first that he meant that Michel had been sent to Schirmeck too, but he shook his head and said 'Gone' again and moved his hand in a sort of chopping motion, and I understood, in shock, that he was implying that Michel was dead.

I was so upset I could hardly speak. I couldn't hold back my tears any longer, and I remember that when he hugged me I could tell by his breathing that he was struggling not to cry too.

Eventually I managed to ask him what would happen to Pierre, and he shrugged and croaked that he'd probably be sent to Schirmeck as well if he got that far.

'You don't know what they're like,' he said again, and it must have been the fourth or fifth time he'd said that, so I asked him to explain. I said, 'Tell me what they're like. I think I need to know.'

'I can't,' he said. 'There are no words.' And then he pushed me away and repeated that this – what we were doing – was dangerous, and that he had to go.

He left me crouching down behind the bushes. I was shaking and crying. I was only just beginning to get an inkling. It will sound strange because these days everyone has seen the photos of the camps, so we know, don't we? But it was all new then. So it took ordinary people – people like me – an incredibly long time to assimilate what was going on. Because, as Matias said, *there are no words*. We had no vocabulary to describe what these people were doing to their fellow human beings, and without words there was no way to picture that kind of brutality, that kind of evil, either. A normal person's brain isn't wired to conceive of that kind of thing and I remember thinking years afterwards that it was one of the worst things the Nazis had done: they'd made us understand for ever more that people, that humans, could behave that way.

I suddenly remembered that I hadn't asked Matias what to do with Leah's baby, and so I ran out on to the street, but it was too late. He was already cycling into the distance. God!

Are you OK?

Yes. I just . . . I just remembered something so vividly . . . I got, you know, one of those flashbacks? It sent a shiver right down my spine.

Can you share it with me?

Of course. It's nothing really, it was so vivid, that's all, like it was just this morning. I remembered that the sun was shining really prettily through the clouds as he cycled away. And I remember wondering how God could allow the sun to shine when everything it was shining on was so hateful.

Yes. That's . . . I like what you said about there being no words that are strong enough. That's powerful.

It's pretty frustrating.

And, look, I'm sorry to interrupt, but my tape is just about to end. Shall I put another one in or have you had enough for today? I can come back another time, if you'd rather do it in chunks?

I think we can carry on for a bit, can't we? It's not even five o'clock yet. But if you want the whole story, then I'm not sure we'll get it finished today.

No. That's what I was thinking.

Ruth. Part Two.

A year went by before anyone could really notice.

When you're young, people you consider to be 'old' warn you how time flies, but trying to tell youngsters to make the most of their youth is a pointless endeavour, partly because the time-flying thing doesn't really become noticeable until your thirties, but mainly because the one thing youngsters are psychologically incapable of is learning from other people's experiences.

Anyway, at thirty-two I was starting to suspect that all the old whingers had been right. Spring, summer, winter. The seasons were passing like days of the week.

Christmas '95 had been a bit lacklustre because despite the supposed thaw in Jake's relationship with Dad, he and Abby had chosen to spend it in Cape Verde instead. So though the rest of the family had been present, Jake's absence meant there was still something of an atmosphere. Because things had felt less fluid than usual, I'd postponed, once again, the big conversation I'd been planning with Dad.

By spring, I was so busy that my plans to contact Grandpa Chris also fell by the wayside.

The first novel by a young author I'd signed in '94, Ellie Day, had finally (after extensive editing) been published, and to everyone's surprise we had a major hit on our hands. In fact twenty-two-year-old Day's *Party Goers* was such a massive success that it was proving hard for a small publisher like us to keep up. In addition to the frustrations associated with our limited size (there were seven of us, including the cleaner) was the fact that our author-and-promotions manager, Miriam, was on maternity leave. The end result was that I ended up having to do all kinds of things that had nothing to do with my job title.

Summer was exhausting but fun, and the fun bit was unexpected. Getting out of my joggers and into heels, sipping champagne in bookshops and chatting to booksellers and journalists made a change. Plus, my ego was loving the buzz that came with the most frequent questions I had to field: 'Who was the first person to read *Party Goers* at Impressionable?' and 'Who discovered Ellie?' Because that person, obviously, was me.

On top of all the buzz around *Party Goers*, getting out and about provided hitherto unimagined opportunities for romance.

So in October I had a fling with a sexy (if over-serious) *Times* journalist. If you're the kind of person who reads the culture pages then you will almost certainly know his name, but for obvious reasons, I'm not going to mention it here.

Just as that one was ending, because yes, he was going back to his wife after all, Dan came along, just in time for Christmas.

Dan was the owner and head chef of Meals on Wheels, the ironically named catering company we'd used for the Christmas book-signing I'd organised at Waterstones. He was fit, good-looking, and because of the circumstances (namely one of their waiters being off sick) dressed rather sexily in a tuxedo. And lord knows, I like a man in black tie.

Dan was funny, cute and flirty, and kept my glass fully filled all evening. It was only once the food and drinks had been packed away and he returned to linger beside me that I realised his attention to my needs had not been purely professional.

When I found myself in his flat the next morning, I fully expected to be kicked out and probably never see him again.

I woke first, and for a while, as I came to, I looked sleepily around his bedroom. I'd been too drunk to take much notice of it the previous night, but now I saw that it was very much a lad's room, but tasteful, arty and cultured with it. There were stripped varnished floorboards, a hi-fi with an expensive turntable and shelves filled with vinyl. But there were also books, which is always a good sign, plus a great Bowie poster and a full-sized reproduction of Hockney's *The Splash*.

I rolled on to my side and studied Dan's features for a bit, making the most of the fact that he was still asleep. His mid-length brown hair had fallen across his eyes and he looked quite angelic.

As I was sighing at my thoughts – at how disappointing it was that the sexy, pretty, good-in-bed ones like Dan never work out – he opened his eyes and smiled at me.

Then he stretched and yawned sexily, if such a thing is possible (which it is) and said, 'God, I was dreaming. I was dreaming about *you*! Can you believe that?' If I'm honest, I couldn't *really* believe that, but I made a determined effort to try.

In the battered kitchen of the apartment, he cooked me poached eggs and spinach on toast. He was sharing with two girls and a guy but we had the place to ourselves that morning. And then he asked me what I was doing for Christmas. That threw me a bit, I must admit, because asking about Christmas breaks every rule of the game.

His parents lived in Portugal, he explained, and his co-renter friends would all be elsewhere for Christmas. He was going to have the place to himself, and was wondering 'even though it was perhaps premature' if I fancied spending Christmas Day in bed. 'I cook a mean nut roast,' he told me, 'if you're into that. Or we could just drink champagne in bed.'

Jake and Abby had just got officially engaged and Christmas – by then only four days away – was to be the first since The Great Falling Out when everyone would be together. So I explained that, though champers in bed and nut roast sounded fabulous, Christmas with my family was non-negotiable.

'How many of you will there be?' Dan asked.

'Tom and Tracey, Harry and Suzie, Eirla and Pippa . . .' I started to count on my fingers, but then paused. 'Including or excluding kids?'

Dan shrugged. 'Include 'em,' he said. 'Let's go crazy.'

I counted to ten and then Dan offered his own fingers to help out. 'Sixteen,' I said, finally.

'Sixteen!' he repeated. 'Sounds amazing. A family Christmas dinner for sixteen! Who the hell does your catering?'

I laughed. 'Are you angling for the job, or to be invited?' I asked, then, 'Oh, you are, aren't you? You really do want to sample Mavaughn's burnt turkey.'

Dan shrugged again cutely and sipped his coffee. 'I really like you,' he said, and I suspect that I failed to keep the surprise from reaching my face.

'Oh, I know, I know . . .' Dan said. 'I'm supposed to play it all cool and disinterested, but since I hit thirty I just can't be bothered.'

'OK,' I said, then, 'Gosh.'

'You see! It's true,' he said. 'Now I've scared you off. If I'd said something like "Maybe see you next summer" you would have been all over me.'

'Not at all,' I said. 'It's just that I tend to assume everyone's got Christmas booked. Especially this late in the day. Plus, most men I meet turn out to be married or something. So a Christmas request . . . Well, that's a surprise.'

'I'm not,' Dan said. 'Married.'

'Or otherwise involved?'

'Nope. Free as a bird.'

'Or confused about your sexuality?'

Dan laughed and grinned salaciously. 'Nope. Totally clear about my sexuality as, hopefully, you noticed last night.'

'OK!' I laughed.

'And you?'

'Which one?'

'Any of them,' Dan said.

'Nope. I'm available,' I said. 'And equally unconfused about shagging.'

'So, do I get an invite or not? If there's already sixteen of you, what difference can one more make? Plus this particular "one more" can cook.'

'Maybe,' I said. 'But you don't know what you're letting yourself in for. The food's terrible and my family are out of control.'

'Mine are very much *in* control,' Dan said. 'Which is why yours sounds like fun.'

'We'll see,' I told him. 'Maybe.'

'Right,' Dan said. 'OK.' His lovely smile had begun to fade.

'Let's see how well you perform over the next few days,' I offered, attempting to reinject a bit of humour into the proceedings.

Dan laughed again and crawled on top of me. 'Oh, I have to *perform*, do I?' he asked, straddling and starting to tickle me.

And though I was telling myself that this was silly; though I was telling myself that I'd only just met him and that falling for him on a first date was utterly ridiculous, I was also thinking, *God, I could maybe fall in love with you.*

◆ ◆ ◆

Other than the fact I surprised everyone by bringing Dan along, Christmas '96 was pretty normal. Everyone was present and with the exception of some heated discussion about kids and passive smoking due to the fact that it was raining too hard to smoke outside, everyone got on just fine.

Abby was disappointed I hadn't brought Gina along, but she quickly took Dan under her wing instead. The two of them got on so well that both Jake and I ended up feeling jealous.

The turkeys were so burnt that by the time all the black bits had been discarded there wasn't that much left to eat. But Masterchef Dan had brought not one but two different nut roasts to the table, which – despite the usual anti-vegetarian vibe in our family – turned out to be quite a hit.

No one brought along Scruples to play, and everyone behaved themselves. The only near-miss was when Eirla, who hadn't been present for The Great Falling Out, quite casually asked Jake where he and Abby were getting married, and whether they were intending to get hitched in a church, or a registry office, or a synagogue.

'We haven't decided yet,' Jake said, sounding nervous.

'So would you have to convert?' Eirla asked, still unaware of the chill sweeping through the room.

Dan gave me a worried glance, and I was impressed that he had picked up on the danger.

'If we decided to get married in a synagogue, I would, yes,' Jake said. 'Why?'

'No reason,' Eirla said, sounding defensive. 'I just wondered, that's all.'

'But it's not on the cards for the moment, is it?' Abby said, reaching out for Jake's hand.

'Thank Christ for that,' Dad muttered, and had Mum not whacked him around the back of the head, I'm not sure how many of us would have noticed.

'What did you say?' Jake asked, his cheeks turning red.

'Nothing,' Dad said.

'Yeah, you did. Say it again.'

'I didn't say anything,' Dad said.

'He was just cheeking me,' Mum lied.

'I didn't hear, Jakey,' Abby whispered. 'What did he say?'

'Nothing,' Jake said. 'Forget it.'

No doubt retrieving a second-hand telling of The Great Falling Out from his dodgy memory banks, Eirla finally twigged. 'So!' he said, clumsily addressing Dan. 'How did you two meet?'

Dan, aware that the hot-potato task of moving the conversation on had been handed to him, cleared his throat. 'We met on a hook-up line, if you must know.'

'A hook-up line,' Mavaughn said. 'What's that?'

'It's a premium number you call to meet other like-minded swingers,' Dan said.

My mother took a sharp intake of breath.

'Well, fancy that!' Mavaughn said.

I elbowed Dan in the ribs. 'He's kidding you!' I announced to general relief. 'We met at one of Ellie Day's book-signing events. Dan was doing the catering.'

'Totally true,' Dan said, and people started to smile. 'But I like my version better.'

'I'm reading that right now,' Mum said. 'The Ellie Day book. It's very good. Quite racy, but funny too.'

'Everyone's reading that right now,' I said. 'And you can forget about opening your Christmas present. Because I can tell that you're not going to like it.'

'Oh, you didn't get me *Party Goers*, did you?' Mum asked.

'She got everyone *Party Goers*,' Dan said. 'I know because I did all the wrapping.'

And though I was annoyed that, just like that, he'd revealed the contents of everyone's presents, I was so relieved the conversation had moved on that I forgave him.

'They are *signed* copies,' I pointed out.

When we got back to my flat that evening, I'd barely fed Buggles when the phone rang. It was Jake on the other end of the line, so I joked that he must be missing me already.

'Guess what Dad asked Abby?' he said, ignoring my little joke and jumping straight in.

'Erm, I don't know,' I said, pulling a face for Dan's benefit. 'What did Dad ask Abby?'

'He asked her if Daniel is a Jewish name,' Jake said.

'He didn't!'

'He did! He said he didn't want to make the same mistake twice.'

I laughed weakly. 'God! And what did poor Abby say to that?'

'That's the best bit,' Jake said. 'She said . . . What did you say, exactly? Hang on, I'll put her on and she can tell you herself.'

There were a few clicks and scrapes and then Abby's voice sounded out. 'Hello you,' she said. 'Long time no see.'

'Hi, Abs,' I said. 'So what did you say to my idiot father?'

'I said that yes, Daniel can sometimes be a Jewish name, but that so could a lot of other common names, such as *Ruth* and *Jacob*! And then I told him that the easiest way to avoid making the same mistake twice was probably not trying to learn the etymology of every single name, but just avoiding making racist or anti-Semitic remarks in general.'

I laughed. 'Burn, baby! And what did he have to say to that?'

'He apologised, and said that yes, of course, I was right. And then he said that, to be honest, he doesn't care if Dan does turn out to be Jewish – he's just relieved you're not a dyke. Because apparently, for a while back there, you had him wondering.'

'Oh God.'

'And then he asked me if Ruth and Jacob are really Jewish names.'

'Oh, Dad . . .' I said. 'He really is clueless, isn't he?'

◆ ◆ ◆

So that's how Dad's latent anti-Semitism (not to mention his newly-hinted-at homophobia) became 'a thing'. No one really discussed it – we simply saw less of each other. Actually, that's not true. *I* saw a little less of everyone than usual. I'm pretty sure the primary members of the family nucleus – comprised of Mavaughn, my parents, and uncles Tom, Harry and Eirla – carried on living in each other's pockets as before. But I definitely increased my distance for a while, and as far as Jake was concerned, I don't think he saw anyone except me for about a year.

Because it went undiscussed, the issue was less present in everyone's minds than it had been during The Great Falling Out but I couldn't help but think the silence implied that the situation was in fact more serious this time around.

But selfishly, I didn't care as much as I should have. Things were going well with Dan, and after decades of fraught, complicated love affairs, the joy of being in a stable relationship with a funny, sexy guy was just about all-consuming.

Still, I waited for the guillotine to fall. For months I lived with a feeling that 'a terrible discovery' was imminent – a discovery that would prove the whole thing had been a mirage. Dan was married, or mad, or an alcoholic. He was a drug addict, or dying, or a con-man or – even though that seemed ever more unlikely the longer I knew him – gay. I didn't know which direction the storm was coming from, but for a while I lived with a sense of certainty that the storm would most surely come, and it would probably come *that day*. But one sunrise after another, Dan continued to prove me wrong.

We both had full-on careers – Dan with his catering business, and me running around after Ellie Day and her many fans. So Dan and I didn't always get to spend as much time together as we would have liked.

Between chaperoning Ellie in Manchester, Edinburgh and New York, while trying to fit everything else into the gaps in her schedule, and Dan's constant crisis management at Meals on Wheels, which had him forever driving somewhere for last-minute fish, or somewhere else to deliver last-minute food, or putting on a tux to replace one of his waiters, the moments when we were available to spend quality time together were few and far between. In February, for example, I think we only got to see each other twice.

Though this lack of availability increased the excitement when we did finally get together, I was still feeling paranoid and thus was able to convince myself that absence was maybe the only reason for all that passion. After all, absence makes the heart grow fonder and familiarity breeds contempt. If we ever managed to spend a full week together, wasn't it still possible that we'd realise how incompatible we'd been all along?

So it was with great excitement, and much trepidation, that I accepted Dan's invitation to holiday together in Portugal.

He'd planned the ten-day break at his parents' house long before we'd met, while I had almost a month of holiday I needed to take before the end of April. There was no way I could manage a month, but ten days seemed doable.

His parents' house was in Faro, a stone's throw from the beach, he said. They would be present for the first and last days of our stay while, for the other eight days, with the exception of Maximiano

– the aged Labrador it was our duty to look after – we'd have the place to ourselves. It sounded like the perfect opportunity to get to know each other, didn't it? A proposition that excited me but which also scared me witless.

◆ ◆ ◆

We boarded our flight on the afternoon of the 17th of April at Luton. It had been raining for a month in London but Faro was forecast to be sunny. I had my bikini packed. I was excited!

I had no intention of expressing my fears; had, in fact, consciously decided *not* to express them. But as we sat and fidgeted beneath us for our seat belts, it just slipped out. 'So are you scared that we'll end up hating each other after a full ten days together?'

Dan laughed. 'Of course,' he said. 'We're halfway there already.'

'Halfway?' I said flatly. 'How so?'

'Well, I already hate you. So all we need now is for you to start hating me back.'

He glanced at the tattered in-flight magazine from the seat pocket and then fiddled with the sticky-looking safety card. He tightened his seat belt and peered out of the window at the runway.

Finally he glanced sideways at me. 'Oh shit!' he said, performing a mock double-take. 'She's being serious! Are you? You can't be?'

And because, in that moment, I realised how ridiculous I was being, I pretended it had been a joke after all. 'Totally serious,' I mugged, pulling a face and nodding. 'And well on the way to hating you already.' And then I rather convincingly slipped into a sexy grin instead.

Dan winked at me and then sighed.

'What?' I asked.

'Do you think Blair's actually going to win?' Back home, everyone was talking about the election, but at a loss as to why Dan was mentioning him now, I glanced around the cabin until I found my answer – a man in the aisle seat had just picked up his copy of the *Telegraph* and the cover was splashed with an unflattering photo of Tony Blair.

'Maybe,' I said. 'Everyone in publishing's rooting for him anyway.'

'Pretty much everyone in London,' Dan said.

'Except my mum,' I said.

'Yeah?'

'Yes, she hates him. She says he's slimy. Actually, *smarmy* was the word she used.'

'Smarmy?' Dan said. 'In that case I guess he's done for.'

The flight went without a hitch and three hours later Dan's father had picked us up from the tiny airport. He was older than I'd imagined – late seventies, at a guess – with a full head of grey hair and skin that was wrinkled like a sun-dried tomato. But he was in shape, I'll give him that. He was tall and thin and sporty-looking with an upright, almost military gait.

He shook my hand vigorously and then shook Dan's too. Being from a family of huggers, that surprised me, but Dan had warned me they were 'control freaks' so I supposed this was just another aspect of that.

The drive to Praia de Faro in Henry's immaculate old Renault took less than ten minutes and as we approached our destination I could hardly believe my luck. When Dan had said that his parents' place was a 'stone's throw' from the beach, I'd imagined the sort of distance estate agents try to minimise by using that phrase, whereas in fact the beach was *literally* a stone's throw away – a toddler's stone throw even, and from any window you chose.

Praia de Faro is a long, thin strip of land which is essentially an island linked to the mainland by a raised roadway or a long, low bridge, depending on how you look at it. The island is comprised of one single, sandy road with beaches either side. That's three miles of back-to-back beach, dotted with houses, restaurants and small, local-looking beach bars.

Their unassuming villa faced the street that ran the length of the island. On the far side was a peeling white wall which was attempting, but failing, to hold back the dunes, and beyond the dunes, the Atlantic, the horizon, the universe. At the rear of the house their garden merged seamlessly with another grassy beach bordering the thin strip of sea that separated the island from the mainland.

'What an amazing place!' I commented as Dan lifted our cases from the hatchback.

'The sand gets in everything . . .'

'*Everything*,' his father repeated.

'But other than that it's pretty much perfection.'

'It is,' I said, spinning on one heel to take it all in. 'Panoramic perfection!'

Dan's mother greeted us at the front door and Maximiano loped out beside her to say hello as well.

Like her husband, Carolina was tall and grey-haired, and she had similar poise. She too shook my hand rigidly, though she deigned to peck her son on the cheek.

If the parents were keeping their emotions in check, the dog most certainly wasn't. He jumped up and licked Dan's face, and then rolled at his feet before licking my toes where they peeped through my sandals and barging me so hard that I fell over.

Once I'd scrambled back to my feet, Carolina showed us to a small, plain boxroom overlooking the rear beach and therefore the mainland.

We dumped our cases on the bed and then Dan kicked the door closed. 'We'll steal their room tomorrow once they've gone,' he said, looking out of the window with me while nudging my hip with his. 'At the front they've got a sea view, balcony, the works.'

'Oh, this is fine, Dan,' I said. 'And that is the sea. Well, a bit of it.'

'Yeah, but the front bedroom's even better,' he said. 'Plus they have . . . a . . .' He wiggled both eyebrows suggestively.

I frowned at him. 'They have a *what*?'

'A waterbed!' Dan said with a wink. 'It's even got a wave-maker thingy that bounces you up and down, so you don't even need to do any work. Just switch it on and wait to see who comes first.'

I stared at him wide-eyed. I couldn't imagine his parents having a waterbed at all.

'Really?' I asked.

'Nah,' Dan laughed, turning to the door again, where Maximiano was nosing his way in. 'T'would be fun though. Come in, Max!'

Max pushed into the room and started snuffling at my crotch. 'The dog's friendly!' I commented, almost instantly regretting the fact that it had the potential to sound like a non-comment on his parents, as in friendly dog (shame about the parents).

'Your folks seem lovely, too,' I added quickly, but it was too late. Dan had spotted the gap.

'They're all right really,' he said. 'They're kind, that's the main thing. They're just not very effusive.'

'I didn't for a minute think anything else,' I told him.

'I think they got Maximiano so that he could express everything they can't,' Dan said, as Maximiano put his front paws up on the bed and started licking the side of my neck.

'Well, some forms of expression are more acceptable from a dog, after all,' I said.

Dan frowned at me, so I expounded: 'I'm just not sure how I would have reacted if your mother had started licking my neck, that's all.'

That evening we went three doors down to a little local restaurant. It was their 'canteen', Henry explained, and once I saw the price list I understood why. Because with filleted snapper and fried potatoes at the equivalent of £1.10, with a carafe of wine at 20p, why would you ever eat at home?

The food was good, too: simple fare, nothing fancy . . . Just pan-fried fish with butter and parsley sauce served with spicy fried potatoes. We were seated on plastic chairs beneath strip lights at a worn Formica table, but the fish was fresh and locally caught, and the potatoes were crispy and chewy at the same time, a combination that's not so easy to achieve. I felt relieved to know that restaurants like that still existed. A back-to-basics sort of vibe, but not in the fake London way at all. Just a place you go to eat.

The conversation with Dan's parents remained clunky, especially compared with the easy chit-chat of my mother's side of the family, but I liked them all the same. They did, indeed, seem kind, and were genuinely interested in me.

So I summarised, as best I could, where I lived in London, and my French/Irish ascendants, and then asked them how they'd come to be living in Faro.

It turned out that Carolina had been born in Portugal and moved to London with her parents as a child. When Dan's maternal grandmother had fallen ill the year they'd both retired, they'd taken it as a sign and moved back so they could take care of her.

'Eventually she died, of course,' Dan's mother said, matter-of-factly. 'But by then we didn't want to move back, did we? Not back to Croydon. Not after here.'

'Yes, I can see the attraction,' I said. 'I think you're incredibly lucky to be here.'

'And your father's French, then?' Henry asked me. 'So you're immigrants in Britain, like Carolina was? How's that working out for you?'

'Well, Dad's totally integrated,' I explained. 'So I never felt like an immigrant at all. You'd never even know Dad was French, actually. Most of the time, I'm not even aware of it. He sounds very much like a Londoner. But Grandpa Christophe can be quite haw-he-haw, especially if he's tired. Actually, if he's had a drink, he can sound like that policeman from *'Allo 'Allo!*

'How old was your dad when he came over?' Dan asked.

I frowned. 'I don't know,' I said. 'Young. Five, ten – something like that.'

'And how did they get on, when they arrived?' Henry asked. 'Do you know why they moved to England in the first place?'

I shrugged. 'I'm afraid I have no idea. We didn't see them a great deal.'

'Oh,' Dan's mum said. 'And why would that be?'

I shrugged again, and felt myself blush. 'I'm afraid I don't know that either.'

'Anyway,' Dan said, addressing his parents. 'What time am I taking you two to the airport tomorrow? It's an early one, right?'

I noted from the way his mother dragged her eyes away that he'd changed the subject because I was sounding a bit weird.

After the restaurant, we walked half a mile along the sandy road to the northern end of the isle, where we sat in a fake-Hawaiian beach bar and drank delicious cold beers. And then, mentioning their early start the next morning, Henry and Carolina went home.

Dan headed off to the loo, and while he was gone I pulled my brand-new Nokia from my handbag and clunkily constructed an SMS to Jake. You had to press an unbelievable number of buttons to write anything back then because every letter required multiple presses.

'HI JAKE; JUST ARRIVED IN FAROBULOUS; QUICK Q: YOU KNOW WHY THE GRAMPS MOVED TO ENGLAND OR EVEN WHEN? I DON'T. IS THAT WEIRD?'

I was quite proud of my eloquent message, specifically the question mark I'd managed to place at the end. But when I clicked on send, the message just sat there on the screen for thirty seconds before a box popped up with 'SEND FAILED NO COVER'.

As I say, the phone was new, and I'd never tried to use it abroad before. Perhaps it wasn't even possible to send messages home from Portugal.

As my message appeared to have vanished, and as there was no way I was typing it again, the question would just have to wait until I got home.

Dan returned then, grinning and carrying two more dewy glasses of beer. 'One more and then home, I reckon,' he said. 'I'm shattered.'

'Sure,' I said. 'Me too.'

'Anything important?' he asked, as I slipped the phone back into my bag.

'Nah, I was just seeing if it works here.'

'And does it?' Dan asked.

'Not in any discernible way!' I laughed, pulling a face. 'But you know, me and technology . . .'

◆ ◆ ◆

The next morning, I woke to the sound of waves and screaming seagulls.

I pulled on yesterday's jeans and jumper and padded my way downstairs to discover an empty house. Dan, I assumed, had taken his parents to the airport. I gave him top marks for having let me sleep in.

Coffee was waiting on a hotplate along with what continental hotels like to call a 'mixed plate' – bread, ham, cheese and butter.

I wrinkled my nose. I don't eat meat if I can help it, and cheese before noon is just madness. But on returning the ham and the cheese to the refrigerator, I found a pot of Nutella-like spread, so all was well.

I wandered around the house, trying to choose the best place for breakfast. There was nowhere to sit in the kitchen and the lounge was too spotless to be a room where anyone might dare eat. But the dining room also had a failing in that the sea view was obscured by a massive dying bush.

In the end, I thought *what the hell* and, barefoot, took my breakfast to the other side of the sandy street, where I sat on top of a dune. From there I could survey both our open front door and enjoy the wonderful blue seascape. And that view, that sea breeze, well, it made that first morning's breakfast quite magical. In fact, to this day, I think it's one of the most memorable breakfasts I've had.

After about ten minutes, Dan drove up in his father's Renault. He paused beside me and, leaning on the open window, grinned up at me. 'Nice breakfast spot?' he asked.

'Perfect,' I called back. 'Amazing!'

A woman walking her child passed between us at that moment and she too smiled up at me and said something that I presumed was 'Good morning' in Portuguese.

Dan parked the car and opened the boot, revealing bags of shopping, so I scooted down the dune to the roadside to help him.

'The dining room's rubbish, isn't it?' Dan said, and I was surprised that he'd worked out why I'd ended up on top of the dune. 'Who wants to sit and eat looking at a dead bush?'

'That's kind of why I crossed the road,' I admitted as he handed me a carrier bag.

'The balcony's the place,' he said, nodding in the direction of his parents' upstairs bedroom. 'That's why we're going to steal the room.'

'They won't mind?'

'They won't know,' Dan said.

'But they *would* mind?'

'They won't *know*,' he said again, more decisively.

Once we'd put the food away and changed his parents' sheets, we poured fresh cups of coffee and went to sit on the balcony. It was small, just wide enough for the tiny table and two chairs, but the view from up there was exquisite. A hundred and eighty degrees of beach and sea and horizon.

While watching some kite-surfers shooting past, we chatted about Dan's parents visiting Paris, and our plan for the day, which was basically to eat and sleep and make love.

'And swim,' I added. 'I presume it gets warmer later on.'

'Sure,' Dan said, with a wry smile. 'About two is probably the warmest.'

'Why are you grinning?' I asked. 'Don't you believe I'll swim? Or are there sharks or something?'

Dan shook his head innocently. 'No, I'm just looking forward to swimming with you,' he said, and I didn't quite believe him.

On the way back downstairs, I paused to look at some framed photos hanging in the stairwell. 'She was pretty,' I said, pointing to a photo of his mother striking a ballet pose. 'She danced?'

'A bit,' Dan said. 'Only amateur.'

'It still shows in her poise, though.'

We continued down a few steps and then Dan pointed to an older photo of another couple in tatty formal clothes. 'That's her,' he said. 'That's my grandmother, the one they came back here to look after.'

'Did you know her?' I asked, prompting Dan to laugh.

'Of course I knew her,' he said. 'She's . . . she was . . . my grandmother.'

'And you were close?'

'Well, yeah,' he said, pulling a face to indicate that my question struck him as absurd.

'Don't be like that,' I said. 'Not everyone is close to their grandparents. I hardly even knew . . . know . . . my father's side of the family.'

'Really?' Dan said. 'How come?'

I shrugged and continued downstairs. 'I have no idea really. I didn't even notice until my grandmother died last year. Which is weird.'

'Yeah, that is weird,' Dan said, moving into the lounge.

I crossed to the sideboard, where even more photos were amassed, and picked up one of Dan's mother with his frail-looking grandmother.

'One of the last ones,' Dan commented, moving to stand beside me and slipping one arm around my shoulder as if it was me that needed comforting.

'It's lovely that they came back to look after her,' I commented.

'Well, someone had to,' Dan said. 'And they were retired, so . . .'

'Sure,' I said, almost adding that I hadn't even known my grandmother had been ill. But because I felt ashamed of the fact, a fact that Dan would almost certainly consider even weirder, I said nothing. Instead, I put the photo back down and pushed from my mind another challenging fact that had popped up: my parents had *no* photos of Dad's childhood that I knew of. There were photos of me and Jake, and lots of photos of Mum's side of the family. But none of Dad's childhood or his parents. Another thing I'd never noticed before.

'So what now?' Dan asked.

'Walk?' I suggested. 'Beach?'

'Sex?' Dan offered.

I wrinkled my nose.

'Oh, wow!' Dan said, feigning offence. 'We've already reached the scrunchy-nose stage, have we? Full-on hatred can't be far behind.'

I gave him a playful push. 'You!' I said. 'No, I just fancy a walk, that's all.'

'Max does need walking,' Dan admitted. 'But I'm not picking up his poo.'

That, pretty much, is how the next eight days were filled. Despite the fact that we did so little, or perhaps precisely because we did so little, it slipped by in the blink of an eye.

We'd have breakfast, walk Max and then return home to cook lunch. We'd eat on the balcony watching the surfers, then have a siesta, followed by luxurious, hour-long sex sessions. Then we'd shower, walk Max again and stop at a bar for a beer. Finally, we'd eat in the 'canteen' next door, walk to the end for a drink in Little Hawaii, and then home.

I missed out the 'swim' part of the schedule because there was a reason that Dan had smirked when I'd suggested a swim: the sea was *freezing*.

Did Dan decide to tell me that, though? Did he choose to warn me? No he did not. Instead, he eagerly changed into his swimming shorts and suspended a pair of swim goggles around his neck. We crossed the road and laid our towels between the dunes before he shouted, 'Last one in's a sissy. Last one to go head-under cooks dinner!' after which we both began to run.

He 'unfortunately' tripped on some grass, which left me powering ahead, and so, laughing, I put everything I had into it and managed my finest sprint in years. I was up to my ankles when I realised how far behind me Dan had fallen, and up to my thighs by the time I understood why.

With a scream, I stopped. The water had barely reached my bikini line but the sensation was like pins and needles. And I've been swimming in Scarborough in May, so I'm honestly no wimp.

'Whassup?' Dan called out. 'Cold?'

I turned back to see him doubled up with laughter at the shoreline. 'It's fucking freezing, Dan!' I said, already wading back.

'Not actually freezing,' Dan said, through continued laughter. 'It's a few degrees above. About thirteen.'

'Thirteen!' I exclaimed.

'It's the Atlantic. Why do you think no one else is swimming?'

Of course, I splashed him. He must have known that was coming, but he nonchalantly glanced back towards the house to make it all seem like a surprise.

On the final day he drove us to the centre of Faro. I was feeling like a philistine for having spent the entire eight days on the beach, plus I wanted to buy something for Mum. By common accord, there were too many people in our family for gift-buying to be inclusive. But everyone knew the one rule that allowed you to exclude everyone else. You *had* to get something for Mum.

The centre of Faro was prettier than I'd expected. I'd feared it would be a bit Benidormy, but it wasn't. The pedestrian streets were elegantly tiled and the buildings low-rise; the shops and cafés looked local-owned, which made a change from Starbucks and Primark back home. With the occasional exception of a restaurant offering 'Fish and chips – English spoken', it still felt authentic and foreign and nice.

As far as gifts were concerned, I couldn't find any local options I could imagine my mother might like. The shops everywhere were full of Chinese-made fridge magnets and, for some inexplicable reason, lace. In the end I settled on a tube of Portuguese custard tarts, or rather *Pastéis de Nata*. On the plus side, I got to test a freebie before I committed to my purchase and it was delicious. On the downside, my choice implied that I'd be forced to visit my parents the next day so that the tarts would still be fresh. Deciding it was wise to keep open the option of just eating them all myself, I grabbed a bottle of Porto as well.

On the way back we picked his parents up from the airport. They looked less rested and were paler than when they'd left eight days earlier, but I suppose that's just what happens when you live somewhere like Praia de Faro and choose to holiday in the centre of Montmartre.

Once home, they carried their cases upstairs, but Dan's mother came jogging back down almost immediately. 'Have you been using our bed?' she asked, glancing between the two of us.

'Who's been sleeping in *my* bed?' Dan boomed. When no one laughed he continued, 'Not at all. Why would we want to do that?'

'Well, you changed the sheets,' Carolina said.

'That was my idea,' I lied. 'Sort of to welcome you home. It's nice to come home to clean sheets, isn't it?'

'Why *would* we, anyway?' Dan asked again, feigning confusion. 'I don't want to sleep in your bed. God knows what you get up to in there.'

'Very funny,' Dan's mother said.

'Maximiano got in there once,' Dan told her, 'which was another reason to change the sheets. I showed Ruth the balcony and forgot to shut the door. So he spent the whole day on your bed.'

'He loved it there,' I said. 'He was stretched out like a sunbather on the beach.'

'He loves anything that's forbidden,' Carolina said, wiggling a finger at Dan. 'Just like you!'

And then as she started to remount the stairs she paused. 'Thank you,' she said, without turning back. 'Thank you for changing the sheets.'

Once she was out of sight, Dan tapped palms with me. 'Great lying. You're hired,' he whispered.

Getting home the next day felt tough. It was raining in London – that dull, grey drizzle that Britain so excels at – and after the blue skies and dazzle of Portugal, it felt like God had forgotten to switch on the lights.

But most traumatic of all was going our separate ways at St Pancras. I hadn't, for some reason, prepared myself for the moment when Dan would say, 'So! This is me . . .' while pointing to a tunnel to the left.

For the first time I saw the obvious advantage of living together. No more goodbyes. No more doubts about when we'd next manage to meet. No more, 'So! This is me . . .'

Feeling choked up almost to the point of tears, I let him hug me.

'Are you really going to schlep out to Walthamstow just to give your mother those tarts?' he asked.

I thought about the drizzle and dragging my suitcase through puddles and began to hesitate. I could always get a taxi to theirs from the Tube station, I supposed, but all the same.

'Too slow!' Dan said. 'You're going to go straight home and scoff them, aren't you?'

'Maybe,' I replied. 'I am struggling to motivate myself to go out there.'

'Buggles'll be happier if you go straight home,' Dan said helpfully. 'He must be missing you like crazy.'

'Thanks,' I said. 'I think you've convinced me.'

'In which case, you should probably give me half,' Dan said.

'Half what?'

'Half the tarts.'

'Oh, no,' I said. 'No, I'm not really going to eat them. I'll just take them out to Mum's tomorrow. They'll survive an extra day.'

'They'll be stale,' Dan said.

'Mum's Irish. She's never eaten a *Pastéis de Nata*. I'll just say that's how they're supposed to be.'

We started to go our separate ways, but then I turned and called Dan back. 'Thank you for that,' I said. 'I had a brilliant time. Really.'

'You don't hate me then?' he said, slipping into a grin.

I shook my head. 'Nah. Saving that for later.'

'Good,' he said.

'And you?'

'Quite the contrary,' he said.

And to my shame, all I did was nod. 'See you soon then,' I croaked. And as tears welled up, I powered off towards the Victoria line, trundling my suitcase behind me. I didn't look back once.

The next morning I woke up to the beep-beep of text messages arriving on my Nokia. Thanks to Buggles, I'd slept really badly.

Though my neighbour had been in to visit him, feed him and cuddle him twice a day, he'd been so overjoyed at my return that he had massaged me for much of the night while purring at full volume. When this had failed to elicit a response, he'd moved on to licking and even biting my nose.

Once I had a mug of coffee in my hand, I moved to the sofa, where Buggles jumped on my lap.

I attempted to focus on my mobile phone. The first text was from Dan at 6.24. It read, 'Morning, sexy. Missing you like crazy already. When's the next saucy siesta?'

I replied, 'NOW? COME OVER!' and a few minutes later he replied, 'Soz. At work. It's a nightmare. Laters.'

The second text was from Jake, offering to meet me for breakfast at Ed's in Soho, an American-style diner he favoured. 'We'll be there from 10–11.30 if you're interested,' the message read.

It was gone eleven by the time I got to Ed's, and Jake and Abby were already eating.

'Sorry, sorry,' I said. 'I woke up late. I think I have jet lag. But I'm here!'

'Can you get jet lag from Portugal?' Abby asked.

'No,' Jake said, speaking through a mouthful of pancake. 'But don't worry. She does know that.'

'Oh,' Abby said, looking confused. 'Anyway, we're the ones who are sorry, aren't we? We're sorry for starting without you. But that's my fault. I was starving.'

'We both were,' Jake said. 'And I'm not sorry at all.'

I ordered a full veggie breakfast from a girl with a fake American accent and then told them all about Faro while I waited.

Once my own breakfast arrived, I listened, while I ate, to their discussion about wedding plans.

Jake explained that they'd decided to have a civil ceremony in a register office, but were going the whole hog afterwards.

'D'you mean circle dancing and jiggling you around on chairs?' I asked.

'Yeah, the hora and everything,' Jake said. 'Dad's gonna love it.'

'Luckily my lot aren't believers or anything,' Abby said. 'But they sure do love to party.'

I smirked at that, and Abby asked me why.

'She's imagining the mayhem of our lot dancing with your lot,' Jake said. 'Or fighting them.' Then, turning to me, 'Am I right?'

'I was actually imagining a combined hora and Irish jig,' I told him. 'Could you circle dance to jig music?'

'You can hora to just about anything,' Abby said. 'And I'd say they're pretty close. So if you want to bring along some Irish fiddlers, they can jam with our Jewish ones. It could be fun.'

'The more fiddlers the merrier,' Jake said, raising an eyebrow.

Once we'd all finished eating, I asked the question that had been bugging me my entire holiday; why did I know so little about my grandparents?

'Well, they came after the war, didn't they?' Jake said, as though this was everything anyone could need to know.

'What year though?' I asked. 'I've been trying to work out how old Dad was when he arrived.'

Jake shrugged. 'He was young.'

'Does he still speak French?' I asked. 'You see, I don't even know that.'

Jake frowned and nodded at the same time. 'I think so. He tried speaking French once or twice in Spain, didn't he? Not that it helped.'

'OK. So, what part of France do they come from? Why did they come to London in the first place? Do you know that stuff? Because I don't.'

Jake sighed. 'Not really. Not in *detail*.'

'Then tell me the bits you do know.'

'OK, look, I admit it. I don't know shit,' Jake said. 'But I don't think that's necessarily abnormal. I mean, they're our grandparents, not our parents. I think plenty of people don't see much of their grandparents.'

'Really?' I said. 'You see, I'm not sure that's normal at all. Unless there's a *reason* why we never saw them.'

'You mean, like an argument?'

'Yeah. Anything that would explain why.'

'Did they go back to France or something?' Abby asked.

'No, Genny moved to Brighton, but as far as I know, Grandpa Chris is still in London today.'

'Even Brighton's not exactly the other side of the planet,' Abby said.

'No,' Jake said. 'No, I suppose not.'

'Maybe your dad was angry because they divorced,' Abby offered. 'That can happen. Happened to a friend of mine, actually.'

'Perhaps,' I said. 'I don't remember anyone ever talking about it though. In fact I can't remember anyone even mentioning the fact that Dad's French.'

'But we know he is,' Jake said.

'Sure. But I don't know how I know.'

'I saw an old passport once, I think,' Jake said. 'Don't you remember that? In that drawer where they had the lighters and screwdrivers and what have you. There was an old passport with a photo of him wearing a suit.'

'Yes, we used to play with it. I used to ask you for your passport to let you into the den. And the year?'

'When they came over, you mean?' Jake shook his head almost unnoticeably.

'He was born in, what, 1940?'

'Yeah, he was fifty-six last time, right? So yeah, 1940.'

'You cannot be serious,' Abby said. 'You don't even know what year your parents were born?'

'Well, Mum was born in '42,' I said. 'We know that one. But we never talked much about Dad.'

'Maybe he, like, had to give it up or something when he became English?' Jake offered. 'Maybe that's why we never talked about it. Because he's not French, anymore. Actually, maybe that's what pissed him off. It would piss me off, losing my nationality.'

'I'm pretty sure you can have both if you're French,' Abby said. 'I think you can have, you know, dual nationality.'

'But we don't have both, do we?' I asked.

'Of course not.'

'But I mean, could we? If we wanted? I'd quite like to be Anglo-French or Franco-British or whatever. It sounds classy.'

Jake shrugged. 'I don't know,' he said. 'You'll have to ask Dad.'

'I'm going to,' I said. 'I'm going to see them right after this.'

'You have such a strange family,' Abby said. 'Sometimes I worry what I'm marrying into.'

'It's only Dad,' Jake said. 'Dad's the only weird one.'

'So, Dad. I have a question for you.'

I'd been there less than five minutes. Mum was still unwrapping her gift.

'Yes?'

'Are you still French?'

He made a face and pulled his neck in as if the question both confused and offended him. 'Where did *that* come from?' he asked.

'You *know* he's French,' Mum said, without looking up. 'What a silly thing to ask.'

She had undone the end of the wrapping paper and, for some reason known only to her, was trying to extract the tube of tarts from within the paper without ripping it.

'I just thought you might have had to give it up when you became British.'

'No, I have dual nationality. But you know that.'

I smiled tightly. 'If you say I do, then I must,' I said. 'But I honestly can't remember it ever being discussed. And I mean ever. And nor can Jake, for that matter.'

'Why would we need to discuss it?' Dad asked. 'Why would it be an issue?'

'Do we discuss me being Irish?' Mum asked, finally extracting the box from the intact tube of wrapping paper, which she suddenly found she didn't know what to do with. She placed it delicately on the coffee table so that it stood up of its own accord and started to examine the box of tarts.

'No, but it's pretty present . . . our Irish heritage . . . I mean, I was certainly never in any doubt. Whereas on Dad's side, no one ever mentions it, which is kind of bizarre, if you think about it.'

Dad pulled a face, implying that I was being silly.

'Like I say,' I continued, 'I just don't remember anyone talking about it. I don't even know how old you were.'

'When we moved?' Dad said. 'I was five.'

'So how come you don't have an accent or anything?'

Dad shrugged. 'Like I say, I was *five*.'

'He does still say *bizarre* quite a bit,' Mum said, smiling lovingly at my father.

'Bizarre?'

'Yeah. No one ever really says *bizarre*,' Mum said. 'Except the French.'

'I say bizarre,' I said.

'Yes, you get that from me. And from your grandparents,' Dad said.

'Erm, I think you'll find that I didn't get much from my grandparents,' I said.

'What's that supposed to mean?' Mum asked.

'I meant from Dad's side. We hardly ever saw them.'

'Ah,' Mum said, relieved that the honour and influence of her side of the family remained intact. 'OK then.'

'And you saw them plenty when you were kids,' Dad said, sounding vaguely annoyed with me. 'You just don't remember.'

'So, what is this?' Mum asked, turning the tube in her hand.

'Um, I have absolutely no idea,' I said sarcastically. The tube was embellished with a massive photo of a custard tart. It even said 'Handmade Portuguese Custard Tarts' in English on the top.

'Really?' Mum said. 'You didn't take a peep?'

Both Dad and I snorted at this. I pointed at the picture and said, 'Mum!'

'But it's not the right shape,' Mum said, opening the end and sliding out the transparent tube of stacked tarts within. 'Oh,' she said. 'I see. I was thinking it looked more like a bottle or something.'

I blinked at her in disbelief. Sometimes my mother scares me.

Dad caught my eye and winked. A few years back he would have made an unsavoury joke about her being Irish, but thankfully these days he just winks.

'So shall I make a cup of tea to go with these?' Mum asked.

'I couldn't, love,' Dad said. 'I'm still stuffed from lunch.'

'Oh, you can have a taste,' Mum said. 'I'll make tea and we can cut them in half. Or do we have to have some special Portuguese drink with these?'

'Tea would be great,' I said, pulling the bottle of Porto from my bag. 'But I also got you this.'

'Oh, lovely,' Mum said. 'That's just lovely. But for the moment I'll go with tea.'

Once she'd left the room, Dad picked up the bottle and examined the label. 'She hates port,' he said. 'But luckily for you, I love the stuff.'

'Well, good. That way you both have something.'

Dad caressed the bottle and put it down.

'So where is everyone?' I asked. I couldn't remember when I'd last seen my parents alone.

'All busy. Harry's at some birthday party in South London. Eirla's taken his lot down to Margate for the day.'

'In this weather?' I asked. The forecast was grey and cold with occasional showers.

'They're going to the funfair, not the beach. And Tom is . . . I can't remember where Tom is. A work thing, I think.'

'And Mavaughn?'

'Oh, she elbowed her way into the Margate trip.'

'Right,' I said. 'That'll be nice for her.'

'It's good to have a bit of peace and quiet, to be honest.'

'You're a rude one!' I said. 'I can leave if you want.'

'Nice to have a bit of peace and quiet *so that I can talk to you*.'

'I saw Jake just now, for brunch,' I told him, subconsciously prompted by my brother's absence from Dad's list.

'Good,' Dad said. 'As long as *someone* knows he's still alive.'

'Oh, he phones *me* twice a week,' Mum said. She'd popped her head back around the door jamb while she waited for the kettle to boil.

'Yeah,' Dad said. 'At least he still phones your mother.'

'So you know he's still alive,' Mum said. 'Don't exaggerate.'

'So how is he?' Dad asked, visibly forcing himself to sound upbeat. 'What's he up to?'

'He's well,' I said. 'They were discussing their wedding plans.'

'It sounds like it's going to be a riot,' Mum said as she returned to the kitchen to finish making the teas.

'Yes, it sounds like it's going to be fun,' I told Dad. 'We were discussing whether or not it's possible to combine an Irish jig with the hora.'

'As long as they don't make me wear one of those silly hats,' Dad said.

'What, a beret?' I asked, being obtuse. 'Because you're French?'

'No, those kippah things,' Dad said. 'Don't even keep your head warm, they don't.'

'It would keep your bald patch warm,' Mum said, returning with the mugs of tea on a tray.

'Yes, I suppose there is that.'

'Can't you just . . . you know . . . ?' I said, wincing. 'Tone it down a bit?'

'Tone what down?'

'The whole anti-Jewish thing? Be a bit respectful? Stop being a knob, maybe?'

'Oh, don't get him started,' Mum said, cutting one of the already small tarts into four and handing me a quarter.

'I am,' Dad said. 'I'm totally respectful. Unlike you. Calling your own father a knob!'

'Only you're not being respectful.'

'Look, if people want to believe in all sorts of nonsense, then that's their business,' Dad said. 'But I've no time for it. No time at all. Ed, the electrician on the job I'm working on . . . he was saying only yesterday—'

'You do realise, don't you, that you don't have to agree with other people's traditions and beliefs to be respectful of them?' I asked, interrupting him. I had no desire to partake of Ed-the-electrician's wisdom. 'That concept has crossed your mind in the fifty-six years you've been on the planet, right?'

'Ah, I'm only having a laugh,' Dad said. 'It's like when I pull Mavaughn's leg about her holy water.'

'Don't you dare turn this one on my mother,' Mum said.

'Look, I'm always respectful of everyone,' Dad said. 'It's just Jake. He gets the hump over nothing. He's always been like that. Sensitive. *Over*sensitive.'

'Only it's not over nothing, Dad,' I said. 'This time you're in the wrong, and you need to think about it until you get it. Otherwise it's just going to go on and on.'

'Is this still about that Abby thing?' Dad said. 'Because that was ages ago. That's all water under the bridge. I apologised to Jake and he said it was fine.'

'I do know what you asked her,' I said. 'What you said to her at Christmas. This Christmas, that is. Christmas just gone.'

Dad was feigning confusion, so I explained: 'You asked Abby if Dan – my Dan – might be Jewish.'

'Oh, you didn't!' Mum said. 'You old fool.'

'I did not.'

'You so did.'

'I did not,' Dad insisted. 'I asked if Daniel might be a Jewish *name*.'

Mum laughed at this and, when she'd swallowed her bite of custard tart, said, 'Ah, now if that isn't splitting hairs, I don't know what is.'

'It's not the same thing at all,' Dad said. 'I was asking about a word. Am I not even allowed to ask the origin of a word anymore?'

'No,' I said. 'No, in this case, you're not allowed to ask, because it's insensitive.'

'It's all this PC nonsense,' Dad said. 'Political correctness. The world's gone crazy.'

'These are lovely,' Mum offered, rather obviously trying to change the subject. She reached for the spare quarter of tart. 'Gosh, who knew the Portuguese could make such lovely custard tarts?'

'It's not political correctness gone crazy or otherwise,' I told my father. 'It's called being sensitive to the issues that affect other people's lives. Millions of people died because they had the wrong names. I think we need to remember that. I think you specifically need to remember that. Because Abby damned well will.'

'They were killed because they were Jewish. Which is totally evil – don't get me wrong. But it wasn't because of their *names*.'

'That's how they knew, Dad. The Nazis knew they were Jewish because they had names like Abigail and Joseph, and surnames like Cohen and Goldman.'

'*And* because they wore those silly hats,' Dad said.

'Dad! Just stop it!'

'All right,' he said. 'All right! I can see your point.'

'So when you ask if a name is Jewish it's insensitive. It's how it all started. Or rather, for millions, very likely including some of Abby's own descendants – I mean ascendants – it's how it all ended. And asking Abby that is incredibly insensitive, especially after that Christmas. And anyway, why ask? What difference could it possibly make to anything if Dan is Jewish or not?'

'Well, it's good to know, isn't it?' Dad said. 'I mean, if I'd known Abby was Jewish . . .'

'. . . then you wouldn't have said something crass and insensitive to her,' I said, completing his sentence for him.

'OK,' Dad said again. 'I give in. Now, can we please just enjoy these tarts?'

'Sure,' I said. 'Whatever. But you need to be much more careful.'

'You do have a bit of a gob on yer,' Mum said. 'Especially when you've had a drink.'

Dad rolled his eyes and we each bit into our tiny quarters of tart.

Mum, I couldn't help but notice, was already halfway through a whole new tart of her own. I forcibly reminded myself that they were my gift to her, so they were hers to do with as she pleased.

'They're good,' Dad said. And though they weren't anywhere near as good as they'd been when they were fresh from the bakery in Portugal, it was true that they were still pretty tasty, especially when associated with a cup of tea.

'Anyway, is he?' Dad asked. 'Just out of interest.'

'Is who what?'

'Your Dan,' Dad said. '*Is* he Jewish?'

'Oh, for Christ's sake,' I said, eliciting a glare from my mother.

'I'm only asking,' Dad said.

'Yeah, well, don't. Because I'm not going to tell you. I'm never going to answer that question.'

'Because he is, then?' Dad said.

'No, because I don't know. Because I've never asked. And I never *will* ask. Because I don't care one way or another. And nor should you. Nor should anyone ever.'

'Tell us about your holiday,' Mum said. 'Tell us about Portugal before I slap this old fool myself.'

And so I did. I told them about the little sandy island and the cheapest restaurant on earth. I told them about Faro and the dunes and Dan's parents. And then I segued rather elegantly into asking Dad where Grandpa Chris was living, and was stunned to learn that he was near the coast in south-west France.

'Is there any particular reason that we didn't get to spend our holidays on a beach in the South of France?' I asked.

'Well, to start with, when you were little, he lived in Vauxhall.'

'Not *the* most fabulous holiday destination,' Mum said in a rare moment of sarcasm.

'He moved there when he retired. Like your Daniel's parents did to Portugal.'

'It's Dan,' I said. 'Not Daniel.'

'Ooh, OK,' Dad said. 'Sorry, I forgot how touchy we're being.'

'I'm not being touchy, Dad. It's just that I don't even know if his actual name is Daniel.'

'You didn't see his passport?'

'I did not.'

'Or his plane tickets?'

I frowned at this. 'Maybe, but I don't think so. Or maybe it just said Dan, so I didn't notice.'

'What do his parents call him?' Mum asked.

'They call him, Dan!' I said. 'Jesus! Everyone calls him Dan.'

'And does he speak Portuguese?' Dad asked.

'He does,' I confirmed. 'Like a dream.'

'It's a funny language,' Mum said. 'It sounds funny. Sort of like Spanish, but drunk.'

'Unlike Gaelic,' Dad said, 'which doesn't sound funny at all.'

'Anyway,' I said, noticing that they'd derailed me from my mission. 'Have you got an address for him?'

'For Dan?' Dad asked.

'For Grandpa!'

'Oh, sure. Of course. Somewhere.'

'And a phone number?'

'That too, I expect. But why?'

I shrugged. 'I don't know,' I said. 'Maybe I fancy a holiday in France.'

'I'd think twice before staying at his place.'

'Why?' I asked. 'Is it awful? Have you been?'

'No, never. But he's a bizarre old bugger.'

'This is your father we're talking about.'

Dad opened his palms towards the ceiling and shrugged. 'Sometime bizarre old buggers have children. And sometimes they have wonderful children like your dad.'

'So was there some kind of falling out?'

'With who?' he asked. 'With Dad?'

I resisted the desire to say, 'Well, that is who we're talking about, isn't it?' Or – a family favourite – 'No, I was talking about the Pope.' Instead I said, 'Yeah, I'm assuming there's a reason why we saw so little of him. And Genny, for that matter.'

Dad wrinkled his nose almost indiscernibly. 'Not really. Other than the fact that they were funny buggers.'

'You're not going to tell me, are you?' I said. I turned to Mum. 'Do you know?'

She half-heartedly shrugged, and then, speaking through a mouthful of tart, an act she delicately hid behind her fingers, said, 'I just don't think they were very family oriented, that's all.'

'That's it!' Dad said, sounding a bit too keen that Mum had come up with an answer. 'They just weren't very family oriented. Not after the divorce they weren't, anyway.'

'But they still lived together, right?'

'In the same building,' Dad said. 'Not *together*.'

'I remember that,' Mum said. 'We went there once or twice, didn't we? He had that funny little bedsit upstairs.'

'So you carried on seeing them, then?'

'A bit. From time to time. But it was . . .' Dad sighed, and frowned with the effort of trying to remember. 'It was like you had to book an appointment,' he finally said.

'Oh, gosh, yes, I remember that,' Mum agreed. 'They hated it if you just turned up unannounced.'

'That is a bit of a French thing,' Dad said. 'People do like you to call in advance. But you're right. They weren't keen. Didn't like surprises.'

'And this is both of them? Either of them, I mean? As they were living in different flats . . .'

'Yes, they were both pretty funny about it.'

'D'you remember that time we surprised them?' Mum said. 'How strange your dad was?'

'Yeah,' Dad said. 'Yes, that was the last time we ever dropped in, wasn't it? We always phoned after that.'

'I'm not sure we went back at all after that,' Mum said.

'Why?' I asked. 'What happened?'

'Oh, nothing really,' Dad said. 'Nothing specific. They were just strange. It was uncomfortable.'

'But if you made an appointment, they were OK,' Mum said. 'They were nice to me anyway. We used to meet them in that restaurant Genny liked.'

'Claude's,' Dad said. 'French place. It's gone now. She used to try to get us all to eat snails.'

'They were fine,' Mum said. 'Your father wouldn't try them, but they tasted a bit like mushrooms. Lots of garlic. Actually, that's all you could taste, really: the butter and the garlic.'

'But you'd all meet up together? Even after the divorce?'

'Yeah. Sometimes,' Dad said. 'Until she moved to Brighton. After that it was usually separately.'

'So they still got on OK? They didn't hate each other's guts?'

'No, they got on fine,' Dad said. 'Better than before, I think.'

'That happens a lot,' Mum said. 'It's the day-to-day grind that kills the passion. It's the dirty socks and the skid marks. And I should know.'

'Cheeky!' Dad said, then, 'So, are you ever going to give us another one of those tarts? Or are you just going to sit there and stuff them down your gullet?' He looked at me and tipped his head sideways, asking me for back-up.

'Yeah, I was kind of wondering that too,' I said. 'They are your gift, Mum. But you may still share if you so wish.'

Cassette #2

ML: *This is Marie Lefebvre interviewing Genevieve Schmitt for* Gai Pied *magazine. Day one, second cassette.*

GS: Perhaps I'm giving you too much detail. I am rambling on a bit, aren't I?

Not at all. I'm really interested in your story and I'm sure our readers will be too. We may have to edit it down a bit for the magazine . . . but for now, I'd like to get the whole thing exactly the way you're telling it, if that's OK?

<Laughs> I'm rather enjoying telling it actually. Perhaps 'enjoying' isn't the right word. So much of it is horrific. But I think it's doing me some good to tell it. You know, no one has ever been that interested.

I find that hard to believe.

Oh, it's true. I can assure you. Of course, bits and bobs. Once every decade someone will say, 'Tell me about the war,' but they don't usually mean it. People want tales of heroism. They don't really want to hear how sordid it all was. You can always see their eyes glazing over after a few minutes.

Well, I really do want to hear. So, you know, just carry on and tell me when you've had enough, OK?

OK then, I shall. Can you remember where I was up to?

Yes, you, um, have Leah's baby back home. Pierre is being held by the police. And Matias has just cycled off into an obscenely beautiful sunset.

Well, it was closer to sunrise than sunset, but . . .

Yes, sorry. Of course.

When I got home, Mum was washing a pile of nappies a neighbour had given her. They stank of mildew, she said. At least the baby had stopped crying.

Mum wanted to know what Matias had said to do with him and I didn't dare admit that I'd forgotten to ask, so I lied and said he'd told me that if we handed him over, he would probably be killed because he was Jewish. From everything Matias had told me about the Germans' brutality, that felt like a reasonable guess, and with hindsight it's what would almost certainly have happened.

Really? They even killed newborn babies?

Absolutely, they did. The Jewish babies who arrived at the camps were ripped from their mothers' arms and thrown straight into a burning pit. They were of no use to the Nazis, so they were either gassed or burned alive.

Jesus! I didn't know that.

No . . . I think some details are so harsh that people don't like to talk about them, even now. But it's true. Anyway, I didn't know that at all, but I suppose I was finally starting to get the picture, and that's what I told Mum. She said that I was being ridiculous and that no one would kill a baby, but I remember she glanced at my father, who rather vaguely wobbled his head from side to side, indicating that it was as likely an outcome as anything.

Mum asked me then if I had any news about Pierre. She seemed to assume that he'd have been questioned and released, just like Dad was. Of course I still couldn't explain to them why that was unlikely so I told her that, no, he hadn't, and that all I knew was that they were still holding him. I added that they were treating him pretty badly, I think, and this made Dad jump into the conversation, asking me why were they holding him. Had he done something? Did he have communist friends? Did they think he was Jewish?

I told him that I didn't know. And then I said that I thought they suspected him of something that he hadn't done.

Dad picked up that I knew more than I was admitting, so eventually I told him that they suspected Pierre of being friends with some queers, which I insisted he 'evidently' wasn't.

'Pierre?' Dad said, outraged.

'People are saying all sorts,' Mum commented. She said that someone had told the soldiers that Monsieur Kastler – the goat farmer – was Jewish, and that it was only luck that the Germans hadn't believed them.

'Can't we just go down there and tell them it's not true?' Mum asked. 'Can't Genevieve just tell them that Pierre's her fiancé?'

I pointed out that Pierre wasn't my fiancé, but Dad was speaking over me, saying that no one in their right minds would go down there for anything, and that – and here was that phrase again – my mother didn't understand 'what they were like'.

He told me in no uncertain terms that I was not to go anywhere near the police station, and then went off to his garage, purportedly to work. As no one was driving much – petrol had become very scarce – and as the Germans hadn't yet commandeered his garage, there wasn't any work for him to do. But as well as having lost a leg, the war had also left him a bit deaf, and the garage was the only place he could listen to the radio without Mum constantly turning it down. He liked to sit in an old armchair he had there and smoke.

With Dad gone I asked Mum something that had been worrying me: if the Germans would be able to tell that Menashe was Jewish.

She said, 'What they've done to his private parts won't help,' which didn't categorically answer my question, but I was too embarrassed to pursue the subject any further. In the afternoon, Mum went out to do her cleaning and—

Your mother was a cleaner?

Yes. It was just a part-time job. She did more when Dad's garage business wasn't doing so well to make up the shortfall – that and her sewing. But most of her clients had either fled, or been evicted, or didn't have money to pay her anymore. There was just one big house left, up in Rebberg, as I recall. The husband was a lawyer, I think. There were a few families like that who seemed to glide through the war without really being affected. They probably had German relatives in high places.

Anyway, Mum left me looking after the baby, and just after she'd closed the front door behind her, she returned and said, 'And just so you know, we're not keeping him. So don't get too attached.'

I told her that I had no intention of 'getting attached,' and it was true. I knew that I didn't want Leah's baby to *die*, but that was about as far as it went. My maternal instincts were pretty non-existent in those days.

'Good!' Mum said. And then she added that, in the meantime, I should choose another name for him.

I asked her what she meant, and she said, 'A non-Jewish name.'

I hadn't thought until that point what a giveaway Menashe was.

Once she'd left again, I sat there trying out names on the baby. I thought about calling him Pierre, as Pierre was obviously very much in my thoughts, but decided that was silly and would be confusing. I thought about what was going to happen to the baby and it started to dawn on me that he perhaps would be with us for a bit, despite what Mum was saying. I decided that he'd probably be safer with a German name – there were lots of German names in Alsace anyway, so I went through some of the names from school in my mind and as I thought of them, I said them to the baby to see if he reacted. I tried Matias and Witter and Willi and Ansgar, and when I said 'Ansgar', he gurgled, and so it stuck. It seemed like a safe choice. You can't get much more German than that.

So Menashe became Ansgar.

Yes. Because he gurgled at the right moment.

When Mum got home from cleaning, I went down the road to the garage. I found Dad tinkering with an old tractor engine he'd been working on for ages . . . He had the radio on and it was so loud I'd been able to hear it from outside, so I ran across the garage and switched it off.

He glared at me and said something about me being exactly like my mother, but he'd been listening to the BBC, and when I explained that I'd been able to hear it from outside, he understood.

I told him that I wanted to talk to him about something important and we both looked nervously out towards the street to check that no one was around. I explained that Matias had heard of someone who helped people escape across the border, and then started to explain further, saying that apparently there was this old carpenter chap and that all you had to do was get to— But Dad stopped me in my tracks, pressing a finger to my lips.

'You mustn't tell me,' he said. 'You mustn't tell anyone.'

I asked him why not, and he said that it was a dangerous thing to know.

So I said I was telling him because I thought that maybe we should be thinking about doing it, because everything *was* getting dangerous, but Dad said he was too old and too slow to try to escape, and he was too stubborn and too proud to let anyone kick him out of his home.

It was really strange, because for the first time ever he'd talked about him instead of us, and I noticed that, because it sounded a bit like he was saying that he wouldn't go, rather than telling me not to.

'If they release your Pierre, though . . .' he said, 'and he wants to go, then that would be a different matter.'

So I asked him how that made things different, and he said it didn't make things different for him, but if Pierre was considering leaving then I might want to talk to him about my own options.

Dad was usually very direct, but we were suddenly having this really strange conversation. It was like he was talking in riddles and leaving it to me to decode what he was saying. So I asked him outright if he thought that I should try to leave and, again, he shocked me, because for the first time in my life, he didn't have an opinion about what I should do. He said, 'You're a grown woman now, and these are exceptional circumstances,' or something like that. And he said I should do whatever I thought was safest, because he didn't have any answers anymore.

Was he maybe in shock from his interrogation?

Yes, I think that was part of it. And I think he was also realising that he *didn't* have answers anymore. He probably suspected already that the Germans were going to come back for him—

Because he'd fought in the First World War?

Yes. So he was starting to understand that even if I stayed, he might not be there to protect me and that he couldn't protect me even if he was still there. I think he maybe regretted not letting me go to London.

It does seem like he wanted you to leave.

No, that would be overstating it. It's more like he said that he no longer knew what was best. He no longer trusted his instincts over mine.

Were you still in touch with Ethel, by then? Was she still begging you to join her?

No. There had been no post since the invasion. I think it started up again a bit later on, but by then they were censoring everything anyway, so a love letter from Ethel would have been a dangerous thing to receive.

What did you decide to do?

Well, I decided to leave, didn't I? But not yet, not at that moment. Because I could never have done it alone. I would have been far too scared. On top of the fact that it was so dangerous to try to leave – if they caught you, I was pretty sure they'd shoot you – but as a woman, in a country full of male soldiers, well, I felt very vulnerable as well. What had happened to Pierre's mother could happen to anyone.

So did you leave with Pierre?

Ah, now you're trying to jump ahead!

And you really are starting to get into telling your story, aren't you?

Well, this is the exciting bit. We're about to come to my moment of glory.

So, go on. Tell me about your moment of glory!

Well, that night, I fed the baby and took him to bed with me again. It wasn't even dark yet, and I didn't think that I would be able to sleep because I was far too upset about Pierre. But I hoped that, snuggled up against the baby, I might at least be able to doze.

I'd just switched the light out when I heard a knock on the front door. It was after curfew, so that was pretty scary to start with. Then I heard the door open, followed by a sob from my mother – more of a gasp, really. And then, straight off, with no resistance whatsoever, she said, 'You've come for the baby, haven't you? He's in there. We only took him in because we didn't know what else to do with him. We found him on the street.'

I hated her in that instant because she hadn't given me any time to think what to do. I considered climbing out the window, but with a baby in tow, that was almost impossible. We were on the second floor, after all. But while I was still looking out at the drop below, I heard a familiar voice say, 'Baby? What baby?' and that set

Mum off on a different track, telling my father, 'God, they've come for you, Bernard – they're here for you.'

I heard Dad tell her pretty sharply to 'shut it', and then the voice – and now I was certain, it was Matias's voice – said, 'No, I just came to have a word with Genevieve, if that's all right?'

I pulled on my dressing gown and opened the door, and there he was, in his policeman's uniform, terrifying the wits out of my poor mother, who was still crying and muttering something unintelligible about what could they possibly want with me.

So I told her that he was a friend, and to my parents' surprise, dragged him into my bedroom and shut the door.

I remember he looked down at my breasts, and for a minute I thought I wasn't sufficiently covered or something, but then I followed his gaze and realised I had the baby in my arms.

'A baby!' he said. 'You have a baby!'

I told him it was a long story and that he wasn't mine.

But Matias was looking weird: sort of shocked and hopeful at the same time. 'But that's perfect,' he said. 'A baby is absolutely perfect.'

Perfect for what?

Well, Matias had worked out a plan to get Pierre out. He was incredibly worried about him, though 'worried' isn't really the right word. I'm not sure there is a word to describe that level of anxiety. His voice went all wobbly and I could see tears welling up as he explained just how precarious Pierre's situation was. The Germans were holding him in a crowded cell, he said, and they were torturing them all to make them give the names of other homosexuals they knew, but so far Pierre had held out. Some of the others were already dead. Others had been shipped out to Schirmeck, where he thought they'd almost certainly die too. Pierre was in a bad way, he said, and it was our last chance to get him out. He said that if he caved in and gave them a single name then he'd be done for.

He explained how a woman had come in two days earlier – how she'd screamed and shouted at the Germans about the fact that they were holding her husband. The soldiers in charge had been so embarrassed by all the fuss that they'd simply released him. They'd arrested her husband by mistake, he said. In their haste they'd been making a lot of those sorts of mistakes.

So he wanted you to pretend to be Pierre's wife?

That's right. And of course, with a baby, he thought it would be even more convincing.

I asked him if it was dangerous, and what would happen if I got caught, and he started to cry properly then, saying that yes, it was true, it was dangerous – it was too dangerous. But my mind kept conjuring up images of those bastards torturing poor Pierre, of him sitting on a cold stone floor in a cell. I asked Matias to tell me the truth about what they were doing to him, and he said they'd pulled off some fingernails. He said they'd done other stuff too, stuff he didn't want to tell me about.

And this rage started to rise up in me, this sense of . . . indignation . . . perhaps, is the word. It felt like it came from outside of me, from God, perhaps, or the universe, or . . . I don't know. I honestly don't know where it came from, but it filled me . . . I felt so . . . so very offended . . . so *outraged* at what they were doing to my friend. I wanted to go straight down and give them what for.

And did you?

No, Matias made me calm down. It had to happen while he was at work, he said. He needed to be there so he could vouch for the fact that I was, indeed, Pierre's wife. So we had to wait until morning.

After Matias left, I didn't sleep a wink. I kept changing my mind about whether it was suicide to go down there, or whether it was simply unthinkable not to, unthinkable to leave Pierre to die at the hands of the Germans. I honestly didn't know whether I was going to do it or not.

In the end, I left the flat just after eight, as instructed, the baby slung over my back in a folded shawl. I marched towards the police station and then, just as I approached it, I had a fit of panic and couldn't breathe, so I walked straight past. But when I got to the corner of the street, I saw two young German soldiers smoking and laughing together – they honestly looked about seventeen – and I thought, *damn them! I'm not afraid of them!* That crazy, fearless feeling had returned so I turned around and marched back in.

The policeman at the front desk was French, and for some reason I hadn't expected that; I'd expected them all to be German, which was stupid of me, because of course, I knew that Matias was still working there. But I was suddenly terrified I'd be recognised, that some policeman from around our way would see me and say he knew my father and that I didn't have a baby. But by then it was too late. It was my turn at the desk.

So I told him that my husband had gone missing – just as Matias had instructed – and I demanded to know if they were holding him.

I gave him Pierre's surname and watched as he went into the office to talk to a German who was sitting there. He was probably SS, but I was so scared I honestly didn't notice. He glanced out at me and then leafed through a book he had on his desk. And then the policeman came back and said, 'He's your husband, you say? Are you sure?'

So I laughed sourly, and told him that of course I was bloody sure, and he said that yes, he was here, but there must have been some kind of mistake.

I started making a fuss then. Matias had been quite specific about how I should start out reasonably and get louder and louder, and so that's exactly what I did. And, honestly, I should have got an

Oscar for that performance. I started to rant and shout about how the hell was I supposed to look after a newborn baby without my husband, and what in God's name were they doing holding him? What had he ever done to anyone other than to mend people's plumbing? I was so scared that my voice was all shaky and I started to cry as well, but I think that only made it all the more convincing. People started to stop and stare. An old woman who'd been waiting joined in, saying something about the fact that it was shameful, taking my husband away. And with a newborn as well!

The baby started to scream then too, and as I could see that was annoying the German, who was struggling to concentrate on his paperwork, I jiggled poor Ansgar up and down, making him scream even more.

Finally, the German rubbed a hand across his forehead, took off his glasses and stood and came out to the desk.

He shouted '*Schweigen!*' at me – silence! – but as planned, I got even louder. More people started stopping and staring at this hysterical woman with a baby, shouting at the German officer, so I started screaming how we'd been happy – happy! – when they'd arrived, because they'd been so polite and friendly and helpful, but that this, this rounding up of people's husbands off the street was absolutely intolerable.

The soldier told me that if I didn't shut up, I'd be joining my husband in the cells, and I told him to do it, to take me. 'At least we'll be together!' I said.

He shrugged then and told the policeman to take me down, and for a terrible moment I thought I'd failed, and I swear my heart stopped in fear. In seconds, I was drenched in sweat, and I was gasping because I couldn't breathe. I thought I'd got it all wrong and now both Menashe and I were going to die. But just as he grabbed me, Matias sauntered in. I think he'd been outside, listening and waiting for the perfect moment.

'Genevieve!' he said, then casually to his colleague, 'Hold on. What's going on here? I know her. Is there a problem?'

The policeman asked Matias if he was sure he knew me, and he said that of course he was sure, we'd grown up together – he'd even been best man at my wedding.

I told him they'd taken Pierre and I didn't know why, and he pretended to be shocked. He made a tiny gesture with his hand, which I didn't at first understand, but after a second or so, I understood that he wanted me to turn it up a notch – he wanted me to make more fuss. So I sank to my knees and hugged his legs and started crying again about how Pierre had been missing for days and I'd been looking everywhere for him, and that he'd been here all the time. I begged him to help us, to tell them that they'd made a mistake, and then he made another gesture to indicate, I think, that I was going a bit over the top. He prised my hands from his legs and went into the back office to speak to the German.

They spoke for a short while and the soldier studied his book again before Matias returned, jangling some keys, and said, 'You'd better come with me.'

He led me through a door and down a long corridor, then some steps and all the way back in the other direction, past all the holding cells. There was a terrible sound of weeping and pleading coming from them.

Finally he stopped in front of one of the doors and unlocked it, and for a moment I didn't understand. I thought that perhaps our plan had failed and to save himself he was going to have to lock me up after all. And then it crossed my mind that maybe he'd tricked me and that it had all been a ruse to get me there with the baby.

The door opened and he asked me to identify my husband.

The sight of that cell . . . God, I don't even know how to describe it to you. It looked like some sort of Armageddon in there. There were six, maybe seven men huddled into the far corner. Some

123

were completely naked and others were still wearing their clothes, but all ripped and filthy. The floor and walls were covered with faeces and glistening with blood, and the men, those men . . . you know, I still have nightmares about them. They were like tiny, frightened animals waiting in an abattoir, which in a way is what the Nazis had reduced them to. I remember thinking that I'd never really believed in evil, or the devil, but that he undoubtedly existed, and was there, in that building, in uniform.

I couldn't see the men's faces because they were all trying to hide from view, whimpering and struggling to get behind each other, so Matias pulled me into the cell. I covered the baby's eyes with the shawl so that he wouldn't have to see that sight.

The stink in there – God, it just came back to me. I can smell it now, I swear – blood and shit and urine and sweat all mixed up. And fear. You can actually smell fear.

And then, quite brutally, because another man was, I realised, watching from the corridor, Matias pulled the men one by one from the huddle, saying, 'Is it this one? Or this one? Is this one your husband?'

One of the men fell at my feet and grabbed my leg and started to beg me to help him and I had to shake him off, which felt night-marish. And when Matias finally pulled Pierre from the group I didn't even recognise him, partly because he was staring at the floor, but mainly because he'd changed so much in such a short time that it didn't seem possible. He was naked from the waist up and shoe-less and filthy dirty and so terribly thin. He'd never had much meat on him, but he was so skinny that it shocked me. He had blood on his face and his hands and one of his trouser legs was deep red with blood as well . . . what they'd done to him . . . it was . . . I can't . . .

Take a moment if you wish.

I'm not sure I can . . .

We can take a break if you want. Really. We don't have to do this right now.

No, I'd rather carry on. But Pierre . . . He just looked so pitiful. It was a terrible shock when I realised it was him.

Matias pushed him right in front of me and asked if I was sure my husband wasn't there, and I began to weep again because I'd realised it was him. At some point I remembered someone was watching and asked Matias angrily what in God's name had he done to my husband.

He asked Pierre if this was his wife, if this was his child, but Pierre just looked stunned. I saw that he'd recognised Matias and panicked he was going to give the game away. He kept looking from Matias to me and back uncomprehendingly. So Matias asked him again, shouting at him this time, saying 'Is this your damned wife?! Yes or no?'

And then the man who'd been clawing at my leg said, 'She's my wife. Aren't you? Please, help me.' And that was when Pierre twigged. I saw the realisation sweep across his face.

I asked, 'What have you done to my husband?' and said that they were animals, and finally Pierre replied, speaking through tears. 'You came. I thought you'd never come.' He told me that they had been accusing him of the most terrible things.

Matias told him he could go, and pushed him towards the door, but I had to pull his arm around my shoulder so that he could walk.

Then, hassled by Matias to get a move on, we made our way back along that corridor and up the stairs, and then all the way back down to the front desk. I was petrified that someone would realise what was happening – that a voice would suddenly ring out and say, 'You! Stop!' or something. Those corridors seemed endless.

When we got to the front desk, the officer I'd seen when I arrived told me happily that he was glad I'd found my husband, as if this was all perfectly routine.

Matias gave me a little push and said, 'Go on then, off you go! And don't hang around, OK? I don't want to see you here again. Either of you!'

The two soldiers I'd seen smoking outside were coming in just as we were leaving. They were still joking and laughing about something, and one of them held the door open for us, so we had to squeeze right past them. And then we stepped out into the sunshine.

It took us for ever to walk home. It was only a few kilometres, but Pierre was limping along, leaning on me, and even then he kept having to stop and rest. He looked absolutely shocking, too, and I became hyper-aware of how visible we were, how utterly conspicuous, especially when the baby started crying on top of it all. Nearly every person we passed stopped and stared. Some looked sympathetic and concerned, but just as many turned away in disgust. Pierre was still naked from the waist up, and shoeless, remember. He had bruises on his face, bloodied hands and feet, and a huge dark stain all down the left leg of his trousers. Most terrifying of all was whenever we walked past policemen or German soldiers – they were everywhere by then. I kept expecting them to stop us and enquire why Pierre looked the way he did, and then most probably take him straight back to the station. But out of all the people we walked past, the soldiers were the ones who seemed the least interested. I can only suppose that they were thoroughly used to the sight of injured, bloodied, crying men.

We went straight past ours to Pierre's place, where his mother opened the door and promptly fell to her knees. I led him into the apartment while she stayed in the doorway saying over and over, 'Oh, Pierre. Oh, Pierre! What have you done?' On about the fourth repetition it annoyed me so much that I shouted at her that he hadn't done *anything*, and would she please pull herself together and bloody well help me with her son.

She stood up then and we took Pierre into the kitchen – lots of people still didn't have bathrooms in those days – and he just stood there limply while we sponged him down. Naked and up close, his body was even more shocking.

In what way?

Oh, the signs of everything they'd done to him. He had some missing toenails – I think it was three or four – and four missing fingernails, two from each hand. He had cigarette burns all down his inner arm, and a wide, deep cut on his cheek. His eye was slowly closing up too, as it swelled. I'd honestly never seen anything like it, and I haven't since, either. Plus he had all this congealed blood stuck down his left leg that was incredibly hard to get rid of. I couldn't work out where that had come from and kept looking for a wound.

As we were finishing, his mother became embarrassed by my presence. I saw it happen, and I'm still not sure what suddenly changed. Perhaps she'd just been in shock until that point and only when she started to come out of it did she realise that this young girl was kneeling, helping her clean her naked son. Whatever the reason, she suddenly stopped, threw her flannel down and pushed me towards the door. She even forgot that the baby was lying on the sofa and I had to push back so that I could return to pick him up.

As she reached for the latch she paused to ask me if it was true.

I asked was *what* true, but I was just playing for time. I knew what she meant. I'd guessed that she'd been told why they'd arrested Pierre, and what she was asking was if he was homosexual. But thankfully, she dropped the subject and instead asked, 'Will they be back for him, or is everything OK now?'

I told her I didn't know, and that I'd try to find out. Finally, as I was leaving, she grabbed my sleeve and pulled me back one last time to ask me, 'Is it his? Is the baby his?'

I stared at her as I tried to run through all the knock-on effects that might result from whether I replied yes or no: the fact that if I said yes, and she believed me, then it might be easier to convince the Germans that we were a couple. But that it was a lie, and a big one, to tell a woman in distress she had a grandson when that totally wasn't true. In the end I sort of shrugged, because I honestly couldn't think how best to reply, and she got totally the wrong end of the stick. She muttered, 'Oh the shame!' or something like that and slammed the door in my face.

Because she thought you didn't know who the father was?

Yes, exactly.

God!

Well, you know, afterwards, I thought about it and realised how that made sense. She'd asked me, and I'd shrugged. So it wasn't an unreasonable reading of my reactions.

I suppose not. But all the same.

I went back home, then. My mother and father were waiting for me in the kitchen and, because my clothes were still covered in blood, I had no choice but to explain. So I told them everything that had happened. My mother went so grey that I thought she was going to be sick.

Once I'd finished, she took the baby from me and started changing his nappy – I think she needed something to do – and my father began telling me off, saying that I shouldn't have gone without him; I was lucky to have got out of there alive. He asked if I had any idea how stupid I'd been or how dangerous it was. Mum stood up for me a bit, I remember. She pointed out that I'd saved Pierre, and I could hardly have just left him there to rot.

I washed the blood off my arms and then went to change into some clean clothes. When I got back my mother was feeding the baby, and she nodded towards the lounge and told me that my father wanted to talk to me in private.

He was standing looking out of the front window, keeping watch, I suppose, and he barely glanced at me when I entered the room. He told me to close the door.

'You realise they'll be back,' he said. 'They'll almost certainly be back for both of you.'

I asked him if he really thought they would and he said he did.

He asked me again if I'd really told them that Pierre was my husband and the baby was ours.

I nodded and said a quiet 'yes' and then he turned to face me properly, and I realised that his eyes were glistening.

'They're going to check the records, aren't they?' I said, and he nodded. 'They're going to see that we're not married.'

Dad nodded again and then cleared his throat and told me he might have to take a trip out to La Vieille-Loye the next day, and my heart leapt into my throat because I knew exactly what he was referring to.

He said he had a customer out there who was having trouble with his old tractor engine. But he needed to find petrol from somewhere first.

I started to cry then so he crossed the room and took me in his arms.

I protested that we should all go together, and he said there was no way that was happening. He said his hillwalking days were long over because of his leg, and I almost explained how injured Pierre was, but then, scared he'd make me leave Pierre behind, that he'd make me leave on my own, I changed my mind.

I told him I was scared, I think, and began to cry again, and I'll never forget what he said. He said, 'We're all scared, Genevieve.

We're all terrified, and we're right to be. We're all going to continue being terrified until this whole thing is over, however long that takes. So you might as well just get used to it.'

I asked him if I really had to leave, and he said that he couldn't tell me if it was safe to leave, but he could tell me that, because of what I'd done, it definitely wasn't safe to stay.

Because he'd stopped speaking, I looked up – I'd had my face buried in his chest – and I realised that Mum had slipped into the room. She was holding the baby against her shoulder, tapping his back to wind him.

She asked what was going on, and Dad said that he had to take a trip west the next day and he was going to take 'this one' with him, meaning me. Mum asked him where, and he said, pointedly, that it was 'over towards the demarcation line'.

'And Pierre?' Mum asked, and Dad nodded.

'And the baby,' I added, and when Mum frowned, Dad explained that it was better we went 'as a family'.

As my mother turned away, I saw a tear slip down her cheek. 'I'd better make you something for the trip, then,' she said, pretending to be very matter-of-fact about it.

Sorry, but just so that I – so that the readers understand – had she worked it all out? Because it sounds like you were all speaking to each other in riddles again.

Yes, we were in a way. I think Dad was being cagey because he didn't want to feel he was pushing me to leave . . . And he didn't want to give my mother any information that could put her, or me, in danger later on.

But yes, I suspect that Mum had heard enough of the conversation to work out what was happening.

But she didn't try to stop you leaving?

No. For those kinds of big decisions she believed in my father's judgement. He'd been a soldier, after all. I think she just trusted him to know better than her what the risks were. She knew how much he loved me, so . . .

But you must have been scared about leaving, weren't you?

Yes, I was – I kept getting the shakes. I kept having these sort of panic attacks where I couldn't breathe, as well. I was terrified. I was only nineteen, remember. I'd never even lived away from home. So yes, it was a very, very scary thing to attempt. I went off to try to find Matias because I was hoping that he'd tell me we were safe, that we didn't need to go after all. But he wasn't in the café and I couldn't see him in any of the other places he was generally to be seen either, so after a while I returned back home. There was no way that I was going to go near the police station again, after all.

On the way back I called in to tell Pierre what Dad was proposing and find out if he was well enough to travel. His mother, who as ever was sewing, told me rather abruptly that he was in his room sleeping, but Pierre shouted out that he was awake so I let myself in and closed the bedroom door behind me.

He was lying on his front with pillows beneath his stomach so that his bum stuck up and I think I made some joke about that which fell very flat. He apologised and said that it was the only position that didn't hurt.

I told him, in whispers, what Dad had suggested, and Pierre said that Matias had dropped in to tell him the same thing – we needed to get out as soon as we possibly could. Pierre said he wasn't well enough to leave and suggested I should go on my own.

I told him the truth, that I was too scared, and as a woman, it was too dangerous to go alone anyway. We talked a bit about postponing it until he felt stronger, but we knew that wasn't an option. We tried to think of places we could hide for a while, but couldn't come up with anywhere sensible.

Pierre wasn't even sure if he could walk, so I helped him from the bed and he limped a little around the room. I asked him if it hurt, and he said that, yes, it hurt, but that wasn't the problem, that the problem was if he started to bleed again.

'Your feet or your fingers?' I asked, and he held out his blood-encrusted fingers and then looked down at his swollen toes and wiggled them and said, 'No, they're OK.'

'You mean your leg?' I asked, looking down at his pyjama bottoms to see if they were bloodstained, and he replied that it wasn't his leg either. That his legs were fine.

I was frowning, I think, so he said, 'Look, Gen, I'm going to tell you this, OK? But then can we please never speak of it again? Ever?'

I think I just nodded . . .

Go on.

Actually, you know, I'm just wondering . . . well . . . I'm not sure your readers need to know this.

No?

No. It's pretty graphic. But then again, it's kind of important in order to understand the rest.

Perhaps just tell me and we can decide later if we leave it in or not, or how we present it, or whatever?

OK.

Are you OK?

Yes, I'm fine. Sorry. I'm just remembering. It's hard. So, Pierre started to cry again. And he whispered it so quietly, I almost didn't hear him. He whispered that they had fucked him.

The soldiers had raped him?!

That's what I thought he meant. And that's what I asked him to confirm because I wasn't sure I'd heard correctly. But he closed his eyes, and looked away. And then as he turned back to face me – God, he was crying so hard, the tears were dripping off his chin. He said, 'They did, but not . . . you know . . . Not using themselves.'

Not using themselves? What does that mean?

I didn't understand what he meant either until he managed to say it – until he managed to tell me that they'd raped him with a bit of wood. I don't know the details – we truly never did speak of it again. But I believe they'd smashed a chair over someone, and then raped him with the chair leg.

He said they'd broken his insides. I remember he said that. That he was 'broken'. And he said that was why he kept bleeding.

My God, that's horrific. I can understand your reticence, to have it in the interview. My feeling is that it's important. People need to know this stuff. To remember. But we can discuss what to keep in and what to leave out at the end. And was Pierre able to walk? Were you able to leave?

Yes. Actually, we had to leave the very next morning.

Why? What happened?

We'd decided to ask Matias if it would be OK to wait a few days – if he thought we'd be safe for that long – because we wanted Pierre to be able to recover a bit first. Pierre was also desperately hoping for news about Johann before he left. We suspected that he'd been shipped to Schirmeck, but it was only hearsay, and Matias had said he'd try to find out for sure. Pierre was still desperately hoping that Johann would be able to run away with us.

As I was leaving Pierre's apartment, I crossed paths with a boy in shorts, sprinting up the stairs, and just as I reached the downstairs street door, Pierre called me back. So I turned around and trudged back up, crossing paths again with the kid, now heading down. I remember thinking it strange that he avoided eye contact.

When I got back to Pierre's landing I found him leaning against the wall reading a note, and he handed it to me. It was very short, it said something like, 'Go now. Go today. Go as soon as possible.' Oh, and, 'If you stay I won't be able to help you'. And it said not to wait for Johann. That he was 'gone'.

I asked Pierre if he was sure it was Matias's handwriting, and he said that yes, it definitely was. And then he started to cry about Johann, saying, 'Gone? What does he mean, gone?'

I hugged him and told him that whatever it meant, we couldn't help him, and that he needed to save himself right now, that it was what Johann would want. We needed to think about ourselves, I said. I told him we'd have to leave and that my father was offering to drive us. I said he should tell his mother what was going on, but Pierre didn't want to tell her anything. He was scared she'd make too much fuss, I think. To say that she wasn't particularly good in a crisis would be an understatement.

I went next door to tell Dad, and by the time I got there Mum had packed a tiny suitcase with clothes and food before going off, as usual, to her cleaning job.

Once I'd told him about Matias's note, Dad decided that Pierre, myself and the baby should go and sleep in his garage. He said that it was dangerous to stay at home and the police might return at any moment. I protested that I hadn't been able to say goodbye, but Dad insisted it was better this way, and more discreet if Mum carried on as usual.

He went off to the garage with my suitcase wrapped up in a blanket to disguise it, telling me to get Pierre and meet him there as soon as we could. He said it was too dangerous for us to all walk together.

And was Pierre able to walk by then? Was it far?

It was about a kilometre, I suppose, and yes, he could walk, just about. The bleeding appeared to have stopped, though what he hadn't told me was that he'd stuffed towels down his underwear. It wasn't until we reached La Vieille-Loye the next day that I realised how bad it still was. His feet were in a terrible state too. God knows how he'd managed to keep shoes on over those toes. He must have been in a lot of pain.

Anyway, he packed his tool-bag with clothes and threw it out of his bedroom window into the garden. He told his mother he was coming next door to see me and they argued about that because she quite rightly didn't think he was well enough to go visiting anyone, but in the end she let him go. The last words she said to him were that he was the stubbornest child she'd ever known.

So he didn't say goodbye to her either?

No. He left her a note, I think. As I recall, he put it in his bed.

He'd dressed in his plumber's overalls and I remember making some joke about that, but it turned out to be a good choice. They were very resistant – they lasted him for ever, those overalls – plus they were what people were used to seeing him in during the day, so in a way it disguised him for the walk to the garage.

We both slept really badly, me and the baby on the seats of the pickup and Pierre in Dad's dirty old garage armchair, and the next morning we waited for him to arrive. He'd said that if he wasn't there by lunchtime then it meant the Germans had come, and we should just do our best to get out of Mulhouse, so that wait was really nerve-wracking. I kept pacing around the garage, chewing my nails until my fingers bled. But he arrived about ten in the morning, carrying two jerry cans of petrol to add to what he had in the pickup. I don't know where he got those from . . . Petrol was really hard to come by. He must have called in a few favours, I suppose.

The pickup had a single three-person bench seat up front and an open flatbed bit behind the cabin, so Dad decided to hide Pierre horizontally in the tiny space behind the seat and have me and the baby sit up front. Pierre looked suspicious, he said, while I looked like the Virgin Mary. We rolled him in a blanket and slid him into the space.

Dad loaded all his tools in the back, piles and piles of them, and winched his old tractor engine on there as well – to give the Germans something to look through, he said – and then piled some more ropes and things on top of Pierre behind me, and then we drove out of town.

No one tried to stop you?

Oh, there were checkpoints. But it was early days still, and the checkpoint troops were still trying to be relatively polite. Dad was a mechanic in his garagist's truck returning a tractor engine to La Vieille-Loye. The soldiers checked our papers and rifled through the tools in the back every time, and when they showed too much interest in the baby I pinched his thighs to make him cry, the poor thing, and told the Germans off for having woken him up. That always worked – they waved us on every time.

And they didn't find Pierre?

No. I had lots of blankets on my lap beneath the baby, and they sort of merged into the one behind us that was covering Pierre. There was so little space behind me that I don't think the Germans thought to look, and he was so slight . . .

You know, he slept during most of the journey. I remember – and this is quite funny – that as we pulled up at one of the checkpoints, I realised he was snoring and had to kick him and tell him to be quiet!

I suppose he was exhausted after his ordeal . . .

Exactly. Though he was more than exhausted. He was suffering from a sort of anaemia from all the blood he'd lost, but we didn't know that yet.

Did you get emotional about not being able to say goodbye to your mothers?

I did. Pierre not so much. They didn't get on so well, plus I think he was still in shock from what they'd done to him at the police station. He seemed a bit . . . I don't know how to put it really . . . a bit *robotic*, I suppose you could say. It was like he'd gone into a sort of survival mode, and everything else was just switched off. But I did – I got really weepy during the drive and Dad kept having to reassure me that it was better this way, because Mum would only have got upset, and we were all going to see each other again soon anyway, weren't we?

Did you still believe that?

Yes, I think I did. I couldn't project anything specific in the future. I had no idea how things were going to pan out, but I didn't imagine for an instant that was it, that I would never see them again.

Are you OK? Do you need a tissue?

Thanks, yes. I'm fine. Sorry. It's just . . . it's still hard. Even after all these years. The fact that I never got to say goodbye properly. I tried to ask Dad to tell Mum that I loved her, but I couldn't even say the words to him. My throat kept closing up. But I remember he said it was OK because she knew. He squeezed my leg and said, 'It's OK, sweetheart, she knows. We both do. That's one thing we got right in this family. We all know how much we love each other.'

It took all day to get to La Vieille-Loye. I hadn't thought to even question how far it was, so I was shocked about that. Normally it would only have taken about three hours, but because we got stopped and questioned a few times, and because Dad took lots of detours down country lanes to avoid as many checkpoints as possible, it ended up taking us twice as long.

He drove without a map and I didn't realise how strange it was that he knew exactly where to go until the afternoon when he turned off the road and started heading down a bumpy dirt track. That was when I realised that neither of us had told him the carpenter was in La Vieille-Loye. Neither of us had a specific address – we'd been too upset and too busy being scared to even think about the details of it all. So it was only then it dawned on me that something strange was going on. I asked him if he was sure it was down that particular track and how he knew and he replied that he'd 'spoken to some people' and that I didn't think he'd put his only daughter in the care of some random person he knew nothing about, did I?

The track was long – perhaps three or four kilometres, and incredibly uneven – so the baby woke up and started crying and then, whenever we went over a really big bump, Pierre groaned as well. My father kept apologising about the bumps.

Eventually we came to a dilapidated stone farmhouse in a clearing, and Dad parked and told us to stay put. He specifically told Pierre to stay silent.

He was gone for ages, maybe half an hour. When he returned and started the engine without a word, I thought he'd decided against leaving us there for some reason – I thought something about the set-up had made him suspicious. But then he drove the pickup across the courtyard and into a huge wooden barn. There were big carpentry tools dotted around the place – you know, drills and saws and one of those big machines for turning table legs and stuff.

A lathe?

Yes, that's it, a lathe. Once we were in, Dad climbed out and dragged the big wooden doors closed behind us.

We pulled Pierre from his niche and unwrapped him and then an old man, a very tall, wiry man with lots of grey hair, appeared through a side door. He was a gruff, rustic sort of person with a huge grey moustache and a very strong accent – but he turned out to be kind, and as soon as he saw Pierre, he offered to hide us until he'd got his strength back.

My father pulled a roll of banknotes from his pocket and peeled off a wad to give to the man. I think it was only a few hundred francs, and they were old francs of course, so it wasn't a huge amount. He divided the remainder into two rolls and put rubber bands around them, telling me to give one of them, the smaller one, to the man once he'd got us over the border, and the rest he said was to help us on our travels.

I hadn't really thought much about the future, about where we were supposed to go, so I asked Dad where we should aim for, and he said he'd heard that the Atlantic coast was supposed to be safe. I was shocked because that was thousands of kilometres away and I had no idea how we were supposed to get there. We didn't know anyone over that way, either. The carpenter – he never told us his name, so Pierre and I started referring to him as Moustache – said he'd heard that too, that the south-west was safest – to the west of Perpignan, but we should avoid anywhere north of Lyon. Even Lyon he'd heard bad things about, he said. He told us not to go near the Italian border either. But then he interrupted himself and said we'd have plenty of time to think about all that, and my father should leave. It was dangerous for us all the longer he stayed.

Dad hugged me and made me promise to write whenever I could. He said never to put my address or my name. He told me to just tell him if we were OK and then sign the letters Nours or something.

Nours?

It was the name we'd given my teddy bear when I was little. So after that I always signed my letters home Nours.

The carpenter insisted that Dad should get a move on, and so we hugged and in a flurry of tears said our goodbyes. Dad told Pierre to look after me, and Pierre joked and said I was going to look after *him*. And then they opened the barn doors and Dad got in his pickup and drove away.

That must have been pretty traumatic, wasn't it?

Oh, totally. It was awful. The whole thing was. Of course, I didn't know then that I'd never see him again. But all the same, yes, it was terrible. I couldn't stop crying and shaking. As you can see, I'm crying now, just thinking about it.

Take a minute, if you need to.

No. I'm OK. It's just that . . . you know . . . when people are dead, once they're gone . . . Well, you always wish you'd said more, don't you? But I didn't know. It took me a very long time – years and years and years. But in the end I managed to forgive myself for that – for not having said more. Because I've accepted that there's no way I could have known.

Of course there wasn't.

Once he'd driven away, God . . .

Take a minute. Take some breaths.

Yes. Gosh, the memories still feel so fresh. Dad driving away, the dust swirling behind his truck . . . Anyway, Moustache led us into the woods, and we walked for half an hour through the trees – I think it must have been a couple of kilometres. Pierre was whimpering from the pain of having to walk and I was in tears because I was so scared. It was very remote, and I wondered if he wasn't just going to kill us or something – but then we came to a small wooden hut. It was made of tree trunks and the forest was so thick around it that you couldn't see it until you were upon it. He told us he'd built it himself from the trees he'd cut and that we'd be safe there. He was very proud of it, I seem to remember.

It was incredibly basic, just a single room with a rough bed made out of planks, and two chairs that he'd hacked out of other bits of tree. There was a wood burner he told us not to light because of the smoke – not that we needed to anyway, it was summer, after all. The shutters were all closed and he said we couldn't open them and we'd have to stay indoors and not go out, 'not even to shit'. I remember he said that. As I say, he was a pretty rustic kind of a guy. There was a bucket in the corner 'to shit in', he said, and there was a jug of water on the shelf. He promised someone would be back with food later on and then started to leave.

Pierre asked him how long we needed to stay there, I recall, and he said rather abruptly that we'd be there until Pierre could walk properly. And then he left.

When we realised he had re-chained and padlocked the door we got quite panicky. Actually, we got very panicky.

You mean, he'd locked you in?

Yes. We went around checking the shutters and realised they'd all been nailed shut. So unless we smashed our way through the door or something – and there was nothing to smash it with anyway – we were stuck there.

We worked ourselves into a frenzy then. We sat on those two chairs whispering about what if he never came back and left us there to starve, or came back with a shotgun to kill us and steal all the money he'd seen my father give me. Pierre thought he was probably off to fetch some Germans and would hand us over in exchange for food or money or something.

Eventually we ran out of theories and even energy to come up with new ones and fell asleep, the three of us, on the bed. It was only a single, and a narrow single at that. It had one of those old-fashioned straw mattresses too, and the straw stuck through the holes and needled you when you moved. But we'd worn ourselves out worrying, I think, so the three of us slept for a while.

Later on, after dark, we were woken by the sound of the chain being pulled off and got scared all over again. There was nowhere to hide, and we had no weapons, so we just sat up to await our fate. We talked about it afterwards and Pierre said he'd been convinced that Moustache had come back to kill us, while I was certain it was going to be Germans. But when the door opened, it revealed this pale, grubby little girl – she must have only been about eight. She had a lantern in one hand and a bag in the other which contained a baguette, a jug of milk – you know, country milk, straight from the cow – and a bar of chocolate.

God, that chocolate. I shed a few tears when I saw the chocolate.

Because chocolate was hard to come by during the war?

No. Well, it was – chocolate was incredibly hard to come by. But when I saw the chocolate, I knew they weren't going to kill us. Because if you're going to murder someone, well, you don't give them chocolate first, do you?

I asked her what her name was, and she said that her daddy had told her no names. She told us, very precisely – because she was clearly reciting what she'd been told – she said to put the lamp out as soon as we'd eaten so no one would see it through the cracks, and she'd be back for it the next day. And then she left, padlocking the door behind her.

And that's how we lived for a week. There was a jar of dried peas on the shelf by the wood-burner and once we'd realised that we were losing track of time, we removed one each day and lined them up on the shelf. We couldn't wash properly because we only had a jug of water, and we only ever spoke in whispers. The baby cried a lot and we did our best to keep him quiet, but that was it. That was how we lived.

Was it always the little girl who came?

Yes, every night, she'd come just after dusk and swap her lit lantern for the one from the day before. She always brought a baguette and a litre of milk, and sometimes a bit of goat's cheese or a slice of ham, or some jam.

But no more chocolate?

No. The chocolate was only that first day and Pierre was annoyed that we'd eaten it. He said we should have rationed ourselves to make it last.

Couldn't you have forced her to leave the door open or to leave you the key, if she was just this little girl, on her own?

Well, we asked her on the second day to leave the door unlocked and she said her papa had told her to lock it. She could lock us in or lock us out, she said, but the door had to be locked. We were hardly going to fight a little girl for the key, were we? So we chose to stay locked in. Plus we were depending on her for food, of course . . .

Do you know why they locked you in?

I can only suppose that it was dangerous for them if we wandered around and got seen. It could have given their whole operation away.

I see. And what did you feed the baby? What about bottles and nappies and stuff?

Well, we fed the baby the milk, straight from a cup. It gave him colic at first, which made him scream, but we didn't have any other choice. I worked out a way to put my little finger in the cup and he'd suck at it and swallow milk at the same time. And for the other end, when we ran out of nappies, we lined his nappy with newspaper. There was a whole pile of old newspapers in the corner for lighting the fire, so we just used those as sort of nappy liners. When they were dirty we put them in the poo bucket and when the girl came she let us empty it in a hole behind the cabin.

Gosh, newspapers as nappy liners? Did that work?

No, not really. They weren't very absorbent and they left newsprint all over his bum, but it was what we had, so for a while we made do. After a few days the girl began taking the dirty nappies away so her mother could wash them, so things were a bit easier after that.

Pierre slowly got better. After a few days, he could use the bucket without bleeding too badly, and on the third or fourth day he was able to walk around the room without too much pain. One of his toes was infected, and hurt a lot, but he was able to walk. He started doing press-ups too, which made us laugh, because I could always beat him. I could always do more press-ups than Pierre.

I thought it was because of all my rowing, but he was still quite weak, I think.

Time must have gone very slowly, didn't it, locked up in the dark?

During the day, it wasn't completely dark. Some light leaked in around the edges of the shutters and if you sat in the right place you could even read the old newspapers. That was peculiar, I remember, reading the papers – all the silly things people used to worry about before the war. It all seemed so . . . frivolous, I suppose. But yes, it did seem a long time.

Is that what you did then? Just read old newspapers?

Well, Pierre slept a lot. He slept for maybe fifteen hours a day. And when he was awake, we talked, endlessly, in whispers. We were childhood friends, remember, so we had lots of things we could talk about – our parents and what they'd be doing or saying. We talked about Ethel in London, and what might be happening to Johann or Leah, which always made us cry, or what it was going to be like once we got over the demarcation line, and whether we'd find ourselves in occupied France or free France. We didn't know then where one ended and the other began and neither did we know how far down the border we'd be crossing. We talked about how we'd explain the fact that we'd lost our papers if anyone stopped us . . .

Had you, then? Lost your papers, I mean?

No. But Dad had made us hide them in the lining of the suitcase. He'd said it was too dangerous to show them, because of course they said that we weren't husband and wife at all. He thought that Pierre would end up on some sort of wanted list as well.

We argued about what to call ourselves – we even managed to have a tiny bit of fun going through names. In the end we decided to call ourselves Mr and Mrs Poulain. Genevieve Poulain and Pierre Poulain.

Can I ask why you chose Poulain?

Yes. <Laughs> It was the name on the chocolate, that's all. It was the brand. It was a bar of Chocolat Poulain, and we liked the name. We liked the chocolate, too, so . . .

And then, one day, when the girl came back – it was eight days after we'd arrived – she said that her papa had told her we were leaving that night and we were not to go to sleep.

Gosh, that must have been a relief, wasn't it?

It actually wasn't. Neither of us felt relieved. Of course, it was awful being locked in that cabin with no sunshine and nothing to do and the smelly poo bucket in the corner. But by then we'd got used to it. We'd come to feel safe. We even imagined staying there for months and then one day someone breaking down the door and it turning out to be an Allied soldier telling us the war was over. So no, we didn't feel relieved. We felt petrified that we had to leave. And of course, there was no one to ask about where we were going and what was going to happen next.

I'm just wondering something . . . The man, the carpenter man who helped you. Was it for money? You said your father paid him.

No, I don't think so. I think that was just what he did, getting people over the border. I think the money – and it really wasn't that much – was just to help feed us, and his family and . . . I don't know, incidental costs. There were perhaps people he had to bribe. That's how things worked during the war. He gave Dad some petrol, too, so it might have been something to do with that.

And did he ever ask you why you were running away? Did he ever ask why they'd hurt Pierre? Do you think he cared who he helped?

Well, he almost asked us. Didn't I tell you that bit?

No, I don't think you did.

Yes, that first day, when he let us into the cabin, he said we wouldn't be able to leave until Pierre could walk properly. He said it was a long walk, and we needed to be fit. And then he asked Pierre what he'd done to 'piss off the Krauts'. I don't know what Pierre was going to tell him – he definitely wouldn't have risked telling him the truth. But before Pierre could even reply, he said, 'Don't tell me. It's better I don't know. You pissed them off, that's all I need to know. And anyone who pisses off the Krauts is a friend.'

I'm afraid my tape is about to run out again. What do you want to do? Carry on, or do you want to call it a day? I could always come back tomorrow.

I am feeling a bit exhausted . . . It's all getting more emotional than I thought it would be. Perhaps we can carry on tomorrow? Oh, isn't tomorrow Sunday? Yes? Could we continue on Monday then? Would that work for you?

Sure, Monday's fine. Same time?

Yes. Or perhaps even a bit earlier? But I am worried: isn't this too long? It's going to be a book at this rate, not a few pages in a magazine.

Yes. Yes, I think it might be pretty big . . . we'll see. We can talk about how to edit it down or whatever once it's done. I'm just thrilled to be able to hear it from you first-hand like this.

Ruth. Part Three.

It took a considerable amount of the kind of repetitive, discreet, low-level nagging that, because of various jobs I have held, I happen to be particularly good at, but finally, in May, Dad gave me Grandpa Chris's address. He couldn't find the phone number, he said, which, knowing Dad's filing system, had about a fifty per cent chance of being true. But I didn't mind – with the name and the address I figured I'd be able to get hold of the phone number with no problem.

I was wrong about that, though. Even Freida, our multilingual Swedish secretary at Impressionable, couldn't track down Grandpa Chris's phone number so, instead, I sent him a card with a folded letter inside telling him a little about my life and saying I felt I'd rather missed out on my grandparents. I closed by saying I'd love to come and visit him one day, and, feeling hopeful, I included my phone number and email address.

A week later I received a low-tech reply in the form of a postcard. The image on the card was of the bay of Arcachon, a photo that looked as if it hadn't been renewed since the 1960s. He said, in the limited space offered by the postcard, that he was thrilled to hear from me, and I was welcome anytime. Sadly he didn't add his phone number, so I wrote back again specifically requesting it and suggesting that perhaps I could visit with my boyfriend in

September, which was the next time I knew we both had holidays booked. This time no immediate reply was forthcoming, which I optimistically decided meant 'I'm thinking about it.'

In the meantime, life continued. I visited my parents every other weekend, generally without Dan, who almost always seemed to be working.

At Impressionable our author manager had finally been replaced (the original one having never returned after maternity leave, joining one of our larger competitors instead). Her replacement started just as the buzz around Ellie Day began to fade, so I'd basically returned to the now-teetering slush pile, working my way through dreadful manuscripts, hoping upon hope to stumble upon the *next* Ellie Day.

This meant that I had more free time than before in which to notice my sweetheart's absence, which is why, that terrible day in Chinatown, I attempted to bring up the subject of our living arrangements.

It was a rainy Sunday in July and the streets were unusually quiet. In my defence, I was premenstrual. I'm not sure what Dan's excuse was but in my humble opinion he needs one too.

'So I've a question for you, sexy boy,' I said, forking a prawn dim sum to my lips. Unlike Dan, who's an expert, I've never been able to get anywhere with chopsticks.

'Oh,' Dan said. 'Sounds serious.'

'Not really. It's just, do you think we see enough of each other?'

'Oh,' Dan said again, deftly chopsticking some bok choy to his lips.

'Don't pull a face,' I said. His brow had furrowed quite noticeably. 'It's just a question. It's not a big deal or anything.'

'Yeah, but it's a trick question,' Dan said, once he'd finished chewing. 'Isn't it?'

'Is it?' I asked, starting to frown myself. 'How so?'

'Well, I have to say no, don't I?'

'Not at all. You can say, "Yes, I see quite enough of your ugly mug, thank you very much,"' I offered, trying to reinject some humour into the conversation.

'OK. Yes, I see quite enough of your ugly mug, thank you very much,' Dan repeated.

'Oh!' I said, crestfallen.

'You see?' Dan said. 'I *can't* say that. And that's kind of my point. It's a trick question. Because I can't say yes but I can't say no either, because then we'd be on to whose *fault* it is that we see so little of each other, and it's obviously *my* fault because I work all the time and you don't. Only I can't do anything about that because I'm trying to build a successful business.'

'Hey,' I said gently, reaching across the table for his hand. 'I'm not trying to trick you. Not at all.'

'OK then,' Dan said, with a sigh. 'But I'm guessing that if you're asking the question, it's because you think we don't see enough of each other.'

'I have more time now, that's all. And I know . . . and understand . . . that you haven't. But I seem to be seeing more of Gina than I do of you lately.'

'So?' Dan asked, sounding vaguely aggressive.

'Will you please just chill?' I asked.

'I hate that word,' Dan said.

'OK. Then will you please relax?'

'I am relaxed.'

'I don't know what you are, Dan, but I can tell you that *relaxed* does not describe it particularly well.'

'OK, then, go for it,' Dan said.

'Go for what?'

At that moment, the waitress swung by our table to ask if everything was all right. We both turned fake smiles on her and insisted everything was lovely.

Once she'd gone, Dan nodded at me, raising his chin as a rather unpleasant way of indicating that I should continue.

'God, Dan,' I said. 'You're being so weird about this.'

'Maybe, but about what?' Dan said, laying down his chopsticks. 'Because I'm still in the dark here.'

'Just forget it,' I said.

'If I knew what I needed to forget, then I might,' Dan said. 'But I'm still waiting for you to spill the beans.'

'Jesus! I was merely going to suggest that if, perhaps, just maybe, we lived together, then I'd see you even when you're working your tits off. Because we'd end up in the same bed every night.'

'Nicely done,' Dan said.

'What was?' I asked. 'Sorry, but *what* was nicely done?'

'The reproach. For "working my tits off".' He made angry little quotes with his fingers as he repeated my words. 'You slipped that in quite deftly.'

'There was no reproach in that phrase, Dan,' I said. 'None. There was merely an offer to live with you because—'

'Yeah, well, sorry, but been there, done that,' Dan said, interrupting me. Which was a shame because I'd been about to end my phrase with, 'I love you'. And of course, once he'd said, 'Been there, done that,' I no longer wanted to tell him that at all.

'Been there, done what?' I asked.

'Um, tried to live with someone who's never happy because I'm always out "working my tits off",' Dan said, making the quotes again. 'And trying to live with someone who's never happy because when I do get home after "working my tits off", I'm too shattered to be any fun to live with anyway.'

'Right,' I said. 'Fine. Well, that's clear, at least.' I turned to look out at the street in an effort to calm my racing pulse. A woman was busy clipping a plastic cover on her daughter's pushchair and the rain looked harder than before. Our silence lasted about a minute and when I turned back, Dan was staring right at me.

'You see?' he said. 'Trick question.'

And it was unreasonable of me, no doubt, but, as my mother would say, the anger was upon me. Something snapped. 'Oh, fuck you, Dan,' I said, standing, and pulling on my coat. 'I don't need this.'

'You're leaving?' Dan asked, speaking through sour, mocking laughter. 'You want us to live together, but we can't even have a discussion anymore?'

'Gimme a call the next time you're not too busy,' I said. I started to walk away, but then turned back. 'Actually, no. Gimme a call next time you're not "working your tits off",' I said, echoing his angry quote marks. 'And when you're not also in a thoroughly shitty mood like what you are today.'

And then I span dramatically on one heel and flounced out of the restaurant, leaving him to pay and wondering if he'd noticed my clunky and grammatically incorrect 'like what you are'.

When I got outside, I stood beneath the awning to button up my coat. As I walked away, I glanced back and saw, to my fury, that he was not attempting to pay at all but was reaching over with his chopsticks, digging into my remaining dim sum. The cold-hearted bastard!

Because I'm very good at sulking and because Dan was too busy to do anything other than phone me – calls I obviously rejected – our silly, pointless crisis lasted almost a month.

Depending on the day of the week, I managed to convince myself that our relationship was over and he'd been my one true love and now I'd be single for ever, or he was a bastard and I was better off without him.

But then, mid-August, I got a text message from him. It said, 'Are we merely sulking or has one of us met someone else?'

Then, a few seconds later: 'That one of us being you, because I totally haven't.'

I sat staring at the screen for a moment as I wondered how best to reply. But before I could even begin, another one arrived.

'And by the way, the answers to your questions are Q1: No and Q2: Yes.' Which gave me a non-committal way into the conversation.

'Sorry, what were the questions again?'

Followed quickly by a softener: 'Plus: hello you!!'

His answers arrived almost immediately, in fact, I was impressed with the speed of his texting.

'Q1: Do you think we see enough of each other?'

'Q2: Would living together be a good solution?'

I started to type a message to the effect that I felt I'd twisted his arm but my phone rang with his incoming call, so I said it out loud to him instead.

We met in the Red Lion, a pub halfway between his place and mine that we'd been to many times before. Despite the fact that it was fairly busy, we managed to get ourselves a booth where we sat opposite each other, nursing our drinks, sheepishly avoiding eye contact.

'Well, that was quite a biggie,' Dan finally said, and I was grateful he'd broken the silence. 'What was that? A month?'

'Almost,' I said. 'We're still a couple of days short.'

'I wasn't expecting it to last that long. I was thinking ten or twenty minutes max.'

'No,' I agreed. 'I didn't think it would end up being quite so dramatic either.'

'I *am* sorry,' he said. 'It's just . . . past trauma, I guess you could call it. These things have a habit of sneaking up on you.'

'Are we talking about the *been there, done that*?'

'Yeah, and that was stupid of me. Because of course, I haven't been there and done that with you, have I?'

'No,' I said. 'Well, for what it's worth, I'm sorry too.'

'For?'

'Um. Well, for starters for telling you to fuck off.'

'Gosh, you did say that, didn't you?' he said. 'I'd forgotten that.'

'Should have kept my mouth shut.'

'Yes,' Dan said. 'Maybe.'

'But mainly I'm sorry for being such a sulker. I am a terrible sulker, sometimes. I hate that about myself.'

'Yeah,' Dan said again. 'Yes, you can certainly sulk.'

'Erm, so can you.'

'I wasn't sulking,' Dan said. 'I was just "working my tits off".' He'd made the quotes again, but this time they'd seemed to be quite friendly. 'Plus I called you,' he continued. 'Not really my fault if you choose not to pick up.'

'Totally true as well,' I said. 'And we don't have to live together, by the way, Dan. We honestly don't. It was just—'

'But I want to. I've thought about it and I want to try.'

'Oh, wow,' I said. 'OK. Could we perhaps talk about that another time, though? Let's just get back on track first, can we?' Going from not speaking for weeks to moving in together just seemed too much of a shift to be achieved within the space of a single conversation.

'Sure,' Dan said. 'Whatever you want.'

'In the meantime I do have another proposition for you,' I said. 'A holiday in Arcachon next month.'

'That's in France, yeah? On the Atlantic?'

'That's the one.'

'The ocean'll be freezing, but then you know that.'

'Yes,' I said, smiling. 'I remember.'

'That's where your grandfather is, right?' Dan asked.

'It is,' I said. 'So it could be weird. Dad says he's a bit strange.'

'Great,' Dan said. 'I *love* strange.'

'Do you still have the first to the fourteenth free?'

'Yep,' he said. 'Amazingly, I do.'

'Me too. So those are our dates.'

I'd received Grandpa Chris's second postcard – with an email address this time, but still no phone number – just a week earlier and had been toying with the idea of going to see him alone. But now Dan was back, I had an ally. And having an ally would make it fun no matter how weird my grandad turned out to be.

So that same evening, after make-up sex, I emailed him suggesting the 1st to the 14th of September.

When after three days he'd failed to reply, I checked the address and emailed him again, saying that we could make it a shorter visit if he preferred.

Finally, in desperation, I went to Mum and Dad's and literally begged my father to look for the phone number. And this time he found it with shocking ease. I suspected he'd known exactly where it was all along.

'No, *I'll* call him,' Dad said, holding the slip of paper out of my reach.

'Let me,' I insisted, jumping to get at the bit of paper. 'I'm the one who's been talking to him about a visit.'

'Yes, but I'm the one with the phone number,' Dad said. 'So it's only polite. Plus I have a feeling.'

'A feeling about what?' I asked, but he raised a finger to silence me and turned to dial the number.

'*Bonjour, puis-je parler*— Oh, sorry. Yes. Of course I do. Can I speak to my father, Chris? Oh, it is? Hi there. Yes.'

Dad's face went a little grey then and he perched on the edge of the sofa for a moment before slumping back into it. 'Yes,' he said. 'Go on.'

Then, 'Yes . . . Yes . . . Yes . . . No! Yes . . . Yes . . . Oh . . . Oh, I see. Oh, God, that— . . . Yes, of course. Gosh, I'm sorry to hear that. Yes, I will.'

Finally he hung up and shook his head. 'I hope you haven't booked tickets yet,' he said.

'Who *was* that, Dad?' I asked. 'And you didn't let me—'

'He's in hospital,' Dad said, interrupting me. 'Your grandfather's fractured his hip. He fell off a ladder cleaning the gutters, apparently. That was a friend of his, Igor.'

'He's in hospital?' I said. 'But that makes me want to go even more.'

'Not much point for the moment,' Dad said. 'He's completely out of it, apparently. And Igor said it's not looking great.'

'What's that supposed to mean?' I asked. 'What do you mean, *not looking great?*'

'He is seventy-six, sweetheart,' Dad said.

'It's only a fracture though, isn't it?'

Mum, who'd remained silent until that point, now looked up from the *Radio Times* she'd been leafing through. 'Hips can be nasty,' she said. 'My grandmother died after she broke her hip.'

'But seventy-six isn't even old,' I said. 'Especially not these days.'

'It is if you've got a broken hip,' Dad said. 'But we'll see. I said I'd call back tomorrow. He was just on his way out the door. I'll keep you posted. But I don't think your little adventure's going to work out. Not in two weeks' time it's not, anyway.'

◆ ◆ ◆

Dan and I ended up in the Lake District, where we spent two nights in a luxury spa complex, followed by a week in a cottage on Lake Windermere.

It was sunny, which was as lucky as it was unexpected, and though it wasn't the South of France, we had a lovely time, lazing around, reading, eating, drinking and, of course, shagging.

Grandpa Chris was on my mind, but whenever I called home, the news was always the same: he was stable but still in hospital. After each phone call, Dan and I would discuss the many things I didn't know about my family, and how strange it all was, and what the possible causes might be for such a void. But we didn't come up with much and our conversations only made me more determined to get down to see Grandpa Chris as soon as he was better.

The holiday enabled Dan and me to reconnect though, and very possibly in a way that a trip to Arcachon, heavy as it would have been with family intrigue, might not have done. So by the time we got back, I felt as in love with him as I ever had.

Meanwhile – a fact that had been perfectly dissimulated by my mother – Dad had flown down to Bordeaux to be with his dying father.

I was pretty upset when I found out, though I hid it well. It seemed to be something Dad and I could have done, or rather *should* have done, together.

Much later on, Mum explained that Dad hadn't intended to go himself, in fact he'd specifically told her, on multiple occasions, that he saw no reason to do so. But as his father's condition had worsened, his emotions had suddenly caught up with him. One morning on opening his eyes, he'd turned to my mother, and said, 'I *have* to go, don't I? And I have to go today.'

I imagine that Mum, who gets the 'family' thing better than she gets just about anything else, will have nodded and stroked his head. 'Of course you do,' she'll have said. 'I'll help you pack a bag.'

Also, in fairness to my father, by that point, by the time it had dawned on him that he needed to go, I was lazing by a heated pool in Windermere. Not wanting to spoil my holiday was an understandable, albeit – in my opinion – insufficient reason for having lied to me.

I didn't find any of this out until after I got back, when I finally went to visit my parents.

I was riding a wave of optimism in the wake of my successful holiday and virtually buzzing with rediscovered passion for Dan.

Surprised to find the house so quiet on a Sunday, I asked my mother what was going on.

'Your father told them all to stay away,' she said, which surprised me even more. 'He wants some peace and quiet this weekend.'

I told her I could go, too, if that was really what they wanted, but she shook her head. 'No, he has something he wants to tell you,' she said. 'He's out in the backyard. Go and talk to him.'

I found him gathering tomatoes from the plants he had nurtured in grow-bags, and we set up two deckchairs by the back wall in the middle of a small square of autumnal sunlight.

'Your grandfather died,' he told me immediately I was seated. 'I've just got back from Bordeaux.'

'Oh!' I said, too shocked to come up with anything more eloquent. I sat in silence for a moment, absorbing the news before asking him if he was OK. And slowly, bit by bit, Dad told me the story of his trip.

He'd flown to Bordeaux airport, he said, where he'd rented a car to drive to Arcachon. But by the time he'd got there, Grandpa Chris had been moved to intensive care in Bordeaux, so he'd turned around and driven right back. Once there, he'd rented a room in an ugly hotel next to the hospital.

Within a few days, Grandpa Chris was officially dying, so he'd decided to stay on until the end. And then once the end had come, he'd decided to stay on for the funeral. All in all he'd been out there over three weeks. 'God knows how I'm ever going to catch up on work,' he said.

'Did you get to talk to him?' I asked.

'Not much,' Dad said. 'He was pretty bad by the time I got there. On oxygen and stuff.'

'Did you go back to his house in Arcachon?'

Dad nodded and pushed his tongue into his cheek.

'Is it nice?'

Another vague nod and a shrug.

'So are you – are *we* – inheriting this place?' I asked. I realised as I said it that it might be misinterpreted as sounding mercenary, and that hadn't been my intention at all. I'd actually been thinking about all the formalities, about the hassles of having to empty and sell an overseas property, and whether that was something I might be able to help him with.

'This Igor chap's living there,' Dad said. 'That's the thing.'

'His friend?'

'Yes.'

'Like a lodger?'

'Yes. But he was also a very good friend, I think. He was widowed quite young, when I was still a teenager. Maybe a bit later, actually. But yes, his wife died. Cancer, I think it was.'

'Oh, I see,' I said. 'So they've known each other for ever.'

'Yes,' Dad said. 'Pretty much.'

'And he's been living there?'

'Yes. It seems that way.'

'Not just on holiday or visiting because Grandpa was ill?'

'No,' Dad said. 'No, I don't think so.'

'But the place must be yours, right? Grandpa didn't have any other children?'

'Not that we know of,' Dad said.

'So it must be. Did this Igor say anything?'

Dad shrugged. 'Look, I feel silly about this . . .' he said. 'But it didn't feel right to ask.'

'Ah . . .' I said. 'OK.'

'He . . . Igor . . . he's just lost his best friend. I feel like I should have . . . you know, asked for more details . . . but I couldn't. He was very upset. More than me, in some ways. There was no . . . space . . . I suppose you could say . . . in which to ask.'

'Of course,' I said, in an attempt at reassuring him. 'That makes sense. That makes perfect sense, Dad. And there's no hurry, is there?'

'No,' Dad said. 'No, we said we'd keep in touch. With Igor. I suppose it will all become clear.'

'There's got to be a will, hasn't there?' I asked.

'Again,' Dad said. 'I couldn't bring myself to ask. It's daft, I know, but there it is.'

He turned away and looked out over the fence, and after a moment I asked him once again if he was OK. 'Of course you're not OK. But has it knocked you for six?'

Dad wobbled his hand from side to side. 'I just feel sad that I never really knew him,' he said. 'I feel sad for whatever it was we should have had but didn't.' And then he stood and returned to his tomato harvest.

I desperately wanted to ask him what he meant by that but I could see that this was not the right moment – there was no space, as he'd say, in which to ask it. That question, too, would have to wait.

The beginning of October was to be the beginning of my experiment living with Dan and I was glad to have something to distract me from thinking about Dad's sadness and my grandfather's death.

Because moving into an apartment that was big enough for both of us was a stunningly complex and expensive endeavour – I owned my flat, or rather the bank did, while Dan's shared rental was a bargain – we'd decided to timeshare between our two places and see how that worked out first. The first two weeks of the month we'd spend at my place, and the second half at Dan's.

The losers in this game were undoubtedly Buggles, who'd have to move back and forth, and Dan's co-renters, who were going to have to put up with me.

It wasn't an ideal solution by any means, both of us could see that, but it seemed to be the best way available to test the waters before having to truly jump in.

Thus, Saturday the 4th of October found us carrying Dan's stuff up from his catering van.

'You're sure this is all going to fit in?' Dan asked, as I unlocked my front door.

'I told you,' I said. 'I've made space.'

We carried the cases and bin bags in and dumped them on the sofa. Dan glanced around the room and I thought I saw him raise an eyebrow at the fact that he couldn't see any evidence of me having made space. Then he lifted a rather elegant old leather suitcase on to the table and undid the straps.

'You said to bring some personal effects,' he said, opening the lid.

I moved to his side and looked down at the random assortment of objects – an ashtray, a Nintendo, a paperweight, a buddha . . . – before selecting a framed photo of Dan with his grandmother, a photo I recognised from Dan's bedroom. I span on one heel and set it down on the middle shelf of my bookcase. 'Here?' I asked.

'Yep,' Dan said. 'One down, fifty more to go. And you're bringing stuff to mine, right?'

'Yes,' I said. 'Of course.'

'Good. Then I'll have hostages in case you refuse to give Granny back.'

Buggles appeared from my bedroom and sat blinking at the light. I've never known another cat take so long to wake up. In that we're perfectly matched.

'What are you looking at?' Dan asked him, then, 'He looks like he's never seen me before.'

And it was true. Buggles was staring at Dan quite intently. Had he understood that Dan was moving in?

'He's just not awake yet,' I said. 'He always stares into the middle distance when he wakes up. He's like me. Can't do anything until he's had his coffee.'

Dan handed me a bin bag filled with folded clothes, which I carried through to my bedroom where I proceeded to add them to his existing stuff already in my wardrobe.

By the time I returned, he'd scattered the contents of the first suitcase around the room. None of the items, I noticed, were where I would have chosen to put them, but I realised that I'd have to be tactful in moving them to less obtrusive spots.

He was holding a frying pan in one hand and an electric whisk in the other.

'Wow,' I said. 'You've brought everything but the crib.'

Dan froze. 'What?' he said.

'What what?'

'What did you say?'

'What, *everything but the crib*?'

'Yeah, that.'

'Oh, it's a Solomas saying. Actually, I think it might be one of Mum's.'

'Ah,' Dan said, visibly relaxing. 'Good, because you had me worried there.'

I frowned at his back for a moment as he continued unpacking the case. Because there had been something of note, hadn't there? A certain hint of urgency that had taken me by surprise.

I thought about Dan's relationship with the children we'd come across. He'd been great with Eirla's lot, and had held Gina's sister's baby without qualms. So I'd just assumed . . . But we hadn't had The Baby Conversation yet, and I wondered if that was a mistake.

◆ ◆ ◆

It turned out that we didn't see a huge amount of each other even when living together at mine.

Dan would get up at six and was out the front door by seven thirty, an hour that had me blinking like Buggles at the daylight.

In the evenings he'd get home at either 8 p.m. or midnight, depending on whether he'd had a function that evening or not, so some days we didn't speak at all.

But it felt nice, all the same. When he got up he left a warm impression in the bed that felt like more than the mere shape of where he'd been sleeping. I'd roll into his musky warmth and inhale his essence and have the most fantastic dreams.

Likewise, though he was rarely in the flat when I was, it too seemed to hold a memory of his presence, a memory that felt comforting and warm. So though, objectively, during the day, I was exactly as alone as before, it honestly didn't feel that way. The atmosphere in the flat felt different somehow. After all, I had his grandmother watching my back.

I decided not to raise the subject of children immediately because I didn't want to upset the first few days of our experiment.

But I knew I needed to at least broach the subject, to find out if we had a problem.

I'd intended to bring it up on the final Sunday morning, just before changeover. But Dan got there first.

He'd returned home in the early hours of Sunday after a Westminster function the night before, so for once, I was up before him.

Unlike Buggles and myself, Dan is a man who wakes up at the speed of a lightning strike. So where my morning mood could be described as soft and blurry, if anything, Dan tends to be on edge.

That morning, he came into the kitchen and pulled out a bar stool while I poured him a cup of coffee.

When I turned to offer him the mug, he was sitting bolt upright, staring at me with such intensity it made me jump. 'Good morning,' he said, then, 'Can I ask you something?'

'Sure,' I said, turning back to the pot to refill my own mug.

'Are you still on the pill?'

'Oh!' I said, pulling a face before turning back, so that he wouldn't see. 'Um, yes, of course. Why?'

'Why?'

'Yeah, why are you asking me this at . . .' I checked the clock. '9.05 on Sunday morning?'

'No reason,' Dan said. 'Just checking.'

'OK . . .' I said, doubtfully. 'And would it be a problem if I wasn't?'

'Erm, *yeah*!' Dan said, sounding sarcastic.

'Erm, *yeah*?' I repeated, copying his tone.

'I just mean that it's something I'd need to know. It's something we'd have to discuss.'

'OK then,' I said, grasping the nettle. 'Let's discuss it.'

'Really?' Dan said. 'Now? At 9.05 on Sunday morning?'

'You started this discussion sweetheart. Anyway, it's now 9.06.'

'OK,' Dan said. 'I suppose now's as good a time as any. So, yeah, I don't want kids. Not yet I don't, anyway.'

'Not yet,' I repeated. 'Well, as it happens, I'm not pregnant, and even if I were, I've heard it can take a while before a baby pops out. Months, some people say!'

'Nowhere near yet,' Dan said.

'Well, I'm thirty-three,' I said. 'So . . .'

'And I'm thirty-six.'

'Yeah, only your testicles don't have an expiry date, do they?'

The discussion did not go well.

I wouldn't say we exactly had an argument, and certainly it was nothing like that awful meal in Chinatown. But let's say that it wasn't the *friendliest* chat I've ever had. Not the friendliest chat at all.

Once it was over and we'd agreed to discuss it further once we'd both had time to 'mull things over', I asked Dan if we were still moving Buggles to his place for the fortnight. I'd bought a new carrier for him the day before. It was made out of cloth rather than hard plastic so was purportedly less traumatic for the cat.

In a way, my question about his plans may have been a strategic error, because it made something that had been definite become a choice.

'Can we maybe have a rain check on that, then?' Dan asked, the final 'then' emphasising the fact that I was the one to have made this optional.

'Do you mean you just want to stay on here another week, or . . . ?'

'The "or" part of that equation,' Dan said. 'Definitely the "or" bit.'

'You're going to your place, you mean? Alone?'

'Yeah, I think I might. Just for a breather.'

Within an hour, Dan was gone, leaving me sitting on the sofa with my cat, struggling to work out what I was feeling.

Buggles purred as loudly as he had in a long time. He seemed quite happy about Dan's departure and eventually, after half an hour or so, I had to admit to myself that my principal emotion was relief. Sure, the baby thing remained problematic, but it didn't need to be dealt with immediately, after all.

On reflection, I managed to acknowledge that I'd been artificially stoking my resentment about Dan not being head over heels about wanting a kid. Because evidently he was supposed to be so totally smitten with me that nothing would please him more than tying himself to me for ever with a child.

But the truth was that I knew how Dan felt, because the idea of a baby made me feel panicky too. Biological clock or not, I didn't feel ready to become a parent either, nor was I one hundred per cent certain that Dan was the right man to do it with.

Buggles abandoned me in favour of a tiny patch of sunshine on the armchair, a patch he tends to track throughout the day, and that made me think about how unhappy he would have been at Dan's. That was a fact I'd known all along but had suppressed because it was inconvenient. Everyone knows how territorial cats are. Everyone knows you can't just cart them around willy-nilly. What a silly, crazy idea that had been!

And while we're on the subject of territoriality, I would have hated living at Dan's place as well. If I'd wanted to live in a flat-share then I wouldn't have crucified my finances with this mortgage, would I? I spent my days alone, at home, with Buggles and the never-ending slush pile. And that was exactly how I liked it.

I wondered what had got into me, into *us*, that we'd made so many bad decisions lately.

I made a cup of tea and stared out at the street for a while. And then, while sitting on the loo, I sent a text to Dan.

I said that I was sorry we'd got each other's hackles up, but the truth was that I didn't feel ready for a baby either.

And then I sent another one saying that the timeshare concept was pretty rubbish because neither of our flats was big enough. So could we please just go back to how things were before?

I was on the train out to Walthamstow when his answer came through.

It said, 'I love you and I do want kids with you and I do want to live with you. But not like this and not right now. Are we OK with that?'

'We're OK,' I replied. 'We're more than OK. We're in love.'

He replied with '<3' and, because I hadn't come across a sideways love heart before, I assumed that he'd typed it by accident. Which is a shame because if I'd understood the message, it would have pleased me no end.

◆ ◆ ◆

At Mum and Dad's it was full house, meaning the ambience was basically mayhem.

Mum, Pippa, Harry and Aisha were squashed into the kitchen, peeling and chopping while drinking cocktails. Actually, as far as I could see, they were mainly just talking, but cooking was their official occupation. Dinner was not going to be happening anytime soon.

In the lounge Dad, Eirla, Tom, Tracey and Suzie were arguing, of all things, about politics and the Irish presidential election. Suzie, for some reason, had taken it upon herself to make everyone mojitos, and she handed me one almost the minute I set foot in the room.

'Thanks,' I said. 'That's, um, a nice summery idea.' It was eight degrees and cloudy outside so it seemed a strange choice.

I listened to them arguing about Mary McAleese for a while, and then drifted out to the backyard where the cousins were discreetly passing round a joint.

'I still think he should call her, just in case,' Harry's daughter Alice was saying as I stepped outside. 'What if it's money or Premium Bonds or something?'

'Who should call who?' I asked, and Alice finally noticed my presence and turned to face me, making a futile attempt at hiding the joint behind her back. Because there's nothing I like more than being hip with the youngsters I beckoned to her until, looking nervous, she handed it over.

'Your dad should call Ethel,' Peter said, answering for his sister.

'Ethel?'

'Yeah,' Peter said. 'Grandma Genny's cousin.'

'I don't . . .' I said, shaking my head and speaking through smoke. 'I have no idea what you're all talking about.'

'Careful,' Alice said, addressing Peter. 'We don't know what it's about. And we're not even supposed to know.'

'Oh, Ruth's all right,' Peter said, then, 'Alice overheard your mum talking to Dad. Apparently Ethel's been trying to get in touch with your dad about something. But he's not interested enough to even phone her back.'

'I would, wouldn't you?' Alice said. 'It could be to do with his inheritance or something.'

'So this is *my* dad's inheritance from *his* mother Genny we're talking about?' I asked, playing catch up as I handed the joint to Peter.

'Yeah,' Alice said.

I shook my head. 'Then I don't know why you're so excited. Even if it was about that – which I doubt – Grandma Genny isn't your grandmother at all. Or your great-grandmother, even. I know everyone called her that, but she's not related to your parents in any way.'

'No,' Peter said. 'No, I know that. But when my mate Tommy's grandad died, they discovered he was loaded. And there was so much dosh that they dished it out to the whole family.'

'Ah,' I said, laughing. 'I see.'

'But even if he doesn't choose to do that,' Alice said, attempting to sound a little less calculating, 'it would be nice for him, for your dad, wouldn't it? To inherit something, I mean? Because he didn't get anything when his dad died, apparently.'

'I met Grandma Genny, and she was not a millionaire,' I told them. 'So I doubt very much that they have some secret stash of gold bars that nobody knows about. And why would Ethel have anything to do with it anyway? I'm not even sure how she's related, but I think the link is pretty tenuous. She's, like, Genny's second or third cousin or something.'

'But they had a business together, in Brighton,' Alice said.

'A restaurant, I think,' Peter said. 'And Dad says Brighton's crazy expensive.'

'So that might be worth a bit.'

'It might be Wagamama or something. Maybe she owns Pizza Express.'

'OK,' I said, frowning at the fact that my cousins knew more about my grandmother than I did. 'I'll, um, see what I can find out, OK?'

'But don't say we told you,' Alice said. 'Even Dad's not sup-posed to know.'

I waited until after lunch to interrogate Mum. I suppose I could have gone to Dad, but he's always been a bit of a clamshell and if you try to get something out of him directly, he just closes up even tighter. Past experience had taught me that the easiest way to ease him open is to go into the attack with pre-existing information. The only thing Dad likes even less than revealing his secrets is not knowing – or rather, not having control over – which bits of the secret you know.

'Yes, she's written to him twice,' Mum said. 'And phoned as well.' She was wiping down the worktop and kept glancing out to the hallway to check that we were still alone.

'But she didn't say what it was about?'

'No,' Mum said. 'I told you. He hasn't called her back yet.'

'But you spoke to her. So you could have asked her yourself.'

Mum laughed at the idea. 'It's not my family, is it?'

'No,' I said. 'I suppose not.'

'And if she wanted to tell me, she would have.'

'Sure,' I said. 'Fair enough. She and Grandma Genny were cousins, right?'

Mum nodded and scooped the gunk from the sink strainer into the bin. 'Not direct cousins, I don't think. Not first cousins, I mean. But they were close. They flat-shared for years.'

'Oh, OK,' I said. 'I didn't know that. Or maybe I did, from way back when. And they ran a business together in Brighton?'

'Huh,' Mum said. 'That'd be news to me. Sounds like you know more than I do.'

'A restaurant, I think someone said.'

'Yeah, perhaps,' Mum said vaguely. 'That does ring a bell.'

'What rings a bell?' Dad asked from the doorway, making us both jump.

Personally, I would have gone for it at that point and tried to extract the cat from the bag, but Mum got there first, saying, 'None of your business. Get out! Honestly! Always thinks it's about himself, that one. If the ladies can't even have a chat in private . . .'

Dad placed the dirty glasses on the worktop and backed out of the room, bowing. 'Sorry,' he said. 'So very sorry, m'lady!'

Once he'd gone, Mum mouthed 'close the door' at me, so I gave it a kick.

'He's always been a bit funny about her,' Mum said, speaking quietly. 'About Ethel.'

'I barely remember her, that's the truth. But in the few memories I do have, she seemed OK.'

'Yes,' Mum said. 'She was always nice enough to me.'

'So you don't know what she wants to speak to him about, and you don't know why he's avoiding her either?'

Mum gave a dismissive shake of the head. 'You know what your father's like,' she said. 'Anything that makes him uncomfortable . . . Well, he just doesn't get around to things, does he? It's called subconscious avoidance, I think.'

'Or conscious,' I said. 'But yeah. He's certainly good at it.'

'You know I always thought it was maybe because she might be . . .' Mum started. But then she wrinkled her nose and started scrubbing at a frying pan instead.

'She might be what, Mum?' I asked.

'No, never mind,' Mum said. 'I shouldn't have said anything. It's just conjecture anyway.'

'What is?'

'Forget it.'

'Mum!' I said. 'You can't do that!'

'I think you'll find that I can,' she said. 'And I'm not saying anything further, so you can forget about making a fuss.'

I found Ethel's number on the phone pad. Luckily my mother is as predictable as she is organised. So I took the pad to the loo with me and copied the number to my phone.

When I got back to the lounge, it was packed solid with bodies and a glance out of the window revealed it had started to rain.

'So the great debate,' Uncle Tom said, when I entered, 'is Cluedo or Pictionary?'

'Or Risk?' Peter offered.

'Oh, God, not Risk,' I said. 'That goes on for ever. We'll be here till next Wednesday if we play Risk.'

'Next Tuesday,' Mavaughn said. 'It's "We'll be here till next Tuesday."'

'You've obviously never played Risk,' I said.

'Exactly,' Tom said, looking smug. 'Which is why it's Cluedo or Pictionary.'

'There are too many people for Cluedo,' Mum said.

'There are too many people for anything,' Mavaughn said.

'Why not Taboo, then?' Alice asked. 'We've played Taboo with massive groups of people before.'

'Taboo?' I repeated. 'That sounds dangerously like Scruples.' Nobody smiled. If anything, the word *Scruples* still had the capacity to elicit a few glares.

'It's not,' Harry said, flatly. 'It's nothing like Scruples at all.'

'Sounds perfect, then,' I said. 'As long as you're sure we can play with . . .' I started to count, but Alice had apparently already done so. 'Fifteen,' she said. 'Seventeen once Jake and Abby arrive.'

'Jake said he *might* drop in for coffee,' I reminded her. 'I'd count them out for this one.' Of late, my brother's visits tended to be rare, fleeting and unpredictable.

'So fifteen, then,' Alice said. 'We can divide up into teams.'

As people moved around the room, reorganising themselves for the game, I thought back to that horrific Christmas and my recall of the argument sparked a new thought – a potential ending for my mother's unfinished phrase. 'You know I always thought it was maybe because she might be . . .'

Because what if she'd been about to say, *Jewish*? Could that really be the reason that my idiot father wouldn't call her? Surely not. Surely even he . . . ?

But then again . . .

171

And then, hating myself for even having the thought, I wondered, *Ethel? Is that a Jewish name?* And I wondered if I dared ask Abby.

◆ ◆ ◆

Unfortunately for my cousins, Wagamama did not belong to Ethel, but she was the proud owner of a Brighton café and it was there that she agreed to meet.

We'd barely spoken on the phone because she'd been in the doctor's waiting room when I'd called, but I didn't mind at all. She'd agreed to meet me – that was the main thing. Finally I was going to speak to someone who might know something about my grandparents' lives, and perhaps even why my father's relationship with them had been so strained.

It was a perfect autumn day – sunny and crisp – and the journey down to Brighton went without a hitch. Watching the countryside slide past felt like a form of meditation, and I arrived feeling optimistic and relaxed.

I was early, so I strolled along the seafront for a while before turning back up through the Lanes until I stumbled upon her groovy café: Roots.

I'm not sure what surprised me so much about how trendy the place was, but surprise me it did. I guess it just comes down to my own misconceptions about the kind of business a seventy-year-old might be running and the kind of person that a seventy-year-old might be. Plus there's the simple fact that our family doesn't really 'do' alternative. We tend to be pretty mainstream and, if anything, a bit old school. Still, I suppose that's what living in Brighton will do to you – or rather *for* you.

Anyway, Roots was dead funky and I liked the place instantly. It was vegetarian and organic and furnished with a beautifully curated selection of mismatched vintage furniture. To top it all, the art on the walls was quirky, bordering on crazy.

The woman behind the counter was, I suspected, the girl I'd seen at Grandma Genny's funeral, though she'd aged a bit and sprouted a few extra nose rings in the intervening years. In addition to the fact that I was happy to see a vaguely familiar face, the idea she'd been working here so long seemed to say something reassuring about the nature of the business my grandmother and Ethel had built. That's if it was indeed her, as she didn't recognise me. Anyway, the girl I may or may not have met before took my order for a cappuccino and a cookie, and at the end, as I was paying, I asked her whether Ethel was around.

'She usually comes in around eleven,' she said, and as she handed me my change we both glanced at the huge station clock on the wall. It was just after ten thirty.

'That's fine,' I said. 'I can wait.'

'But it can be as late as twelve sometimes,' the girl said.

'We, um, arranged to meet here at ten thirty,' I told her. 'So do you think I should call her, or . . . ?'

'Oh God,' she said. 'Oh God, I'm sorry. I forgot. You're Genny's daughter, aren't you? Of course you are.'

'Granddaughter,' I corrected her, trying not to feel – but above all not to *appear* – offended.

'Right!' she said, firing an imaginary gun at her temple. 'You're clearly way too young to be her daughter.'

'Clearly,' I said, with a little laugh.

'I shouldn't have taken your money,' she said. 'Ethel's going to be annoyed about that. 'Cos you're her guest and everything. *And* family.'

'Don't worry,' I said. 'We won't tell her.'

'If you don't mind,' she said. 'Because cancelling the receipt is a right kerfuffle. It's a new till . . . But the next one'll be on the house, I promise. And if you've arranged to meet her, then she'll be here. She's good about that sort of thing. So I'd just take a seat and enjoy your coffee.'

I glanced around the room as I tried to decide where to sit. Only two seats were occupied, one by a hipster with a beaded beard and the other by a suited man reading the *Guardian*.

I'd just chosen to sit on the long seat they'd installed under the window when Ethel strode up to the door.

To say that she also looked hipper than I'd expected would be an understatement. She was wearing a faded red linen dress with a thick wraparound grey cardigan over the top, accessorised with an orange hessian bag and Jackie O sunglasses. Of course, the only time I'd seen her in recent years had been at a funeral, but I suppose even then she'd been wearing a flowery dress. Maybe she truly *was* hip.

'I'm late,' she said, once she'd closed the street door behind her. 'Am I late?'

We all glanced at the clock again.

'Two minutes,' she said, as I replied, simultaneously, 'No, you're exactly on time. I was early.'

'Can't stand being late,' she muttered, as she crossed the room.

Because of my mother's tendency to hug everyone, I expected that Ethel would too, so I opened my arms. That was awkward because instead she just patted my shoulder and turned towards the counter. 'Morning, Janine,' she said. 'My usual, please.' And then to me, 'Come. We can sit over here by the radiator. I'm frozen. Severely underdressed, as it turns out. I see sunshine out of the window and my brain says *summer*!'

I followed her to a little corner table and she eased herself gingerly into her seat.

'Are you OK?' I asked.

She let out a suppressed gasp as she completed the movement, and then looked momentarily confused before saying, 'Oh . . . yes. It's my bones, they're rubbish.'

'Rubbish bones,' I said. 'That sounds inconvenient.'

'Osteoporosis and arthritis. It's a nightmare, to be honest. I'm basically falling apart as we speak. If we talk for too long, you may need to stick some bit of me back on.'

'Oh, gosh,' I said. 'I'm sorry to hear that.'

She shrugged. 'Still the last one standing, I suppose.'

'After losing Genny and Christophe?' I said. 'Yes, that must be hard.'

'Amongst many,' she replied, glancing soulfully out at the street. 'But yes. It has been hard without them. It's been really hard. They were everything that made life worthwhile.'

'You were close to both of them, then?' I asked. 'I'm not that up on our family history, I'm afraid.'

'No,' she said. 'No, I bet.'

Janine came over then with Ethel's usual, which was apparently a cup of green tea. 'It's packed with antioxidants,' Ethel told me, following my gaze.

'Not a big fan of green tea, myself,' I told her. 'Antioxidants or not.'

'No,' Ethel said. 'Me neither. It's medicine, supposedly. So tell me, what's this all about?'

Because I'd forgotten that it wasn't me she'd been trying to contact but my father, her question momentarily flummoxed me. 'I just . . .' I said, struggling for words as Ethel smiled at me serenely and sipped her tea.

'You know, I have a photo of you somewhere,' she said, deciding to save me. 'When you were about this high.' She held her hand out to indicate the height of what would probably be a five- or six-year-old. 'You were cute. And shockingly polite.'

'I'd like to see it,' I said. 'We have so few photos from when we were little. And I still am.'

'Cute?'

'No. Shockingly polite.'

'That's good,' she said. 'Politeness is a good thing. And I'll find it for you. It's in . . .' She cleared her throat. 'I still need to go through all her stuff,' she said. 'Genny's stuff. And yes, I know it's been years. But it's just . . . well, sometimes I think that maybe if I hang on a bit longer I won't have to bother and someone else can do hers and mine together all in one big session.'

I didn't really know how to react to that, and by the time I'd decided I should probably have said she'd be around for a long time yet it was too late, because she'd moved on to talking about the weather.

'Anyway,' she said, when she eventually interrupted her own rambling. 'Why are you here? I'm assuming there's some kind of reason?'

'I suppose I just wanted to talk to you,' I said. 'There's a bit of a black hole in our family history I'd like to fill. A few of them, actually, and I'm not really sure why.'

'You're not sure why you want to fill it?'

'No, sorry. Why there's such a void in the first place.'

Ethel smiled and nodded, encouraging me to continue.

'I, um, feel like I really missed out by not getting to know my grandparents,' I said. 'And I feel sad about that. And *bad* about it – guilty, I suppose you could say.'

'Oh, you shouldn't feel guilty,' Ethel said. 'It takes two to tango, after all. But you did miss out. They were wonderful.'

I wasn't quite sure what she meant by the two-to-tango thing, but I decided to save it for analysis during my train journey home.

'And you seem to have known them both pretty well, so . . .'

Ethel snorted at this and then immediately apologised for having done so. 'Sorry,' she said, 'but it's just a bit of an understatement, that's all.'

'Yes,' I said. 'Yes, I'm sure.'

'I don't think three people could have known each other any better. But there's no reason for you to know that, is there? If nobody ever told you, then nobody ever told you, right?'

'Right,' I said. 'Well, nobody did. Nobody ever told me anything. So how did that come about? That you all knew each other so well? I mean, I know you and Genny are related, but—'

'Well, for starters, we knew each other from school,' Ethel said, interrupting me. 'We went around as a trio. Best friends.' A wistful expression had come over her as she forced herself to remember. 'And then we were separated because of the war. My parents sent me to London while Gen and Chris stayed behind. And then, after the war, we all shared a flat together in Vauxhall. It was too small for three people – well, four people if you include Guillaume, but we were broke so we didn't have much choice. People don't retain much mystery when you live in that kind of proximity.'

'Guillaume,' I said. 'God, I even forget that's Dad's name. I've only ever heard anyone call him Billy, or Bill, my whole life.'

'Yes, well, William is the English equivalent. I think he just got bored spelling it out for people.'

'And you all lived together with the baby?'

'He was five by the time they got to London, but yes. We all shared a flat. And then in '49 I was well off enough to be able to finally move out.'

'That must have been a relief.'

'Oh, it was,' Ethel said. 'You have no idea.'

'What year did they divorce?' I asked. 'You see, I don't even know that.'

'Fifty-nine,' Ethel said. 'And from that point on I shared with Gen.'

'Was that for financial reasons too?'

'More or less. There was no way a single mother in London could rent a flat on her own.'

'I'm guessing that you must know why they divorced as well?'

'Of course,' Ethel said. 'I was there.'

'Can you tell me?' I asked. 'Because no one has ever talked about that either.'

Ethel nodded thoughtfully. 'They . . . I suppose you could say – and it's a bit of a cliché – but they wanted different things.'

'What sort of things?'

'Oh, all sorts of things. It had been a . . . a bit of a . . . a marriage of convenience. That's what people say, isn't it?'

'Because of the baby, you mean? Was it what people call a shotgun wedding?'

'The baby was part of it, definitely. But there were lots of other circumstances too.'

'What, like money and housing and the war?'

'Yes. Stuff like that.'

'I see,' I said.

'I doubt you do,' Ethel said, mysteriously.

'Because?'

'Oh, I just mean that it's a very long story. You can't describe fifty years in five minutes.'

'No,' I said. 'I'm sure. But at least this is giving me some idea. But you all stayed friends? Even after the divorce?'

'Oh, totally,' Ethel said. 'They were everything to me. Everything.'

'Did they stay friends too?'

'Yes,' Ethel said. 'Yes, they were very close, always.'

'I . . .' I said. But I was struggling to find my words.

'Um?' Ethel prompted me after a moment.

'I suppose . . .' I stammered. 'Look. Don't get me wrong. I'm not criticising them at all in any way. But they didn't seem that close to Dad. And if they weren't . . . well, it doesn't sound like it's because they were cold-hearted people or anything.'

Ethel laughed at that, a laugh that morphed into a cough. 'Cold-hearted?' she said, when she was able to speak again. 'No, they weren't *cold-hearted* at all. They were the most loving, kind, caring people I've known. The sacrifices they made for each other, for me, for your father, were just huge.'

'Right,' I said. 'So why was there so much distance?'

'With your father?'

'With all of us.'

'Oh,' Ethel said. 'That's a bit more complicated to explain.' She turned and looked out at the street for a moment until we were both startled by the door bursting open behind us. A woman edged her way in with her Zimmer frame, bumping tables as she passed by.

'I guess not everyone is meant to be a parent,' Ethel finally said.

'You mean . . . Are you saying the pregnancy was unplanned?'

She smiled broadly then. 'Yes,' she said. 'Yes, you could say that.'

'So they didn't really want Dad in the first place?'

'Oh no, no . . . no, dear. I wouldn't say that at all,' Ethel said. 'They loved your father deeply. We all did. He was a wonderful child.'

'But?' I said. 'I'm sensing there's a but.'

'I suppose I'd say that they weren't ready. So it was hard for them. Having a baby rather cramped their style.'

'He *cramped their style?*' I repeated, a bit shocked at her turn of phrase. 'That must have been hard for Dad, if he sensed that.'

'Not as hard as it could have been, believe me.'

179

'I'm sorry, but I'm not sure I follow.'

'Well, they escaped from Alsace, dear. *Nazi-occupied* Alsace. God knows what would have happened to them all otherwise. A lot of people died, either in the streets or in the camps.'

'Right,' I said. 'Of course. I don't really know much about that either, I'm afraid.'

'Well, we can save that for another time,' Ethel said. 'But know that they gave up a lot to keep your father safe. And like I said before, it takes two to tango.'

'Meaning?' I said.

'Meaning that, no matter how nice they are, not everyone ends up being a huge fan of their parents.'

'So you're saying that Dad didn't do much to stay in touch with them either?'

'Yes,' Ethel said. 'I'm sorry, but it's also a part of the reason there was so much distance, as you put it.'

'Oh, please, don't apologise,' I told her. 'Because I can totally believe that's true.'

'Also – and it's not a criticism – but your mother's family did suck him in a bit,' Ethel said.

'Yes, they do have a tendency to do that.'

'And I think that, truth be told, he preferred them. He preferred her family to his own.'

'Was that upsetting for Genny and Chris? It must have been, mustn't it?'

'It wasn't nothing to them. But like I said, they had their own lives to live. Raising children is a big deal. It's a huge deal. People, children especially, tend to think they're the whole thing. But they aren't. People, parents, do have other desires and ambitions.'

'Like opening this place?' I asked, glancing around.

'For instance,' Ethel said, with a shrug. 'But once your father was married; once he was smitten with your mother's side of the family, well, they were happy to let him choose his own path. A part of love – part of good parenting – is knowing when to let go.'

'I'm just wondering – is that why they didn't divorce until '59?' I asked. 'For Dad's sake?'

'Yes,' Ethel said. 'That's exactly why. They wanted him to have a stable home as long as it was necessary.'

The conversation became a bit clunky from that point on and I didn't manage to extract a great deal more information from Ethel, which was disappointing.

She seemed suddenly tired and perhaps even a bit emotional, and I had to remind myself that she was in her seventies, and in pain, and I was asking her to talk about her two dearest friends, one of whom she'd lost only months before.

'I'm going to have to leave you soon,' Ethel said, after a short lull in the conversation. 'But I need your help with something, so . . .'

'My help?' I said. 'Yes, anything.'

'I've been trying to talk to your father.'

'Yes. I heard about that through the family grapevine.'

'Oh, you did, did you?' Ethel said, smiling at me wryly. 'Well, I have something I need to give him. For some reason he's being very elusive.'

'He can be like that, I know. So, would you like me to take something to him?'

Ethel shook her head. 'No, I need to talk to him first. I need to make sure he wants it.'

'OK,' I said, thoughtfully. 'Am I allowed to ask—?'

'What it is?' Ethel said, finishing my phrase. 'No, my dear, you may not. But ask him, or rather, *tell* him to call me. Tell him it's important. And tell him that if he hasn't been in touch by . . . I don't know . . . the end of the year . . .' She paused and swallowed with visible difficulty, and I wondered if she wasn't going to cry.

'Just tell him,' she finally continued. 'Tell that stubborn little man to phone his Aunty Ethel.'

'I will,' I told her. 'I'll make sure that he calls you, I promise. And can I call you again? Can I phone you and have another chat? Or maybe come back another time? It would be great to have an excuse to visit the seaside again. I love it down here.'

'An excuse to visit the seaside . . .' Ethel repeated flatly.

'That came out wrong,' I said, wincing. 'That's not what I meant. I'm sorry.'

'No,' Ethel said. 'OK.'

'So can I come and talk to you again, sometime?'

Ethel shrugged and smiled. 'You can certainly try,' she said.

I wasn't quite sure what she meant by that, but before I could ask, she was standing, holding the door open for me, saying how lovely it had been to see me.

I was shocked about my sudden forced exit. I'd even been hoping to have lunch there, but it seemed that wasn't to be.

As I walked back towards the seafront in the sunshine, I wondered if I'd offended her, but I couldn't really think how. I hadn't been *that* pushy, had I?

I started to think about all the questions I hadn't asked, and felt annoyed with myself that I perhaps hadn't been pushy *enough*.

But after a while I started to slot together the snippets that I had learned, and like a puzzle, my grandparents began to take form. I might not have learned as much as I would have liked, but at least I knew more than before.

Cassette #3

ML: *OK, the tape's on. This is Marie Lefebvre, interviewing Genevieve Schmitt again, cassette number three, second day.*

GS: Oh, before we start, I've been meaning to ask you, and I keep forgetting. How many of these have you done so far?

These interviews? You're my third. And then I have two more after you. So we're hoping for five, all in all.

And the overall theme is survivors of the war?

It's gay memories, really. No one has ever bothered to document gay people's experiences before, so our narrative of the war to date has been almost exclusively heterocentric. But the two I did before were far shorter – they lasted about ten minutes each. So yours is by far the most detailed. And the most interesting! I'm so grateful your waitress put me in touch with you. That was such a lucky coincidence. Anyway, I suppose we'd better get on with it. Do you remember where we left off on Saturday?

We were in the cabin in the woods, weren't we? Waiting to be taken over the border. Are you absolutely sure you don't want that cup of tea?

No, thanks. I really don't. I had a can of Coke just before I got here.

Well, as long as you don't mind me sipping mine.

Not at all. Sip away!

I will. So . . . the cabin, yes?

Yes. The little girl had said it was time to leave.

Yes. My God, we were terrified! We'd come to feel safe in that cabin, you see. Once she was gone, we waited until late into the night. Incredibly – to me it seemed incredible anyway – Pierre fell asleep. So while he snored on the bed, I sat on the chair and rocked the baby and waited. I was way too scared to fall asleep! I felt quite annoyed that Pierre was able to sleep, if I'm honest.

After the longest wait – it was about one in the morning, I think – I heard the sound of footsteps crunching through the undergrowth, and then the noise of the padlock and chain being removed. It was Moustache who opened the door, and that surprised me. I don't know why, but I'd been expecting someone different, someone younger.

'The little one thinks you're fit to go,' he said. 'Is she right?'

No 'Hello'. No 'How are you after a week locked in my shed?' Just the strict minimum.

Pierre, who had woken up by then and was rubbing his eyes, said that yes he was fine now, which was something of an exaggeration. He was better . . . but he certainly wasn't fine.

The carpenter told us to get a move on. It was a perfect night for it, he said, because it was cloudy, so no moonlight.

As before, I slung the baby over my back in the shawl, and he felt heavier this time. As we picked up our things and followed Moustache to the door, I wondered how much weight a baby could put on in a week.

He told us he wanted absolute silence. 'Not one word. Not a groan. Not a sneeze, not a yawn.'

And then, once we'd both nodded solemnly that we understood, he headed off into the woods.

We walked for a while, following the vague glow of his lamp, and though I didn't realise it until we got there, we were heading back to his farmhouse. When we got there, he led us around the far side of the building to where an old flatbed truck, not unlike my father's, was waiting.

He told Pierre to climb on to the back, and I joined him in the cabin with the baby.

He turned around and we went bumping off into the forest, and I mean, quite literally, *into the forest*. There was no road or even a dirt track. He simply drove off into the trees.

With no moonlight, everything was pitch-black, and the only light came from the yellow headlamps of the truck, which, in those days, were pretty useless. At one point we startled a magnificent stag which, for a split second, stood its ground, staring at the headlights, before bolting off into the darkness. That seemed, for some reason, to be a good omen, and I remember turning in the hope that Pierre had seen it too, but his back was against the window and he was facing the other way.

I had so many questions I wanted to ask that man – about where we were and where we were going, and what he thought we should do once we got there. I didn't even know where we'd be once we got over the demarcation line, and it seemed utterly ridiculous – it *was* utterly ridiculous – to be setting off without any plan whatsoever.

Sorry, but I'm just wondering, what exactly was the demarcation line? I'm not sure readers will know. I'm not sure I know, truth be told.

Oh, OK. It was the border where the prohibited zone ended and the rest of France began. France had been divided into two – occupied France in the north, and Zone Libre in the south. But Alsace and that whole strip down the right-hand side, which the Germans had decided to re-annex, to make part of Germany, had its own border with the rest of France, and we didn't know how far down we'd be crossing over and whether we'd find ourselves in the occupied area at the top or the free one down south.

So I started to ask him at least that, but he hushed me. 'I know it's hard for you ladies,' he said rudely. 'But this is one occasion when you really do need to shut up.' Above the rattle of his engine, I couldn't see what difference my little voice made, but I did what he said and kept quiet.

After about ten minutes of slow progress, he turned his head-lights off and continued to drive even more slowly through the trees. I have no idea how he managed to do that, because I honestly couldn't see a thing. I think he must have been driving from memory. It was pretty scary, anyway, and once or twice he had to brake suddenly because we were about to crash into a tree.

One of these emergency stops upset the baby enough to make him start crying, and Moustache whispered to me that I needed to make him stop before we reached the river.

I tried giving the baby a finger to suck, but he wasn't interested, so when Moustache complained again, I asked him what exactly he expected me to do.

'Just feed him,' he said. 'It always worked with ours.'

I realised that he'd assumed I'd been breastfeeding Ansgar from the start, so I explained that I couldn't; I told him that he wasn't my baby.

He insisted that I needed to do something, because there was no way he could get me across that river with a crying baby. He asked me if he needed to turn around and take us all straight back to Mulhouse.

In desperation, I unbuttoned my blouse so that I could put little Ansgar to my breast and not only did he begin to suckle, but he went quiet. It felt shockingly intimate, in both a wholesome way and a weird, uncomfortable, icky way, if that makes any sense, plus it hurt far more than I'd expected . . . It was a strictly zero-calorie meal for the poor thing too, because of course I didn't have any milk. But it worked, anyway. He didn't make a sound after that.

Eventually, we parked up in the middle of a circle of trees and Moustache turned off the engine.

In the hope that the baby would continue to suckle and remain silent, Pierre helped me strap him to my front instead of my back, and then we followed the carpenter off into the brush.

Walking without light was really hard going. I could barely make out Pierre's silhouette in front of me, but somehow we stumbled along and after fifteen minutes we reached a clearing. From the sound of running water I could tell that we'd reached a riverbank.

Moustache dragged some branches away, revealing a wooden boat – a sort of flatbed canoe – which he slid down to the river with surprising ease. Climbing in was a messy, wet business, but in the end, half soaked, we all made it in, and then he started to paddle us towards the other side. It looked like really hard work because the current was pretty strong, but as there was only one paddle we couldn't help. An owl hooted somewhere nearby, making me jump, and then halfway across, the moon – shining through a passing gap in the clouds – suddenly lit up our surroundings. Being able to see was a relief at first, but just as I was thinking how beautiful everything was in that strange light, and feeling a sort of gratitude that I'd had that glimpse, that snapshot to remember this moment by, I saw our guide glancing left and right and realised the moonlight was putting us in danger.

By the time we'd reached the far side, it had gone dark again. The owl hoot repeated, and this time our guide replied, prompting the owl, who was in fact a woman, to step out from behind the trees.

The carpenter handed her my suitcase and she gave him a small package in return. I don't know what it contained but it was the size of a big lump of cheese, or a sandwich or perhaps even a gun, and was wrapped in a piece of chequered cloth like a tea towel. Then he gestured that Pierre and I should follow her. As he turned back towards his canoe I grabbed his sleeve and tried to press the roll of banknotes my father had given me into his hand, but he refused to take it and gestured that we should follow the woman, Marie. I assumed the second payment must be for her.

We headed on into the woods, and on that side of the river it was even harder to walk. There were fallen branches all over the place, and the undergrowth was much thicker. At one point my foot snagged on some brambles and I fell forwards, flat on my face, squashing poor Ansgar in the process.

Just then, we heard someone shouting in German in the distance, which was utterly terrifying. I didn't dare move a muscle. I just lay there, holding my breath and trying not to put too much weight on the baby – amazingly, he didn't make a sound.

After a minute or so, Marie prodded me with one foot and signalled that we should move on as quietly as possible, and because Ansgar still wasn't making any noise or even moving, it was as much as I could do not to burst into tears. By that point I thought I'd knocked him unconscious, or even killed him, you see.

When we finally stepped out of the woods on to a proper tarmac road ten minutes later, I had to steel myself to be brave before I could check if he was still alive.

That was the first time I realised how my feelings for him were growing, I think. Up until then I'd thought of him more as a burden that had been thrust upon me, and sometimes even a sort of alibi. But when I thought I'd hurt him I felt devastated.

Anyway, I pushed a finger into his mouth and he started suckling and I shed a few more tears because I knew that all was well. I've always wondered – actually, I still wonder – was he silent because he was scared when I fell? Babies do that, apparently, if they get a shock. I've heard they can even stop breathing for a while.

Yes, I've heard that too.

Or maybe he somehow knew to be quiet. Perhaps he sensed that his life depended on it. Anyway, we started walking single file along the road and, even though there was no one around, it made me feel visible and really vulnerable. It seemed like a very reckless thing to be doing.

Marie dropped back and whispered to me that there was no choice but to walk along the road, but there were bushes up ahead. 'Just pray the police don't decide to go for a night drive,' she said.

I was horrified and asked if we were talking about German police and she laughed and said, 'No, French police. But they can be bastards too.'

Pierre, who'd been listening, caught up with us and asked if we were in the occupied zone, and Marie shook her head. 'No. I'll explain it to you when we get there,' she said. 'Now walk. We need to get a move on.'

We reached the bushes and ducked out of view and after another ten minutes along a muddy country footpath, we reached an isolated chalet with a barn, to which Marie led us. It had horses in a stable area at the rear and she pointed to a ladder and told us we could sleep on the mezzanine bit above them.

'You're safe here,' she said. She would have let us stay in the house, she explained, but we wouldn't be able to get out in time if someone unexpectedly came.

She said not to make a noise and not to go wandering off, and that she'd bring us some food in the morning, when we could talk about what came next.

I asked her if she had milk for the baby, and when she looked surprised and asked why *I* didn't have milk for the baby I had to explain, again, that the baby wasn't mine and I couldn't breastfeed.

She went off to the main house and returned with a proper baby bottle filled with warmed milk. I remember that she wished us sweet dreams, and though I thought that was most unlikely, I did sleep through until quite late the next morning, when she returned with some bread and a pot of ersatz coffee.

Ersatz coffee?

Yes, it was this sort of fake coffee substitute. It was made out of chicory, I think.

Like Ricoré?

Exactly, only not quite as good. But it's what we had to make do with. There was no real coffee during the war.

Pierre woke up when she arrived, and it was only when he stood up that we realised he'd been bleeding again. The crotch of his overalls was stained red.

Marie commented that *someone looked like they needed a doctor* and Pierre asked if such a thing was possible.

Marie said of course it was, and she'd be back with one as soon as she could. As she was leaving she told us that he was a friend, but we shouldn't tell him where we came from.

I asked her why we couldn't tell him, and she said, 'Because you should never put a friend in that kind of predicament.'

The doctor, when he arrived, was a pleasant young man with bottle-bottom glasses. He spoke to Pierre discreetly, and then asked us for some privacy so that he could examine him. Marie led me around the back of the farmhouse to her vegetable patch, where we laid the baby in the undergrowth while we picked runner beans for lunch.

While we were doing that, she explained what she'd meant about the French police being bastards, even in Zone Libre. She said Pétain's France wasn't as free as the name implied. There were German spies everywhere, she said, and plenty of people helping them out. I must have looked crestfallen, because she added, by way of reassurance, that from the look of Pierre, it was almost certainly less dangerous than where we'd come from. She asked me if we were Jewish, and when I said no, we weren't, she told me that was lucky for us, because they'd starting registering and rounding up Jews, even in the Free Zone.

I asked her if they were persecuting other groups as well, and she said that yes, they were. Members of the resistance, communists, trade unionists, gypsies . . . anyone the Germans didn't like. She told me with disgust that Zone Libre was getting more like Germany every day and eventually it would be indistinguishable.

She surprised me then by asking me if I knew why Pierre was bleeding. 'That was a lot of blood,' she said.

Because I couldn't think of anything else to say, I told her straight up the Germans had raped him, and that didn't seem to surprise her at all. 'They're animals,' she said. 'Animals!'

The doctor told Pierre not to eat any solids for a few days, and to move as little as possible. Marie seemed to have no problem with us staying on in her barn – she liked the company, she said. But the not-eating thing was torture for Pierre.

He'd been skinny before the war and seemed to have lost weight during the short time he was being held by the Germans too. Our rations in the carpenter's shed had been minimal, to say the least, so he hadn't exactly built up any reserves there either.

But the doctor said he needed to rest what Pierre started to jokingly refer to as his 'bum hole'. A few days without food, and as little movement as possible, and it would probably heal just fine, he said.

In the end we stayed there for five nights, I think, and all Pierre consumed was milk. Personally, I ate as well as I had in years. Marie had chickens and rabbits, she had beans and potatoes, and she even baked us some bread.

She told me where I could walk and where it was best to avoid, so I'd leave the baby with Pierre and head off for my laps around the fields in the sunshine. After our week in the dark, that felt heavenly.

On the fourth day, I think it was, Pierre ate two eggs and a potato as a sort of test, and we waited nervously to see if he was better. Sorry if this sounds vulgar, but we became very relaxed about discussing Pierre's 'bum hole'. We had to. It came up rather a lot.

The next morning, he announced that though going to the toilet had been painful, there had been, for the first time, no blood. This was the sign the doctor had told him to wait for and that meant it was time to move on.

Had you decided where you were heading? Were you going to the Atlantic coast, after all?

191

No, we decided to head for Cannes in the end. Pierre had a cousin there, and Marie seemed to think that Cannes was reasonably safe. The Italians had only gone as far as Menton by then, so she said there were a few towns they'd have to go through before they reached Cannes. We knew so little ourselves that we were happy to take her advice.

And, I'm just wondering, was she living on that farm by herself?

Yes. It was a big place, too. She had huge fields of wheat behind her house. She'd left her kids with her sister somewhere, I think. She said she wanted them as far away from the Germans as possible. I remember that because I asked her why she'd come back – why she hadn't stayed with her kids – and she'd said it was because of the animals. She had dogs and cats and horses and goats and she couldn't just leave them to die.

But no sign of a husband?

No. No, she never mentioned her husband. Not once.

Did you ask where he was?

No! Most of the time a missing husband meant a dead husband or a husband in a prison camp. So no, you learned pretty quickly not to ask women where their husbands were.

Of course. I understand. So what happened next?

Well, the next morning, as Pierre still seemed fine, Marie wrote us a list of detailed directions and sent us on our way.

She wouldn't accept any money from us, but after much debate with Pierre, I hid a hundred francs in her coffee jar. Pierre was quite concerned that we'd run out of money and starve to death, so a hundred francs was the compromise we agreed on. It wasn't much.

Weren't you as worried about money as Pierre?

No, I was. We had just over two thousand francs left. I think – maybe less. Oh, I'm not sure anymore, but it was the equivalent of about a month's salary, anyway, so it wasn't a huge amount. I knew it wasn't going to last for ever, but I suppose I've always believed in a sort of what-goes-around-comes-around thing. These days people would call it karma, you know? And after Marie having been so good to us, after she'd taken so many risks to look after us, I just couldn't bear the idea of appearing ungrateful.

She explained that she didn't want to be spotted with us, and then led us through the wheat fields to a point where we could see the main road in the distance, and it was there, surrounded by the crop waving in the wind, that we hugged and said our goodbyes. We wished each other good luck, and then, blinking back tears, continued on across the fields.

Once she was out of earshot, Pierre said, 'Well, she was reasonably pleasant,' and I burst out laughing.

Sorry, but why did that make you laugh? I think I missed the joke.

Oh, it was just a thing Pierre liked to do . . . He'd say something ridiculously understated – it was a sort of trademark of his. It was the first time he'd cracked a joke in ages too, perhaps even since the beginning of the war, so I was happy he seemed to be feeling better. I laughed, and I remember the baby gurgled too, and that made both of us laugh even more. It was as if the baby had understood the joke, you see.

It took us about half an hour to walk to the outskirts of the town – I think it was Mont-sur-Vaudrey, or it might be Mont-sous-Vaudrey. Anyway, it was this small town where the train station had been closed for years, so we hunted around for ages, trying to get our bearings, trying to find the correct bus stop for Poligny, and when the bus arrived, it was so stuffed full of soldiers that I didn't think we'd be able to get on board. But the soldiers all laughed and joked and squashed in a little more so that we could climb aboard – considering France had been defeated, they seemed in a surprisingly good mood but I suppose they were just happy to be going home to their families in one piece. One of them started making a fuss over Guillaume and got a photo—

Sorry, Guillaume?

193

Oh, yes, sorry . . . We changed his name again. The German name had seemed like a good idea in the German zone, but now we weren't so sure. So we changed his name to Guillaume at that point. That was Pierre's choice. I wanted to stick with Oscar – the French version of Ansgar – but Pierre said it made him think about Oscar Wilde, and Oscar Wilde made him think of persecution and prison. In the end we plumped for Guillaume.

Any particular reason?

No, I think it was just a name we both liked. We didn't have that long to think about it.

OK. Gosh, that poor baby must have been so confused!

Yes. I'm sure he was. Anyway, the soldier got a photo of his own baby out to show me. He asked me where we were heading and Pierre jumped into the conversation and replied that we were heading for Lyon. Marie had warned us repeatedly not to trust anyone, and never to say where we were from or where we were going and I think Pierre had guessed, quite rightly, that I was about to give the game away and tell everyone on that bus that we were going to Cannes.

At Poligny we bought a ticket to . . . was it? . . . Do you know, I can't remember? Bourg-en-Bresse, maybe . . . I do remember we had to buy a new ticket for each leg of the journey. I'm not sure if that was a war thing, or if that's just how things were in those days, but I definitely remember having to buy fresh tickets over and over again. We were terrified every time that the train would be full, or there would be some rule about essential travel and we'd have to justify ourselves or . . . I don't really know what we were frightened of, but buying tickets always felt nerve-wracking.

And the trains *were* full, too. Everyone was trying to get some-where back then . . . troops going home, people wanting to get away from the border, people attempting to join their families . . . people trying to return *to* the border now the fighting was over . . . The whole country seemed to be in movement and the trains were filled way over normal capacity. But other than that terrifying squeeze to get in – and sometimes you'd still be hanging out of the door as the train pulled away – it was fine. We managed it every time.

How long did it take to get to Cannes?

Two days.

Two days?!

Yes. Two full days of crowded trains and stations with a crying baby. We ate the picnic that Marie had given us, and I warmed Guillaume's bottle up by stuffing it down my blouse.

We slept on a pile of those wooden railway sleepers behind one of the sidings – that was in Lyon, I think. We went back to using newspapers as nappy liners, and the poor thing got a rash and started whingeing even more.

It was sunset by the time we got to Cannes the next day. I remember that because as we were trying to find Pierre's cousin's address I caught a glimpse of the sea down a side street and begged Pierre to allow a detour so I could get a proper look. I'd never seen the sea before, not once; I'd only ever seen it in black and white at the cinema, or on postcards. But we had our bags with us and the baby was crying, and Pierre was obsessed about finding the address before it got dark. The streets were eerily empty, too, so we were worried there might be a curfew in Cannes, in which case we feared we'd be stopped and questioned, or even arrested for being out after dark.

We asked an old man for directions and then found the place quite easily – it was only about half an hour from the station. But instead of the welcome we'd been hoping for, the cousin, Francine, seemed dismayed by our arrival. She grudgingly let us in and introduced me to her aged mother, Pierre's aunt Jeanne, who was living with her because of the war.

Francine kept muttering, 'They just can't do that . . . they just can't turn up like that . . .' over and over again, as if she was talking to some invisible person, and I wondered if she wasn't a bit mental.

Pierre's aunt made no bones about the fact that she didn't want us staying either, and at one point the two of them – mother and daughter – had a raging argument in the kitchen. Aunty Jeanne was shouting that we couldn't possibly stay, and what would we eat? And where would we sleep? And cousin Francine was agreeing, saying that yes, she knew that, but what the hell was she supposed to do? Throw us out?

For Pierre, the whole thing was mortifying and, when their shouting set the baby off, he decided he couldn't take any more. He marched into the kitchen and told them in no uncertain terms we were leaving and that all he needed was the address of a hotel. That offer turned out to be the one thing that could calm everyone down, and in the end they fed us and let us sleep in one of the beds, though they insisted it would be for one night only.

I whispered to Pierre that I really would rather have gone to a hotel, and he said that if I had my way we'd spend everything on a few days of luxury in Cannes and then starve to death the following week. And you know what? I reckon he was probably right about that. He was always better with money than I was.

The next morning, I woke up to the noise of squawking seagulls, and that sound made me feel so happy – it seemed to promise so much. We'd arrived, and we'd arrived not just anywhere, but in *Cannes*.

I was alone in a comfortable bed for the first time in ages and before I got up I remember allowing myself to luxuriate in the sensation for a while, listening to the sounds of the birds.

But then I suddenly realised that Guillaume was missing and I panicked about his whereabouts so I jumped up and ran into the sunlit kitchen, where I found Pierre busy bottle-feeding him.

'I've just been telling Aunt Jeanne about your condition,' he said, tapping a fingernail against the baby bottle as a clue.

'My condition?' I said, using that special flat tone of voice you use when you're trying to catch up on whatever lies someone's been telling in your absence. I took the baby from Pierre, and the warmth of him, the smell of him, the sensation of having him in my arms, it made me feel calm again.

Pierre said he hadn't been able to recall what 'my condition' was called, and his aunt asked me if it was mastitis, because if it was mastitis then that shouldn't stop me producing milk altogether.

'Oh, no,' I told her. 'No, the doctor didn't say it was anything like that. He didn't really seem to know why I've stopped at all.'

'Doctors!' she said. And then she declared that it was almost certainly just the worry. As proof of this, she said her own mother had stopped lactating for a whole month when her father had died.

I agreed it probably was just because of all the worry, and Pierre nodded at me to indicate that I'd done well.

'Anyway, I'm going to write to them,' his aunt said, apparently returning to a previous conversation. 'I'm going to give them a piece of my mind.'

Pierre explained his aunt was furious that she hadn't been invited to our wedding. Aunt Jeanne threw me a curveball then, by asking when it had taken place.

I glanced at Pierre, who shrugged almost unnoticeably, indicating I was free to choose. 'The third of September,' I said, for no reason other than it was the first date that came to mind.

'The day we declared war?' Jeanne said, sounding doubtful, and I realised that was the reason that date had come to mind in the first place.

'The third was a Sunday. Surely you didn't get married on a Sunday, did you?'

'Sorry, I meant the fourth,' I said. 'The day after.'

She frowned at me suspiciously and counted on her fingers, working something out. 'So when was this one born?' she asked, nodding towards the baby, and I panicked for a moment that I'd chosen a wedding date that implied we'd had premarital sex. That was still a huge deal in the forties.

'Mid-June,' Pierre said. 'The thirteenth. It didn't take us long, did it?' He winked at me reassuringly, and I'm pretty sure I blushed.

Even though I was still attempting to count the months without using my fingers, Pierre's aunt seemed satisfied, so I assumed that Pierre's timing was probably fine.

'Anyway, that's why we couldn't invite anyone,' Pierre said, taking the ball and running with it. 'Because we did it on the spur of the moment. Because of the war.'

Jeanne said that was all very well, but he could at least have written to give her the news.

'I know!' I told her. 'We should have. But what with the war and everything.'

'Plus that's why we wanted to visit,' Pierre added. 'So you could meet Genevieve and little Guillaume.'

Jeanne pulled a face at that. 'Oh, you're here for my sake, are you?' she said. 'I did wonder.'

We escaped the flat and Jeanne's questions as soon as we could, and made our way down towards the seafront.

During the walk, Pierre explained all the other lies he'd had to tell in response to his aunt's questions. He'd told her that he'd had to run away to avoid being enlisted in the German army, and because she'd noticed his missing fingernails, he'd claimed the Germans had tortured him because of his reluctance to enlist. Finally, he'd explained our missing wedding rings by saying that we'd pawned them in order to pay for the train tickets.

It was strange really, because that line about running away to avoid being enlisted in the Wehrmacht turned out to be prophetic in the end, because the Germans *did* end up conscripting the men from Alsace. It's just that it hadn't happened yet.

They made French soldiers fight for Germany?

Only the men from the annexed zone, but yes. Hitler considered Alsace part of Germany, so Alsace men were German men, as far as he was concerned. Towards the end, when they were losing, they freed men from the concentration camps as well so that they could fight.

I didn't know that.

Well, no one talks about it much. Being French and having fought for the Germans was considered pretty shameful, I expect, even if the men involved didn't have any choice in the matter. Plus, not a lot of them survived to tell the tale. They were mostly sent to the Russian Front as cannon fodder. I don't think many came back.

God, how awful. Surviving a concentration camp and then dying fighting for Germany.

Yes, I know. It's dreadful. Everything the Nazis did was dreadful.

And what was it like being in Cannes in 1940?

Oh, gosh, it was so beautiful. I'd never seen anywhere so pretty. And other than the refugees everywhere, things felt quite normal. The shops were mostly still open – the bakeries had bread and so on. Things changed later on, of course, especially once the Nazis took over the Free Zone. Once that happened people went hungry because they shipped all the food off to Germany to help with the war effort. But in July 1940 things felt relatively normal. We bought croissants and ate them sitting on the seafront.

And seeing the sea for the first time?

Oh, it took my breath away. I'd been feeling pretty emotional anyway because for the first time in days we felt relatively safe. We were walking down beautiful sunlit streets and then we turned a corner and there was this glimpse of blue in the distance. I couldn't take my eyes off it. And when we stepped out on to the Croisette – oh, I remember this so clearly – our view of the whole thing opened up into this crazy blue panorama. It was . . . I can't think how to describe it other than to say it was blue and fresh and so *big*. We crossed the road and I had to sit on a wall to catch my breath. There was the sound of it, of the waves . . . I hadn't expected the sea to have a sound. And the smell, too – that lovely fresh iodine smell. I'd never seen anything so wide or so far away or so blue. The biggest expanse of water I'd ever seen was a lake. So I really had never seen anything so beautiful.

I handed little Guillaume to Pierre and ran down on to the beach so that I could sift the sand through my fingers. When I saw a child paddling at the water's edge, I turned and asked Pierre if I could do that too, and he laughed and said that of course I could. I was worried there might be things in the sea that would bite me, and that made him laugh even more.

I pulled off my shoes and stockings and paddled, and you know the way the wet sand crumbles through your toes? That felt wonderful. I still love that sensation, even now, and it always makes me think of Cannes.

It was only when I turned back to beckon to Pierre that I looked at the seafront for the first time. I'd been so smitten by the sea that I hadn't noticed the palm trees and those grand hotels. It was all so incredible to realise we'd escaped from Nazi-run Alsace to the luxury seafront in Cannes that I burst into tears.

When I joined Pierre on the wall again, I told him I'd fallen in love with Cannes, and I wanted to stay there for ever, and he said that he hoped I realised we couldn't stay with his cousin. Of course I knew that already, but I asked if we could please, *please*, try to stay on in Cannes and Pierre said it might be possible, but only if we could find somewhere to stay, and only if one of us could find some work to pay the bills. It's funny really how we fell into those old-fashioned heterosexual roles of me wanting things and him trying to work out how to make them happen, because until we'd left Mulhouse I'd always been fiercely independent. But Pierre had a reassuringly practical nature, and I tended to bow to his suppos- edly greater wisdom. He could see which problems needed to be solved in order to do something far more quickly, and more clearly, than I ever could. Perhaps that came from all the problems he had to solve as a plumber.

Anyway, we spent the rest of the day trying to find a cheap hotel room or a bed and breakfast or even just a bed in a hostel, but every single place we tried was full. To stop people bothering them, most had 'no vacancy' notices on the door. We went into shops at random and asked if anyone knew of someone with a spare room, but no one ever did.

Why was that? Surely it's not just because it was summer?

No. Thousands of refugees had fled the occupation and had arrived in the south just before us. They'd taken every available room and there were people sleeping rough all over the place.

By the time we got back to his aunt's place, we were exhausted from walking, and disheartened because we hadn't found anywhere. Pierre was looking quite ill.

His aunt greeted us with a fresh barrage of questions about had we found somewhere to stay? And why not? And we didn't think we could stay with her, did we? Because anyone could see that the place was too small for the five of us. When she started ranting like that, the words flew out of her mouth like bullets from a machine gun. But before we'd even attempted to reply, I heard a thump and a crash come from behind me and turned to see that Pierre had collapsed, taking the coat-stand down with him. He'd just handed Guillaume to me, thank God.

In a way, Pierre fainted at the perfect moment, because that indisputable proof of illness was probably the only thing that could break all the ice around Aunty Jeanne's heart.

You mean she was nice to him after that?

<Laughs> No, I really wouldn't say she was nice. In fact I'm not sure that she even had the capacity to *be* nice. But she was nic*er*. She was less horrible, let's say.

She didn't stop harping on about how inconvenient it was that we were staying, but she did at least let us stay. And she arranged for Pierre to see a doctor as well.

The doctor diagnosed Pierre with anaemia, which had almost certainly been caused by all the blood he'd lost. He prescribed iron pills, and told Pierre to eat liver at every meal for a month, as if there wasn't a war on, as if you could just pop down to the butcher's and buy two kilos of liver.

But the iron pills played havoc with Pierre's tummy, and because of all the problems he was having down below they turned out to be an absolute no-no, so we went in search of liver.

Francine, it turned out, had a rather unpleasant friend called Jean-Noel – a slimy man with slicked-back hair and a flashy suit – who could, for a price, get anything. So we dipped into our reserve funds and in exchange he delivered the goods: an outrageously overpriced lump of liver delivered to our doorstep every couple of days.

But Pierre remained weak for months, really. If he exerted himself, he'd faint – actually, if he stood up too quickly, sometimes that was enough to make him faint. But he got quite good at it. He got to know when he was about to faint and sit down first. Sometimes people didn't even notice.

And how long did you stay in Cannes?

A bit more than a week, I think it was: seven, maybe eight nights. Francine got ruder and ruder about it as time went by. She was furious about having to share a bed with her mother, who she claimed snored, and they both carped constantly about all the nappies we were washing and drying all over the place. Kids today have no idea how much time their grandparents spent washing shitty nappies. It really is a non-stop job.

Pierre's aunt kept insisting that I attempt to breastfeed the baby, too, saying that my milk would never come back if I stopped trying, so

I had to do that in the evenings as well. The little bugger used to suck so hard trying to get at my non-existent milk it made my nipples bleed.

In the evenings the atmosphere was pretty tense. Everyone was on edge and there were a lot of arguments about how hard we were or weren't trying to find somewhere else to live. So it wasn't ideal, by any means.

But by day it was wonderful. We'd go out and . . . God, I was so happy . . . The sun was shining and we'd walk along the Croisette; we'd sit on the beach and dunk baby Guillaume's feet in the sea. He loved that. Pierre even went swimming a couple of times.

I sent a postcard to my parents every morning – every single morning without fail. God, I hate myself for those postcards. They must have been so painful for my mother.

I'm sure she was happy to know that you were OK, wasn't she? I'm sure they both were.

No. No, my father was gone by then, wasn't he? Obviously, I didn't know that yet, but he was – he was long gone. And my mother . . . my poor mother . . .

Um, you do realise that we haven't covered that yet?

Covered what?

What happened . . . to your parents . . . I know how difficult it must be to talk about it but—

Yes, it is pretty hard. Perhaps you can fill that bit in for me? I know I told you roughly what happened before we started all this.

Perhaps you could tell me again, if it isn't too painful?

I think . . . Look, I'm sorry, but I don't think I'm going to be able to go through all that without getting upset.

 . . .

You're looking . . . I don't know . . . doubtful.

I do know how hard this is, Genevieve, but I think it would be better if you could tell me what happened, for the record. I know you told me that they died, but even then . . . I don't know much more than that.

Perhaps we could do it another day, then?

We could certainly cover that another day if you wish. I have . . . I only have about ten minutes left on this tape anyway, so what would you like to talk about? The rest of your time in Cannes?

. . .

Genevieve?

Actually, let's just do it. Let's get it over with, and then we can call it a day, OK?

If you're sure that's how you'd like to tackle things . . .

My father never made it home. That's the thing.

He never made it home from . . . ?

From . . . God, this is hard! He, um, never made it back to Mulhouse. After driving us to La Vieille-Loye.

Take your time. There's no hurry.

Look, I don't know the details – no one does. In a way, that's what's so hard. Actually, I'm not sure that's true. I'm not sure knowing for sure would be any better. But I think . . . I suspect, let's say, putting two and two together, that he ran out of petrol just after Belfort. What we do know for sure is that he never made it back home.

How did you find that out?

A policeman came – a neighbour told me this after the war, by the way. So, a policeman came to their flat a few days after my father had left us in La Vielle-Loye. He didn't know that Dad was missing, he just came to ask him why he'd left his pickup at the side of the road, near Altkirch. That's between Belfort and Mulhouse, and it was close to one of the checkpoints, apparently. The policeman didn't know why the pickup was there and he didn't know where my father was either. All he knew was that it was there and it was out of petrol and that the Germans wanted it moved.

So your poor mother had just been sitting there, waiting for him to return?

Yes. That was all she could do. She sat and waited for him to come home, for months. And he didn't. He didn't come home. He never came home. It must have been awful. And she probably . . . God . . .

I'm so sorry.

She must have run out of money, waiting, that's the thing . . .

She must have found herself alone, living under German occupation with no man, with hardly any income – her cleaning didn't pay that much – with just these stupid, *stupid* postcards coming from her stupid daughter saying how wonderful everything was in Cannes.

That must have been so hard.

It was hard. In the end it was too hard.

Too hard?

Yes. She wasn't strong enough to cope.

I'm sorry, I . . . ?

She, um, killed herself in '41.

Sweet Jesus.

It . . . <Coughs> It was a neighbour who found her. She was on the floor with her head in the oven.

It was quite a common way to do it, in those days. They changed the gas in the sixties, I think, but in the old days, when it was coal gas, it was perhaps the most common method people used to do that sort of thing.

God, I'm so, so sorry. I can't even imagine how awful that must have been for you when you found out.

No. There are no words. There are still no words.

For a while, I liked to convince myself that Dad had escaped and that he was living it up in Switzerland or on the Riviera or something. But the truth is that he probably died in a ditch at the side of the road. My guess is he ran out of petrol and came across some angry Germans who worked out that he'd lost his leg in the First World War, and they shot him at the side of the road or . . . I'm sorry. It's just that . . . well . . . I suspect that he knew when he left us there . . . that he didn't have enough petrol to get home, I mean. So I . . . God . . .

It's normal. Getting upset is totally normal. How could you not get upset?

I know.

But . . . Look . . . This is an awful thing to ask, and I'm sorry to be the hard-nosed journalist, but was he never found? Weren't you ever able to bury him or . . . Do you have anywhere – a place, I mean – to visit, to grieve?

No, he just disappeared. My mother was buried in Mulhouse, and I've been there. I've seen her grave, and I tend to think of it as where they're both buried even though that's not the case. But no. Dad just vanished. Thousands of people in Alsace just vanished and no one knows where they went or what happened to them. It wasn't even that unusual. But I didn't know so I just kept on sending those damned postcards.

For the longest time, I hated myself for having sent them. And I blamed myself for my father's death. I blamed myself for both their deaths, really. Because of course, if he hadn't driven us . . . And then if she hadn't lost my father, then she wouldn't have done what she did either.

But you know, I think that's enough for today. I'd like to stop now, if that's all right? Can you turn that thing off, please?

It's about to run out any— [tape ends].

Ruth. Part Four.

A week after my meeting with Ethel it was Dan's birthday and as, for once, he had Saturday night free, I took him to a swanky restaurant called /fu:d/ near Clapham Common. It was all white starched tablecloths, silverware and branding.

There we ate a selection of delights such as asparagus tartlets and avocado and hazelnut verrine, and though the prices were as eye-wateringly excessive as the portions were tiny, Dan was thrilled to bits. His great passion in life was cooking, after all, so all those mini jabs at his tastebuds turned out to have been the perfect gift.

Over dinner, he asked me about my meeting with Ethel, so I told him the little I'd learned.

'So did you find out why they came to England?' Dan asked, once I'd finished.

'Not really,' I said. 'I actually forgot to ask.'

'Or why your grandparents divorced?'

I shook my head. 'Her answers were pretty minimalist. She said they wanted "different things".'

'Wow,' Dan said. 'Different things. There's a non-answer, if ever there was one.'

'Perhaps she wanted to move to the seaside and open a café,' I offered.

'Yeah, I suppose,' Dan said. 'I quite fancy the idea myself. And the thing she wants to give your dad?'

'She wouldn't tell me that either,' I said. 'She wasn't the easiest person to talk to, but I liked her all the same. There was something calm and kind about her, if that makes any sense. Something very solid, too. The kind of person that's lived through so much shit, she's not taking any now. Do you know what I mean?'

'I do,' Dan said, 'but she sounds cagey.'

'Yeah,' I said. 'She was a bit.'

With dinner, we downed a bottle of Prosecco, followed by another of white wine, so by the time I came to pay, I was sufficiently sloshed that I didn't think too deeply about paying £270 for two meals – two meals that had left us feeling hungry.

But like I say, Dan was happy – ecstatic, almost – and, as I slumped against him in the taxi home, he burbled on about various dishes and how he was going to try this or that combination himself.

'You know, it might be easier if we didn't have to decide,' he said, after a pause, and I twisted my head backwards to look up at him. His smile, seen upside down, looked a bit horror-filmy.

'I'm sorry?' I asked. I was thinking about food and menus and wondering if he'd come up with some new concept whereby customers wouldn't have to choose what to eat.

'All that my-place-or-your-place stuff,' he said. 'It might be nice if we didn't have to decide. If it was just obvious we were going back to ours.'

'Oh,' I said. '*That.*' The discussion at the taxi rank, in the rain, had taken at least a minute and we'd both got wet in the process. In the end, despite my overpowering guilt about leaving Buggles on his own, I'd caved in.

Dan looked out of the side window and I closed my eyes and basked in the sensation of his arms around me and the pretty patterns the passing streetlights were casting across my eyelids.

Back at his place, Dan poured two glasses of sambuca, which he flambéed with a coffee bean, restaurant-style.

We snuggled on the sofa together until one of his flatmates came home earlier than expected, whereupon we were forced to move to his bedroom.

Dan started to roll a joint, and I shuffled around until my head was resting on his chest.

'Don't you think?' he asked.

'Think what?' I said. I was mainly trying to concentrate on stopping the room from spinning.

'Don't you think it's time?'

'That we lived together?'

'Yeah,' Dan said, and I thought about how nice it was to feel the vibrations of his words transmitted directly from his chest cavity to my head.

'Maybe.'

'Maybe?' Dan laughed.

'You were the one who got cold feet, last time,' I pointed out. 'So, I guess the subject makes me a bit nervous. Maybe we can talk about it another—'

'Yeah, but I got over all that,' Dan said, interrupting me. 'I had a really great conversation with Clive about it a few weeks back.' Clive was one of Dan's flatmates, and was heavily into his self-help books. 'He really, like, changed my perspective on it all.'

At that moment, I was torn between three different desires: sex, sleep and finding out what life-changing revelation flatmate Clive had imparted. Unfortunately for me, I chose to inquire about the last one.

'Oh, it's nothing that profound,' Dan said, licking the joint and lighting up. 'It's just . . . you know, *commitment*. The whole concept of commitment. Because that's all it is, isn't it?'

He handed me the joint and, though I was worried it would make me feel even sicker, I accepted and took a minimalist puff. 'I'm not following,' I said, handing it straight back. 'What's all what is?'

'Commitment,' Dan said. 'It, you know, makes men feel trapped. It makes them feel scared.'

'Oh, OK,' I said. 'Well, if it's any help, it makes plenty of women pretty nervous too.'

'But it's just a concept, that's the point. It's not real.'

I reached over for my glass, only to realise that I'd already finished my sambuca, so I put it back down and shifted positions so that I could look at Dan while I was speaking to him. Something about the conversation was turning serious.

'I'm not following,' I said. 'How is commitment not real?'

'Well, you can still always leave,' Dan said. 'That's the point. Even *married* people – people who've vowed to stay together for ever – even they divorce. People with kids walk out, too. So it's just the reality of the matter. Commitment only ever lasts as long as both parties want it to. So it's not such a cast-iron trap after all.'

I blinked at him slowly and tried to think about what he was saying. And then I had one of those flashes where you realise that if you let your mind go there, it's going to upset you. It was Dan's birthday, and we were drunk, and we'd had a lovely, crazily expensive meal. And I'd been enjoying the moment, there on the bed, and thinking about sex. I really didn't want to spoil it all, and was probably too drunk to discuss anything logically anyway.

'Oh, just shush thee and come here, will you?' I said. 'Let's get that birthday bang going before we both fall asleep.' And thankfully Dan laughed, put the joint down and did exactly that.

Afterwards, as we were falling asleep, he said, 'You should probably stop taking the pill, too.'

The thought *Because even with a kid you can still walk out?* popped into my mind, but once again, I quite consciously pushed it to the edges where I could pretend it didn't exist.

'Shh,' I said. 'Go to sleep.'

'You're weird,' Dan said, pulling me tighter.

'You're weirder,' I said, and I tried to make it sound like a joke.

'Those verrines were just amazing,' Dan said softly. 'I think I'm definitely going to have to get into verrines.' And though I think he carried on speaking, that was the last thing I heard.

By the time I got up the next morning, Dan was in the kitchen, experimenting. He was busy pureeing asparagus with various other ingredients and dolloping it into tumblers.

'I thought the green bit was supposed to be avocado,' I commented sleepily as I poured myself some coffee.

'It was avocado and hazelnut last night,' Dan said, 'but I thought I'd try asparagus, shallot and lime with an almond-butter crumble.'

'Yum,' I said. 'Sounds fab.'

As I sat at the kitchen table, he handed me the first completed verrine and asked me to tell him what I thought.

'Um, would you be really offended if I just had toast?' I asked. 'You know . . . hangover and everything.'

'Sure,' Dan said, snatching the verrine back and nodding at the toaster. 'Knock yourself out.'

By eleven we'd gone our separate ways, Dan out to an industrial kitchen in Wapping he used for his bigger functions, and me home to feed Buggles before heading out to my parents'.

There I joined Mum, Harry and Suzie in the kitchen, where they were making two of the biggest lasagnes I'd ever seen. One was going to be loaded with the cheap, fatty mince Mum favoured, but the second one, to my relief, would be veggie.

I was quickly put on onion-chopping duties, and as I chopped, Suzie told us about her brother's new place and we all did our best to sound enthusiastic about him having chosen to live in Ashford.

Once she'd finished, I explained about Dan's change of heart, which everyone agreed was good news, and then his reasons for having done so.

Mum declared that she would have given him a good punch on the nose, which was a lie, as Mum's never punched anyone in her life, and Suzie agreed with Mum, saying that birthday or not, describing commitment as a mere concept was definitely a 'punchable offence'.

Their remarks made me feel a bit upset about the whole thing so, once the lasagnes had been assembled and loaded into the oven, I stayed behind to wash up. This was partly so I could calm myself down a bit, but mainly to avoid having to continue the same conversation with ten extra people in the lounge.

After less than a minute, Harry returned to the kitchen, where he lingered in the doorway, drinking his beer straight from the bottle. We had virtually never found ourselves alone together, and I wondered why that was.

'I just wanted to say,' Harry said, when I finally paused scrubbing a pan to look at him, 'that I think your fella is right.' He glanced nervously back at the hallway then, to check we were alone.

'Oh,' I said. 'OK.'

'But don't tell Suzie. I don't want to get a punch for my wickedness.'

I dried my hands on a tea towel and then turned to face him, leaning back against the worktop. 'So your commitment to Suzie and your kids,' I said. 'Are we suggesting that's just a concept?'

Harry glanced over his shoulder again and then looked back at me and shrugged. 'I never really thought about it before, but yeah, I think it is.'

'Oh,' I said.

'Not in a flippant way,' he said. 'I actually think your man's being quite clever. I mean, look . . . we all like to think we're these brilliant, infallible moral beings making everlasting pledges left, right and centre. But we're not. We're just . . . you know . . . human.'

'If you're . . . um . . . about to tell me something I shouldn't know, then don't,' I said.

'Oh, I'm not,' Harry said, laughing. 'Not at all. I'm just . . . look . . . I'd love to be able to say I'll stay with Suzie for ever, no matter what—'

'Which *is* what you promised the day you got married.'

'Yes, I know that. Don't you think I know that? And I have. I'm still here, aren't I? But that's still just what people say when they get married. The truth, your Dan's truth, is that there are a whole load of get-out clauses no one mentions.'

'Get-out clauses,' I repeated dubiously.

'Yes, reasons why I would leave her and it would be totally reasonable to do so.'

'Such as?'

'Jaysus, I don't know,' Harry said. 'Suppose I found out she was a criminal or a murderer or something. Suppose she told me she's been in love with someone else for years or she turned full-blown alcoholic like Mavaughn's brother did and screamed the house down every night. She could start doing heroin or selling it, or I could find out she's a terrorist or—'

'OK,' I interrupted. 'I get your point, but none of those are very likely.'

'Maybe,' he said. 'Or I could have my own reasons. *I* could go bat-shit crazy. Or meet someone and fall in love in some mad, obsessional way that left me feeling like I was dying if I couldn't be with her.'

'OK,' I said again. 'And your point is?'

213

'Plus, those things aren't *that* unlikely. They happen to people every day. But your Dan's point – I think – is that if you see commitment as this cast-iron rule . . . if you see it like a legal text and you don't know about the get-out clauses – and that is how men tend to see marriage – then the concept can be terrifying. It can start to sound like a prison.'

'Right,' I said. 'Got you.'

'But like you said, these things aren't that likely. Plus most of them are within the control of whoever the contract is with.'

'In your case Suzie.'

'And in yours Dan. So I'd say . . . and I reckon that this is his point . . . that the probability that terror of commitment will destroy the relationship – that fear of having to stay with someone *whatever happens* – is far greater than the probability of Suzie turning into a serial killer or something. And the probability Dan's *fear* will destroy your relationship is far greater than the probability that you'd ever give him an actual reason to leave.'

I was suffering from a bit of brain fog still, so I really wasn't sure I got his point. But Suzie came looking for him then, effectively saving me from our discussion.

After lunch, I managed to corner Dad. I admitted to having copied Ethel's phone number from the pad and meeting her in Brighton, but he didn't seem to mind that much, or even be that interested in what had been said. At least I'd passed on the message about her having something she wanted to give him.

'I'll call her,' Dad said, sounding curt. 'I just haven't got around to it, but I'll call her.'

'That's not really true though, is it?' I said.

'What isn't?' Dad said. 'Which bit?'

'That you haven't got around to it. Because the truth is that you've been avoiding her like the plague. And you had no intention of phoning her back at all.'

'Not avoiding her, *as such*,' Dad said. 'It's just . . .'

'It's just what, Dad?'

'I've never been that keen, if truth be told.'

'You've never been that keen on Ethel?'

Dad nodded vaguely. 'That is what I said.'

'Because?'

Unexpectedly, he raised his voice. 'Jesus, do you like everyone?' he asked. 'Do you get on with abso-bloody-lutely everyone?'

'No,' I said, taken aback. Dad never really raises his voice like that and so it actually made me feel a bit scared.

'I've told you. I'll call her,' he said. 'Now, *basta*!' And then he stomped off out into the backyard to join the smokers.

Harry, who'd caught the last few seconds of the conversation, asked what it was about, but I just forced a smile and shrugged.

That evening, I joined Gina for drinks in a new bar that had opened in Notting Hill. She had her eye on the ridiculously pretty barman – her reason for the choice of venue.

I ordered my traditional hangover pint of orange and lemonade and then explained the whole commitment debate to her. Once I'd finished, Gina raised both eyebrows and shook her head.

'Fuck me,' she said.

'Yeah, I know, right? It's twisted.'

'No,' she said. 'No, it's . . . I don't know. But no, not twisted at all. It's really quite deep.'

'Deep?' I said. 'Explain.'

'Well, *I've* left relationships because I felt cornered. I think you have too. I think everyone has. Actually, that's pretty much why I left Johnny when he asked me to marry him that time. D'you remember? And Evan. *And* Pete.'

'Pete didn't ask you to marry him, did he?'

'No,' she said, sipping at her gin and tonic. 'Don't be daft. But I felt like I was being sucked in.'

'So are you saying that might have ended differently if you'd only realised how commitment is *just a concept*?' I asked, using a silly, pompous voice.

But Gina wasn't laughing. 'Yeah,' she said, earnestly. 'Yeah, maybe.'

'I still don't get it,' I told her. 'I really don't.'

'OK, so it's like, I left because . . . I suppose I left because I thought I couldn't leave, yeah? Or because I was scared I wouldn't be able to leave at some point in the future. I mean, that's what feeling trapped is about, right? But it wasn't true, was it? And I kind of proved that by leaving. D'you see the point? As soon as you leave a relationship because you're feeling trapped, well, you didn't need to leave after all. Because the fact that you've left proves you weren't.'

'Oh!' I mouthed silently, belatedly understanding what everyone had been trying to explain to me. Of course it was Gina, lovely Gina, who finally put it in words I could understand.

◆ ◆ ◆

I didn't see much of Dan during the final weeks of November both because he was working hard and because I had a stinky cold that Dan couldn't afford to catch. But on the last Wednesday of the month, we finally managed to spend an evening at mine.

Dan had brought a selection of his newly developed verrines, and with the addition of a single crispy baguette, these made up our supper. And Dan had totally pulled it off: they were every bit as good as the exorbitant ones we'd sampled at /fu:d/. In fact, the tomato and tapenade version has to be one of the most delicious things I've ever tasted.

Later, as we were brushing our teeth side by side, bumping heads as we tried to access the tap, he pointed at my blister pack of Ovranette and spluttered, through toothpaste, 'Still taking those, then?'

'I am,' I spluttered back.

Once in bed, instead of the sex I'd been looking forward to, Dan continued the discussion. 'Did I upset you the other time,' he asked, 'when we talked about commitment?'

I forced a laugh. 'I'd be lying if I said no,' I said. 'But in the end I worked out what you meant, I think.'

'But you're still taking the pill.'

I shrugged. 'We hardly ever see each other, Dan. And you did remind me of all the get-out-clauses that mean you might leave at any moment.'

Dan frowned at me and said, 'Get-out clauses?'

'Yes, you . . . Oh! Sorry, that was Harry. We had a very similar discussion about marriage and he listed all these unwritten get-out clauses that mean wedding vows don't count. But he was totally on your side on the whole commitment-is-a-concept thing.'

'And what were these clauses?'

'I'm not sure it would be strategic on my part to give you the full list.' I laughed. 'But they were things like your partner becoming a serial killer, or a junkie . . . or a smack dealer. Stuff like that.'

'Right,' Dan said. 'Are you intending to do any of those?'

'Not in the *immediate* future,' I said. 'Though apparently there's quite a lot of money to be made.'

'In smack dealing?'

'No, serial killing. On a contract basis, of course.'

'Right,' Dan said. 'Of course.'

'But the truth is, sweetie, that we just don't see much of each other. That's not a criticism, honestly. Not at all. It's just a statement of fact. So I'm still not sure where a kid fits in.'

'Well, things would have to change,' Dan said.

'Everything would have to change. But I'm not sure you're ready for that.'

'I'm ready if you are,' Dan said.

I shrugged.

'Well, are you?' Dan asked.

'I'm not sure.'

'Oh, *you're* not sure?'

'I guess I'm ready if you are,' I said.

'Cool, that's sorted,' Dan said. 'So let's do it.'

Because the very next thing he did was to roll me on to my back, I wasn't one hundred per cent sure if he'd meant, 'let's move in together and have a child and do the whole shebang,' or merely, 'let's *do it.*'

The next morning, when I got up, the blister pack was missing. Rather sleepily, I hunted for it, surveyed by Buggles from the open bathroom door.

Thinking that maybe I'd inadvertently carried it elsewhere, I searched the bedroom and the lounge before finally returning to check the bathroom dustbin, where I found it, lying on top.

I stood with my foot on the bin pedal for some time, perhaps two or three full minutes, just staring at that blister pack and thinking about all the different aspects of the situation. How did I feel about Dan taking it upon himself to bin my contraceptives? Was that cute, or pushy, or full-blown narcissism on his part? Did I feel we'd discussed the subject enough for Dan to feel justified in doing such a thing? After all, it was all very well Dan being ready, but was I?

And then a sort of combined *what-the-hell/fuck-it* feeling rose up in me so I allowed the lid of the bin to slam shut. 'Sometimes you just have to go for it,' I told Buggles as he preceded me through to the kitchen, where he'd correctly assumed he was about to be fed.

Dan had rather sweetly laid out breakfast for me and tucked into my empty coffee cup was a slip of paper ripped into the shape of a love heart.

Yeah, I thought. *You'll do, Danny boy.*

We set things in motion quite quickly, in fact no later than the following weekend.

On Saturday morning, I phoned two estate agents and booked them to work up estimations on my place. Meanwhile Dan went to Nationwide to ask how much he could borrow. The answer to that question was, sadly, not much. Banks do not favour the self-employed in these matters. In the afternoon we phoned around various estate agents to request they inform us of any suitable properties on their books.

As our joint criteria included that it needed to be in a lovely area, near park or woodland; that it had to have two (or preferably three) bedrooms, a massive kitchen and a lounge that got direct sunshine, plus the obvious one that we had to be able to afford it, I wasn't holding my breath. This was London, after all. Property prices had been going crazy ever since Thatcher had first got in and there were no signs that they were going to crash under Blair. The only upside was that the value of my flat had also skyrocketed.

Christmas '97 we spent at my place, and that was a first for both of us.

In a way, I saw it as a test. Could Christmas with Dan possibly rival Christmas at my parents' place? The answer, it turned out, was yes. Though I don't think two experiences of Christmas could really be more different, it definitely wasn't a downgrade.

Of course, I missed seeing the family and all the fun and games. But Dan cooked the most incredible veggie dinner and did so without any of the burnt bits or fuss that characterised Christmas dinner at Mum's.

After we'd eaten, he gave me a pretty coral bead bracelet, and he had even wrapped a cat toy for Buggles. Though Buggles preferred the wrapping paper to the toy, that was a sure-fire way to my heart.

We got drunk on champagne that Dan had pilfered from one of his jobs and then fell asleep in a big, warm huddle on the sofa.

Meanwhile, in the corner of the room, my unreliable TV worked just long enough to beam *It's a Wonderful Life* at our three snoozing bodies. And though you'd probably say that I'd drunk too much, and though you'd almost certainly be right, I swear that final detail, that lovely film, just filled my living room with Christmas.

◆ ◆ ◆

The package arrived on the 11th of January 1998.

I'd been working, reading a manuscript set in an apocalyptic landscape where everything and almost everyone had been lost to various catastrophes provoked by the millennial bug.

Though the story was well written and was reasonably exciting, it needed major revision before publishing, and I wasn't entirely sure we'd be able to get that done in time to monetise the whole thing by December '99. Because whether the novel turned out to be fiction – if 2000 went off without a hitch – or prophetic – in which case we'd all be dead – I was struggling to see how it could sell beyond that point.

So I was sucking my pencil, wondering if I could find a way to save author Gail Windrush from year 2000 oblivion when the UPS guy phoned.

He made a right old fuss about having to deliver to a non-commercial address – something he was not paid to do, he insisted – but eventually agreed to meet me on the pavement outside. Quite what was so difficult about delivering it to me rather than the shop I was standing in front of, I really do not know.

Back in the flat I emptied the contents on to the worktop.

Six tiny Dictaphone cassettes fell out, along with a handwritten card that read: *Ethel wanted you to have these. Best wishes. Tony.*

I pushed one of the tapes around the worktop with the tip of my finger, driving it like a toy car as I tried to think about the whys and wherefores of this strange delivery.

The mini-cassettes had been labelled simply GS#1 to GS#6 and as I didn't have (nor had ever had) a Dictaphone machine, they were destined to remain a mystery for the time being.

I re-read the note and, with a shrug, began to dial Tony's phone number from the UPS label.

But then something about the covering note struck me. That past tense – Ethel *wanted* you to have these.

I made myself a cup of coffee and steeled myself before dialling the number. A man answered immediately, saying rather camply, 'Sex addicts anonymous, how can I help you today?'

'Oh,' I stammered. 'Um . . . I think I may have—'

'I'm just pulling your leg. It's a private joke. This is Tony. How can I help you?'

'Oh, right. Sorry. This is Ruth Solomas.'

'Ah! You got the tapes, then?'

'Yes. I did. But can I ask why was it you who sent them? Why didn't Ethel do it? She's not ill, is she?'

'Oh, you didn't hear?' he said. 'She left us. I assumed that somehow you would have heard.'

'I'm sorry?'

'She died, honey. I actually thought she'd told you herself.'

'God,' I said. 'I didn't know. But I don't understand. How could she have told me?'

'I'm not sure I . . .'

221

'Unless she knew she was dying when I met her.'

'Oh, hon,' he said. 'She . . .'

I heard a gasp, then, and the line went quiet for a moment before Tony's partner picked it up.

'Hello, this is Glen. You probably don't remember me, but we met at Genny's funeral.'

'Yes, I do. Of course I do. Hello, Glen.'

'I'm sorry about that. Tone still gets very upset. He loved her to bits. We both did. It's just that my heart is made of steel. That's what he says, anyway.'

'I'm in shock here. What happened?'

'She had a bit of a send-off and checked out,' Glen said, his voice gravelly with emotion.

'She checked out,' I repeated.

'Yeah . . . Massive heroin overdose, hon. No one knows where she got it, but apparently it's a hell of a way to go.'

'You're saying this wasn't an accident?'

'Oh, no. It wasn't an accident at all. Like I say, she had a good-bye party. Everybody knew. Radical right up to the end, our Ethel.'

'Just to be clear, you're telling me she killed herself?'

'Yes. If your father had taken her calls, he would have known, I suppose.'

'But why? Why would she do that?' I asked. 'She seemed so full of . . . *life*.'

'Oh, she was in pain, hon. A lot of pain. That wears you down. She kept breaking bones and stuff. She was sick of it.'

'But all the same.'

'And she just felt she'd lived through enough, I suppose. She felt she was *done*, I think. But, mainly, she just couldn't see the point going on without the others. She wasn't bitter or sad or anything. But she felt that she'd had enough.'

'When you say "the others", you mean without Genny and Chris?' I remembered her telling me something to the effect that life had no meaning without them back in November, but I would never have imagined that foreshadowing this.

'Exactly. They were everything to her. I mean, it's not that flattering for the rest of us, but sometimes you're just a bit player, right?'

I could hear the bitterness in Glen's voice, and I thought about how hard it must be to realise that your friendship wasn't enough for someone to want to stick around.

I asked him to confirm that my father wasn't aware and he told me he didn't know. 'There might be official channels or something,' he said. 'But your guess is as good as mine.'

Only as I was saying goodbye did I remember the cassettes, so I asked him what was on them, but Glen didn't know that either.

'When I saw her in November, she had something she wanted to give Dad,' I told him. 'Was this what she meant? I mean, were these the things she wanted him to have?'

'I don't know,' Glen said. 'But I assume that was the plan.'

'So I should probably just give these to Dad?'

'Hang on,' Glen said. 'This isn't really my . . .'

There was a rustle and a crunch as he laid down the handset and went off to consult Tony.

'Tone says just do whatever you want with them,' Glen said when he returned. 'He says there's no one left to care. Though his language was a little more fruity.'

On that note, we said our goodbyes and then I laid down my phone and lined it up perfectly with the six little cassettes before allowing myself a few tears.

I hadn't known Ethel well, but I'd known her as long as I'd known my own parents, plus I'd seen her recently and had liked her.

Once I'd dried my eyes, I tried phoning Dan to ask him if he had, or could borrow, a Dictaphone. When he didn't call me back immediately I decided I was too intrigued to wait, so I nipped out to Dixons and handed over £9.99 instead.

Back home, I inserted a cassette, only to discover it was all in French. My little trip out had been for nothing.

I texted a few friends to see if any of them spoke French, but they either didn't reply or replied in the negative. I thought briefly about just taking them to Dad, who I suspected still spoke enough French to understand, but I feared he'd take them from me and I'd never hear of them again.

So though I felt bad not telling him about Ethel's death immediately, I waited. I felt I needed to know what was on them before having that conversation.

On the Friday I took them in to Impressionable so that Freida could have a listen.

After about thirty seconds, she pressed stop. 'They're some sort of interview,' she said in her sing-song Swedish accent. 'Something about the war, maybe?'

'Oh,' I said. 'Right.'

She rewound the tape to the beginning and listened to the start. 'Yes, an interview,' she said. 'With someone called Genevieve Schmitt. Ring any bells?'

'Genevieve, yes,' I said. 'Schmitt not so much.'

'Well, they're one and the same person,' she said, thinking that I had misunderstood. 'Genevieve Schmitt. First name last name.' She even made chopping gestures with both hands, placing the words in the visual space between us, just in case I still wasn't getting it.

'Yes. Gimme a minute,' I said, stepping out into the hallway and dialling my parents' number.

'Mum!' I said, when she answered. 'Quick question. Do you know Grandma Genny's maiden name?'

'Um, Le-something,' she said. 'Why?'

I lied and told her I was filling in a visa form and it required my grandparents' maiden names.

'Oh, gosh,' she said. 'That's a tricky one. I wouldn't even know those for myself.'

I heard her open the lounge window and shout out to Dad. 'It's Lecomte,' she said, when she returned. 'See? I said it was Le-something.'

'Not Schmitt, then,' I said.

'Schmitt?' Mum laughed. 'No, why would it be Schmitt? She was French, dear, not German. Where did you get that from?'

'I don't know,' I said. 'I just thought I'd heard that name somewhere.'

Once the call was over, I ducked back into Freida's office to ask if she could recommend a translator. She said she was happy to do it herself, though not, obviously, during work hours.

So we agreed a cash price of 4p per word, and she promised she'd get on it as soon as she had a free evening.

As I couldn't reasonably hold off telling Dad the bad news any longer, I schlepped out to Walthamstow straight after work.

If I'm honest, Dad had been so uncommunicative about them all that I half expected him to say he knew about Ethel and had decided not to tell me. As the Tube train trundled along, I found myself hoping that would be the case. After all, who wants to be the bearer of that kind of news?

They were watching a hysterical documentary about all the money Tony Blair was intending to spend on the Millennium Dome when I arrived, and when I turned it off so that I could talk to them, Dad seemed annoyed.

'I've got some sad news,' I said. 'And maybe you already know it and maybe you don't.'

'I don't,' Dad said.

'How do you know until she tells you what it is, you old fool?' Mum said, at which Dad just rolled his eyes.

'Aunt Ethel died,' I announced, studying his reaction closely just in case he might try to dissimulate some kind of lie.

But Dad didn't know – that much was clear. He stared at me, frowned, and then blinked repeatedly. 'What?' he finally said.

'She died, Dad,' I said. 'A friend of hers from Brighton phoned me.'

'Nah,' Dad said, paling before my eyes. 'That can't be right.'

'I'm sorry, but she actually killed herself, Dad.'

My mother's mouth dropped open in a way that would have been comical under other circumstances.

'Suicide?' Dad said, frowning deeply.

I nodded. 'She was in a lot of pain, apparently. Osteoporosis and something else . . . Arthritis, I think it was. She kept breaking bones. And she couldn't see the point in carrying on. Especially once Grandma Genny was gone. They were in business together, so . . .'

'Jesus, Mary and Joseph,' Mum said, crossing her heart quickly.

'But how can I not know this?' Dad asked. 'And how come you do? When's the funeral? When did she die?'

'You never even liked the poor—' Mum said, but her phrase was interrupted by a killer glare from Dad.

'The funeral was a few weeks ago, I think. And I'm not sure of the exact date when it happened. But it was planned, apparently. She told pretty much everyone. She even had a sort of leaving "do".'

'That's why she kept calling then,' Mum said. 'Jaysus. You told me that you'd called her back. You *said* it was nothing.'

Dad shot her another glare. 'That's hardly important now, woman, is it?' he said.

'Oh, woman, is it?' Mum said. 'Someone's feeling defensive.'

'You've gone a bit green, Dad,' I told him. 'Are you OK?'

'No,' Dad said, leaping from his armchair. 'No, I need to get some air.'

'Shall I come . . . ? Dad!' I said. But the front door had already slammed behind him.

'Leave him,' Mum said. 'There's no good going after him when he's like that.'

'You think?' I asked, twisting my head to watch through the lounge window as my father strode away.

'Just sit yourself down and tell me what you know,' Mum said. 'Old Ethel, gone to meet her maker, eh? I can hardly believe it myself.'

◆　◆　◆

January slipped into February in a blur of dreary property visits. Our search was not going well.

Though neither Dan nor I had expected to stumble upon our dream property on day one, we hadn't been prepared for quite such a depressing experience.

I won't bore you with all the details, but highlights were a downstairs flat that shook so much when the trains passed it felt like an earthquake was happening, and a flat above a kebab shop that reeked of dodgy meat. Best of all was a place off Edgware Road that could only be accessed by walking through a greengrocer's. And I do mean *through* a greengrocer's. 'It makes it very safe for madam if she's home all day alone,' the estate agent told us as we were leaving. 'There's an eighteen-hour-a-day presence, after all.'

'It would certainly make the evening shop easier,' Dan said, trailing his fingers across a butternut squash as I followed him out the door.

The flat-hunting business was miserable and exhausting, but above all time-consuming. When combined with the fact that I had a full-time job, I hardly thought about the cassettes at all. In fact, the only times they really crossed my mind were when I saw Dad and felt guilty about not having told him, or when I noticed how ashamed poor Freida looked about the fact that she still hadn't started the translation.

Then, one morning, late February, my computer got stuck. I was trying to download my morning emails over a brand-new 'high-speed' 56k modem, but every time it finished its interminable series of bings and bongs and whistles, the computer just sat there saying, 'Downloading'.

I phoned Dan, who said I might have a big email blocking things. 'Property propositions maybe?' he suggested. But I had another idea.

I phoned Freida immediately, and she confirmed that my theory was correct: she'd emailed me the transcripts of the first two cassettes.

'It took me one whole hour to send it,' she said, 'so you're just going to have to be patient.'

I set the whole thing going again and went off to take a shower and do my hair, and by the time I got back to the lounge they were there, sitting in my inbox.

If I'm honest, I started to read with what I suppose you'd call casual interest. A part of me was reading what was on the page, while the other half, the professional half, was thinking about the style, spotting typos and analysing the quality of the translation.

However, as I started to get into the story – the beginning of the war, their fear of invasion, the annexation of Alsace – I began to worry about the fates of Pierre and Genevieve and Johann.

As I read, a strange feeling rose up in the pit of my stomach, and I even paused at one point to wonder if I'd eaten something dubious. But it wasn't until Ethel left Mulhouse for London that the feeling became tangible, that the thought crystallised and became a conscious one. Because if Ethel was Aunty Ethel, how could Genevieve be anyone other than Grandma Genny? Then again, the name Schmitt meant nothing to me, nor, to anyone's knowledge, had Genny been gay. So none of it made any sense.

I'd intended to visit my parents for Sunday lunch that day, but I phoned to cancel because not only was I unable to tear myself from the transcript but, until I understood what we were dealing with here, I didn't feel I could face them.

So I made myself a sandwich and moved my clunky ThinkPad to the couch so I could continue to read in comfort. Buggles wasn't thrilled that the computer had stolen his favourite spot on my knees, but he eventually – after much headbutting and walking on keys – settled for the arm of the sofa. His only condition was that I had to caress him constantly.

When I read about Genevieve's escape to La Vielle-Loye I thought instantly of Grandpa Chris's wolf story. A search on Altavista revealed it was a tiny village in France that seemed to be of no real note for anything. So how could that specific place name cropping up in one of our most-told family tales be just a coincidence?

But then Menashe became Ansgar – not Guillaume, as I'd been beginning to suspect – and Genevieve Schmitt became Genevieve Poulain – which was neither Lecomte nor Solomas – and my pre-monitory feeling morphed to one of utter confusion.

When I'd finished reading I closed the lid of my laptop and Buggles looked up at me with what looked like a question in his eyes.

'No idea,' I told him. 'It's like some demented puzzle, babe.' But then Buggles jumped down and ran to the fridge, revealing that his actual question had been far less challenging. All he wanted to know was whether I was going to feed him.

At the beginning of March, I came home from Impressionable one Thursday to discover that the 'For Sale' sign the estate agent had fixed to my lounge window had sprouted an exact twin next door.

I phoned immediately but it was only a small one-bedroom unit, so of no use to us at all. It was an 'unfinished conversion', the estate agent told me. The developer had gone bust halfway through.

The price troubled me though, as on a per-square-foot basis it was twenty-five per cent cheaper than mine. No wonder I'd had no visits.

I didn't see Dan all week, but when I finally did mention it to him he got excited. With a tiny bit of help from me he could buy the place, he pointed out, and then we could simply knock through, effectively joining the two flats.

We visited it the following morning and, though it really was unfinished, the unpainted plasterboard walls at least felt bright and clean.

It had a brand-new kitchen/dining room, which Dan said he could 'make work', plus a bedroom/lounge he suggested could become our new lounge/dining room, leaving my existing lounge as a second bedroom/nursery.

Because I was struggling to imagine the finished project, I told Dan he'd have to draw me a floor plan when we got home.

He started pacing out the rooms and taking notes of their approximate dimensions and while he was doing this I noticed that there wasn't anywhere for a toilet.

I strode through to the lounge where our naughty estate agent, who'd forgotten to mention this nugget of information, was talking on his mobile phone. Eventually I got bored waiting, so I moved into his line of vision, whereupon he apologised to whoever he was talking to and hung up.

'I can't work out where the toilet's supposed to go,' I said, and I noticed he looked caught out.

He led me through to the bathroom – originally half the hallway from before the first floor had been divided into two flats. It had been beautifully tiled in those white Paris Metro tiles and had some drains and pipes sticking out, but otherwise was bare.

'I assume you'd stick it in here,' he said, nonchalantly.

'There's not enough room.' I turned to see that Dan had joined us. He started pacing out the space.

'Clearly the shower is meant to go here,' he said, waving his arms around as much as the tight space permitted. 'Because that's the drain, right there. And then . . . washbasin here . . . So, toilet where?'

'Yes,' the estate agent said. 'I agree it's tight. You'll probably have to be inventive.'

'Inventive,' I repeated.

'Perhaps have the toilet somehow share the shower space?'

'Erm, that won't work,' Dan said.

'Maybe a fold-out washbasin or something?' the estate agent offered, fiddling with the massive knot of his tie.

'A *fold-out washbasin?*' Dan said. 'Have you ever seen such a thing?'

'No, well . . .' the estate agent said. 'I've never seen electricity or radiation, but people assure me they exist.'

Back at mine, on the backs of the pages of one of the worst submissions I'd ever read, Dan excitedly drew some of the worst sketches I'd ever seen. Discovering that he was so very bad at something made me love him even more.

By the end of the week, I was getting impatient for news of cassette #3. The tapes had started to pop into my consciousness at random moments during the day and I was becoming desperate to understand the dichotomy of how these people could be who they seemed to be – my grandparents and my Aunt Ethel – while having characteristics, life stories and even names that were entirely unfamiliar. Which version of our family history was the true one – the one I'd grown up with, or the one recorded on the cassettes? And if this new narrative *was* the true one, how much did Dad know? Was it humanly possible that he was entirely unaware?

But beyond the family intrigue, I felt gripped by the story. I felt as if Genevieve and Pierre were stuck in limbo, locked in darkness in that horrible wood cabin in La Vielle-Loye and, because it seemed almost an act of cruelty to leave them there, I began texting Freida to egg her on.

After a few more days, I thought about them again, and realising Freida still hadn't replied, I decided to phone her instead. It was nine in the evening, but she answered immediately, saying she was working on them at that very moment. She'd 'done' tapes 3 and 4, she said, and was giving them a last read through.

'Please, just send them, faults and all,' I begged. 'I really don't care about typos.'

But Freida was nothing if not professional. 'You'll have them both tomorrow morning when you get up,' she said. 'I promise.'

'Just tell me about that bloody cabin. Do they get out?'

'Yes,' she said. 'Don't worry, they get out.'

'Thank God,' I said. 'Thank God for that.'

'And do not worry,' she said. 'I'm on holiday all next week, so the next instalments will be somewhat expedited.'

I hung up the phone and smiled. Every now and then Freida would come up with these phrases – phrases that were perfectly good English but were simply forms or phrases we never use in speech.

'Somewhat expedited,' I repeated out loud, grinning to myself.

Cassette #4

ML: *Hello. This is Marie Lefebvre, talking to Genevieve Schmitt, cassette number four, I think? Third day.*

Hi, Genevieve. I'd just like to apologise for last time. I feel that I pushed you too hard, and I realise that was upsetting for you, so I'm sorry. If I do that again, just—

GS: You know, really, it's fine. Let's not, um, dwell on that. Let's just get on with it, shall we?

Of course. But I am sorry. So thanks for having me back. When we left off, you were still in Cannes. How did you come to move on? Because I don't think you were there for long, were you?

No, we stayed for just over a week. Pierre spent his days trying to find work, and I spent mine trying to find a room to rent. But neither of us managed to find either. There were thousands of refugees and they were all looking for work and places to live. The only time we ever found a horribly overpriced room for rent, the woman didn't want anyone with a baby.

I was sad we were going to have to leave Cannes, but I understood that the situation was untenable. We were clearly going to have to try a different town, even if we were in no great hurry to do so.

But then something happened that made us get a move on. We returned to the house for lunch on the Saturday to find Francine's neighbour from across the landing in the process of telling her the police had been by. They'd been looking for a Monsieur Meyer and a Mademoiselle Schmitt, she said, and she asked if that was us.

Now the fact that they'd used my surname was doubly scary because it meant that not only did the police know where Pierre was living, but they knew we weren't really married. Because, of course, I'd been telling everyone my surname was Meyer.

Not Poulain?

Oh, no, we'd had to switch to Meyer. Because Pierre's cousin knew he wasn't called Poulain.

Of course she did! Silly me.

I'd been going by Pierre's name, Meyer, so that really scared us.

There were incredible rumours going around about everything back then. I don't think I've ever heard as many rumours as I did during the war. So we'd heard that the Italians were about to take Cannes, and that Pétain had started rounding up the Jews. We heard the Germans were about to invade the Free Zone, and it was said that the French police were arresting people willy-nilly and handing them over to the Germans.

At a later date, virtually all of those rumours came true. Back then, in July 1940, most of them really were just rumours, but we were terrified all the same. And I don't know if Jeanne and Francine believed we were in danger or not, but seeing a chance to get rid of us, and sensing our fear, they certainly didn't hold back from whipping us into a frenzy.

You know, these days, I wonder if the police had just come to deliver a message from my mother. Perhaps they simply wanted to inform me that my father was missing and my mother wanted me home. If my mother had compared notes with Pierre's parents she could have guessed at where we were staying from the fact I was sending postcards from Cannes, where they knew Pierre had a cousin. But we never got to find out why they were looking for us because we left that same day.

Francine went out and returned with slimy Jean-Noel, who announced, rather theatrically, that he'd solved all our problems. He had a place we could rent – a perfectly idyllic-sounding country house up in the back country. It had two floors and an open fire-place. The garden was full of wood we could burn and had a river running along one side. For the paltry sum of one thousand five hundred francs, we could stay there for a whole year, he said. And the war would probably be over by then!

When Pierre baulked at the cost, Jean-Noel added that, included in the price, he would drive us up there and even provide bedding and groceries to 'get us going'.

By chance, that sum was most of the money we had. With hindsight, it seems obvious that Francine had found and counted our stash of cash, and together they'd fixed the price to fit. But we were so desperate to leave, and his offer was so perfect, solving as it did every one of our problems, that it truly didn't cross our minds.

Jean-Noel wanted half the cash up front, he said, so that he could get our groceries on the black market. He needed cash to bribe someone he knew for petrol, as well. And rather naively – very naively, really – we handed the money over and waited for him to return.

And did he ever come back? Because that does sound pretty trusting.

Oh, it was. It was a ridiculous thing to do. We didn't even like the man, so God knows why we trusted him. But we needed to believe, I think. We were scared and out of options, that's all.

But he did return, late that afternoon. He had borrowed a butcher's van, and in the rear, as promised, there were blankets and pillows and pots and pans. There was a hamper of food, as well, including a surprising number of luxury items that were incredibly

235

difficult to come by, and that all seemed so kind of him that when he asked, we handed over the rest of the cash.

You gave him the cash before you'd seen the house?

I know. Don't . . . I never forgave myself for that.

And, what happened then? Did the house even exist?

Oh, it existed all right. It just wasn't quite as we'd imagined.

To start with, it was so far away. That was the first surprise. We drove up and up, through Grasse and then on, higher and higher into the Alps. I hadn't even known there were Alps behind Cannes. We drove past little hilltop villages, and every time we saw one I thought we'd arrived, but no, it was always further.

After a couple of hours driving, he drove down a winding dirt road, and then down another really bumpy dirt track, and there, behind the trees, in the middle of a clearing, was a tiny stone hut.

A hut, you say? Not a house?

Well, it had a front door and an upstairs window, so in a way it looked like a tiny house, but it wasn't really a house at all. It was an old shepherds' hut that, until recently, someone had been using to rear rabbits. In a lot of ways, it fitted the exact description he'd given us, so it was hard to accuse him of lying. I mean, there *was* a river running along the bottom of the garden, it's just that the garden was a chunk of forest. It *did* have two floors, only to get upstairs you had to climb up a rickety ladder. The front door was rotten, full of holes and didn't close properly, and the ground floor was of beaten earth mixed, judging by the smell, with lots and lots of rabbit poo.

There was a battered old table and two chairs, and an open chimney that was more like a campfire made of stones. And that was it.

A stone hut, with two chairs and a table.

Yes. There was no electricity, no toilet, no kitchen, no sink. It didn't even have running water.

Oh my God. What did you do? How did you react?

Well, Pierre laughed. He said something like, 'Well this is a tad more basic than I imagined,' and then got this crazy fit of the giggles. He really sounded quite mad.

And you?

I did what I always do when I'm stressed. I cried.

We all got into an argument, then, with everyone shouting at once.

I pointed out there was no water and Pierre that there was no electricity.

Jean-Noel smilingly batted away each criticism as if he was playing a game with us, pointing to the spring water which flowed across the land – water that he claimed was the purest water in France – and producing a battery radio from the back of the van as proof that we didn't need electricity.

I asked how I was supposed to wash nappies without a sink, and he said there was a communal *lavoir* in the village.

'There's not even a bed!' Pierre shouted, and Jean-Noel pulled the heap of blankets from the van, saying, 'You'll be really comfortable on that lot. You'll be like baby birds in a nest.'

'Light!' I said. 'There's no light! Are we supposed to go to sleep like birds, when the sun goes down too?' and Jean-Noel magicked up a paraffin lamp.

'There's no cooker,' I said, and he delved inside the van to produce a single burner army camp stove.

Pierre begged him to be reasonable. He said there wasn't even a toilet, not even an outdoor one, and Jean-Noel scuttled comically behind the house to fetch a shovel. 'You want an outdoor toilet?' he asked, gesturing at the surroundings. 'The biggest toilet in France. You can shit in a hole, or shit in the river. Out here you can shit anywhere you want.'

And the funny thing was that, faced with his complete lack of anger or remorse, or even apparent self-doubt – in the face of his absurd salesman's confidence – I was beginning to doubt myself. My complaints, to my own ears, were sounding more and more like those of a petulant child.

'It's in the middle of bloody nowhere!' Pierre said. 'What are we supposed to do for food? For meat? For vegetables? For bread?'

Jean-Noel opened the lid of the hamper and pulled out a jar, then, looking skyward, he said, 'I give them foie gras, my Lord, but they want bread!'

Eww.

I'm sorry?

Oh, it's just, you know, foie gras . . .

Ah, yes, I know. I wouldn't touch the stuff these days, but back then we didn't know much about how things like that were produced. No one talked much about animal cruelty. Plus, I suspect it probably wasn't quite so brutal in the old days. I'm sure they force-fed them and everything, but I expect they lived outside and not in those awful tiny cages.

Anyway, I told him we could hardly live on foie gras so he produced a pack of those dry slices of toast as well.

'There's a village ten minutes down the lane,' he told us. 'You can get anything you want from there. Just relax, will you? Look around. Look at how beautiful it is here!'

I asked if there was really a village and Pierre got angry that I was even considering believing the man. Even if there was a village, he said, how would we buy things now Jean-Noel had taken all our money?

'Only I haven't taken it all,' Jean-Noel said. 'You've still got five hundred left. That'll buy you *plenty* of bread. *And* goat's cheese from the farmer over that way . . . And potatoes.' We didn't think until much later how strange it was that he knew exactly how much money we had.

'And when that runs out?' Pierre asked, at which Jean-Noel just shrugged and pointed out, quite reasonably, that what we did once we ran out of money wasn't really his problem. 'But a young man like you, you'll find work in the village,' he said. 'You'll trade labour for food. You'll find a way.'

He was a very smooth operator but, though his strategy was starting to convince me, it wasn't working on Pierre at all. He was still furious and adamant that this simply wasn't acceptable. Jean-Noel, he said, was not an honest man.

That accusation of dishonesty finally struck home, so that even Jean-Noel ran out of steam. He shrugged and, looking genuinely hurt, started putting the stuff back in the van.

I surprised myself by feeling panicky about that. I'd been on the verge of convincing myself we'd be fine here, that this was indeed the best of an admittedly awful set of options, but the best of them all the same. I'd imagined myself bathing in the sparkling river and working for a farmer in exchange for eggs and cheese. I think, above all, I'd imagined how relaxing it might feel being that far from the madness of the war – actually feeling safe.

'So, shall I take you back to Francine's place?' Jean-Noel asked, jangling his keys. 'Because I'm not sure she's going to be thrilled to see you.'

And there was that great truth: we could not return to Francine's place. So I started to address Pierre, asking if he was absolutely certain that we couldn't make this work. He looked at me as if I was a crazy woman, and in retrospect I think I probably had gone a bit mad. I'd certainly lost my objectivity.

'Or perhaps you'd like me to drop you straight at the police station,' Jean-Noel said, managing to make the offer sound generous. 'I'm sure *they'll* be happy to put you up for a few nights!'

'Pierre,' I said. 'We can't go back. You know we can't. Surely we can stay here for a while, can't we? Surely we can at least stay here until we work out a better plan? It'll be like camping. It'll be fun.'

Jean-Noel told him he should listen more to his wife. He said anyone could see I was talking sense.

Pierre handed him the baby then, and led me down to the river so that we could talk in private.

He was angry with me, and he said I needed to stop undermining him. He said it was crazy to stay, even if I couldn't see that. He ran through all those same objections, that there was no electricity and no water, and no bed, and we didn't even know if it was true that there was a village down the way. And I countered that we had a lamp and a stove and a rushing river right next to us, and there was bloody water everywhere. Even if it did turn out to be a bad choice, then we could just move on, I said.

Pierre said that with no money we wouldn't even be able to move on and we'd probably starve to death here, and I asked him where we'd sleep if we were to go back to Cannes, and how he knew we wouldn't starve there.

But then something caught the corner of my eye, and we turned to see the butcher's van bumping its way along the track emitting a blue plume of smoke from the exhaust pipe.

We ran as fast as we could, me because I was worried about the baby and Pierre because he really didn't want to be stranded there.

I was faster than Pierre by a long stretch, but though I managed to bang on the rear window as the van accelerated away, even I couldn't get in front to stop him.

I finally gave up running and doubled over to catch my breath as the van accelerated into the distance. And then Pierre caught up with me and shouted a breathless 'Bastard' at the van, which by then was almost out of sight.

'He's taken Guillaume!' I cried, and it was then that I realised just how profoundly I'd bonded with the child. The idea that he was being driven off to an uncertain fate filled me with dread beyond anything I'd experienced up until that point, and let's face it, things hadn't exactly been dread-free.

Pierre, though still breathless, managed to smile. He said I was being ridiculous, and why on Earth would he have taken Guillaume?

'Knowing him, he's probably going to sell him,' I said. 'Knowing him, he probably already *has* sold him!'

Pierre shook his head in disbelief. 'Relax. He'll be back at the house . . . hut . . . shed . . .' he said.

So I started my way back up the track, and when I heard Guillaume crying I ran full tilt and swept him up in my arms from the pile of blankets where Jean-Noel had left him. And do you know, in that instant, I didn't care about the war, or the house, or the lack of a sink, or any of it? In that moment I was entirely happy. Guillaume was the only thing I cared about.

When Pierre reached us, he stroked Guillaume's cheek and said, 'You see? He's fine,' and then he looked around desolately, sighed deeply and picked up the box of groceries to carry it indoors. 'Do you want to know what I think?' he said. 'I think Jean-Noel's motives might not be entirely altruistic.'

So, I'm assuming you had to sleep there?

Yes, we had no choice. Jean-Noel had driven off, and the sun was about to set.

So we sat at the old table and picnicked on dry toast and foie gras. We ate some tinned fish too . . . it was mackerel, I think. The items Jean-Noel had provided were all pretty strange. None of it was very practical, but it was what we had, so we made do.

And what about the baby? Did you have milk?

Jeanne had packed me a baby bottle, and Jean-Noel's hamper contained half a litre of cow's milk plus a can of the sweetened, condensed stuff. So the first night Guillaume got milk, and in the morning I think I gave him the condensed. He was such an amazing baby. He didn't even make a fuss.

Though we had a paraffin lamp and a stove, we didn't, it turned out, have any matches. And so that first evening, we went to bed just as soon as it went dark, sleeping on the blankets to start with, and then moving under them as the night got colder.

That was a bit of a shock – the fact that even in late July it was still cold up there. That should have given us a clue as to what winter was going to be like, but it didn't. We were young, I suppose, and inexperienced.

We both slept badly, in part because of all the weird noises coming from the forest, but mainly because we didn't have a bed. Because, of course, we had to use the blankets as, well, *blankets* rather than as a mattress. So we ended up sleeping on the planks.

You said there were noises? Were you scared?

Yes, a bit. There were all sorts of horrible screeches and strange shrieks and we had no idea what kinds of animals were making them. Pierre withdrew the ladder at one point, 'just in case', and once he'd done that, I did feel a little bit safer.

By morning, we were both absolutely shattered and the first words Pierre said – and I remember this like it happened yesterday – the very first words he said the next morning, were, 'This is shit.' He said we were going to Cannes and we were going to get our money back.

I'm guessing that by this point you no longer disagreed?

No. I'd spent one of the worst nights I'd ever spent anywhere.

But then we got up and climbed down the ladder and stepped outside. And the morning, that morning in the forest, was so very beautiful, it sort of stopped us in our tracks.

Can you describe it to me?

I'm no poet, but I can try. The sky was a very deep blue and there were some big mountains towering above us, because we were right down at the bottom of a valley. The stream was sparkling in the sunlight and there were birds tweeting, so many birds . . . The grass was knee high and bright green, almost fluorescent really, and it was dotted with wild flowers.

It does sound heavenly.

You know, in summer, that place was heavenly.

We bathed in the stream – which even in summer was icy cold – and Pierre saw some trout dart past and said it was a shame he didn't have a fishing rod. We ate more of our toast things for breakfast, along with a lump of Camembert and some olives. I fed the baby his condensed milk and then let him suckle on my breast until he was calm. And then we set out to find the village.

Was that to buy food, or did you want to find a way to leave?

By then, I was starting to want to stay again, I think, but Pierre was still determined to leave.

That's starting to sound like a bit of a theme between you two?

Yes, it's funny really, because he always had this view that I was the high-maintenance one out of the two of us – that if someone was going to blow all our money on luxuries, it would be me. But I was far more adaptable to the idea of living in a very basic way than he was. In the end, he was always more scared of running out of toilet paper or whatever than I was.

The footpath to the village weaved along the river's edge, cutting occasionally through the trees. There was wildlife everywhere and just on that first morning we saw deer and a squirrel and a hare. There were eagles and buzzards soaring above. It really was quite magical.

Evidently, the village was farther away than we had been told, and it took well over half an hour to get there. And even from a distance we could see it was little more than a collection of houses, most of which were ruins.

There was a stone *lavoir* filled by an ice-cold spring-water fountain where you could wash clothes – that much at least, had been true. We passed a tethered donkey in a field, and some pigs in a boarded pen as well, but those really were the only visible signs of civilisation. There didn't seem to be any people around and there certainly weren't any shops.

We turned into the little alleyways that weaved between the houses and eventually we heard the sound of someone hoeing the earth.

When we tracked her down and Pierre said 'Hello', the woman, in her fifties, jumped in fright.

She was incredibly suspicious of us at first, keeping her distance and scowling, but as always, the baby helped break the ice. No one ever seemed able to resist a woman with a newborn baby.

As our only reference points were trees and the river, we struggled for some time to explain where we were staying, but eventually the woman seemed to understand that we were in what she called the 'Rebuffel refuge', though we didn't know if we'd explained that to her correctly or not. There seemed to be a lot of very similar stone huts dotted around.

We asked her where we could buy food, and when we mentioned shops she just rolled her eyes.

The 'main' village, she explained, was up behind the rocky outcrop that towered over us, but even in the village there were no businesses of any kind, merely a grocery van from a neighbouring village, Sigale, that came to town on Saturdays.

I asked her how we could get up to the main village, and she sneeringly replied that we could either walk or, alternatively, we could walk.

Pierre told me to forget about groceries and asked the woman how we could get back to Cannes.

She explained that if we walked to the village then the grocer would take us back to Sigale, and from there we could catch a bus to Nice, and from there another to Cannes.

Pierre looked at me and nodded, as if to say that was all decided then, and I realised he'd missed a crucial bit of information.

'But you said he's only there on Saturdays, right?'

The woman nodded in reply. We were stuck there, she announced sourly.

Pierre turned to me then and, looking genuinely fearful, said, 'I told you. We really are going to starve to death.'

On cue, Guillaume gave out a little cry, prompting me to point out that it was he who would starve to death first. Because the woman was frowning, I explained that, for some strange reason, I currently had no milk.

She nodded at this information thoughtfully, then said that Lucienne would give him a feed, if we had money. '*Do* you have money?' she asked.

I shrugged and admitted we did still have a little.

'Ah,' she said, smiling for the first time. 'Then tell me what you need, and I'll see what I can do.'

Did she mean that Lucienne would be willing to wet-nurse him?

Yes. Yes, I hadn't realised that, but that's exactly what she meant. And Lucienne turned out to be her daughter. So she was effectively negotiating rental of her daughter's breasts.

Gosh. It sounds like people were pretty mercenary back then.

Do you think they are less so now? I'm not so sure . . . But anyway, it was a war, you know? People were trying to find ways to survive. And no one really knew if they'd make it to the other side.

Yes, I can understand that. And so, is that what you ended up doing? Did Lucienne breastfeed Guillaume?

I'm never quite sure if I'm supposed to feel ashamed about this, but, yes, that's what we did.

I can't see why you should feel ashamed.

No? Me neither really. But I always do feel a bit strange about it. People are often funny about it when I tell them. But in the end, it was a matter of survival. The baby needed feeding, and I had no milk. Lucienne had more milk than her own baby would drink and appreciated the little money we were able to pay.

So yes, for a couple of weeks she fed him three times a day. Quite soon I ended up leaving him with her for the whole day. It was easier than going back and forth. Then in the evenings, I'd give him goat's milk. But I always had to take him to my own breast afterwards. It was the only thing that would ever put him to sleep.

So you stayed for weeks, in the end?

Ha! We ended up staying for the duration.

You mean the duration of the war?

Yes.

Oh, I wasn't expecting that.

No, I don't think we were either. But the following day Pierre trekked up to the main village. It was a difficult forty-minute hike from the hamlet, along a steep forest path up the side of the mountain. I did it myself hundreds of times and it was so steep that even in midwinter I'd be soaked in sweat by the time I got to the top.

But though he got dizzy a few times, he managed it.

Up in the village, Pierre sought out the mayor. His intention was to ask if anyone had any kind of transport so that we could get out sooner than the following Saturday. He was itching to get back and have it out with Jean-Noel, but the mayor had other ideas.

They got talking and got on instantly, I think. And it turned out that the mayor was desperate for someone to do public works in the village.

You mean, he offered Pierre a job?

Yes, ultimately, he did. Once he found out Pierre had all the practical skills that came with being a plumber it was a done deal, really.

There hadn't been that many young men living in the village before the war, I don't think, but those that had been there had mostly vanished by the time we arrived.

They'd been killed?

No. I think one woman's husband might have died, but most of them simply weren't back yet from having been mobilised. The Germans had taken almost two million men prisoners of war. Plus, the few able men that were still present in the village had other essential jobs, working for the Ponts et Chaussées – that's the organisation that maintained the roads. Those mountain roads were very crumbly and rocks were always falling on to them. Keeping them open without all the tractors and what have you that they have these days was pretty labour-intensive. The men would head off on foot with just their spades over their shoulders, so sometimes just walking to wherever the job was would take half a day.

Other men had different jobs they'd returned to, too. There was a builder chap who used a mule to carry his bricks and things around, and there was a goat farmer who sold us milk and cheese. But there was no one to help the mayor, so he saw Pierre – who was both light enough to hop around on roofs to mend leaks, and clever enough to fix the water supply when it suddenly dried up – as a godsend.

Pierre really fell on his feet, then.

He did. Particularly because the mayor turned out to be exceptionally sensitive to our situation.

When you say your situation . . . ?

I mean that he worked out almost immediately that we hadn't ended up in the middle of nowhere for no reason. He could also tell, no doubt from Pierre's accent, that we were from Alsace, and

everyone knew what the Germans had been up to over there . . .
So right from the start, he'd asked if putting Pierre on the books,
paying him officially, was going to cause him any problems, and
Pierre took the risk of trusting him and admitted that it might well.

It turned out the mayor had a contact – I think it might have
even been his brother – who worked at the prefecture in Grasse,
and he was able to get us fresh paperwork.

So that's what happened. We wanted to call ourselves Poulain,
but the mayor thought something more regional might be better
and suggested Solomas, which was a very common local name.

And while we were at it, Pierre, who said he'd always hated
his first name, used his second name instead. So that's how Pierre
became Christophe Solomas. The mayor put Monsieur Solomas on
the payroll, and then set out about getting the required papers for
all of us. I became Genevieve Solomas, and our baby Guillaume
Solomas. So we were finally, officially, a family.

*That's amazing. And were these fake documents? Forgeries? Or
were they official?*

Do you know, we weren't really sure for years? There was always
this terrifying doubt that if we had to produce them, they'd be compared to some official register and a problem would be flagged up,
but it simply never happened. For months, I kept slipping up and
calling Pierre . . . well, Pierre, rather than Christophe, too.

After the war we had to get fresh copies so we could request
passports, and we honestly didn't know what would happen. But
we asked for them through the normal channels and they handed
them over as if nothing untoward had ever taken place, as if those
were the people we had always been. It was only then that we knew
we were officially in the system.

Do you have a marriage certificate too?

I do. Look, it's here in my *livret de famille*. I dug it out so that
I could show you! You see? Genevieve Lecomte married Christophe

248

Solomas on the fourth of May 1939 in Le Mas. That was the name of the village where Pierre, or rather Christophe, was employed.

May 1939? I didn't think you got there until 1940.

Yes, but they backdated the certificate so we were married before the baby was conceived.

That really does look official. What about Lecomte? Where does that name come from?

Oh, we pulled that one out of a hat, too. It seemed like using my real maiden name – Schmitt – might be dangerous. So I went for Lecomte.

Gosh, all these name changes. It's quite confusing.

Yes, I'm sorry about that! It was confusing for us, too, if that's any help! <Laughs> Actually, I'm sure that I must be still listed somewhere as being born as Schmitt in Mulhouse as well, but it has never caused a problem. That's the town hall stamp at the bottom, see? Ethel's the only person who never changed her name. She's still Lambert.

Of course. And did you stay in that same house then – in the hut, I mean – the whole time?

In the end we did, though it wasn't our intention.

The mayor had said that once our papers came through it would be safe for us to move to the village. He even had a place we could use. It was still pretty basic, but it at least had a proper front door and a stove.

But before we were able to move, word came that the government – Pétain's Vichy government – had been forced by the Germans to reintroduce a sort of obligatory scout movement to replace the French national service. It was called Les Chantiers de la Jeunesse, and all young men had to spend six months training, getting fit, hunting and gathering and competing in sports events . . . Often they had to camp in the forest for months on end. It was all terribly virile and Christophe would have hated it.

It sounds a bit like the Hitler Youth.

Well, you know, certain chapters were a lot like that, depending on where you lived. It was very much the luck of the draw. In some regions they enthusiastically shipped their young men off to Germany to help with the war effort. But others were associated with the resistance and saw their role more as one of preparing men to fight when the day finally came to kick the Germans out. So it was a very mixed bag.

Anyway, the mayor of Le Mas seemed to think it was much safer for Pierre – sorry, I suppose I can call him Christophe now, can't I? – to vanish from view before he got enrolled in Les Chantiers and got his name added to all sorts of lists. Especially because he hadn't received the paperwork with his new identity yet.

So he told us to continue living in our forest hideaway for the time being. He found us a mattress and a wood-burning stove – he always had a contact for everything – and eventually Christophe even put in an outdoor sink. But it was always incredibly basic, and in winter quite stunningly cold.

So even once your papers came through, you still weren't able to move?

No. Unfortunately, things never did get any safer. They only ever became progressively more dangerous. Pétain passed anti-gay laws, the first since the Revolution, and started shipping trainloads of so called 'undesirables' – mainly Jews – to the camps. Then in '42 the Germans simply took over the whole of France, so there was no free zone anymore. They began conscripting French men then, and sending them to work in German factories. They didn't often bother coming as far into the mountains as Le Mas – there weren't really enough people there for them to be that interested – but when they did occasionally visit, Christophe would take a day or two off, and we'd hide out in our little house in the forest. Unless someone tipped them off, there really wasn't much chance anyone would stumble upon us living out there. And thankfully no one ever did.

Can you tell me a bit about what life was like up there? It must have been very different to the lives you'd been living in Mulhouse.

Yes, of course. Well, in summer, and in spring and autumn, Christophe worked most days. There was always something to be done around the village, fixing the water supply, or helping someone who was planting or harvesting . . . Some days he'd be fixing roofs, or electricity or . . . I don't even remember really . . . he was a general sort of dogsbody and the tasks he had to do were very varied. In summer he'd work quite literally from dawn to dusk and fish for trout on his day off. We ate so much trout that, even now, I can't stand it. Just the thought of trout makes me feel queasy. And then in winter, he often couldn't work at all because of the snow.

And how was Christophe's health? It sounds like the job was quite physical.

His health has always been very on and off. He'd have a couple of good months where he'd think all that was behind him and then suddenly he'd have cramps or bleeding again. He used to get these twinges of pain, deep inside, that were bad enough to make him gasp, but luckily they never lasted for long. But his anaemia went away, and that was the main thing. Within six months he'd stopped fainting.

And what about you? How did you spend your days?

Well, we made a vegetable patch down by the river – everyone had to grow their own vegetables during the war. So we had potatoes and carrots and beans. We planted tomatoes – though they never did very well – and chard, and even rhubarb. Once the initial tilling of the land was done, the vegetable patch was my job. We built a chicken coop too, so we could feed them the peelings and have eggs. Bottling vegetables for winter, cooking, sewing, mending . . . those were all my responsibility. Plus I had a baby to look after, of course, the feeding . . . the nappies . . . All of that is shockingly time-consuming, Well, it was a shock to me, anyway.

But in winter, we'd get snowed under, sometimes for weeks on end. Often we couldn't even get out the door to go to the toilet without shovelling away the snow first. When it was like that, we couldn't get to the hamlet, let alone the village. So during those periods, we lived like Canadian trappers: we'd huddle by the stove and read books or listen to the radio. We'd play with Guillaume and talk about our plans for after the war.

That sounds incredibly cosy.

<Laughs> I get that; I really do. I know that's how it sounds because, though I lived through it, it does sound cosy, even to me. Memory does funny things to the past. It erases a lot of the awful bits and leaves you with pretty memories of reading by a flickering lamp while snowflakes drifted down. But it wasn't cosy at all. It was absolutely dreadful. Especially that first winter.

Why the first one in particular?

Well, for starters, 1940 was a terribly cold one. They were all cold, those winters: '39, '40 and '41, which was one of the coldest ever recorded, if I'm not mistaken. But on top of that, 1940 was our first winter there and we hadn't known what to expect. So it was the one for which we were the least prepared.

The hut had been built of local stone and in places the wind whistled through the gaps. The roof, above that upstairs room, had no insulation. We did that the following summer, using straw. So up there it was quite literally freezing.

The temperature outside went as low as minus fifteen Celsius that first winter and I think we had below minus twenty a couple of times in '41. And when it was that cold outside, you could build the biggest fire the stove would take and still be able to see your breath when you spoke. It really was utterly dreadful.

The baby would scream and scream. When he was teething, he could scream for days on end, and I would panic that I was doing something wrong, or that he was upset because I wasn't his real mother . . . I definitely remember feeling very scared that I didn't know what I was doing, and that fear lasted for years, really.

Christophe and I argued a lot, too. The extreme conditions and the screaming baby and the lack of sleep put us both on edge. You have to remember we hadn't chosen each other. We were best mates, not soulmates, not lovers. So sometimes, especially when we were shut up together in winter, we really didn't get on at all. Sometimes we'd sulk for days on end.

There was never any romance? Even though I'm assuming you were sharing a bed?

Yes, we were. We only had one mattress. But no. God, no! Christophe liked – likes – men, and I've only ever been attracted to women. You know, there were loads of films in the seventies where gay men suddenly fell in love with the women they were hanging out with – quite often because they were forced to share a bed, or because they were drunk or something. And that always struck me as ridiculous. Anyway, it certainly never happened to us. And there were plenty of times when we were drunk. But no, seriously. Never even a hint of a hint. We came close to blows, once or twice, but that was about as physical as things got.

OK! And what about feeding the baby in all of that? You didn't trek through the snow to Lucienne every day, did you?

Oh golly! I haven't told you about my miracle, have I?

No, I don't think you have.

So, as I explained, those first few weeks, I took Guillaume to Lucienne so she could feed him, while in the evenings I gave him goat's milk.

But he was always demanding my breast. He would never go down unless I'd let him suckle for a bit first. So I got into the habit of doing that every evening. Christophe would put the radio on, I'd read my book, and Guillaume would suck away.

And then one morning over breakfast, Christophe started staring at my chest. When I looked down, I realised I was leaking. The front of my dress was soaked.

At first I assumed it was blood, or even some kind of puss from all that suckling. But it was milk! I'd started to produce my own milk.

I didn't even know that was possible.

Well, neither did I! Because I'd never been able to tell anyone that Guillaume wasn't mine, no one had ever explained to me that it was possible to have your milk come on without having been pregnant first. When it first happened, I honestly thought it was a miracle. We both did. We thought it was like the virgin birth or something, and again, because we couldn't explain to anyone how we believed it shouldn't have happened, we didn't discover that it was quite normal for years. I'm sure it will sound silly, but I secretly believed it was because I'd come to love him so much. I thought I'd made a miracle happen out of love.

How incredible. I've never even heard of that.

I know. It's funny, because over the years, as I've told people that story, lots of people haven't believed me. Even modern, educated women don't necessarily know it's possible. I often think that women's bodies are one of the last great taboos . . . But yes, if you stimulate the nipples enough, your milk can come on, so be careful! Men with certain health problems can have their milk come on too. Even now, it seems miraculous to me. Not miraculous as in something that's impossible, but a miracle of nature – a miracle of the female body, if that makes any sense.

That makes perfect sense.

If I'm honest, I'd struggle to explain how I felt about it. I was very conflicted. Sometimes, it made me feel a bit queasy, as if I was turning into a cow or a goat or something, and other times, I believed I'd manifested a miracle and had channelled some ancient, miraculous female power. It calmed Guillaume down a bit too, thank God. I don't think he really accepted me as his mother until my milk came on. I sensed – and this might sound silly – but I sensed he didn't trust me properly until I was able to feed him myself. It was the moment he started loving me back. Plus, locked in that cabin, in winter, God knows what we would have done otherwise. I expect I would have had to leave him with Lucienne.

And this all continued for the duration of the war? You lived like that until 1945?

Yes, pretty much. We made the place a little more liveable over time. Christophe had some access to building materials because of his job, so he was able to plug the gaps in the walls and that kind of thing. We insulated the roof with straw. We dug a latrine in the garden and Christophe built a sort of shed over it to keep the snow off. He put a stone sink he'd recovered from someone's garden just to the left of the front door and ran a pipe to it from the spring that spurted out at the top of our land. But it all remained incredibly basic. We never had electricity or hot water. We never had any kind of bathroom and, with a baby and later a toddler, that was very, very hard work.

In summer, none of those things really mattered. We'd bathe in the river and spend our time outdoors and sometimes it could really be quite lovely. Christophe was away a lot, working, so that was the one downside to summer. You know, no one ever talks about how boring child-rearing can be. Being alone with a toddler can be quite numbing. I felt like my brain had melted, sometimes. But at least we could get out and about. Once he started walking he'd run around chasing birds while I tended the vegetables, or he'd splash in the river while I did the washing. But the winters remained terrible. Being stuck in that cold hut was horrific.

Guillaume must have been growing up. By the end of the war, he was how old? Five?

Yes, he was five. He was gorgeous when he was five. So cuddly. So funny.

Actually, we never knew the exact date of his real birthday, and that was my fault for not being able to remember when Leah had given birth. I tried so hard to remember, but so much had been going on back then . . . I suppose it wasn't that surprising that I'd forgotten the date. But when the mayor had offered us the option of fresh paperwork, we'd had to choose a birthday for him and had plumped for the fifth of June, which can't have been far from the truth. So, officially, he would have been four the day before D-Day, and almost five in '45 when the Germans finally surrendered.

It was wonderful seeing him become this little person. The first time he called me Mama, the first time he stood, walked, helped me with the vegetable patch . . . Despite all the screaming and tantrums and poo, you never forget those moments. Once he started speaking it was just the best thing ever. He had so much character. He was so funny. With every stage of his development I loved him a little bit more.

So when was the south liberated? Did you leave the minute you were able?

No, not quite. The south was liberated in August '44, so we could have left then. But it was summer, and I'd have to admit that we were enjoying it. Plus, Mulhouse was still occupied. The Battle of the Ardennes didn't end until January the next year. So we stayed on until the summer of '45. It was only when the Germans finally capitulated in May that we were able to accept it was safe to move on. We discussed it a lot, I recall, the risks, our safety, Guillaume's safety . . . So even though we were both desperate to see our families, we stayed until it was really, finally, over.

You still didn't know . . . about your parents . . . ?

No. I had no idea. I was what people like to call 'blissfully ignorant'.

And presumably you were still desperate to find Ethel?

I was, but you know, it had been so long; so much had happened . . . I'd half convinced myself that she would have moved on to someone new in the meantime. I was protecting myself against disappointment, I suppose. But, you know, you're making me jump ahead. First, I need to tell you about our pilot. I need to tell you my most exciting memory of the war.

Your pilot?

Yes! At the end of May '44, an American bomber crashed right near us. There was a mountain behind where we lived called the Col de Bleine, and they crashed into the trees near the peak after a bombing raid. There were ten people on board, I think, but four went down the south side of the mountain and got sold to the Germans by the locals.

Sold?

Yes, if you handed people over, they'd give you food or cigarettes or whatever, so those four probably ended up in the camps. But the other six got lucky. They came down our side of the mountain, and all got saved, including two who ended up in our village. To keep them safe, they used to move them around at night. Almost everyone in the village was known to be sympathetic to the cause by then, but there was one woman that nobody trusted. There were rumours she gave information to the Germans and, as she always seemed to have cigarettes and tins of food, everyone was suspicious. And that meant there was real danger for the poor Air Force men they were hiding as well as for anyone caught hiding them.

Now, the mayor, of course, knew we were safe.

Because he'd provided you with fresh identities?

Exactly. We were compromised, so to speak. Plus, we lived in one of the most isolated houses in the area. So one night, in June

'44, there was a knock on the door and when we opened up it was the mayor with this pilot chap, Sam. They'd disguised him as a French farmer, but that's what he was, an American Air Force pilot.

He stayed with us for a week and he was absolutely gorgeous. He was kind and funny and, you know, relaxed in that special way Americans can be sometimes. There's a naive sort of confidence about them, I suppose. He was funny too – he had that Jewish sense of humour.

Was he Jewish, then?

Yes.

So being caught by the Germans would have been pretty bad for him.

Oh, I think it would have been anyway. But yes, you're probably right. It would have been even more dangerous for Jewish airmen. But did I mention he was also rather handsome? So Christophe, in particular, was smitten.

Oh gosh. And was Sam gay?

No, he was perfectly heterosexual – he showed us photos of his wife and child on the first morning he was with us. So Christophe did his best to keep his feelings under wraps. But, honestly, it was so funny watching him swoon around Sam . . . Christophe would hang on his every word and laugh too loudly at all Sam's jokes. Often, when *I* laughed, I was laughing at Christophe's reaction rather than whatever joke Sam had told.

So did Sam speak French? I'm just wondering how you communicated.

Not one word! But we both knew some English from school. It was pretty rusty, but with a lot of miming, we got by. And in the evenings, we'd sit around and talk, and he'd tell us all about Georgia, where he came from. He liked to tell us all these little details about his life back home. He liked bowling, I remember, and dancing to rock 'n' roll and reading. His favourite author was John

Steinbeck, and after the war I read quite a few Steinbeck novels, and that was entirely thanks to Sam.

Guillaume was quite smitten, too, but Sam couldn't pronounce Guillaume properly – he called him Guy-home, so that caused much amusement. In the end we told him the English equivalent was probably William, so he started calling Guillaume William, and then Will, and then finally Bill, instead. He used to dance to rock 'n' roll around our tiny room with him and Guillaume used to laugh and laugh. When Sam left, he even asked if he could take Guillaume with him.

He was joking, I hope?

Of course he was joking! I told him he should take them both – said he'd be doing me a favour if he took Guillaume *and* Christophe with him, and Christophe said, 'Yes, please take me!' That was the closest Christophe ever got to telling Sam how he felt.

And how did Sam react?

Oh, he just cracked some joke about how if he had bigger pockets he'd take us all with him. But that week was a real highlight for me, for all of us. And that's why I wanted to tell you about it.

Yes, I can see that must have been exciting.

And you know how I was saying that memory plays tricks? How it erases, or at least attenuates, all that miserable coldness, all those arguments, all the boredom . . . But it also enhances the good bits, so that week, when we hid our pilot, well, I remember it as if it was yesterday. And I remember it as if it lasted for months, whereas in fact he was only with us for a week.

Any idea what happened to Sam after he left you?

No, none. You were never told what was next, just in case someone ended up interrogating you. But I believe they mostly got them out over the Pyrenees. The only thing I know for sure is that he did get out. He was definitely OK.

And can I ask how you know that?

Because I gave him a letter to post for me when he got to civilisation. But that's a whole different story. For later.

Fair enough. Can you describe the day that Germany surrendered? What was it like? Were there celebrations? Did people dance in the streets?

<Laughs> You know, for us, where we were, it was incredibly low-key. We were happy; we were more than happy. It's just that, without trekking all the way up to the village, there weren't enough people to have a party. And there weren't really any streets to dance in either. But we went and clinked glasses with Lucienne and her family. Her extremely drunk neighbour was there too.

How did you get the news? Do you remember?

Oh, you know, that sort of thing – the end of a war – well, you never forget a single detail.

We found out over the radio in the afternoon. Christophe was back earlier than usual that day. He'd been helping the Ponts et Chaussées people with a rockslide that had partly blocked one of the roads leading into the village and they'd finished clearing the blockage earlier than expected. So it was about four or five o'clock.

I was boiling water for fake coffee – we had a gas burner by then. It was only a single cooking ring, but it was much better than the army stove.

You had gas there but no electricity?

It was bottled gas. It came in those huge metal cylinders. The grocer used to bring them to Le Mas during his Saturday trip, and then the builder would transport it down to us in the valley on the back of Eglantine, his long-suffering mule.

Anyway, I was making coffee and Christophe switched on the radio. It was unusual that he would switch it on during the day. It ran on an accumulator, and the charge didn't last for long, so we had to ration ourselves. But that day, he switched it on – he said afterwards that he'd had an intuition – and De Gaulle's voice rang out. He was in the middle of a whole speech about Germany's surrender, so it took us a moment to work out that was what he was saying. The first phrase we heard clearly was something about the French people saluting their valiant allies.

And how did you feel when you realised? What did you say to each other?

We were dumbstruck. We just sat and stared at each other with tears in our eyes. And then eventually Christophe broke the tension by saying, 'Well, that's got to be fairly good news, don't you think?'

We spent a week saying goodbye to everyone and organising our affairs. We gave away some of the things we'd collected over the years and I told Lucienne she could have our chickens and that she should help herself to the vegetables from the garden.

Did you feel sad to be leaving?

No. Not at all. We were sad to say goodbye to some of the people, I suppose. And Guillaume was heartbroken when he understood he couldn't play with Cathy – that was Lucienne's daughter – anymore. But no, mainly, we were just happy. Happy that it was over. Happy we could go home. Happy we weren't going to have to spend winter in that hut ever again. Happy we were going to see our families . . .

And how did you travel?

Well, we hiked up to the village on foot. We were pretty used to it by then. I had the suitcase I'd arrived with and Christophe had a sack – you know, a hessian one – slung over his shoulder. We left with about the same amount of stuff we'd arrived with.

It was a Saturday and everyone had gathered around the grocer's van, so we said goodbye to all the people we knew up there, and then he drove us – the grocer, that is – to Sigale, where his shop was. Oh, I just remembered, he had this crazy contraption on the back of his van that somehow made it run on wood. I think it heated the wood to make gas or something . . . And he had to stop every now and then to add logs to this oven-thing at the back.

Because there was no petrol by then?

Exactly. I don't think there was much petrol for years.

From there we took the bus to Nice – I think it ran on wood-gas as well – and then from there a series of trains and buses back home.

Was the mayor sad to lose his number one employee?

I suppose he must have been, but he didn't say anything. The war was over. Everyone was moving all over the place. People expected change.

As we were leaving, the mayor took Christophe to one side and asked if we were intending to revert to our old identities. And Christophe asked if we could wait a little while to decide because we weren't sure.

You weren't sure? I would have thought that would be the obvious thing to do.

Well, to all intents and purposes, homosexuality had been made illegal, hadn't it? We assumed all the awful laws that had been passed, the laws against the Jews and the Roma, and the communists . . . that they'd be cancelled now that the Germans had been defeated. But we had to be sure. We had to wait and see. No one really knew quite what was coming next.

And were they cancelled? Those awful laws?

Most of them were. All the racial ones were, at any rate. But sadly not the anti-homosexual ones. The Allies decided, in their wisdom, to keep those. Germany's gift to the nation!

My God, that must have been upsetting, wasn't it?

It was more than upsetting. It was absolutely shameful. But you know, that was the one thing the Allies agreed with the Germans about. Nobody liked the homosexuals. And they didn't just keep them for a few years, either. They kept those laws for decades. In

France it wasn't until a few years ago – '82, I think – that Mitterrand finally removed the last of the anti-homosexuality laws from the statute books.

Yes, I wrote a piece about that. It's crazy.

But you know, even here in England, right now, in 1986, there are still people who don't want their kids to know about homosexuality. I'm not sure if you've been following it, but in Haringey there have been parents protesting about schools teaching kids about gay relationships just this week. There's an election next year and if the Conservatives win again they want to stop schools and libraries even *owning* books that mention homosexuality. So we're not that far from burning books all over again. But anyway . . . I'm getting sidetracked here, aren't I? It's just that it all makes me so angry. I can't even remember where I was up to, now.

You were just about to leave Le Mas, I think.

Right. Well, we said our goodbyes, and then spent two days getting back home, travelling almost exactly the same way we'd come five years earlier. The only difference was we travelled via Nice rather than Cannes, because that was where the bus went.

You didn't fancy popping in to see Francine and Jeanne, then?

Ha! No. We thought we'd give that pleasure a miss.

What was it like being back in Mulhouse? That must have felt strange, didn't it? You'd been away for so long.

It was awful. It was truly awful in every way. I get the shivers even now, just thinking about it.

Because that was when you found out about your parents?

Yes, that was without a doubt the most awful moment of my life. But even before that, being back in Mulhouse felt dreadful.

Lots of buildings had been bombed or burned to the ground and there were still German signs dotted around the place. There were refugees everywhere: people still pouring in from the east, Poles, and Roma and Jews who'd only barely survived the camps;

people who'd lost everything for one reason or another. Everyone, everywhere, looked poor, and starved; downtrodden and sad. The whole town felt really shocking and I remember thinking that it would never be the same again.

When we got to our street, we went our separate ways. Christophe hugged me and said it was weird, and that he felt as if he was saying goodbye, and in a way, I suppose he was. We had no real plan to stay together beyond that point but, although we were sick to the back teeth of each other's company, we also loved each other quite profoundly. So it was hard to envisage our lives alone.

I know a lot of marriages like that.

Well, quite! It had become very much like a marriage.

The front door to my building had been smashed in, and trying to imagine how that had happened made me nervous.

As I climbed the stairs with Guillaume, a downstairs neighbour who'd known me since birth – Madame Deloye – peeped out at me, but when I said 'Hello' she just closed the door in my face. I can only assume that she knew what had happened and didn't want to be the one to have to tell me.

I knocked on our front door, and when I heard footsteps inside my heart leapt. I was so convinced my mother would be the one to open the door that I started to cry in anticipation.

But a very old, frail-looking woman I'd never seen before opened it instead. She didn't seem to speak any French, and so we had this weird unintelligible conversation on the doorstep until eventually I got frustrated and pushed my way past her into the apartment.

The furniture was all ours, though they had moved some things around. But almost everything else had changed: the knick-knacks, the clock on the mantelpiece, the clothes, the pots and pans. Hardly any of it was familiar.

So I felt like I'd fallen into a dream. That sensation of being in the right place, which was simultaneously *not* the right place, felt nightmarish. Guillaume, who tended to pick up on everything, started to cry, and I ended up trying to calm him while simultaneously shouting at the old woman, demanding answers. Where were my parents? What had she done with my clothes? Why was she wearing my mother's slippers? And eventually, Madame Keller, the neighbour from across the landing, came out to see what all the fuss was.

I told her rather hysterically that the woman had 'stolen' our apartment and wouldn't tell me where my parents were, and she led me into her place, where she sat Guillaume and me down on the sofa so that she could give me some answers.

That can't have been easy for her.

No.

But for you . . . I can't even imagine.

You know it's really very strange, but I remember all the wrong things about that day.

What do you mean by the wrong things?

All the irrelevant things. I remember that she served me mint tea. I remember the way the light was filtering through her net curtains, the way the steam was rising from the tea, the way the dust motes floated in the sunlight. I remember that she smoked a Gitanes cigarette and I remember the smell and the way the grey smoke twirled as it rose. I remember the feel of her beige corduroy sofa beneath my fingertips and the way Guillaume squeezed my hand as she spoke. But I honestly couldn't begin to tell you what she said, or what I said by way of reply. I can't remember anything about the conversation or how she actually told me.

It must have been just about impossible to hear.

Yes. It was unbearable. That's a word we use willy-nilly, but I mean it literally. It was unbearable, as in the sense that what she told me was impossible to bear. I don't think I said much. I just sat there running my fingernail across the material covering the sofa. And then I thanked her and got up and left without drinking my tea.

As I was leaving, she offered me a place to stay. Our flat had been re-rented to the Polish refugees I'd seen, so she offered to put me up. But I just wanted to leave. I wanted to get out . . . That need to escape the building . . . it was physical. I just couldn't breathe there.

When I got downstairs I found Christophe sitting on the door-step. His parents had given him the news, so when he saw me he stood and tried to hug me, but I pushed him quite brutally away. I was scared that . . . I'm not that sure what I was scared of. Perhaps that I would . . . I don't know . . . melt down, or collapse, or some-thing. I had this terror that if I allowed myself to feel anything at all I'd just . . . vanish, or perhaps stop breathing. It wasn't that clear a thought; it was more just a sensation of fear.

I was aware that I had a young child holding my hand, and nowhere to live, and no future, and in a way, no longer any past. And it simply wasn't possible to let myself feel anything until I'd found practical solutions to all of those problems. So I pushed him away.

I remember I kept thinking, *I'm an orphan*. I kept on and on thinking those words. But not in a moving, upsetting sort of way. It was more of a cold, logical revelation. *I'm an orphan*, I kept think-ing, and then trying to work out what that might mean.

Christophe took me to a horrible, cheap hotel and I lay there comatose for three days while he looked after Guillaume.

I don't know what they got up to, though, in a way, by deduc-tion, I can probably work it out. We didn't talk about it, but he must have gone looking for Johann, and then Leah and Matias. But he didn't tell me what he'd found out. I expect he realised that I wasn't strong enough to hear any more bad news. So without argument, he just let me stay there, staring at the ceiling. He didn't try to talk to me about his own pain, and I still think of that today, of that amazing sensitivity in not asking for anything and not trying to help me either; in not even attempting to talk to me, or make me listen, or think, or do, or express anything whatsoever. It was one of his finest moments. He really was an exceptional friend to me.

A few days later, and I'm pretty sure it was the morning of day three, I sat up and declared I wanted to go.

Christophe rolled over to face me – it was really early in the morning – and said, 'Oh, you're back with us, are you? Good.'

He asked if I wanted to leave the hotel or Mulhouse, and I replied that I wanted to leave both, and preferably the country as well.

'You want to go to London,' he said.

He reached into the drawer of the bedside table then, and pulled out a pile of letters and postcards and told me that I probably needed to read them first.

Sorry, these are letters sent by who? I'm confused.

He'd gone back to my parents' apartment for me and had spoken to the Polish woman's son. So this was all the post they'd found in the letterbox when they'd taken over the apartment.

Most of it was from me: the letters and postcards I'd sent to my parents. But there were letters addressed to me too – letters Ethel had posted from London. There were lots from 1940 and a few from 1941, and then hardly any from that point on, and they just got shorter and shorter as time went by. I tortured myself by reading through them all in order, from her early declarations of undying love until the final one, posted in 1943, which was painfully short and to the point. It said she didn't know if the war would ever end, and she didn't know if she'd ever see me again, but if I was receiving her letters I needed to know that she was well, that she was having to move around a lot, and if I wanted to contact her I should write to her care of her cousin Hannah. That letter was so cold, so business-like . . . I knew she couldn't be too expressive because of the censors, but all the same, it really upset me. It was a letter from someone who'd got bored writing letters to someone who had never replied. It was a letter from someone on the point of giving up.

Hadn't you written to her at all?

No, I had. And that was the problem. I had written to her from time to time, both at her parents' address and care of her cousin in London. So my letters clearly hadn't got through.

I read through all of Ethel's letters repeatedly, and I finally let myself weep for her, for my parents, for all of it. Christophe tried to comfort me for a while but then gave up and went out for the day with Guillaume – he simply let me get on with my grieving.

When he got back that evening, I told him I needed to visit Ethel's parents, and it was only when he told me they were gone – and the whole Jewish quarter was like a ghost town – that I realised I'd been lying on my bed for three days, and during that time I hadn't even thought to ask what Christophe might be going through.

So I asked him if his parents were OK, and he said that they were alive but not OK at all. He said they'd wanted nothing to do with him.

How could they not want anything to do with him?

I'm not sure if I told you, but they were devout Catholics. And of course, his arrest meant they'd found out he was gay. I believe they'd asked him if it was true that he was a sodomite, and that had so upset him – because it was the same word the Germans had used – that he'd told them that yes, he was. He never wanted to talk about it much, but from what I could gather, it was very much their opinion that he'd brought his bad luck upon himself.

Poor Pierre! After all that he'd been through as well!

That's funny. I kept calling him Pierre in Mulhouse, too. It was as if, as long as we were there, he'd gone back to his previous identity for me.

I asked about Johann next, but he hadn't been able to find anything out. No one had seen Johann since 1940. And then he started to cry as he reeled off a list of all these people we'd known, saying, 'Lala's missing, probably dead. Michel and Matias are dead.'

Matias, his policeman friend? The one who helped you?

Yes, he was one of the few where we were able to find out for sure what had happened. He'd been shot for conspiring with the resistance. I just prayed that it wasn't because of us, but I suppose we'll never know.

Johann's ex-boyfriend, Jean-Paul – the boy he was with before he dated Pierre – he was in prison. And that's one of the most shameful stories of all.

Prison? Why?

At the end of the war quite a few homosexuals were transferred from the concentration camps straight to prison. Most survivors were obviously freed, but often the ones with the pink triangles, the homosexuals, were transferred to prisons so they could finish serving their sentences.

I don't understand why?

For the simple reason that homosexuality was still illegal almost everywhere. Many courts even refused to consider the time these men had spent in the camps as counting against their sentences. So there were gay men, particularly in Germany, who'd been arrested in, say 1938, and sentenced to five years in prison. And if they were lucky enough to have survived until 1945 – and very few did manage to survive that long – but if they *had* made it until the liberation of the camps, they got transferred straight to prison so they could finish serving their time.

But that's outrageous! That's totally inhuman!

Yes. It is. And that's what happened to Johann's friend, Jean-Paul. He survived Schirmeck and Dachau, only to be arrested when they liberated the camps.

In fact, Jean-Paul was the person who was finally able to tell Christophe what had happened to Johann. Christophe went back for his father's funeral – in '53, I think it was – and he ran into Jean-Paul somewhere. Jean-Paul had been in Schirmeck with Johann, so he knew all the awful details.

And what had happened to Johann?

Are you sure you want to know this?

From the fact that you're asking, I'm guessing that I probably don't . . . But tell me anyway, just for the record.

He was eaten by dogs.

Christ . . .

Yes, he was mauled to death by German guard dogs.

You know, a terrible thing is happening. I'm getting to the point where these horrors don't even surprise me anymore, and that feels kind of tragic.

It's called compassion fatigue, dear, and it's both tragic and entirely normal.

Was Johann trying to escape from the camp or something?

No, they just set the dogs on him for no reason. Jean-Paul said that they'd stripped him naked and tied him to a post before setting the dogs on him. They did it in front of the whole camp, apparently, so Jean-Paul was forced, along with everyone else, to stand and watch. It was fairly common practice, I believe. They liked to do that kind of thing to the homosexuals in the camps. If you were a Nazi it was what passed for fun back then. They used them for target practice, too. They'd strip them naked and release them in the woods and have fun chasing them and shooting them dead. Plus the horrendous so-called experiments. The list is endless, really.

The medical experiments?

Yes, they were horrific. And there was nothing medical about them. They tested mustard gas and nerve gas on inmates and filmed them as they died in agony. They injected dyes into their eyes and did lobotomies and amputations without anaesthetics. They even sewed pairs of children, twins, together to make conjoined twins – what they used to call Siamese twins back then. How utterly obscene is that?

That is utterly, utterly disgusting.

I think it's what's so hard to get one's head around – the unbridled cruelty. I mean, even if they had been real experiments – which they weren't – and even if it had been justified to experiment on people against their will, or on children – which it totally, absolutely, wasn't – to choose to do it without anaesthetics on top of all the rest was just . . . evil is the only word I can think of, but it's really not up to the job. It's the stuff of horror films, only it wasn't a horror film, it was real. They starved people and froze them; they removed bones to see if they'd live or die. They smashed people's limbs with massive mechanical hammers, sterilised women and gave the men electric shocks until it killed them. But for the gay inmates, their speciality was attempting to cure them of their homosexuality. Specifically, there was a Danish doctor called Carl Værnet who went to Buchenwald camp, where the Nazis gave him free rein. His speciality was injecting hormones into the testicles of gay men or castrating them and inserting hormone implants under their skin. These were all supposedly attempts at finding a way to 'cure' them of their 'unnatural' desires. And do you know, at the end of the war Denmark helped that bastard escape to South America? In a way, I think people like Matias were the lucky ones. He apparently died in front of a firing squad. What they did to the people in the camps was quite literally hell on Earth. And then at the end of it all they would kill them anyway and perform autopsies. The twins, the gay men, the women, the children . . . there was never any mercy for anyone. They all suffered horrifically and then were killed. It's beyond imagination.

I'm sorry, but I feel a bit sick.

That's a good thing. That means you're a human being.

You know so much about this all. So much detail, I mean.

Well, how could I not? All three of us grasped at the tiniest smidgen of information, our whole lives. We always wanted to try to understand what might have happened to our families, our friends . . . But the more you find out, the worse it is. That kind of information never provides any kind of closure. So in a way, I can see why people don't want to talk about it. But the problem if you don't is that people forget, and if people forget then the whole thing can happen again.

So how . . . I mean . . . Someone like this Jean-Paul . . . How did he manage to survive? Do we know?

Yes, we do because he told Christophe. He survived by becoming a dolly-boy.

A dolly-boy?

Yes, he was good-looking and young, and he used it to his advantage to survive.

You mean he serviced the Germans?

Yes. He survived by having sex with one of the SS guys who ran the camp, as far as I can remember. Or it might have been one of the kapos. Either way, he did what was needed to stay alive.

The hypocrisy of that . . . The SS throwing them in camps because they were gay and then simultaneously abusing them sexually . . .

Yes. I know. But that's how Jean-Paul survived anyway. At least in body.

You mean that he lost his mind?

Lost it might be overstating things, but I know Christophe said that he was an utterly broken man.

How could he be anything but, after that? But we need to take a pause there. My cassette is about to run out.

Good. Because I think that after re-visiting Mulhouse, I could do with a cigarette break.

Ruth. Part Five.

By the time I had read to the end of cassette #3, my eyes were distinctly humid. That Genevieve's father had died saving them – that he'd died because he'd driven them to safety – was quite simply heartbreaking. And had he known, as Genevieve hinted, that he hadn't had enough fuel to get home? If so, then what a terrible choice he'd been faced with. And what a terrible sacrifice he had made.

I closed the laptop and went to the bathroom to sprinkle water on my face, before returning to the kitchen to make a cup of tea.

I had a sense of foreboding about tape #4. I'd been certain for a while that Genevieve and Ethel were no other than my grandmother and her supposed cousin. But what I wanted, what I needed, was for it to be stated explicitly. Because once it was stated, then perhaps I could find a way to discuss it with Dad to find out how much he actually knew.

Armed with a fresh cuppa and with Buggles by my side, I reopened the laptop to continue reading.

When Pierre and Genevieve morphed into Christophe and Genevieve Solomas, I'm pretty sure I gasped out loud. My name, my surname . . . finally, there it was in black and white. With the pilot's arrival, even Guillaume had become William and then Bill. It was all beyond doubt. Our entire family history had been faked, and the sadness, the trauma, the misery . . . these were ours. My grandparents had lived through these horrors and still somehow managed to bounce us up and down on their knees.

I had to pause to take in the enormity of what I was reading, so I stood and crossed to the window, where I stared unfocusedly out at the street. It was drizzling, so I watched the raindrops chasing each other down the pane. And then I crossed the room decisively and called Dan.

'It's me,' I said, then without further ado, 'Can you come over?'

'I'm kind of busy,' he said. 'How about tomorrow?'

'I . . . Look . . .' I said. 'If it's impossible then it's impossible. I understand.'

'It's not impossible,' Dan said. 'It's just—'

'Then please, just come. I've never asked you to come over immediately before, have I? So please, this once, just come.'

'Do you want to tell me what's happening?' Dan said. 'Because you're kind of freaking me out.'

'Don't freak out,' I said. 'There's no reason to. Not for you, anyway. Just get your arse over here, will you?'

'OK, OK,' Dan said. 'I'm on my way.'

While I waited, I finished cassette #4 and cried all over again as I read how my grandmother had learned of her parents' – my great-grandparents' – deaths. And poor Grandpa, losing lovely Johann, losing all of his friends . . . How could anyone live through that much sorrow? How could human beings do such things? How could other people have allowed such things to happen?

An hour later, Dan arrived, muttering something disparaging about the Circle line. I'd more or less patched my face up by then, but Dan told me I looked terrible all the same.

I made a fresh pot of coffee and then we sat down together at the dining table. This didn't seem to be the kind of story that could be told from the softness of a sofa.

Once I'd finished summarising what I'd read so far, Dan looked at me and blinked slowly while shaking his head, as if dazed.

'What do you—?'

'Hang on,' Dan said, interrupting me. 'Just . . . I'm trying to get my head around it all.' He circled one finger in the air.

I left him to think whatever he was thinking and made us sandwiches. On the kitchen worktop two submissions I was supposed to read caught my eye, something that clearly wasn't going to happen now.

I returned and plonked the plate down on the table. 'Thanks,' Dan said, grabbing a sandwich. 'I'm starving.'

'So what are your thoughts?' I asked. 'Because my mind is officially blown.'

Dan shrugged and shook his head slowly. He licked his lips and opened his mouth to speak twice, but said nothing.

Finally he closed his eyes and frowned for a bit before opening them and saying, 'So, just to get this clear . . . Because there were a lot of name changes in there.'

'There were,' I said. 'Fire away.'

'So Genevieve . . . Schmitt? Who's the one being interviewed, became Genevieve Poulain, and then Genevieve Solomas. Which just happens to be your grandmother's name.'

'It doesn't just happen to be . . . but . . . yes.'

'And Pierre . . . Meyer? Right? He becomes Pierre Poulain, and then Pierre, sorry, Christopher Solomas. Who's your grandfather.'

'It's Christophe, not Christopher, but otherwise a perfect rendition.'

'And Ethel Lambert, who was supposedly your grandmother's cousin, was in fact her girlfriend/life partner/whatever. Which means that your grandfather was gay, and your grandmother was gay, and your father . . .'

'Was adopted.'

'Yeah,' Dan said, then, nodding exaggeratedly, 'And Jewish, right?'

'Yep.'

'What was his name again? His birth name, I mean?'

'Menashe.'

'And did you say Rosenberg?'

'Rosenberg would have been his mother, Leah's, maiden name. I don't think she mentions the father's name but I'll have to re-read it to check. Or it could be in one of the later cassettes I haven't received yet.'

Dan took a bite of his sandwich then, and I saw he was stifling a thoroughly inappropriate smile.

'What?' I asked, feeling a bit dismayed.

'Sorry,' Dan said, speaking through crumbs. 'There's so much tragedy in there, I feel terrible. It's just . . .'

'Just what, Dan?'

'It's just your dad,' he said. 'I'm trying to imagine . . . Can you? Imagine?'

'His reaction, you mean? When he finds out he's Jewish?'

'Well, yeah!'

'You're assuming he doesn't know then?'

'Aren't you?' Dan asked.

I shrugged. 'Can he *not* know something like this? I just don't see it.'

'Sure. But then again, if he knew, could he still say the things he says?'

'Well, quite,' I said. 'Either way, it's crazy.'

Dan's smile faded. He exhaled and wrinkled his nose. 'Isn't it though?' he said. 'Isn't it just a bit *too* crazy?'

'You think it might not be true?'

Dan shrugged.

'There's a lot of detail in there,' I pointed out. 'And it all seems pretty accurate. The stuff about Alsace and everything . . .'

'I wouldn't know,' Dan said. 'Did you learn this stuff at school, then? Because I don't think we did.'

I shook my head. 'But I've read a lot of historical fiction. I have to.'

'Yeah,' Dan said, then, with meaning, '*Fiction.*'

'Do you really think that?'

He shook his head vaguely. 'I don't know. I mean, just . . . maybe do a search for it on the worldwide web before you say anything to your dad. See if there are records of any of this . . . check she didn't copy it all from some book.'

'From a novel, you mean? You think she could have just lifted the whole story from somewhere else and changed the names?'

'Or maybe she was mad. We just don't know her that well, do we? She could have been, like, really *nasty*, or something. Or so offended by your dad's anti-Semitism she decided to fuck with his head.'

'It crossed my mind that it could have been a sort of fantasy. But—'

'Yes, you see. That's what I mean. It's not necessarily absolute truth.'

'But I don't think so. It's pretty convincing.'

'I still think you should check.'

'Yeah,' I said, thoughtfully. 'The first thing would be to see if that magazine . . . *Gai Pied* or whatever – see if it really exists.'

'They might have published the interview if it's true,' Dan said. 'How long did you say it is?'

'Oh, it's massive. Way too long to be a magazine piece.'

'You see?' Dan said. 'That's dodgy.'

'Yes, I know. But if you'd read it, you'd see. It reads like an interview that's sort of turned into something else as they were doing it because she had so much to tell. And she says something about it being part of a series, so there will have been other interviews. Shorter ones.'

Dan nodded and pushed his lips out. 'OK. But definitely check the magazine exists before you tell your dad, that's all I'm saying. Maybe even speak to the journalist if she's around.'

'Now *that*,' I said, 'is an excellent idea.'

Dan checked his watch so I told him, 'It's OK, you can leave. I just needed to tell someone. Actually, that's not true. I needed to tell *you*.'

'It's fine,' Dan said, brushing the crumbs from his lips and standing. 'I'm flattered. But I really do have to go.'

'Oh, before you do,' I said. 'You know the flat next door? I think we should make an offer on it.'

Dan finished pulling on his coat and then froze. 'Where's this coming from?' he asked. 'You were all angsty about it after the visit.'

'I don't know, really,' I said. 'I'm just thinking that . . . well, we can afford it. And it would be big enough. And one day it could even be lovely. And I feel as if . . . I don't know . . . It seems like a sign, doesn't it? The flat coming free next door at a good price . . . And I feel like a spoilt kid, you know, sort of stamping my feet and saying, "No, mister universe. That's still not good enough."'

Dan raised one eyebrow, revealing that he thought I was being bizarre, which undoubtedly I was. But then he said, 'OK, whatever, I'll phone the bank and see. That's the first step, anyway. To see if they'll lend on that property.'

It was only after he'd left, as I sat staring at the rain running down the window, that the origin of my change of heart came to me. It had been seeded while I'd been reading about that tiny stone hut in the forest.

It had crossed my mind how spoilt we are, having never known war or suffering or even hunger. That's certainly the case for many of us in the West, at any rate, but we complain all the same. I'd imagined my grandparents living – hiding – in that freezing mountain hut with no bathroom and no electricity, and I'd thought, *Honestly what are we like?*

A new thought popped up then. If all of this was true, were Genny and Chris even my grandparents? And then another thought that required a quick call to Dan before he vanished into the depths of the Underground.

'Dan! If Dad was Jewish, would that mean Jake and I are too?'

'Hum,' Dan said. 'Not sure. But I think it goes by the mother. The phone's gonna cut out soon, by the way. I'm already in the train.'

'So if your mother's Jewish you're Jewish,' I said, speaking quickly, 'but if only your father's Jewish then you're not?'

'I think that's how it works,' Dan said. 'But—' And then the line cut out.

Cassette #5

ML: *Marie Lefebvre, interviewing Genevieve Schmitt, cassette number five, third day.*

We're doing well today, Genevieve!

GS: Yes. But I'm realising that we're still not going to finish, are we? Not even today! And I hope you're not spending too much on all these tapes?

Oh, they're only £2.99 for three. I buy them in multipacks at Woolworth's. But I may have to buy another set if you carry on chatting like this!

Aren't you concerned about how you're going to use all of this? Aren't you worried about the length? Because it's got to be much too long for your magazine, hasn't it?

Oh, I'm not even thinking about that anymore. I'm just enjoying the story. So we'll cross that bridge when we get to it. Oh, please don't think that I'm not going to use it. I'll definitely do something with it, even if it ends up being a much shorter piece. Even if I have to edit it down.

I'm not worried about that at all. Use it or don't use it . . . It's honestly all the same to me. As long as you're finding it interesting.

I am. It's incredibly interesting.

Good. So where were we?

Mulhouse, 1945.

Yes.

I was wondering . . . It's just that in Mulhouse you still had Guillaume with you . . . So I'm left wondering if you'd decided to keep him by then? I mean, clearly, you had. But at what point was the actual decision made?

I'm not sure there ever was a specific decision. Things were never that clear-cut. I was very torn about Guillaume the whole time. We both were.

If I'm honest, I'd have to say that I tried very hard to avoid thinking about all the reasons we might have to give him up. He was so very much my child by then – our child. He'd spent the first five years of his life with us. I'd breastfed him. We'd taught him to walk and talk and . . . I don't know . . . We'd toilet-trained him . . . everything, really. I loved him so much. That bond was incredibly powerful by the time we got back to Mulhouse.

So the idea of losing him was unthinkable. And yet, at the back of my mind, I knew it was still a possibility. I knew he wasn't mine, and that if we found Leah I'd almost certainly have no choice but to hand him over.

So how hard did you try to find Leah? Honestly.

<Laughs> Well, you've said it all really, haven't you? Not very hard. Not very hard at all. Because finding her, for me, would have been a disaster. Luckily Christophe's a much more moral person than I am, and he was far more diligent about looking for Leah than I would have been. He spent days searching high and low for any remaining members of Leah's family.

Does that mean you think he was less attached to Guillaume than you were?

No, I wouldn't say that at all. He loved him to bits. But in a way – and I'm sure he would admit this if you asked him – I don't think he saw Guillaume as quite such a permanent feature of his life as I did, if that makes sense. He was more rational, in that way that men so often are. He knew Guillaume wasn't ours. I don't think he ever let himself forget that. And I wasn't ever planning for it to be permanent either. In my case it was simply that I'd come to a point where I couldn't imagine the future without him. Do you understand what I mean? When I pictured the future, any kind of future, Guillaume was in it.

But anyway, like I said, Christophe looked for Leah. He looked really hard. He asked everyone he could find in the Jewish quarter and not a single member of Leah's family had returned. I tried again to track her down much later, in '53, and—

Why? Sorry, but why in '53?

Oh, it was because Pierre's father died. Oh gosh, I've gone back to calling him Pierre again, haven't I? It's whenever I talk about Mulhouse. Anyway, he was really grief-stricken about his father's death. Despite everything that had happened between them, he was absolutely wiped out by it. And that made me think even more than usual about Leah, I suppose, and about her grief. It made me think about the fact that if she had survived the horror of the camps, then she needed to know her baby had survived too. I wasn't sure how, or when or even *if* I'd get in touch with her, but I did set things in motion by contacting the Red Cross and the Jewish Relief Unit and, eventually, they found them in the records. The Nazis kept very detailed records – shockingly detailed. Did you know they recorded how many grammes or calories or whatever of food they gave each prisoner? They wanted to work out the absolute minimum they could give them before they keeled over and died. Death was a shockingly scientific business for the Nazis. But anyway, the news was all horrific.

Because the whole family had died?

Yes. They'd all died in the camps – or rather had been murdered. I hate the way people say they died . . . It makes it sound like it was an accident, don't you think? But yes, they'd all been slaughtered by the Nazis except for Joshua, that's Leah's brother, but he was living in America. So I went from trying to find them to wanting to protect Guillaume from ever having to know about all that horror instead.

Did you struggle with that decision – the decision not to tell him? Did you never consider that he maybe had a right to know about his heritage?

Oh, definitely. We always imagined we'd tell him one day. Well, I did, anyway. It seemed obvious. As you say, he had a right to know. That's indisputable. But not at five. And not at ten, either. You can't tell a ten-year-old that their entire family ended up in the gas chambers. Nor a fifteen-year-old, for that matter. And then, by twenty, or thirty . . . I don't know . . . By the time they're old enough to perhaps understand, and old enough to potentially take that kind of shock, they're *too* old . . . the lie has been going on too long. It becomes almost impossible to say, 'Hey, I've been lying to you your whole life and you're not my son, and you're Jewish, and you're an orphan.' So it's a tough one. There's never a right moment for that sort of thing.

Of course. I can understand that perfectly. Going back to the decision to keep Guillaume, it sounds like it was pretty much taken in Mulhouse, when it was confirmed that Christophe couldn't find Leah?

Well, even then, we only knew we weren't going to find her at that moment. But we didn't know we would never find her. We didn't know that until 1953 or so. But in a way you're right. Because by the time we left Mulhouse I'd decided to at least try to keep him. That's why we had to return to Le Mas.

Oh, you went back there? I'd assumed the next stop was London?

Well, we were heading for London, ultimately. But in those days, in the provinces, it was the police who issued passports. So if we'd asked for them in Mulhouse—

You'd have had to request them under your real identities.

283

Exactly. And Guillaume wouldn't have been able to go on my passport either, because he was clearly not my son. So we had to request them in Le Mas, where no one knew who we really were. Or rather, where everyone knew us as the Solomas family.

Gosh. I see. And Christophe decided to come with you? I'm surprised by that.

Yes. It was a surprise for me too. But he was terribly upset by the way his parents had rejected him, and literally heartbroken by the disappearance of Johann and all of his other friends. He had nowhere to live in Mulhouse anymore, and no job either, because he'd worked in his father's business before. I wouldn't say he was particularly motivated by the idea of returning to Le Mas, and even less so of travelling to London. It was more the case that he felt at a loss to know what to do with his life, I think. So coming with me, with us . . . helping us do what *I* wanted . . . that provided him with some kind of purpose, albeit temporary. But he was surprisingly flippant about the whole thing. It was very much one of those 'What the hell/why not?' kind of decisions. I think the war had made everyone a little crazy and Christophe was no exception.

So you went back after all?

Yes. We had to. And the journey back to Le Mas that time was absolutely hellish. It had been pretty bad the first time, but this was just a nightmare.

The trains were all full again – the number of people criss-crossing the country was shocking – but one thing had changed and it made everything that much harder. That wartime solidarity of squeezing in to help others get onboard had vanished, and it was suddenly a case of every man for himself.

Why do you think that was?

You know, there was a lot of bad feeling after the war . . . Most people were grieving for someone, of course, but there were lots of other complex feelings too. People felt awful about the way their government – the Vichy government – had collaborated. The way they'd been ordered not to resist, and the way they'd obeyed that order. Others were ashamed about the fact that they'd had to be liberated by the Allies. Some hated their neighbours because they'd collaborated, and others neighbours who'd resisted . . . People resented family members who'd lost nothing, or they blamed someone else for the fact they'd lost everything . . . The country felt very fractured, very messed up, so perhaps that had something to do with it.

Whatever the cause, the end result was that for a while people weren't that nice to each other. And we missed multiple trains because we simply couldn't get in the door. Even when we tried to sleep on the same pile of railway sleepers we'd used five years earlier we got moved on by a grumpy station guard. The hotels we tried all seemed to be full, and so we spent that whole horrible night walking the streets of Lyon, sitting on benches, then being hassled and having to move on. Christophe almost got into a fight with a Lyon policeman at one point, and if I hadn't intervened I think they would have come to blows.

Anyway, the end result of all these delays was that we arrived in Sigale not early Saturday morning, as planned, but on Sunday. And that meant that the grocer couldn't take us to Le Mas because on Sundays he went in the opposite direction to sell his wares in a market in Roquestéron instead. There was no way we could walk there with Guillaume. It was about twenty kilometres to our place, as I recall.

By using little Guillaume to make the locals feel guilty, we at least found a bed for the night, and the next morning Christophe convinced a chap with horses to take us to Le Mas.

Twenty kilometres on horseback?

And I'd never ridden a horse before! Christophe convinced me it was easy – that all I had to do was sit down. As you'll know if you've ever ridden a horse, that's an absolute lie.

The roads down to Le Mas were rocky and steep and if you fell off there was generally a ravine below you'd fall into and die. So while Christophe and the owner of the horses shouted random instructions at me – none of which helped – I bounced around on my bloody pony, and by the time we somehow made it to Le Mas, I felt as if my buttocks had been definitively broken. As an aside, Guillaume, who travelled on Christophe's horse with him, absolutely loved the whole thing. Our five-year-old's superior horsemanship was something Christophe teased me about for years.

When we got to Le Mas, I refused to go any further. I'd almost fallen off on multiple occasions, and the track from the main village down to our hamlet was the steepest, most dangerous part of the journey. I was damned if I was doing it on a pony with a penchant for walking right along the edge. So despite Christophe's protests – and we did argue about that quite violently – we paid the horse chap there and then and finished the journey on foot.

On arriving at the house we got another surprise because we discovered that Lucienne had moved in – we could hear her daughter screaming as we walked up the footpath. She was in the middle of a proper floor-slapping five-year-old temper tantrum. But the cute thing was that the second we opened the front door and she saw Guillaume she stopped crying, got up, and ran to the door to hug him.

Lucienne was in the middle of cooking supper and was mortified to have been caught red-handed living in our house. Of course, in reality, it was no more ours than it was hers. We hadn't paid any rent since 1940, after all. But she didn't know that and we – needing somewhere to stay – weren't going to be the ones to tell her.

So in a flurry of tearful apologies, she threw a few things in a bag and then, promising to return the next day to clear out the rest, she rushed out the door, leaving her dinner still bubbling on the stove.

It turned out to be a delicious chicken stew that she'd made using the carrots and onions and potatoes that I myself had planted. It was only halfway through the meal that it dawned on me we were eating one of our own beloved chickens, and the next morning I understood that we'd in fact eaten the last of them. Still, at least we got a hot meal out of it.

I was in pain for days after that pony ride but even though I could barely move, it felt lovely to be back in the country. I think we were even happier to be back than we had been to leave.

The next morning we bathed in our river and relaxed on the grass in the sunshine, recovering slowly from the horror of Mulhouse and our journey from hell. We talked a lot, I remember, about how awful it was living there in winter. I suspect we were both afraid that we'd be lulled into staying on there if we didn't constantly remind ourselves of all the significant downsides.

During the week, Christophe hiked up to the village to talk to the mayor about getting passports. He wanted to check that requesting them wasn't going to result in our being thrown in prison for having faked our identities or something, but the mayor was able to reassure him that was unlikely.

Christophe told me that when they first laid eyes on each other, the mayor got all choked up. He assumed Christophe was back for his old job, and was so happy at the prospect that he cried! Once Christophe explained that we were only back to get passports, the mayor offered him his old job back anyway, but on a temporary basis, and because we needed as much money as we could for our trip, Christophe accepted. So that's what happened in the end. He went back to working for the mayor and that lasted right through to mid-September.

Mid-September? So you ended up staying for months?

Yes, that's how long it took to get passports in 1945.

But in September, just as it was getting cold and we were beginning to worry about winter, our passports arrived. We went up to the village one Saturday morning to buy food from the travelling grocer, and the mayor was there with our passports in his hand. He joked that he'd considered hanging on to them until Christophe had finished laying some pipes he was working on, and Christophe felt so guilty that he offered to stay until it was done. But the mayor had already found someone else for the job, I think, so we were finally able to leave.

You had to say your goodbyes all over again.

Yes. The only difference this time was that we told Lucienne she and her daughter could move back into the hut. I also told her the truth about how we'd rented the place from Jean-Noel for one year only, back in 1940. We didn't want her to get into trouble if he turned up one day with new renters, after all.

And do you know what? When we told her that, she laughed so much that she cried. Because it turned out the hut had nothing whatsoever to do with Jean-Noel. It had never belonged to him in the first place.

So who did it belong to?

To a previous mayor who'd moved away many years before. Lucienne had thought we'd rented it from him – that's what everyone had assumed. Apparently he'd been friends with Jean-Noel's father or something – I can't remember the details – but that was the only reason Jean-Noel even knew the place existed. No one had ever tried to live in the place, let alone rent it, because before Christophe had fixed everything, the place had been considered a ruin. He was known in the village, too – Jean-Noel, I mean. Everyone knew what a shady character he was. I haven't thought about him for years . . . I wonder what became of him? You do rub alongside so many people in a lifetime . . . so many different stories without endings . . .

I expect he's a millionaire now and owns some awful corporation or something.

Yes. I think you're probably right about that. I expect he probably does.

And next, you travelled to London?

Yes, we arrived on the 29th of September, 1945. It was a Saturday. I remember that, because the next day, everything was closed and—

Sorry to interrupt you, but how did you travel? Did you . . . I don't suppose you could fly in 1945, could you?

Oh, OK. No, we went on the train, or rather a whole string of trains. And no, I don't think you could fly back then. At any rate, if it was possible to fly from Cannes to London, it certainly wasn't for the likes of us. Cheap air travel didn't happen until the seventies, I don't think. The late seventies, even.

So yes, we travelled by train. I think it was Nice to Marseille, and then Marseille – Lyon, then Paris, where we stayed in a horrible hotel just opposite the Gare du Nord. I remember that because it had bed bugs and we all got bitten to death. It was ghastly.

And then the next morning, we went from Paris to Rouen, then Rouen – Dieppe, and finally we got a ferry from Dieppe to . . . Newhaven, perhaps?

I'm sorry, but I really wouldn't know.

It doesn't matter that much anyway. But I think that was it. Dieppe – Newhaven, and then more trains to London Victoria.

That all sounds utterly exhausting.

Oh, it was! But it was also incredibly exciting, and when you're excited you don't notice how tiring things are. It took four days altogether, I think, but the only bits I really remember are that awful hotel in Paris and the boat trip. Because that was one of the most wonderful things I'd ever experienced.

You'd never been on a ferry before?

No, never. Neither of us had. So seeing your country slip away and then shrink into the distance . . . then seeing another island appear on the horizon. Well, that was just so exciting I could barely contain myself. You have to realise just how exotic foreign travel was back then, before cheap flights and the EEC and all of that stuff . . . My heart was all of a flutter. Plus we were incredibly lucky, because it was a beautiful day. There wasn't a gust of breeze and the sea was like a mirror. So we stood on the deck in the sunshine for the entire trip. Guillaume loved it too.

Arriving in England was really scary because neither of us had ever been to a foreign country. Speaking English, explaining ourselves to the passport police, changing our francs for pounds . . . it was all pretty challenging.

And did you cope OK? Speaking English, I mean?

<Laughs> Just about. Barely, sometimes. Christophe kept pushing me forward so I had to do all the talking. And that was utterly ridiculous because his English was far better than mine. We'd found that out when the pilot was staying, so we knew his was better. But Christophe never wanted to say a word if he could avoid it, so he'd stand behind me whispering clues in my ear and pushing me forward – it always came down to me.

I'd forgotten you'd practised your English with the pilot.

Yes, but he was American, not English. And from Georgia, to boot. So he'd spoken much more slowly than the English did. They all had these terribly clipped accents in the forties, and they seemed to speak at a rate of about a thousand words a minute. Especially once we got to London, where everyone seemed in a permanent hurry.

People were helpful, don't get me wrong. It's just that they wanted to be helpful in the fastest, most efficient way possible. But we found people to help us change money and buy tickets. People pointed us to the right platform and told us when to get off. And so, somehow, we made it to London.

We arrived at Victoria Station, and the first thing we saw when we stepped outside was a pub. I think it was called the George's Arms or something. It was one of those very standard pub names. Anyway, it had a sign in the window that said 'Food/Drink/Rooms/ Entertainment'.

By that point I was starving hungry, we were utterly exhausted, and Guillaume had started to cry. So I pointed at the sign and nudged Christophe, and he laughed and said, 'All four in one place! OK! But only if it's not too expensive. Otherwise we look further afield.' And we were lucky because it wasn't expensive at all.

Was this hotel better than the one in Paris?

Thankfully, it was. It was basic but clean and comfortable. And above all, no bed bugs.

We ate our first ever English meal in the pub downstairs. It was so exotic to us . . . it's funny really.

Do you remember what you ate?

Absolutely, I do! It was sausage and mash with gravy. The gravy surprised us a bit. We'd never seen mashed potato swimming in that strange brown sauce before. But we hadn't known what to order and a man at the bar was eating sausage and mash so I'd pointed and said we'd have two of those. Christophe asked the barman for a 'good English beer' and he served the poor thing a pint of bitter.

Is that bad? I'm not much of a beer drinker, myself.

It was bad for Christophe. Turned out he hated it. But he forced himself to drink it because he was afraid of offending the barman. I didn't realise until later on why he worried about that so much.

We had to leave the pub-restaurant bit by six thirty, and as far as I can remember that was because we had Guillaume with us. So we found ourselves in our little room pretty early that evening. We talked a bit about how we were going to tackle looking for Ethel the next day, and then Christophe surprised me by declaring that he was going to pop back downstairs and have another pint of horrible beer with the handsome barman. That really shocked me.

Sorry, what shocked you?

Well, Christophe hadn't said anything like that since Mulhouse in 1940. He hadn't once mentioned finding someone attractive since he'd been tortured by the Germans. Obviously, I'd noticed that he'd liked Sam, but he'd never said anything to me about it. So I was really shocked and, surprisingly, a bit upset.

I'm sorry, but I'm not getting this. Can you explain why you were upset?

Oh, it's perfectly normal you're not getting it, dear. I'm not even sure that I understand, to tell the truth. Because you're right, there's no reason that should have shocked me at all because, before the war, he'd been incredibly cheeky. He was always commenting on men's bums or muscles or whatever. He had quite a thing for moustaches at one point and could barely walk past a man with a moustache without saying, 'I'd kiss him until he suffocated,' or some such. He was very, very naughty.

But since Mulhouse, since 1940, he had never mentioned finding any man attractive. And then suddenly, we were in London, and the old Christophe was back. And the thing was, the thing that I didn't want to admit to myself, was that it made me feel jealous!

Jealous? Oh! I see.

Yes, shocking, isn't it? We'd been pretending to be this married couple with a child for so long that it was almost as if I'd convinced myself it was true!

But you still weren't attracted to him? You weren't in love with him?

Attracted? Absolutely not. As for 'being in love' with him, that's more complicated. It's just that I knew him so well by then. I knew his moods and his foibles and his weaknesses. I was so used to spending time with him – so used to *depending* on him, as well. We were linked in a way by Guillaume, too. It truly felt as if he was our son. And then suddenly here was Christophe talking about men, and I had to remind myself that my relationship with him was temporary and tenuous – in a nutshell, that he wasn't 'mine' at all. And that made me think about Ethel and how much was riding on the fact of whether she was still waiting for me or whether she'd met someone new.

So while Christophe went down for his drink with the sexy barman, I lay next to Guillaume and tried to work out all my mixed-up feelings.

And how did it go for Christophe?

Oh, I don't know. I fell asleep pretty quickly and he never mentioned it the next morning. But I don't suppose anything happened. I expect he was just your typical flirty barman.

OK. And what was your plan? To find Ethel, I mean?

Well, the plan A was to visit her cousin Hannah. That was the only address we had in London, after all. But I was scared she'd refuse to help me find her.

Did you have any specific reason for thinking she might refuse?

Yes. Ethel had told me they'd fallen out, remember? In one of the last letters I'd got from her before we fled Mulhouse, she said she'd told Hannah the truth about us and that she was probably going to have to move on. In the subsequent letters I'd picked up from home she'd said she was having to move about constantly and that I should write care of Hannah, but I *had* written a few times, and she didn't seem to have ever received my letters. So I suspected that Hannah wasn't exactly on our side.

And how did it go? Did you find Hannah?

The whole thing was pretty awful. We went out there by bus, to Golders Green. We were too scared to use the Underground at first – for months, actually. We didn't understand how it worked and without landmarks it was hard to work out where you were. But there was a bus that was almost direct and the bus journey was wonderful. I'd forgotten about that. It was a double-decker, which for us was quite the novelty, so we sat on the top floor, looking out over London. It was thick with cigarette smoke up there, but we loved it. Guillaume was thrilled too.

When we got to the address, it turned out to be a mansion – a huge place surrounded by a lovely garden. In London. Imagine! A maid answered the door, and I mean a proper maid in a uniform. She led us into the drawing room, and because Hannah no longer lived there – she'd got married in the meantime, I think – she got Hannah's dad to talk to us instead.

Now, Hannah's father was an orthodox Jew with the beard and the payots and everything—

Payots?

Yes, those braids they have dangling down. He was unfriendly from the start, and before he would even talk about giving us Hannah's new address, he demanded to know how we knew her.

Christophe explained that we were friends and we'd shown Ethel around Mulhouse during her stay, and from that he deduced the entire story almost instantly. He pointed at me and said I was Ethel's something-or-other, and then at Christophe and said that he was something else. I didn't understand the words he used for either of us, but I suspected they were some kind of insult, in English or perhaps even Hebrew. From the curl of his lip you could definitely tell they weren't compliments anyway. And then he began staring at Guillaume, who'd been sitting there good as gold, and demanding to know where he came from. He started looking back and forth between our faces as if mentally comparing us with Guillaume, and I became overcome with fear that he was in the process of working out that Guillaume was Jewish and wasn't our child at all. I got panicky that he was going to try to take him from us because of some special Jewish law I didn't know about.

Those things were impossible though, right?

What things, dear?

Spotting that Guillaume was Jewish. Or taking him away from you, for that matter.

Oh, my fears weren't rational at all. But they were very real to me all the same.

So what did you do?

Well, we just left. We left as fast as we could. And we never went back there.

That must have been so disappointing.

It would have been. Only, just as we rounded the corner at the bottom of the road, the maid from the house caught up with us. She'd been eavesdropping on the conversation, I think, and had felt sorry for us.

She didn't know Hannah's address, and said she'd only started recently and so had never met Ethel either. But then she asked us something important, something amazing: she asked if we knew Ethel's American friend.

Her American friend?

Yes. She said a handsome GI had come looking for Ethel and Hannah's father had given him an address. She didn't know if that was Hannah's address or if he perhaps knew where Ethel was living, but Hannah's father had definitely given him a piece of paper with something written on it.

Am I right in thinking this is Sam?

Yes! We couldn't be sure of that, but I assumed it was him as well. I was so happy then that I burst into tears. Because I'd given Sam a letter for Ethel, and it seemed he'd tried to deliver it by hand. And presumably because he was a man, and American, and no doubt in part because he was Jewish as well, they'd not turned him away as they had us.

OK. But I suspect I'm missing something here. I get that you'd given him a letter, but I don't see how that helps you find her. Because even if Ethel got it, there's still no way for you to find each other, is there? Not with you staying in a hotel in Victoria.

Ah, well! That would be because I haven't told you yet what I wrote in my letter. Because luckily – thanks to Sam – I'd written something really, really clever.

Sam helped you write the letter?

Not as such. But he helped me think about what to put. I hadn't told him Ethel was my girlfriend, though I suspect that despite Christophe and the baby being around, he had his suspicions . . . Instead I'd told him she was my best childhood friend and that I planned to join her in London after the war. I'd told him that Hannah didn't like me much, and I was worried she'd not been forwarding my letters.

The first draft had said merely that Ethel should write to my parents with her address and I'd come and find her, but when I'd explained this to Sam, he'd pointed out that it was likely she'd return home to find her own parents, and even if she didn't, everyone was moving around all the time because of the war, so any address she gave me might not turn out to be permanent. He asked – with terrifying clairvoyance – how I could even be sure my own parents would still be at the same address by the time the war finally ended – or that my own address even still existed. I suppose he must have known how heavily Mulhouse had been bombed.

So even though it was impossible for me to imagine they might be anywhere else – let alone imagine the horror of what *had* happened to them – I'd redrafted the letter, saying that I'd look for her first in Mulhouse, and that if she wasn't going to be there she should write to me care of my parents and send me her address anytime she moved, so that I could join her in London wherever she was. I added that if for any reason I didn't find her in Mulhouse, and the address she'd given me didn't work – because my letters weren't getting through or she suddenly had to move – then I'd meet her at a landmark on the first Sunday of the month after the war had ended.

I added that if I hadn't tracked her down by the first Christmas after the end of the war, then I'd meet her back in Mulhouse, outside the boathouse, or if that no longer existed, down by the canal where we'd first kissed.

Gosh, you really covered all the bases, didn't you?

Yes, thank God! And that was largely thanks to Sam, who kept pointing out all the things that might go wrong with what I suppose you might call military precision.

You mentioned a landmark. Which one did you choose?

Speakers' Corner. That was Sam's idea. At first he'd said to put Big Ben, but he was worried that it might get bombed, and that it represented too big an area in which to meet someone, so I changed it to Speakers' Corner instead. The final version said that if I didn't find her in Mulhouse, and I hadn't received an address, I'd go there – to Speakers' Corner – at twelve o'clock exactly, on the first Sunday of the first month I could get there.

But how would she know which month that was?

Well, she couldn't know, could she? *We* didn't know that it would take so long to get there. So I just hoped she'd be motivated enough to go there repeatedly, once a month.

But you're right. It was a lot to ask. I'd never expected getting passports to take so long. And there were so many other things that could go wrong: had Sam even found her? Was she still there or had she been travelling home at the same time we'd been travelling to London – had our paths crossed, so to speak? And even if she was there, was she even able to get to Speakers' Corner? What if she had a job waitressing or something, and had to work on Sundays? So I was more than aware how unlikely it was. But I couldn't help hoping all the same.

But the fact that Sam had been to Hannah's father's house . . .

Yes. That at least shifted things into the realms of possibility.

So come on, tell me. What happened?

Well, the first Sunday of October was a week away, so the most urgent thing was to find somewhere cheaper to stay. Christophe found a boarding house in Vauxhall that was half the price, including half board, so we moved there.

Half board?

Yes. Breakfast and the evening meal were included. Breakfast was only a cup of weak tea and a slice of toast with either butter or jam and dinner was always pretty awful, but it was something, at least.

That boarding house was run by a dreadfully authoritarian woman, and she had rules about absolutely everything. There was this huge list pinned up in the porch, a list of all the dos and don'ts. It said things like do keep your room immaculate, and do behave politely to other guests, and don't play the radio so loud it can be heard outside your door, and don't congregate in communal areas . . . There were so many things on that list . . . hundreds . . . and I remember Christophe saying that no human being could possibly remember them all.

But the houses two doors down had been bombed to rubble by the Germans – there were bombed-out houses everywhere because of the Blitz – so it was cheap.

But tell me what happened at Speakers' Corner. I'm dying to know!

<Laughs> I will, don't worry. But there's one more thing that happened first. An important thing.

OK. Go on.

One night, after I got Guillaume to sleep, Christophe asked if I minded if he went out for a walk. I said I didn't mind at all, but if he did so, the next night it would be my turn. There was so much to see in London, and it was pretty claustrophobic in that room.

Just after eleven, I was woken by a tapping noise on the window. He'd had to climb up the drainpipe because one of the many rules on that list we hadn't read was that guests had to be in by ten thirty, after which the door would be locked, and not opened under any circumstances.

Gosh, that is strict.

So I got up and helped him climb in the window, and I could see immediately that he was terribly excited.

It turned out he'd stopped at the first pub he'd come to – a place called the Royal Vauxhall Tavern – and at first, because there were so many soldiers there, he'd assumed he was in a military pub. He'd been 'enjoying the view', as he liked to call it, sitting in the corner, watching all the young soldiers chatting to each other, when suddenly, they'd turned a spotlight on the stage, and a drag queen had appeared. Can you believe that?

<Laughs> Are you saying that he'd stumbled upon a gay pub?

Yes! Isn't that the funniest thing? And in 1945, I suspect it was the only gay pub in London.

Yes, I can understand why he was excited.

Especially because, unlike in Paris, say, homosexuality had been illegal in Britain since the 1500s. So to just stumble on a place like that . . . The next night . . . Actually, let's see if you can guess what happened the next night.

Um, it was your turn to visit the pub?

<Laughs> No! Try again. Let's see how well you know your gay men.

Ah! Christophe wanted to go back again, even though it was his turn to babysit?

Yes.

And you let him.

Yes, I did. We'd been through so much misery, you know? So just to see him looking happy, like that . . . Plus, if I'm telling the truth, going out didn't appeal that much to me.

Why didn't it appeal?

Well, for one, I was still grieving for my parents. And if anything excited me it was the idea of finding Ethel the following Sunday. So the proposition of a night out didn't really do much for me at all.

But Christophe loved it – he went back every night that week. He'd get home just minutes before the landlady locked the door and he always had a smile on his face.

Did he tell you what he got up to?

No, and I didn't ask. I could guess, anyway. I knew the kind of shenanigans that made Christophe grin that way.

On the third or fourth night, he slipped into his bed beside me and said, 'Christ, I love London!' And I realised that if I was going to lose Christophe at some point in the future it would be because I had to go home, rather than him wanting to return to Mulhouse. And so I prayed that Ethel was still in London, so I could find a way to keep them both.

On the Sunday, we left the house early so we had time to find Speakers' Corner. As we crossed the hallway the landlady came out and said something about how she was happy to see we were good God-fearing citizens.

She assumed you were on your way to Mass?

Yes. Christophe said, 'Just imagine if she knew what sinners we are!' and we giggled about it all the way.

We got to Hyde Park ridiculously early. We didn't know our way around London at all, and we had no idea how long anything would ever take, but it only took about half an hour to walk there so we did laps around Hyde Park with Guillaume. There were still piles of sandbags where the anti-aircraft guns had been, and the wartime allotments they'd created were still there too, so we spent some time identifying the various vegetables people were growing.

There was a pond, too, so we watched a family feeding the ducks, and then Guillaume started to run around with a little boy and in the end they played together at the water's edge for almost an hour even though they couldn't communicate at all.

I'm telling you this because Christophe said something that stuck with me. He said how it was funny because if you put three children together – one English, one French and one German – they'll simply play together. 'I wonder what happens when they're older,' he said. 'I wonder why they all end up killing each other?'

I suggested that it was precisely because they couldn't communicate with each other that they got on. I said it was hard to argue, or start a war, if you can't even speak each other's languages. But Christophe said he thought it was the opposite. He said he thought that wars happened because people from different countries didn't mix and communicate enough. But it's true, isn't it? That thing about kids and how they'll just play together. It's like society teaches them to be nasty at some point.

Hum. You say that, but the other kids were pretty horrible to me at school.

Ha! Touché. That's true, too. Children can be cruel little buggers.

But please, can we get to Speakers' Corner? I'm dying of anticipation here!

Sorry, yes, I'm getting sidetracked. So we went, and Ethel wasn't there.

Oh no. I'm so disappointed!

So was I, as you can imagine.

There was a man with a strong accent – Russian, or something like that – ranting on about Winston's Iron Curtain, and because of our poor English and his strong accent, we could barely understand a word he was saying. Certainly we had no idea what he was talking about when he said 'Iron Curtain'. That wasn't a phrase either of us had ever heard before.

But he shouted on and on about it, and people wandered up, listened for a while, and then drifted off. Someone shouted that he was a 'bloody communist', and someone else told the heckler to shut up. Because that's what Speakers' Corner turned out to be – a simple street corner where anyone was allowed to say anything.

We must have got there about a quarter to twelve, and we listened to his incomprehensible ranting until after one, at which point Christophe and I started to argue – me, of course, wanting to stay, and him wanting to leave. Ethel wasn't there, he said, which was indisputable, and Guillaume was hungry and getting irritable. He said we'd find a way to earn some money and return there the following month, but I was scared that if we left that wouldn't happen, and certain that if I took the decision to walk away, I'd burst into tears. So I just hung on and on.

Finally the Iron Curtain man got off his soapbox – and it literally was a soapbox in those days, it said Lifebuoy on the side – and a Frenchman replaced him, so I lied and told Christophe that I wanted to hear what our fellow countryman had to say.

He started by telling us that he wanted to talk about the Jewish Question, and because of his French accent he was much easier for me to understand. He claimed the Allies had known about the gas chambers but hadn't done anything, and people drifted away until hardly anyone remained. At that point, the man beckoned us forward. He was a bit scary, really, with a wild, unkempt beard and crazed blue eyes, but he was very insistent so in the end we sheepishly obeyed and moved forward.

Christophe started to argue with me again, saying it was time to leave and that Ethel wasn't here, and if I didn't make a move he'd leave me there and I'd just have to find my way back on my own. When he paused for breath we realised that the Frenchman had stopped speaking too and was staring at us intently. I assumed it was because we'd been talking during his speech and so I apologised to him, quite naturally speaking in French.

He frowned at me, and then at Christophe, and then at Guillaume, and then finally back at me before saying, 'You're not Genevieve, are you?'

I nodded that I was, and he asked, 'Genevieve from Mulhouse?' and I nodded again, wondering how he knew me.

'She said you'd be alone,' he said, still speaking French. 'I'm sorry, but she said you'd be alone. That's why I didn't recognise you.'

He pulled a folded slip of paper from his pocket, then, and held it out so that I could take it. And before it had even reached my fingers, tears started to well up, because I knew, finally, that I had found her.

The address on the paper was in Islington – not that either of us had any idea where that was. Personally, I didn't even know it was in London.

So I interrupted the poor Frenchman, who by then had resumed his speech, to ask how far away it was. He shrugged and told me that he didn't know. I asked how he knew Ethel, and he said he didn't.

Christophe tried to lead me away at that point, but I shook him off, telling him I didn't want to go and find somewhere to eat, that I wanted to go to the address on the bit of paper I was waving around, right then.

He very reasonably tried to point out that we didn't know where that was, and we didn't know how to get there. He explained it was likely that it was either a long way away, or Ethel was out somewhere working, because otherwise she would simply have come to Speakers' Corner herself. He said we should go and find something to eat, and then make a proper plan about how and when we'd travel to Islington.

But I was too excited. I *couldn't* calm down. So I interrupted our Frenchman again to ask him why Ethel hadn't come: was it because Islington was a long way away, or was it because she was at work?

Clearly annoyed, he shouted that he didn't know where Ethel worked or when she worked or even *why* she worked and he didn't know what size shoes she wore either, so now would I please shut up and let him speak.

It was a thoroughly deserved telling-off, and I knew it. Especially because the subject of his speech – firing squads and gas chambers – was far from frivolous. So I blushed and apologised to him and the few people who had gathered to listen, and finally let Christophe drag me off to a workmen's café for egg on toast. The owner kindly let us consult his *A-Z*, and we were relieved to see that Islington was no more than a few miles away.

Christophe tried to get me to temper my excitement by pointing out that we didn't know how old the tatty scrap of paper was; we didn't know if Ethel still lived there, or even if she had ever lived there. It was perhaps, he said, just a forwarding address.

He started to add something else then, but I interrupted him. I knew exactly what he was going to say – it was entirely possible Ethel had met someone new in the five years since we'd last seen her – but I didn't let him finish. I was as excited as I'd ever felt, and that excitement felt wonderful. I didn't want to temper my hopes, I wanted to revel in them.

I hurried Christophe and Guillaume through their meals and then nagged them to walk faster once we were outside. But it was all quite pointless because when we found the place an hour later, there was nobody home anyway.

The address was a bit of a shock. I'd expected some kind of run-down boarding house like our own, but it was a splendid Georgian town house. There was a small green opposite, half of which had also been turned into allotments, and so we crossed the road and sat on a bench while we waited.

I remember asking Christophe if he thought we had the right place, and he said we definitely had, but he agreed Ethel almost certainly didn't live there. 'Unless she's married some nice Jewish doctor,' he said jokingly, and for a few seconds I was so angry with him for even suggesting such a thing that I couldn't speak.

After an hour or so, Christophe wanted to leave. He'd walked Guillaume around the green at least ten times by then and he'd had enough. We could come back later, he said.

But I was physically unable to leave the spot, and he laughed and said he could understand why, so we waited, turning our heads right and left every time someone entered the street from either side. Christophe joked that we looked like we were watching a tennis match.

Eventually an elderly woman with a kind face stopped outside number twenty-three and climbed the steps, so I jumped to my feet and ran across the road to question her. She was visiting someone called Irene at the same address who wasn't home yet either. So I invited her to join us on our bench.

She shook hands with Christophe and introduced herself as Joan. Then she ruffled Guillaume's hair and asked me if we were Quakers too.

To my shame, I didn't know what the word even meant, so I replied that no, we were French, and felt embarrassed when she laughed in a way that made me realise I'd probably said something silly.

'But your friend,' she said slowly, so that we could understand. 'She's a Quaker, yes?'

I looked at Christophe, who shrugged, and so she explained that it was a religion. 'I just assumed,' she said, 'because she seems to be staying with John and Irene.'

I managed to express that I doubted Ethel was a Quaker, but after five years anything was possible, and so she asked, 'Oh! She's not one of Irene's Jewish girls, is she?'

Irene arrived just then, cycling up the street on a pushbike, and so Joan introduced us all and explained to her that we were looking for Ethel, so Irene invited us all indoors to wait.

She was a middle-aged woman with short grey hair and one of those serene smiles that makes you feel instantly at ease, so we followed her into the house and perched on her sofa while she made tea.

I managed to tell her that we'd lost touch with Ethel during the war, and didn't really understand her situation, and so she explained, as we supped our cups of tea, that Ethel was a lodger. She had a number of Jewish girls staying but Ethel was the most recent. She was a lovely girl, she said, and we agreed that indeed she was.

She wanted to know how we'd fared during the war in France, so I did my best to explain, but it was all terribly stilted. I was much too excited about Ethel's imminent arrival – too busy listening for the door really – to concentrate on speaking English, and Christophe, as ever, was too embarrassed to help out.

Eventually footsteps approached and the front door opened, but Irene winked at me and shook her head and said, 'Not yet.' A young man peeped around the door, said 'Hello' in a very casual manner, and then ran upstairs.

It was unbearable, sitting in that lounge, waiting, and I started to realise that I'd been better off waiting outside. Not only would I have seen Ethel enter the street, and thus gained a few extra seconds with her, but I'd be able to lose myself in that precious moment without having to think about the fact that we were being watched by strangers.

I was trying to think how to say politely that we would prefer to return to our bench when I heard fresh footsteps approaching and the sound of keys jangling. This time Irene stopped speaking and smiled at me wide-eyed. 'Now, *that's* Ethel,' she said. 'She gets the keys mixed up so I can always tell when it's her.'

My eyes started to water then – the tension of the moment was unbearable – and Irene looked at me quite intensely and I saw her understand that the moment was not without significance. 'Go!' she said, smiling. 'I can see how eager you are. Go! Open the door for her before she changes her mind and goes somewhere else!' And so I jumped up and ran to the hallway.

By the time I got there she was closing the door behind her and fumbling with the clasp of her handbag. She looked so different that for a moment I thought it was another lodger – that Irene had made a mistake. Her hair was the shortest I'd ever seen it and she was wearing a skirt and a tweed jacket. Because she was fiddling with her bag, her hair had fallen forwards, too, so I couldn't see her features at all.

But then she straightened, shook her hair from her eyes, and looked straight at me.

She didn't say a single word, she just gasped. I suspect our mouths fell open, and for a few long seconds we just stood there at opposite ends of the hallway, staring at each other.

Finally she managed to say my name, but when I tried to reply, when I tried to say the word 'Ethel', nothing came out.

She bit her bottom lip for a moment and then said, 'My God! It's you!'

We met in the middle of the hallway and hugged rigidly, and then she held me at arm's length so she could look at me better. She started to say how she couldn't believe that I'd found her, but something behind me distracted her and I turned to see Christophe standing in the doorway, his hands on Guillaume's shoulders. 'God,' she gasped. 'Pierre!'

'It's Christophe now,' he said, winking at her. 'I changed my name.'

Ethel shot me a puzzled glance and then kissed Christophe on the cheek before crouching down so that she was at Guillaume's level. 'Hello, little man,' she said, then, glancing between Christophe and me, 'Is he yours?'

Christophe started to answer, but I beat him to it. 'Yes,' I said, forcefully, because Guillaume, after all, was listening. 'Yes, this is our wonderful baby boy, Guillaume.'

Ethel straightened then and said, rather coldly, I thought, that we clearly had some catching up to do. She leaned into the lounge to ask Irene if it was OK, and then we followed her to the top floor, where her tiny attic-room was located.

'I can't believe this,' she said repeatedly. 'I just can't believe that you're here.'

She sat Christophe, Guillaume and me on the bed and then positioned herself cross-legged opposite us as we started to attempt to catch up on the five missing years. There was so much to tell that we jumped back and forth as we tried to reorganise all the events into some kind of cohesive story. We told her about escaping from Alsace, and the winters in Le Mas, and Christophe's family rejecting him when we got back; the only subject we avoided really was Guillaume, because, of course, he was present.

But Ethel seemed to be elsewhere for much of the conversation and I was never sure if she was listening. It was bizarre. You know when someone ums and ahs in the wrong places? Well, she was doing that.

I tried to explain about my parents, but failed. It was still hard for me to say the words without breaking down. But as it turned out, I didn't need to. Ethel had been home already. She'd visited Christophe's parents just a week after we'd returned to Le Mas and she said they'd told her everything.

I asked her about her family, and she told us that her father was missing, presumed dead. He'd been shipped to Schirmeck and then Dachau, whereupon he'd vanished from view. By then, we all knew what that meant. Her sister and her sister's fiancé were missing, too, as were most of her aunts and uncles and cousins. In the end it turned out they'd all died in the camps, every single one of them.

God, she must have been heartbroken.

She was devastated. It's the kind of trauma you never recover from. She's had a visceral hatred of Germans her whole life. I remember, once or twice, people have tried to reason with her about that. They'll say that the Germans of today aren't the Nazis of yesterday, but for much of our lives, of course, they were. Many of those responsible are alive and kicking right now in 1986. So it's hard and it never really gets easier. But at least her mother slipped through the net. She was alive and living in Mont-de-Marsan with a surviving aunt. 'She won't even discuss the fact that the others might be dead,' Ethel told us, shaking her head. 'Especially Dad. She just can't accept the possibility . . . But one day there'll be a piece of paper, I suppose, and then she'll have no choice. At that point we'll have to deal with it.'

'She's in denial,' Christophe said.

'Exactly,' Ethel agreed. 'But who can blame her? I'd quite like to be in denial about it myself, but I can't. I can sense it . . . that he's gone.'

After an hour or so, Irene knocked on the door and handed Ethel a plate of sandwiches and a jug of lemonade for us all, so once she'd gone, Ethel told us about her, too, and about all the other Quakers who had helped her.

I know Quakerism is a religion, but if I'm honest, I don't know much more than that.

Sure. Well, it's a branch of Christianity, really – Protestant. But I like to think of them as sort of real Christians in a way, if you know what I mean?

Real?

The way Christianity maybe ought to be, if you went right back to the source. There's none of the pomp or circumstance of Catholicism, for instance, about the Quakers. They don't have fancy churches or gilded altars. They believe in non-violence and helping others . . . And during the war, they did everything they could to help the Jews. But I'd never heard of them either until that day.

Is there a specific reason the Quakers helped the Jews? Is there some sort of link between the two religions?

No, not really. It was just their Christian desire to help others, I think. And perhaps for some it was a way to make up for the fact that, being non-violent, they couldn't fight. But they certainly did help thousands during the war. It all started with the Kindertransport in '38, when they began evacuating all those Jewish children from Germany. The Quakers convinced Britain to let them in, and organised transporting them and placing them once they arrived. There were over ten thousand of them, I think.

Later on they sorted out accommodation for adult refugees who'd managed to escape as well; they provided financial guarantees to convince the British government to let them stay on . . . No one really wanted Jewish refugees, not even Britain. There were so many of them and there was so much prejudice towards the Jews. But the Quakers basically did anything they could to convince people and house people and help. They were very, very involved.

And Quakers organised the Kindertransport? I didn't know that.

Not alone. There were British government officials involved, too. And all the Jewish organisations, obviously. But the Quakers were incredibly active. Groups of them even travelled to Nazi Germany to bring the kids away to safety.

And had Ethel converted? Had she become a Quaker?

No, by the time the war was over she was certainly friends with a lot of Quakers and I know she volunteered in the kitchens they ran and stuff like that. But no, she didn't convert. I think once she'd seen the horrors of war, she became a fully-fledged atheist. She used to say that if God existed, then he or she would have intervened. And if God *did* exist and had chosen not to do anything, that wasn't a God she could worship.

Yes, I can see how a person could feel that way.

Anyway, when Ethel's uncle kicked her out, a friend had advised her to ask the Quakers for help, and they'd been looking out for her ever since.

How exactly did they help her?

Well, with work, and housing . . . with all the paperwork that was required in order to stay . . . Those sorts of things.

So Ethel told us about all of that. She explained how the first Quaker house she'd stayed in had been bombed and she'd had to move repeatedly before ending up at Irene's. She told us about the air raids and hiding under the table during the Blitz and all the nights she'd spent in the bomb shelters and how terrifying it was emerging to all the firestorms and bombed-out buildings. She told us how she'd worked as a seamstress the entire time – how she'd sewn uniforms and parachutes, and she showed us the callouses on her hands to prove it.

But though it seemed like she was telling us everything, it still felt like she was holding something back. There was something missing from our reunion, and the more I thought about it, the more I suspected that Christophe was right, and that she'd probably met someone new. It felt like there was, you know, an elephant in the room, as the English say, that none of us were able to talk about.

At dusk, Christophe said he was going to take Guillaume back to the boarding house, and Ethel volunteered to walk with us. After a few hundred yards she tugged at my elbow to slow me down so we could speak privately, so I braced myself for the revelation I felt certain was about to come. I was almost in tears even before she started. But instead of telling me about her new love, she wanted to know more about me and Christophe. 'I don't understand,' she said. 'Explain it to me. Explain about you two.'

I frowned at this and even laughed a little, I think. It seemed so obvious to me that I couldn't possibly be with him that I couldn't believe that was what she meant. But she did. She really thought we were together.

'I couldn't believe it when his mother told me,' she said. 'I just couldn't believe that you were married . . . And married with a kid, as well.'

It was only then that I understood why our reunion had been felt so strained. She really hadn't been listening.

I told her more explicitly how we'd faked our marriage, and explained that Guillaume wasn't really our son – he was Leah's. Amazingly, Ethel wouldn't believe me at first, and that upset me a lot.

I told her how we'd done it all in order to stay alive, about Christophe being tortured and Leah leaving the baby with me. I explained how dangerous it had been to be people like us in occupied France and I saw that she was finally starting to doubt the story in her mind – the story that Christophe's parents had told her.

'So Guillaume's not yours, then?' she asked. 'Because Pierre's mother said . . . even you said that he was yours when you arrived.'

So I repeated again that obviously Guillaume wasn't ours, but Guillaume didn't know that, and I didn't want him to know it either. And I told her again how Christophe's parents had wanted nothing to do with him because he was what they termed 'a sodomite'.

'And you're saying the marriage isn't real?' she asked, and I got angry and shouted at her about the fact that I kept having to tell her the same things.

'OK, but do you love him?' she asked, finally. 'Because I've been watching you, and you look like you do.'

I laughed at that and told her that, yes, I loved Christophe, but more like a brother; I wasn't *in* love with him, because in case she hadn't noticed, I preferred girls.

My laughter upset her so I had to explain I wasn't laughing at her, just at the silly idea that I might be in love with a man.

'The only person I'm in love with is you,' I said, in the hope of breaking through. And that finally had some effect, because she stopped walking and turned away from me.

Once I'd circled back and lifted her chin so that she was facing me, I saw she was crying properly.

'But they said . . .' she told me. 'They said . . . His parents . . . they said you were . . . And I . . .' She was crying too much to finish her sentences.

I told her that I understood, but nothing they'd said had been true. That it had all been just to hide their shame.

'I've been waiting for you for so long,' she finally managed to say. 'The war went on for *so long*. And then I went back and they said that . . . They said all that . . . And I believed them . . . and I just felt so alone, so abandoned. Do you understand? And now . . .'

'And now I'm here,' I said.

I asked her why she thought I'd come all the way to London – who did she think I was there for, anyway? Why did she imagine we'd gone to all the trouble of getting passports and organising to meet with her at Speakers' Corner? And finally, through the tears, she managed a tiny hint of a smile. And for the first time that day, she looked like the Ethel I knew.

Ruth. Part Six.

It was Monday the 12th of April and I was downloading that week's workload via the landline when Dan called me on my mobile.

Impressionable had started accepting submissions via email, and these were now simply forwarded to me by Freida every Monday so that I could read them on my laptop. We were doing our bit to save the trees, and all that. Like a lot of Scandinavians, Freida was of an ecological bent.

Though the Monday morning download was now part of my weekly ritual, the process had become no more reliable. BT had been talking recently about introducing a sort of permanent, high-speed internet service, and I suddenly was able to see the point – that Monday my modem had already lost the connection repeatedly. But at least mobile reception in my street had improved dramatically that year, so I was able to chat while I downloaded.

'They accepted our offer,' Dan told me excitedly, the second I answered his call. The download bar on my laptop screen ticked up one notch to a tantalising ninety-nine per cent. 'So it's ours if we want it.'

'That's brilliant,' I said. 'Now we just need the bank to join in the fun.'

At that moment, the download bar vanished, and my list of fresh email was revealed. Three of these were entitled simply 'Submission' but the top entry was called 'Cassette #5'.

'The bank won't be a problem,' Dan said. 'They've already given me an agreement in principle.'

'Um,' I said. 'If you say so. I just never thought it would happen this fast.'

'But that's good, isn't it?' Dan said.

'Yes, I guess it is.'

'You don't sound very enthusiastic,' Dan complained, and I realised that he was right. I'd started reading cassette #5 and I hadn't sounded enthusiastic at all. We women like to think we're brilliant at multitasking, but in my case it's not true at all.

I slammed the laptop lid shut and sat up straight, the better to concentrate on the news from my beloved. 'Sorry, I got distracted,' I told him. 'But seriously, that's great news! What happens next?'

Once I'd convinced Dan that all was well – which took considerably longer than you might imagine – I returned to the next instalment, and quite literally devoured cassette #5.

It felt like reading a novel, but also levering open the heavy shutters that had been concealing my past. Because this was where I'd come from, after all. Here they were, finally, in London. Chris, Genny, Ethel and Guillaume/William/Bill. *This* was why I was a Londoner, then. This was how Dad had survived the war. Ultimately, this was the reason I existed.

I understood only in that moment the exact nature of the void I'd been living with. Because, yes, I had known that my father was French. By deduction, I'd known that he had travelled to London as a child, too. But in the absence of context, in the absence of the whens and the whys, none of that knowledge had ever made sense. It had all been meaningless, which was why my brain had pushed that knowledge aside. The subject had become blurry and vague – in fact, it had become taboo. But suddenly here it all was, here *I* was, roots and all.

Once I'd finished reading, I distractedly made myself lunch.

Even if the precise nature of my job was jumping from text to text, I knew I'd be unable to jump from what I'd just read into a dark murder mystery set in Amsterdam. So I ate slowly, thoughtfully, and then fed Buggles, before finally calling home.

Dad answered the phone. 'Hey,' he said. 'You just caught me. I only nipped home for some tools. Everything OK?'

'Yep,' I said. 'Yep, everything's fine. Our offer got accepted on the flat.'

'The one next door?'

'Yes.'

'That's great news,' Dad said. 'I'd better clear some space in my agenda. I'm pretty sure you'll be working me to the bone.'

'Yes, I'm sure I will,' I said. 'But Dad. Quick question: did you ever live in a stone hut somewhere in the South of France?'

'When I was a kid, you mean?' he asked. 'During the war?'

'Right,' I said. 'So you did. I thought someone had mentioned it. Maybe Grandpa Chris in one of his stories?'

'Probably,' Dad said. 'Why?'

'Oh, I just, um, had a weird dream. And it reminded me of that. But I wasn't sure.'

'I don't remember it really,' Dad said. 'I was too young. But they talked about it sometimes. So I remember snippets.'

'Yeah? Like what?'

'Oh, nothing really,' Dad said. 'Your grandpa liked to tell his stories, but he never said much about anything real.'

'OK. But you said they talked about it. What did they say?'

'It was just one of those little jokes they had,' Dad said. 'If ever someone complained about the cold, they'd laugh and say, "This isn't cold. That hut in Le Mas was cold."'

'Le Mas?' I repeated. When details tied up, it still had the capacity to shock me.

'It's the village where we stayed during the war. It was freezing cold, apparently. In the Alps, I think.'

'Right,' I said. 'Well, I'm sure that's why I had that dream. He must have told me a story.'

Afterwards, I attempted to work. I was behind with my reading, and I really did need to get on with it all but, still unable to concentrate, I moved to the sofa and gave in to cuddling Buggles instead, while I thought about freezing huts and name changes and journeys to London.

Did I have enough detail to be one hundred per cent sure? And if I did, then was now the time to tell Dad? Or did I need that final cassette, just in case – as Dan had drunkenly suggested one evening – the final phrase was 'And then she woke up and realised it was all a dream.'?

About five, I gave up trying to work and phoned Jake to ask if we could meet. He didn't ask what it was about. I suspect he was too busy to care.

Instead he told me he was meeting Abby in The Grenadier at 6.30 and I could join them if I wanted. If I hadn't known my brother so well I would have taken umbrage at his snappy tone.

If you've never had the joy of visiting The Grenadier, it's a rather funny, lovely little pub tucked in the streets behind Wellington Arch. It is, to this day, a favourite of Jake's, because he works nearby and has a thing for their fish-finger sandwiches. Which is what they were both eating when I arrived at ten to seven.

'We gave up on you and started,' Jake said, wiping tartare sauce from his beard with a napkin. 'You're late. Again!'

'Yeah, sorry,' I told him. 'I got delayed.' I'd actually had a time-consuming discussion with Dan just before leaving about whether telling Jake was wise.

We kissed hello and then I went to the bar for a glass of wine before returning to sit opposite. I had my back to the room, which is something I hate, but as they were still eating it seemed rude to ask one of them to swap.

'You're not eating?' Jake asked.

'Maybe later,' I told him, glancing over my shoulder. 'It's a bit early for me.' The truth was that my stomach was queasy with nerves.

'How continental of you,' Jake jibed.

'So, I have something to tell you,' I said. 'Something pretty shocking.'

'You're pregnant,' Jake said.

'Nope. And why would that be shocking?'

'You've bought a flat?'

'We have, but that's not it.'

'Ooh, tell me,' Jake said. 'Is it the one next door?'

'No. Later. This other thing is more important. And stop guessing, because you're never going to get it.'

'You're scaring me,' Abby said. 'Is it good news or bad news?'

I held up my palm in a stop sign. 'Stop it, both of you,' I said.

Jake elbowed Abby in the ribs and pulled a face. 'She's gone all serious,' he said. 'Must be getting married.'

'Jake!' I exclaimed. 'Shut up!'

'That's his third pint,' Abby said. 'He gets excitable. Sorry.'

Jake sat up and crossed his arms like a schoolchild. 'OK,' he said. 'I can be serious too. Fire away.'

'Dad's Jewish,' I announced.

Abby's features slipped into a frown, but Jake remained like a statue. I swear not a single muscle moved.

'I'm sorry?' Abby said eventually.

'Dad,' I said, then, gesturing between Jake and myself, 'Our father, Bill: his birth name was Menashe. And he's adopted. And Jewish.'

'What?' Jake said, making the W and the H whistle.

'I know,' I said. 'And there's more.'

◆ ◆ ◆

To say that Jake's reaction surprised me would be an understatement.

Firstly, he had absolutely no problem believing what I was telling him was true, and secondly, he kept laughing, clapping his hands and saying it was 'Just brilliant, just fucking brilliant.'

I'm going to give him the benefit of the doubt and say that he was amused by the irony of our anti-Semitic father turning out to be Jewish, and I suspect the alcohol he'd ingurgitated contributed too. But all the same, it surprised me. He shocked me and in a way he disappointed me. A little shock and sorrow wouldn't have gone amiss, after all.

'You have to tell him,' he started insisting, quite manically gripping my arm as we were leaving the pub. 'You have to tell him so we can finally sort out our wedding.'

Abby explained that they'd been worried about Dad offending all her relatives at the reception. They'd even been discussing whether it was necessary to invite him.

'So if you don't tell him, I will,' Jake slurred.

At the taxi rank, I made him promise he'd wait until we had the final cassette, and then I asked Abby, who was far more sober, to control him if he forgot that promise.

As I walked off in the direction of the Tube station, I phoned Freida to ask how much of a bonus I would need to pay her to get that final cassette #6 done right away.

'Oh, it's done,' she told me. 'I sent it this morning just after tape number five. You didn't get it?'

'No,' I said. 'No, I only got number five.'

'I will send it again then, right now,' she said. 'It will be with you within half an hour.'

Cassette #6

ML: *And we're off! This is Marie Lefebvre, talking with Genevieve Schmitt, cassette number six, fourth day. Hello again, Genevieve.*

GS: Day four! You must be getting bored with me by now, aren't you? I think I'm getting bored with the sound of my own voice. I'm a bit hoarse today. Can you hear that?

I can! I'm sorry if I'm wearing you out. And no, I'm not bored at all. But – and I know this is extremely difficult to estimate – but I am going to have to ask you if you have any idea how long you think we still need? I just need a vague idea.

So you can buy more cassettes?

Well, there is that too. But no . . . the thing is that I only set aside a day for this at the start. So I'm getting behind with the other interviews I have lined up. My editor is starting to complain, too.

Oh, I see. I knew I was being too chatty!

You're really not. But if we go on beyond today then I might have to come back at a later date. At the end of the month, maybe, once I've caught up with everything else I need to get done.

Actually, I don't see why we can't wrap it up today. If you help me stay on track, that is! Most of the shocking bits are past us now anyway . . . The rest is just . . . you know . . . normal life.

Sure, though I gather your lives weren't actually that normal, were they?

No. Perhaps not. I suppose it depends on what one considers normal.

Maybe we can see how things go today and decide what happens next. When the last tape ended, you'd finally found Ethel. And you'd managed to convince her you weren't in love with Christophe.

<Laughs> Honestly! How could she even imagine such a thing? But yes. She cried a lot when it finally sank in that she was the one I loved – that I'd been waiting for this moment for five years . . . I cried too, and eventually Christophe realised that he'd lost us and doubled back with Guillaume, and he ended up crying as well. Predictably, the fact that three adults were crying set Guillaume off, so we ended up in a strange comedy moment of hugging and crying, all four of us in the middle of the street, as people passed by. But in 1945 I don't think it was even particularly unusual. People were finding out things that made them weep all the time back then – who had died, who had lived, what had happened to their loved ones, good news as well as bad.

We got all the way to Vauxhall before Ethel announced that she wanted me to return to Islington so I could spend the night with her – she couldn't bear to leave me, she said. But I was too worried about what Irene might say. I was scared I'd have to walk back all over again, only this time on my own. So we arranged to meet the next day outside Ethel's workplace instead.

Where was Ethel working by then?

In a workshop – a small factory, I suppose it was really – near Smithfield Market. She was sewing clothes for Polly Peck. She loved it there, in fact she worked for them until the late fifties. And that's where we met the next day.

Was this all of you, or just you and Ethel?

Just the two of us. Christophe thought, quite rightly, that Ethel and I needed some time alone, so he volunteered to look after Guillaume. I was pretty desperate to kiss her. That's what I kept thinking about: getting naked and kissing her. I was craving physical contact with her skin.

We went for a drink first – I think we both thought that some alcohol might help. And then we travelled to Islington by bus. Irene was out – Ethel had known that she would be – and so we ran upstairs and locked the door. No prizes for guessing what happened next.

And how did that feel after all these years?

<Laughs> Awkward is how it felt. Very, very awkward. It was as if we were all elbows and knees, as if our bodies were all angles and no longer fitted together properly.

Did that worry you?

A tiny bit, I suppose. But I still loved her so much. That hadn't changed at all. And I could tell that it was reciprocal. We cried every time we looked into each other's eyes. We just felt so lucky to have survived, to be reunited . . . It felt like a miracle, really.

Afterwards we lay naked on the bed and tried to fill in all the gaps – everything that had happened since 1939. But there was so much ground to cover that process ended up being almost continuous. Even years afterwards, we'd sometimes say, 'Did I ever tell you about when . . . ?' and discover we'd found another gap we needed to plug.

And then she shocked me by asking me when I was going back to France – how long did we have together? That caused a bit of a moment.

A moment?

Yes, that's what we used to call them, Ethel and I. When, you know, there's a misunderstanding and suddenly everyone's bristling . . . I got up and pulled my clothes on, I remember. I felt too vulnerable naked to have that discussion with her. Because she'd assumed that I was only visiting and I assumed that meant she didn't really want me to stay . . . Anyway, we had a 'moment', and we both got dressed and crossed our arms and glared at each other for a bit. But then we talked it through, and I told her that I didn't care where we lived as long as I could live with her.

And Guillaume in all this?

Well, exactly! That's what made everything so complicated. Because we had Christophe in the equation, too, plus Guillaume tying the two of us together.

I knew that I'd never give Guillaume up, but I had no idea what Christophe wanted. He'd been raising him as if he was his child for five years too, and yet we'd never discussed their future. So we agreed, in the end, to meet up the next day and talk it all through with Christophe. And we agreed we'd have the conversation in English so that Guillaume wouldn't understand what we were saying.

I walked back to Vauxhall to tell Christophe all this, and that led to a pretty fiery discussion between the two of us. He'd already been thinking about all the possibilities during my absence, so we gave Guillaume a sheet of paper and a pencil – he loved to scribble – and went out on to the landing so that we could talk.

'I know that now you've found her you just want me to vanish . . .' Christophe said. That was his opening gambit! It was so aggressive that I was stunned into silence for a bit. I hadn't been expecting that at all.

I tried to explain that wasn't what I wanted but, as if he hadn't heard me, he carried on arguing with this other version of me inside his head, saying he knew it was what I wanted, and he'd already thought about it, and that he'd love to give me what I wanted, but he just couldn't do it because he'd realised that he would miss Guillaume too much.

After a while I managed to calm him down to the point where he could hear what I was saying, and he asked me, sounding jealous, sort of challenging me, to deny that I wanted to be with Ethel. I admitted that obviously I did, but I had no intention whatsoever of taking Guillaume away from him.

'So we all have to live together,' he said. 'That's the only solution I can see.'

I was so happy I threw my arms around him, and then did this little dance on the landing.

I asked him then where he wanted to live: in London or back in Mulhouse, or some other place that we hadn't tried yet, and he made me laugh by saying, 'Vauxhall. I want to live in Vauxhall. Preferably I want to live in the Vauxhall Tavern.'

So the discussion the next day with Ethel turned out to be a terribly simple one. Both she and Christophe wanted to stay in London, and I didn't care where I lived. As long as I could be with Ethel and Guillaume, I would have lived on the North Pole.

And Christophe?

Yes? What about him?

Did you still want to live with him?

Oh. I . . . He . . . Look, if I'm honest, perhaps not. After five years, I felt a bit sick of him. Does that shock you? I wouldn't have minded a break. You know, you mustn't ever tell him this. Or print it, for that matter! But that's the truth.

OK. But you said you danced for joy when he said you'd all live together.

Well, yes. Because any other configuration was impossibly complicated. What I wanted was to live with Ethel and Guillaume. But I wouldn't, couldn't, ever have tried to take Guillaume away from Christophe, or Christophe away from Guillaume. Plus, two women living together, in the forties, with a child . . . it wasn't just frowned upon, it would have been almost impossible to even find somewhere to rent. So Christophe being happy for us to all live together solved almost every problem we had. It provided a very neat way forward.

So that's what happened. And it all worked out pretty well.

You all just moved in together?

Yes. Irene's husband had a brother, Tom, and he rented us a flat he owned above a Lloyd's bank. We used to joke about drilling down into the safe . . . It was only a dingy two-bedroom place, but it had lovely high ceilings. Anyway, it felt like a palace to us.

Christophe and I rented it as a couple, and we had my 'cousin' Ethel come and live with us.

Did you have to lie in that way?

Oh, of course we did. There was no way we could have lived as an openly gay couple. And Christophe needed the cover too. The police raided the bars and the cruising grounds he went to all the time. They were always stomping in and whacking everyone with their truncheons; rounding men up and throwing them in prison. And of course, Pierre was terrified of that because of what had happened to him in Mulhouse. So our fake marriage reassured him because he thought that if anything happened I'd be able to save him all over again.

And did you all work?

Yes. Christophe got a job working on the rebuilds.

The rebuilds?

Yes, all the houses that had been bombed, I think it was one in three houses or something. The scale of destruction was mind-blowing, and they all had to be rebuilt, and they all needed re-plumbing. So Christophe got a job almost immediately – he answered an advertisement in the newspaper, I think, and ended up working for Walter and Sons plumbers. The sons had both died in the war but that was what the company was still called. People were always assuming his father was Mr Walter. He worked for them for a decade. Ethel carried on as a seamstress for Polly Peck and I was a stay-at-home mum. But I did piecework from home for Polly Peck, too. Officially, Ethel got paid for doing overtime, but secretly it was me. So between the three of us we got by.

Did Guillaume have to go to school at some point?

Yes. I home-schooled him until he was seven – because, of course, he didn't speak English at first – and then through a friend of a friend, it was something to do with Irene again, I think, we got him into the local primary school. And then, when he was ten, we managed to enrol him in the French Lycée. And that was just amazing, because it was a brilliant school, plus he got to use both English and French. The original school buildings had been used by de Gaulle for his government-in-exile during the war, too, so that had a sort of poetry about it. I liked the idea, anyway.

You mentioned Irene again. Did you stay friends with her?

Ethel did, right up until when Irene died. But she was always more Ethel's friend than mine. For obvious reasons, I did my best to keep to the shadows.

Because Irene never knew you were a couple?

Oh, I think she probably suspected. But in that kind of way where you know something without really knowing it. I don't think she would have been surprised, but that doesn't mean she would have approved. I'm not sure how Quakers were about that sort of thing, back then . . . But you know, in those days, it just wasn't done to put people in that position. What we were doing was criminalised, and frowned upon, and putting friends in a position where they had to go against society to support you felt bad. That's just how things were in the forties and fifties. In the sixties, too, really. Everyone was very careful. You had to be.

And Christophe? Did he have a boyfriend? Or boyfriends plural, perhaps?

<Laughs> Christophe had lots of boyfriends. Mostly they were just ten-minute affairs, but occasionally he'd fall in love and it would last longer.

Did you ever meet any of them?

A few, but only ever once or twice before they vanished. There was a Didier with sad eyes – he was French. And Thomas – he was fun. But they never lasted more than a few weeks, I don't think. Not until much later on.

Is there a reason for that, do you think?

Well, relationships are hard, aren't they? Even nowadays, even straight relationships, where everyone approves – they're hard. Which is why so many marriages end in divorce.

But when the very essence of who you loved was illegal . . . when you could be thrown in prison just for loving another man . . . when your families would almost certainly disown you – or in Pierre's case, already *had* disowned him – and you'd lose your job and be kicked out of your lodgings if you got caught . . . Well, that's a hell of a lot of pressure to heap on any relationship. Especially on top of all the normal stuff.

So I think that made it easy – very easy really – to decide that your momentarily annoying boyfriend wasn't worth it . . . wasn't worth all that fear, and risk, and rejection and shame . . . Do you see what I'm getting at?

I do.

It's why Christophe and most of his peers struggled to have proper relationships. That's my theory, anyway. Plus, he was officially married to me. He lived with me. We shared a bed. We had a child. None of that made things any easier for him.

You still shared a bed?

Well, it was two singles side by side, but yes, we were officially still a married couple.

Can you explain to me how that worked?

Sure. Well, we had two bedrooms. So Christophe and I slept in one, and Guillaume shared the other room with Ethel.

Oh gosh. That must have been frustrating, wasn't it?

Yes, it was. But when Guillaume was little he used to sleep like a log. So I'd carry him to Christophe's bed and slip in for a night with Ethel. The problem was that Pierre had terrible nightmares. He still has them these days, though I don't think they're quite as frequent. At the beginning, in Le Mas, they used to be every single night. He used to scream and scream in his sleep.

Did he ever tell you what they were about?

He didn't like to talk about them much, but I gather they were about being tortured by the Germans. And about Johann, too. I think he spent a lot of nights imagining what they'd done to him.

Poor Johann. And poor Pierre! Losing his first love, like that. It's all so sad.

I know. It's awful. It never stops being awful, that's the thing. Anyway, in '49, when we had enough money coming in, we rented the bedsit upstairs, officially for Ethel. So from that point on, Guillaume had his own bedroom, and I could slip upstairs to join my sleeping beauty.

That sounds really complicated.

I know it sounds it, but other than having to rush back downstairs whenever Pierre had a nightmare, it really wasn't that bad.

And how long did you live that way?

Oh, for years! Until '59, when Guillaume got married and moved out.

Gosh, he got married at nineteen, then?

Yes, nineteen. It was just after his birthday. He fell madly in love with Patricia, a lovely Irish girl out in Walthamstow, and her uncle, who was quite well off and in property, rented them a place out there. He gave Guillaume a job, too, redecorating the apartments he rented out. Once Guillaume was gone, we swapped around right away.

How do you mean, swapped around?

Well, Christophe moved upstairs to the bedsit, and Ethel moved in with me.

How did you explain that to Guillaume? Or did you just tell him the truth?

No! No, we never told him the truth.

Would that still not have been socially acceptable?

It was absolutely not acceptable. Lesbianism wasn't illegal per se, purportedly because Queen Victoria refused to imagine such a thing. Only sex between men was illegal, I think, though any kind of same-sex relationship was certainly frowned upon. But Ethel was my cousin, remember? So we were just two old maids – little old divorced me and my cousin, living together.

How did Guillaume react to all of that? What was his understanding of the situation?

We just told him that we were sick of each other – Christophe and me, that is. But I think he was a bit confused by it all, especially because we visibly remained on such good terms. We still used to take him and his wife out to restaurants as a threesome – stuff like that – and he'd say, 'I'll never understand why you divorced,' and I'd reply with something light-hearted like, 'Your father snores too much,' or 'farts too much', and make a joke of it.

But I think Guillaume ended up resenting 'Aunty' Ethel a bit, which was unfair on her. He perhaps sensed that she had taken me away from his father, which of course, in a way, she had. Only Christophe wasn't his father, Ethel wasn't his aunt, and I wasn't his mother, either. So really, if he'd known, he could have seen his relationship with Ethel as quite extreme generosity on her part.

But it didn't cause major ructions. He was living his own life as a newly married man. Patricia got pregnant with Jake quite quickly.

He was too busy to spend much time worrying about our living arrangements, especially as our fake divorce hadn't made anyone unhappy. Quite the contrary, in fact.

You were all happier living this way?

Oh, it was a revelation! I was thirty-eight years old, and it was the first time in my life that my living arrangements had matched who I really was. We all felt the same. It was wonderful! Ethel and I finally lived as a couple – we only ruffled the sheets in the second bedroom if Guillaume or someone else came to visit. And Christophe was able to bring men back to his bedsit as well.

Shortly after that he met Igor and, you know, I've always thought that he met Igor at that moment because he was able to. Because they finally had somewhere they could spend time together.

Igor? That's a pretty unusual name, isn't it?

Is it? I suppose . . . His parents were originally from Hungary, I think. He inherited their emporium – it was a junk shop really – a wonderful place, piled high with furniture and boxes of knick-knacks and electrical goods and paintings . . . Anything you needed, Igor could find it somewhere. So Christophe went in there one day looking for a paraffin heater, and their eyes met over the top of all that junk . . . And I suppose you could say that Christophe found *exactly* what he needed.

And what year was this? When Christophe met Igor?

It would have been '58, I think, or early '59. Like I said, it was around the time that Guillaume moved out.

Tell me about Igor. What was he like when Christophe first met him?

Oh, he was wonderful – a real character. He was a bit younger than Christophe, maybe four years younger, and he had this wonderful Hungarian accent – not strong, but just enough to make him sound exotic. He looked a bit like Christophe, only darker, and younger. He had a pointy beard and a long moustache he used to twiddle all the time whenever he was thinking or listening to music.

And was he nice? Did you like him?

Yes, I did. Ethel wasn't so keen at the beginning, and to be honest I'm not really sure why. I think they were maybe too similar to get on straight away, though later they became best friends. But I liked him a lot. He was very funny – he had this very dry, rather dark sense of humour which was very much like Ethel's.

He was mad about classical music and had a wonderful collection of tapes – you know the old-fashioned reel-to-reel ones you had to thread through the little wheels . . . So he had a whole stack of those tapes and he'd play classical music all day long in the shop, though I only ever remember hearing Rachmaninov. He had a real obsession with Rachmaninov, and even these days I still can't hear a Rachmaninov piano concerto without instantly thinking about Igor and wondering how he's doing.

I'm assuming Igor was single?

Which is proof that you should never assume anything!

Oh! He wasn't?

No, he was married to a woman called . . . I'm sorry, the name escapes me. It was Laura or Gina or something like that. One of those American-sounding names. She always looked ill, really, even when she wasn't. She always looked pale and thin and unhappy.

Could that have been because she was married to a gay man, do you suppose?

<Laughs> I don't think it helped. But you know, I always got a gay vibe off her too. I always suspected that, had she not been so devoutly religious, she would have liked to be with a woman. But she always looked shocking, and in fact she probably was already ill by the time I met her, even though we didn't know it yet. She died of cancer in . . . maybe '60 or '61 . . . when Igor was in his mid-thirties.

Oh, that's sad. How did that affect Christophe and Igor's relationship?

Well, Igor was terribly upset. Christophe was a bit surprised by that, because he and Igor were very much in love by then. But Igor clearly loved Dana too – that was her name! Dana. It came back to me. I suspect Igor loved her in much the same way I love Christophe. And even if that's not true love, it is still quite a powerful sort of thing. As for Christophe, I suspect he was secretly relieved when Dana died. That will sound awful, I know, and I don't think he'd ever admit it. But once Dana was out of the picture he got to see Igor all the time. They ate together pretty much every evening, I think, and on Saturdays Christophe would spend the whole day at Igor's emporium. On Sundays they'd go off to auctions and classical concerts and things. I think that was when Christophe was happiest – in the sixties. They were both young and full of beans, and suddenly Igor was free . . . It was lovely to see them together.

Did Guillaume meet Igor? Did he know about Christophe's relationship?

I'm sure he bumped into him a few times, but no, he never knew. As far as Guillaume was concerned, Igor would have been his father's friend, the same way he believed that Ethel was my cousin.

It must have been hard work hiding all that stuff, wasn't it?

Not as hard as you'd think. Guillaume was living out in Walthamstow by then with his wife and son. And since my 'divorce' from Christophe, he'd been quite distant towards all three of us. This is a bit sad to admit, but because we were all finally living these lives that we'd only dreamed of before – me living with Ethel, and Christophe dating Igor – that distance suited us. I know how selfish that sounds, because Guillaume really was like a son to us, but him popping round every five minutes wouldn't have suited anyone. It wouldn't have suited Ethel and me if he'd caught us snuggling on the sofa, for instance, and it wouldn't have suited Christophe and Igor getting caught in the act, or having breakfast, or whatever else they got up to. I think the drift away from us started when he couldn't get his head around our divorce – when he couldn't understand why Christophe had moved out. But at the same time he was being pulled in a different direction, towards his wife's family – which was pretty tightly knit – and towards his own new family, his own children, as well.

What I'm trying to say is that there were all these invisible forces simultaneously pushing him away from us, and others pulling him into a new, different orbit out in Walthamstow. And though it's sad, we just let it happen. Because it indisputably suited us all.

You sound like you maybe feel a bit guilty about that.

Yes, I suppose . . . Actually, no, I don't. Oh golly, I don't know! In a way, I do, because it's sad how little we saw of him, especially once we moved to Brighton. I saw him from time to time for lunch when I was up in London, but I'm not sure Ethel *ever* saw Guillaume after that. But in a way, our own lives had been on hold for so long . . . we'd been so constrained by the war, and then by society and all the stupid rules and laws about what we were and weren't allowed to do – who we were and weren't allowed to love . . . Plus, in the midst of that, we'd made incredible sacrifices to provide Guillaume with something that at least looked like a traditional family. So I felt, also – I think we all did – that it was our turn by then, do you understand? Guillaume was sailing off towards his own destination, his own adventures . . . And we felt, quite rightly, I think, that we'd given *everything* to allow him to do that, to let him live whatever life he wanted; to live full stop, in fact. So we sort of watched him sail off, and then turned our attention to home, to ourselves, to our partners, and to the lives we wanted to live. I think we all breathed a huge sigh of relief in a way.

What year did you move here to Brighton?

In 1971, dear, to this very house! It cost us just over £5000, and we haven't moved since. We love it here.

I can understand that. It's gorgeous, especially with that little garden out front.

That's Ethel's passion – the gardening. Can't stand it myself. I got my fill of gardening during the war.

Did you come here because of the gay culture?

Yes, I suppose you could say that, though it wasn't gay per se when we moved here. But Brighton always had a very liberal vibe about it, and that certainly drew us – the idea of being able to be more open about our relationship and everything. But it was Ethel, really, who wanted to move. She got laid off from her job and she wanted a change. We both wanted to get out of London. We both love the sea . . . She had a dream of opening a café . . . so here we are.

Of course. It was your waitress who put us in touch.

That's right. We're semi-retired now so we have some lovely youngsters running the place.

That's not where Ethel is now, then?

Now? <Laughs> No, she's in Mont-de-Marsan, visiting her mother.

She stayed there, then, after the war?

Yes, she never got over losing her husband and the rest of her family. It made her go a bit mad, which is understandable. Plus, she's eighty-seven now, and in a nursing home, so Ethel has to go down quite often. I'll be joining her out there next week.

And Christophe? I don't suppose he stayed with Igor, did he?

Yes, he did. They split up in . . . oh, I don't know . . . the mid-seventies, I think it was, but then they got back together, and they've been together ever since. They live on the coast near Arcachon.

They moved back to France?

Yes. Well, Christophe did. Igor was born in Hungary, so it wasn't moving back for him. But yes, they retired to a village near

Arcachon, on the edge of a big nature reserve. It's gorgeous. They have cats, lots of cats. Igor wanted dogs, but I think Christophe still has a problem with dogs.

A problem?

Yes, because of what happened to Johann.

Oh, of course.

But they treat their cats like children. They spoil them rotten. I think they have three or four now.

Arcachon is quite near Mont-de-Marsan, isn't it?

Very good. Your geography is better than your history. It's about an hour and a half away, but it's the same corner of France.

I think my grasp of history is pretty good now, thanks to you. Well, about the Second World War in Alsace it is, at any rate. But I'm so glad they're still together. Gosh, I feel a bit tearful about it! That's lovely. Did you all keep in touch?

Of course we did! After everything we've been through, how could it be any other way? I'm flying down to Bordeaux on Monday to join Ethel and then we're going to rent a car and drive over to stay with them.

With Christophe and Igor? Oh, that's wonderful. That's such a great way to end my piece.

Are we at the end then?

I'm not sure. I just assumed . . .

I suppose we are, in a way. That went quite fast, then, didn't it?

Perhaps you could just . . . Maybe you could get me up to speed on Guillaume? Tell me what he's been up to?

Of course. Well, Guillaume and Pat are still together. They're very happy, I think. She's a bit obsessed with her family, but I think he likes that. They have two children, Ruth and Jake. Though they're not children now, of course. Ruth must be twenty-two or so and Jake's a bit older.

Jake, that's Jacob, right? So aren't those both Jewish names?

Yes, I think they might be. Which is funny, really, if you think about it.

That's not because you told Guillaume about his origins, then?

No. No, we still haven't told anyone anything.

OK. Look, I know we've kind of covered this, but perhaps you could just explain to me one more time why? Because times have changed so much. Attitudes, I mean, have changed.

You're right. They totally have, thank God. But it's rather like I said before: when is the right time to tell your child that he's a) not really yours and b) your marriage is fake, and c) your surname isn't really Solomas, and d) that his family died in the gas chambers, and . . . where are we up to? e)?

Yes, e). You just did d).

And e) that you've spent his whole life pretending to be heterosexual.

Yes, I can see that, but—

Plus, you have to remember that for much of his life, until Guillaume was almost thirty, it was illegal for Christophe to be who he really was. Men got thrown into prison. Just think about that: in prison! And even when the law changed in . . . I think it might have been '67 or '68 . . . But even after that it took another fifteen years before attitudes changed, and even then, even now, there are still plenty of homophobes around. So by the time it felt possible to tell him, it seemed like it was just too late, I suppose. At least, that's how Christophe has always felt about it.

Would you have been more inclined to tell him the truth, do you think, if it hadn't been for Christophe?

Perhaps, I'm not sure. Out of the four of us, I'd say Ethel and Igor were always most in favour, and that makes sense really. After all, they didn't look after him almost from birth. They're not the ones who would lose him if it went wrong, are they? They're not responsible for all the lies, either. I've always thought that he needs to know about his real mother at some point, but I've never found the right moment. Finding the right time – finding the perfect moment to drop a bombshell like that . . . bombshells plural . . . well . . . I've just never managed it. Plus, Christophe has always been dead against, and I could never take that decision on my own.

And you must remember – and please make sure this comes out in your article – you must remember just how much difficulty Christophe faced over the course of his lifetime because of his sexuality. Rejection from his family, from the state, from lawmakers . . . Rejection and pain. Actual physical danger, too. He was tortured because of it, remember; his friends, his first true love, were all slaughtered because of their sexuality, so we're talking huge, very real trauma. Even now, I think it would be reasonable to say that it's still an incredibly difficult subject for him. He's probably lived with some form of post-traumatic stress disorder his whole life. I think we all have, if you get down to it. So it's pretty understandable he's never wanted to risk ruining his relationship with his son.

OK, I understand. I get it.

But you know, I may still tell him. One day, I may just write that letter, or arrange a meeting. I still think about it sometimes. Perhaps I'll send him a copy of your tapes. I'm always full of surprises, me!

And will you tell Christophe about this interview?

I'm not sure. Do you need to speak to him, do you think?

No, not really. I don't think I can use any more. I already have way too much for a magazine piece.

Perhaps not, then. I still haven't decided. I'll probably wait until I see the edited-down result so that I can judge how we all come out of it . . . How flattering, or otherwise, it looks!

I'll make you look like heroes, I promise. Because that's how I see you; that's what you are. You're the heroes of your own lives. So, I promise, I'm going to make you look great.

Well, you'd better, dear. You'd better!

Ruth. Part Seven.

The minute I got home, I connected to the internet, and by the time I'd finished grilling cheese on toast, cassette #6 was sitting in my inbox waiting to be read, and that felt like a miracle of technology.

I settled on the sofa with my comfort food, my cat and the computer, and began to read, and for fifteen minutes I was lost inside Genevieve's story.

When finally I finished, I closed the lid of my laptop delicately, as if jolting it might disturb the ghosts within.

I sat staring at my reflection on the TV screen for a while and it crossed my mind that I looked older, or perhaps *felt* older, as if being supplied with a comprehensive back-story had finally made an adult of me. It was a strange thought, but in that moment it seemed real.

So Grandpa Chris had found love after all, had he? That bit of news had brought tears to my eyes. And Igor, the famous Igor, who my grandfather had been living with all these years in France – the same man my father had met at the hospital – he'd been my grandfather's life-partner, and in a way, my dad's stepfather? And he was alive. There was still time to know him, at least.

The distance, that inexplicable sense of void between my father and his parents, between Jake and me and our grandparents

– finally it made the tiniest bit of sense. Because they'd been living a lie, hadn't they? Everything they'd shown the outside world had been fake. But the thing that had surprised me the most had been coming across my own name there in the text. To discover that Jake and I had been written into Genevieve's life story had shocked me, and I wasn't quite sure why. Perhaps because it made their story definitively *our* story. Or maybe it was simply the final detail needed to lay to rest any remaining doubt.

Oh, I hadn't ever really believed it was all fiction, of course I hadn't. But I had still been carrying a remote, lingering fear around with me, a sense of terror at the idea of telling my father something this radical only to discover that I was mistaken in the way I was interpreting it all.

But here we were. The story, our family story, was up to date. A line had been drawn, right from my grandfather's youth in Alsace through my father's improbable survival and on to my own birth here in London. And every detail felt, to my editor's eye, utterly convincing. This was all true. This was all absolutely true, I was sure of it. And the fact that it led all the way to me, to here, to now, made me feel, for the first time, that I was a legitimate custodian of that story. I too had a right to read it and help decide what happened to it next.

Just after ten, Dan phoned me from a private party he was catering. They'd just served dessert, he said, so he had a break before they had to start packing up.

He asked me how things had gone with Jake, and once I'd told him about my brother's surprising reaction, I went on to summarise the contents of the final cassette.

'You sound pretty sure now,' he commented.

I told him that I was.

'So what happens next?' he asked.

'Next I have to find a way to talk to Dad.'

'You know you don't have to talk to him about this. I just want you to keep that option in mind.'

'Erm, I kind of do have to,' I said.

'He's lived quite well not knowing,' Dan said. 'I think you should remember that.'

'You're still assuming he doesn't know, but—'

'Well, if he already knows, then you *definitely* don't need to tell him,' Dan pointed out.

'True. But if he doesn't, then . . . well . . . we have Jake and Abby in the picture now. And Jake's definitely going to want to talk about it.'

'Which is why I didn't think you should tell him.'

'Yeah, OK. But I *did*. So now I have to talk to Dad.'

'Unless you and Jake agree not to,' Dan said.

By the time I'd hung up I felt like I'd had a half-hearted, pointless argument with him – pointless because despite what Dan might say it was unthinkable that I might try to keep this from my father.

Still, Dan had said one useful thing. He'd suggested once again that I should check the existence of *Gai Pied* magazine – something I'd been unable to do so far – but more importantly, he'd told me about a new search engine I could try called MSN, which, unlike Altavista, came up trumps.

These days you can find pages and pages of stuff about just about anything online, but in the days before Google, even the internet had the capacity to disappoint. And that was particularly likely if you were enquiring about anything beyond the borders of the USA. So back in 1998, the only thing MSN came up with was the following one-line entry:

Gai Pied was a French magazine aimed at homosexuals. It was published monthly, and later weekly, between 1979 and 1992.

Minimalist, admittedly, but it was more than enough for me.

To buy time, I lied and told Jake that I was still waiting for the final transcript. The question I needed to ponder wasn't so much if I would tell Dad, but *how* I could tell him. Even after a full week of mulling it over, I was unable to even imagine how that conversation might go.

At work on Thursday, I got Freida to use Impressionable's brand-new laser gizmo to produce a single bound copy for my father, and the following Sunday I slipped it into my chunkiest handbag and headed out to Walthamstow.

But the whole family was there and I realised the second I arrived that it wasn't the right moment to have such a challenging conversation. It was one of those times when I felt annoyed with myself for even having considered such a silly idea.

So I left with my still-heavy handbag as early as I politely could and instead phoned Dad once I got home to ask him if he'd mind dropping in one night during the week.

'Is it about knocking that door through?' Dad asked. 'Because I've told you, you need a proper builder.'

I told him that I needed his advice as a painter-decorator about where best to put the door before I could ask for quotes.

◆ ◆ ◆

Dad took a swig of his beer as he studied the wall. He was wearing an expression that, in our family, we call 'plumber's face'. It involves scanning the problem being discussed while alternately chewing the inside of your cheek and sucking air through gritted teeth. 'I don't see where you can put it other than here,' he finally announced, rapping the wall with his knuckles in the exact spot we'd chosen for the future door. It was, quite clearly, the only place the door could possibly be installed.

'Great. Well, everyone agrees then,' I said, caressing the folder I'd positioned on the arm of the sofa beside me. 'Come and sit down for a bit.'

But Dad continued studying the wall. He's always been more at ease with DIY problems than with conversation and I suspect he'd subconsciously detected the tension in my voice. My hand was trembling so I squashed it flat against the folder to steady it.

'Dad,' I said again. 'Sit down and drink your beer.' When he didn't react I added, 'I want to talk to you about something.'

Instead he walked to the window and looked out at the street below. 'It's a nice area, I'll give you that,' he said. 'A good place to invest. You won't lose money on this one.'

'Dad!' I said again, only this time there was enough urgency in my voice that he turned to look at me.

'Jesus!' he said. 'What is it?'

I pointed at the armchair. 'Sit down,' I told him. 'You're making me feel nervous.'

Once he'd sat in the armchair opposite, I cleared my throat.

'Well?' he prompted.

'I've something I need to tell you,' I said, my voice sounding unintentionally brittle. 'Something difficult.'

'OK,' Dad said, then, 'You're not ill, are you?'

'No, I'm fine,' I said. 'Everyone's fine.' I took a massive sip of wine before attempting to continue. 'I . . .'

Dad raised one eyebrow comically, took a swig of beer and then grinned at me. 'What? Are you pregnant?'

I shook my head in disbelief. 'Why does everyone always think I'm pregnant?' I asked.

'So, what then? I'm not a mind-reader, sweetheart.'

I took a deep breath. 'It's not . . . it's nothing like that. It's . . . Look . . . You know how Ethel was trying to get in touch with you before she died?'

342

Dad pushed his tongue into his cheek. His smile had already vanished.

'She wanted to give you something,' I continued as Dad's brow furrowed. 'She wanted to give you this.' I lifted one corner of the folder and then smoothed it back down with my hand.

'OK . . .' Dad said, sounding dubious.

'But she couldn't seem to reach you, so . . .'

'I called her. I've already told you. But—'

'This isn't about that, Dad,' I interrupted. 'No one's reproaching anyone here. I'm just trying to tell you about this.' I stroked the folder again. 'Because she ended up arranging for someone to send it to me. Because it's important.'

Dad scratched at the corner of one eye. 'I don't . . .' he said, shaking his head confusedly.

'It's your life story, Dad. Well, it's Grandma Genny's life story. But they end up becoming one and the same thing.'

'What, in that folder?'

I nodded. 'Everything from Alsace before the war through to that café they had in Brighton. The whole shebang.'

'You're saying she wrote a book about her life?'

'Yes. Well, it was an interview, actually. On cassettes. In French. I paid the secretary at work to translate it and type it up. It cost me over two grand in the end.'

'Two grand? Jesus! Why?'

'Because it was worth it.'

'Worth two grand?' Dad said, looking doubtful. He clearly hadn't grasped the gravity of the moment. 'Is it interesting, then, this book? Are you going to publish it or something?'

I licked my lips and swallowed. 'It is interesting,' I said. 'It's actually more than interesting, Dad. It's quite . . . um . . . mind-blowing. And I think you need to read it.'

Dad laughed lightly at the idea. 'Oh, you know I'm not the world's biggest reader,' he said. 'But I'm sure your mother will enjoy it if it's any good. Or you could just give me the tapes, I suppose. If I find time, I'll have a listen.'

'If you find time . . .' I repeated flatly. I sighed. 'You're not really getting this. So, it's an interview, OK? With a magazine. With a French magazine called *Gai Pied*. Have you ever heard of it?'

Dad pouted and shook his head.

'OK, well, it's a gay magazine,' I said, watching him closely to see any signs of recognition.

'Oh, OK,' Dad said, lightly.

'God, this is hard,' I said. 'Do you *really* not know any of this?'

'Any of what?' Dad asked, leaning forward.

I blew through pursed lips. 'So, there's a reason. There's a reason she was interviewed by a gay magazine. It's because Grandma Genny was gay.'

'Oh,' Dad said again, looking confused, but not shocked. 'OK.'

I was struggling to decide whether his lack of shock meant he already knew, or simply didn't understand what I was saying. 'Ethel wasn't Grandma's cousin at all. She was her partner. Her life partner.'

Dad grimaced at me but said nothing, so after a moment I asked him if he'd heard me.

'Yes, but . . .' Dad said, still looking confused but also faintly amused.

'Genny and Ethel were a *couple*, Dad. They were lovers. And so were Grandpa and his friend Igor.'

Dad laughed out loud at this. 'No,' he said, simply. 'They weren't. I don't know where you got that from but—'

'It's all in here, Dad,' I said. 'That's the thing.'

'This is . . .' Dad said, then, 'What are you up to here?'

'I'm sorry?'

'What do you think you're up to?' he asked. 'What's this about? Because I don't—'

'I'm not up to anything, Dad. It's the truth. Genny and Pierre pretended to be a couple their whole lives, but they weren't. Genny and Ethel were a couple. And so were Pierre and Igor.'

'Pierre?' Dad said. 'Who's Pierre?'

'Pierre was Grandpa Christophe's name before he changed it. And his family name wasn't Solomas either. It was Meyer.'

Dad put his beer down with precision and stood with studied calmness. 'This is . . .' he said. He scrunched up his nose and shook his head. 'I'm not sure what you think you're up to, but it's really quite unpleasant.'

'Dad, sit down,' I said, then, 'Dad! Please sit down. I haven't finished.'

'I think I'll just go home now,' he said, sounding so everyday that he seemed a bit mad.

'You were adopted, Dad,' I said as he pulled on his jacket, hoping to stop him in his tracks. 'They saved you. Genny and Pierre saved you from the Germans by pretending to be a couple and adopting you.'

And just for a moment, with one arm in his jacket, Dad paused. 'I don't even know a Pierre,' he said. 'You're talking nonsense.'

'I just told you,' I said. 'You're not listening. Pierre Meyer. That was Grandpa's name before the war. He changed it to Christophe, and he was Grandma Genny's best friend. Her *gay* best friend. And when the Germans invaded Alsace they saved you.'

But it had all gone wrong, and I thought about the fact that the reason I'd been unable to imagine how the conversation would go was because the reality was this: the conversation simply could not happen.

'Dad,' I said, as he crossed to the door. 'Dad!'

But then my front door slammed shut.

Buggles, who'd picked up on the atmosphere and had hidden beneath a dining chair, peeped out, glanced at the door and then back at me.

'Sorry, Bugs,' I said. 'That's not how that was supposed to go.'

My mother phoned me at eight thirty the next morning. It was when I knew my father generally left the house for work so I was in no doubt as to the reason for her call.

'What's wrong with your father?' she asked without further ado. 'What did you do?'

'I didn't do anything,' I said, childhood reflexes kicking in.

But over the course of the next hour, I told her exactly what I had done. I told her everything. And she was as furious as I've ever known her to be.

'Why the hell didn't you tell me first?' she kept saying. 'You stupid, stupid girl!' She could have managed him, she insisted. She alone knew how to manage my father. And I had to admit that she was probably right about that.

The one thing she didn't do at any point was cast doubt on the veracity of Genevieve's revelations.

'I always knew there was something dodgy about that lot,' was her only real comment. 'But now it all makes sense.'

'Dodgy?' I repeated.

'Yes, dodgy.'

At the end of the conversation, she asked me for a printed copy of the interview and I promised I'd drop one over during the week.

'But it'll have to be while your father's out,' she told me. 'I don't want one word about this from anyone. And I mean not one word, or so help me God, I'll never speak to you again.'

The problem, evidently, was Jake.

346

He phoned me on Saturday evening, so I told him what had happened, and what Mum had said.

'No way,' he said, immediately. 'There's no way I'm pretending this didn't happen. I don't care how much they want to stick their heads in the sand. Not talking about this is not an option.'

'Please, just wait a bit,' I pleaded. 'And please just talk to Mum first.' I pulled a face at Dan, who'd just arrived and was looking at me accusingly.

But Jake would not wait. Instead he stormed over there first thing on Sunday, and demanded that my father discuss his Jewish heritage. Which was almost certainly the worst possible way for that particular snippet of information to be revealed.

Thus was born The Second Great Falling Out.

In the end, Dad – who I suspect genuinely believed Jake and I had lost the plot – threw Jake out of the house. It was the only way he could shut him up, I think. And I don't mean he 'threw him out' figuratively. Jake, by all accounts, ended up on the pavement with a nosebleed.

Sad times had fallen upon our family, and I couldn't help but wonder if Dan had been right all along. Perhaps Dad hadn't needed to know. Certainly no good seemed to have come of my telling him.

Dad apparently became depressed. I say 'apparently' because all family get-togethers had ceased by then. 'Your father isn't up to it today,' Mum told me for the first three Sundays in a row, and by the fourth we'd got the message and had stopped asking.

Within two months Jake had announced his wedding for the following September while quite spectacularly not inviting Mum and Dad, a gesture that caused alternating ripples of alienation and allegiance that would spread far and wide, so that by the time his wedding took place not one family member felt able to attend without falling out with everyone else. The deal breaker for me had been the fact that he'd refused to invite Mum and Dad. I'd attempted to blackmail him into submission by refusing to go without them, but my plan had failed. He'd simply un-invited me too.

The wedding drama had led to a unique combination of sadness on my mother's part for having missed it and unpleasant smugness on Dad's side at the fact that none of us had 'bothered to go', as he liked to put it. The atmosphere back home felt so sad and toxic that even I stopped visiting them for a while.

The cassettes had been like a neutron bomb, and they had ripped the heart out of our family. And it was all my fault, because, after all, I'd been the bomber pilot, hadn't I? I had pressed the big red button that had released havoc on the whole family.

In a strange repetition of my father's own history, where he'd turned his back on the confusing drama surrounding his parents' divorce, each branch of the family span off to form their own independent satellite, turning inwards to concentrate on themselves while blanking out all those uncomfortable feelings provoked by everyone else. And it worked. It turned out, shockingly, that it was perfectly possible to slip on a pair of family blinkers. In fact, it was more than possible, it was easy.

To give you some idea of just how radical the change was, I'll tell you some things that took place over the next few years:

Dad had a full-blown breakdown and took three months off work with depression, the first time he'd taken sick leave in his life. It took a combination of therapy and Prozac to enable him to even return to work.

Abby got pregnant, had a miscarriage, and got pregnant again, finally giving birth to baby Nathan on Boxing Day 2000.

Uncle Harry discovered a melanoma on his ear, but had it successfully removed before it could spread and so narrowly avoided chemotherapy.

Pippa set fire to her kitchen with a chip pan and a tea towel with the result that they had to move to a rental property until the entire house had been redecorated and refurnished.

And finally, Suzie caught daughter Alice smoking a joint in the garage and kicked her out of the house. As a result, Alice moved in with Mavaughn for six months. A more unlikely combination for a flat-share would be hard to imagine.

My point in telling you these things is not that they happened, though. It's that I didn't hear about any of them first-hand at the time. Information in our family had ceased to flow laterally from brother to brother, from cousin to cousin or even from family to family. Instead it trickled on a strict need-to-know basis vertically, *resentfully*, up and down the family tree via Mum. That's how badly the lines of communication in our family had been disrupted.

As far as Dad's breakdown was concerned, he was so embarrassed about it and so incapable of discussing the cause that my parents made sure no one knew anything at all.

Looking back, I wonder how I filled the void my absent family had left behind. But the answer, again, is that it just wasn't as hard as one might think.

For one, Dan and I were busy buying the flat next door. We were getting builders' quotes on knocking a door-shaped hole in the wall, a process during which we discovered we needed planning permission (something no one had ever mentioned to us). We requested said planning permission (twice), got refused (twice), and eventually Dan found a Polish builder who didn't care about planning permission and discreetly knocked our door through anyway.

While we decorated our newly enlarged flat, I thought I was pregnant (three times) and found I wasn't (twice), before giving birth to our daughter, Lauren, in June 2002.

With Lauren's arrival there was finally a joyful reason to visit Mum and Dad, but even then, those visits were coloured by everything else that had taken place. They became defined not by the fact that we were seeing each other again, and not even by the fact that my parents were getting to spend time with their gorgeous baby granddaughter, but by everything that *couldn't* be discussed. The interview could not be mentioned. My grandparents could not be mentioned – in fact, even the word 'grandparent' seemed dangerous and best avoided. France could not be referenced, and nor could the French language, gayness, Jewishness, Jake, Abby, baby Nathan, weddings, funerals, magazines, cassettes . . . the list went on and on.

So the things we could talk about ended up feeling like fillers for everything that was forbidden. Their enthusiasm about seeing Dan and me, or even Lauren, ended up feeling strangely fake.

The situation was unbearable, and I couldn't see how it would ever end.

But then one summer day in 2003 Mum leaned in towards my ear and said, 'He's read it. I just want you to know that he's finally read it.'

I was pre-washing dishes while she stacked them in her ancient, lazy dishwasher.

'I'm sorry?' I asked, pausing and turning to look at her.

'He's read it,' she said again. 'All of it.'

'You mean . . . ?' I asked. The subject had been taboo for so long I couldn't even bring myself to say the words.

Mum nodded quickly. 'And then he listened to it as well. To the original tapes. Just to make sure.'

'To make sure it was really his mother's voice?'

Mum nodded. 'And to make sure the translation was right, I think.'

'And what did he say?'

Mum raised her hand in a kind of half-hearted stop sign. 'Just give him a bit more time,' she said. 'He's digesting it all. He's working through it all with that shrink of his.'

'Shrink?' I said. 'Dad's seeing a shrink?'

'Yes,' Mum said. 'But don't ever say that I told you so. Just give him some time and I'm sure he'll talk to you about it eventually.'

'Oh,' I said. 'OK. Sure.' I resisted the desire to make a joke about more time. After all, it had only been five years.

◆　◆　◆

It was two years after that, the 7th of July 2005 – the day of the London bombings. It's the kind of date that, if you were anywhere near, you simply don't forget a thing.

I'd been watching Sky News going round in circles all morning, filling airtime with very little content. Simultaneously, I'd been trying to phone my parents, but the line had been continuously busy, so by the time I finally did get through it was five past eleven and I was in tears.

'God, you're alive!' Mum said. 'I've been trying to call you!'

'And I've been trying to call you!' I replied. 'Why didn't you just leave a message?'

'Because I didn't *want* to leave a message,' Mum said. 'I wanted to know if *you* were OK!'

Once Mum had confirmed that everyone else in the family was alive and well, she put my father on the line.

'Why aren't you at work?' I asked. 'Is it because of the bombings?'

'Yes, the Underground's closed, isn't it?' he said. 'I can't get in to pick up the van. But I've nothing that urgent on anyway. Horrible business, though. Awful. Actually, they're bloody bastards is what they are.'

'It is,' I said. 'And you're right. They are.'

'But now I've got you on the phone . . . Well, I've been thinking about things. And I think it's time.'

'Time,' I repeated. 'Time for what, Dad?'

'I need to see you. I need to talk to you and Jake. Together. So do you think that you can arrange it?'

'Oh!' I said. My mind was so monopolised by the horror of the bombings I was struggling to even think about the curveball he'd unexpectedly thrown my way.

'Oh?' Dad repeated. 'Is that it?'

'It's just, *with Jake*?' I said, doubtfully. Though Dad had seen Nathan when Abby had dropped him off with Mum a few times, Jake hadn't spoken to Dad one-on-one since before the turn of the century.

'Not this week, obviously,' Dad said. 'Let this all calm down a bit first, eh?'

'Assuming it does.'

'I'm sorry?'

'I just mean assuming it does all calm down.'

'Oh, sure,' Dad said. 'Of course. It doesn't need to be right away. But soon. Can you do that for me?'

'Getting Jake to come might be a bit of an ask,' I said.

'Yes, I know. Which is why I need you to organise it. Maybe do it at yours and don't tell him I'm coming or something?'

'Maybe,' I said. 'What's it about?'

'You know what it's about,' Dad said.

◆　◆　◆

On reflection, I couldn't bring myself to trick my brother into the meeting. It felt like that would be a breach of trust that our already fragile relationship might not survive. What's more, I didn't think it would work anyway. I could perfectly imagine Jake storming out the second he laid eyes on our father.

Instead, I told him the truth and simply begged him to come. And he surprised me by saying, 'Sure, yes. Of course.' I suspect the bombings had concentrated everybody's minds on what was important in life and what wasn't.

After much discussion with Dan about the pros and cons of a private versus public meeting place, I booked us a booth in a pub that did great food. It seemed to provide a perfect combination of enough privacy for us to talk freely, while being public enough to head off any actual shouting.

It was a warm summer evening and would have felt pleasant if there hadn't been troops with machine guns everywhere.

Once I'd been thoroughly frisked by a security guard, I went inside to find Dad already seated in our booth.

'You're early,' he said, leaning over the table to peck me on the cheek.

'You're earlier,' I replied.

'No Lauren?'

I shook my head. 'She's with Dan. She's fine. Enjoying a night with Daddy. I thought it was better this way.'

'Yes,' Dad said. 'Of course.'

While we were waiting, we ordered a bottle of wine and chatted about Lauren and Dan, and then the attacks and the soldiers, and by the time Jake arrived at half past seven the wine had cushioned me suitably for whatever was coming next.

I'd seen far less of Jake over the previous few years and I remember being shocked at how much weight he'd put on. He'd always been one of those pointy, foxy-looking men, all angles and jawline and stubble, but here he was, a forty-four-year-old, rounded-looking daddy. I thought the extra weight suited him, and I said so. It seemed to make him look kinder, or less harsh, a thought I kept to myself.

Once he'd sat down and removed his suit jacket, he stretched his fingers and cleared his throat before looking across the table at Dad. It was only then I realised he'd managed to cross the entire pub and sit down without looking our father in the eye.

'So, Dad,' he said. He cleared his throat again. 'Long time no see.'

'Yes,' Dad said. 'Yes, it's been too long. It's been much too long.'

Dad asked after Abby and Nathan, and then Jake inquired about Mum and Dan and Lauren. Everyone was being so polite that it was making my teeth hurt, so I felt relieved when Jake finally interrupted the chit-chat by asking Dad why we were actually there.

'I need your help with something,' he replied. Then, turning his attention to me, he added, 'Yours too. I need help from both of you.'

Jake raised both eyebrows. 'Help?' he said. 'I wasn't expecting *that*.'

Because I sensed that he was about to go off on one, I discreetly patted his thigh beneath the table in the hope of calming him down.

'You've both read it, I assume,' Dad said. 'The interview thing?'

At the realisation that Dad was going to address the elephant in the room, I sensed Jake relax a little beside me.

'Yes,' I said. 'Of course. A number of times.'

Jake nodded solemnly. 'Me too. But just once.'

'So I wondered if you could both help me with something. Well, with two things really.'

'Fire away,' I said, thinking that he perhaps wanted extra copies or a typed transcript of the untranslated original.

'I wondered if you, Jake, could help me try to track down Joshua in America. If he's still alive, that is.'

'Joshua?' Jake said. 'Sorry, but I read it a long time ago. Years ago, actually.'

'He was Leah's brother, wasn't he?'

'Yes. My uncle, really,' Dad said. 'And you're very good with all those search engines and things, Jake. So I thought you might be able to find out if he's still around.'

Jake cleared his throat but quite noticeably did not reply, so to move the attention away from him I asked Dad what he wanted from me.

'I thought you might accompany me on a little trip,' he said. 'To France.'

'To see Igor?' I asked, already feeling excited.

Dad nodded. 'I feel that I need to talk to him while he's still around.'

'Oh, totally,' I said. 'I'd love to! And I'm sure Jake will help you track down your uncle, won't you?'

'Um, actually, that depends,' Jake said. 'I think there are other conversations we need to have first.'

'Oh,' Dad said. 'Go ahead.'

Jake laughed sourly. 'You haven't said *anything*, Dad! No apology. Not one word about the tapes. Nothing about the fact that you didn't believe Ruth when she told you. Nothing about missing my wedding. Nothing about making my entire family boycott it. Nothing! So don't you think you might start there before asking me to *help* you?'

'I never made anyone boycott your wedding, Jake,' Dad said, which, though it could hardly be said that he'd encouraged anyone to go either, was at least factually correct.

'And in all fairness,' I pointed out as gently as I could, 'Mum and Dad didn't *miss* your wedding either. You didn't invite them. Subtle difference.'

'No, *you're* the one who missed it,' Jake said, turning his glare on me. 'You were invited and refused to come without Mum and Dad. And if that's not Dad's fault, then I imagine it must be yours.'

I raised my hands in surrender. 'OK,' I said. 'But I think you know that was a bit more complicated too. But OK. Whatever.'

'Anyway, you're right,' Dad said. 'I'm sorry. That's what I should have said first. I'm sorry for all of it. I should have apologised ages ago. But it's been hard. It's been really hard. A shock . . . to the system. A big one.'

'OK,' Jake said. 'That's a start.'

'Those tapes . . . they . . .' Dad shrugged, and I felt really sorry for him. These kinds of conversations had always been hard for him, and I sat there trying to think of a way to subtly remind Jake of just how much effort Dad was expending even trying to talk to us this way.

'Are we admitting that it's all true, then?' Jake asked. 'Because you haven't said that either.'

Dad nodded and fidgeted in his seat. 'Yes, I think it probably is,' he said.

'So Grandad and Grandma were gay. And in a fake marriage. And you're adopted, and an orphan, and Jewish. And our family name isn't Solomas at all?'

'Jake!' I said. 'Jesus . . .'

'Well, it's true, isn't it?' Jake said. 'If we're saying what's on the tapes is true.'

'But you don't have to be so brutal about it, do you? There are ways of saying things with kindness, you know.'

Jake looked away and blew through pursed lips. 'OK,' he said, after a moment. 'Sorry. Sorry for being so brutal.'

'This is all still pretty hard for me,' Dad said. 'So I'm sorry if I'm . . . not . . . how I'm meant to be or whatever. You know what

356

I mean. But yes, you're right. All of those things you said would appear to be true.'

'And I'm supposing the hardest bit is the Jewish thing, is it?' Jake asked.

'Jake,' I pleaded.

'The Jewish thing?' Dad repeated.

'Yeah, being Jewish. Seeing as you hate them so much I would imagine that's particularly hard to stomach.'

Dad gasped and shook his head. 'Is that what you really think of me?' he asked.

'Yeah,' Jake said coldly. 'It is, actually.'

'Jake?' I pleaded again. 'Please? Can we just try to show a little . . . I don't know . . . *compassion* here? This isn't easy for anyone.'

'No,' Jake said. 'No, it's not easy, that's for sure.'

'I have no problem with the Jews,' Dad said. 'And no problem if I'm Jewish. None.'

'Yeah,' Jake said sarcastically. 'Right.'

'No, really,' Dad told him. 'It's neither here nor there to me.'

'So why throw me out of the house when I tried to tell you? Why all the Jewish jokes when we were kids, eh? Why all that anti-Semitic shite?'

Dad sighed. 'Do you want to hear anything from me, Jake? Or do you just want a really good fight? Because if that's all you're after here, I can oblige.'

'Of course he wants to hear, don't you?' I said, gently nudging Jake with my hip.

'Sure,' Jake said with a sigh. 'Go ahead.'

'So the jokes and things were wrong,' Dad said. 'For what it's worth, I don't think they . . . you know . . . were as bad as you made out. But they were wrong. So I apologise.'

Jake nodded. 'Right,' he said, sounding unconvinced.

'But you don't know everything about me,' Dad said. 'There are . . . I don't know . . . reasons, I suppose. For everything.'

'Reasons,' Jake repeated.

'They called me Jew-boy at school,' Dad said. 'That's probably a tiny part of it.'

'Who did?' I asked.

'The other boys,' Dad said. 'Because they saw, in the showers. So they all started calling me Jew-boy.'

'Because you're circumcised?' Jake asked.

'Yes, I thought it was, well, a medical thing . . . Sometimes it is, it can be. So that's what I thought. But the other boys took the mickey out of me. And they started calling me Jew-boy.'

'I don't see what that's got to do with anything,' Jake said. 'It just sounds like another excuse.'

'It's a . . . I suppose you could call it a defence mechanism,' Dad said. 'That's what the shrink called it anyway. I'm not justifying it. I'm just trying to explain.'

'A defence mechanism?'

'Like an attempt at fitting in?' I offered.

'Yes,' Dad said. 'It was a way of telling everyone I wasn't Jewish, I suppose. So I always told those jokes. I collected them, in a way, so that I could use them. To defend myself.'

'So you *were* ashamed of being Jewish,' Jake said.

'I didn't know that I was Jewish, Jake. So how could I be ashamed? I still don't know really, do I? I suppose I probably am. And I don't care. Really, I don't. If anything, I feel sad that I know so little about it all, about what being Jewish even means. But I need you to at least believe that. I'm not anti-Semitic. I promise you I'm not.'

'So what's so hard if it's not that?' Jake asked, still sounding harsh.

'I'm sorry?'

'You said it's been a shock. That it's been hard. So if it's not finding out that you're Jewish, then what?'

Dad glared at Jake and shook his head. 'What is wrong with you, boy?' he asked. 'Where's your goddamned empathy gone? When did you get to be so cold?'

'My empathy?' Jake said. 'Oh, I think I lost that somewhere. Maybe during that wedding where none of my family showed up.'

Because things seemed to be spinning out of control, I put my wine glass down and reached out so that I could touch both their wrists at once, forming a symbolic bridge between them. 'Can we please just take a breath at this point?' I asked. 'Can we please just try to remember that we're family, and deep down we love each other, and just, I don't know, chill out a bit? And can we please try to listen to each other properly? I think it would help.'

Jake sighed deeply. 'OK,' he said. 'Fine. So tell us, Dad. Tell us what was so hard for you.'

'The betrayal, mainly,' Dad said.

'*My* betrayal?' Jake asked.

Dad laughed. 'No! My parents' betrayal. They lied to me. They lied to me every day for my whole life. In fact, my whole life has been nothing but a long list of lies. I have no idea who I even *am* anymore . . . Can you imagine how that feels? Actually, there's no reason you should be able to imagine how that feels. But maybe you could try.'

'Sure,' Jake said reluctantly. 'OK, I get that.'

'Do you?' Dad asked. 'Do you really? Because, you know, I worked it out. There were more than twenty thousand days when they could have told me. That's twenty thousand days each. Twenty thousand occasions when they decided to just carry on lying.'

'I think it was really hard for them to find the right moment,' I offered in my grandmother's defence.

'*Hard*,' Dad said. 'Yes, I'm sure it was. But you know, life is full of hard stuff. And if you have any balls at all, you find a way. On one of those twenty thousand-odd days, you find a day – you find one hour in one day to do that hard thing that needs to be done. To do the *right* thing.'

'So you're angry,' I said. 'You're angry with them.'

'I'm . . .' Dad said. He looked around the room and for a moment I thought he'd finished, that he'd exceeded his word quota for the year and was simply going to beckon over a waitress and order dinner. Knowing Dad, it was perfectly possible. But then he turned back and, staring at the table, continued, 'Yes, I'm angry, and grateful, and sad, and disappointed. I'm confused and resentful as hell. I feel lucky and saved and . . . violated, I suppose, in a way. I feel cheated, and . . . I don't know . . . *bereaved*, perhaps, is the right word. And a bit undeserving as well.'

I glanced sideways at Jake and saw his eyebrow twitch at the shock of what had undoubtedly been the most heartfelt sentence my father had ever uttered to us.

When I turned back to face Dad, he was dabbing at his eyes, and I started to cry as well. Because Jake wasn't the only one who hadn't fully realised the extent of what had happened to my father at the moment he'd read that transcript. I realised that, faced with Dad's silence on the subject, I'd probably spent more time thinking about how these revelations changed my own sense of identity than how they might have affected Dad. Compared to the earthquake he'd endured, I'd suffered nothing more than a few ripples from a distant tremor. Only now was I understanding quite how profoundly his life had been swept from under his feet. His identity: gone; his family: gone; mother, father, grandparents, surname, culture, belief system, date of birth: all gone. Every essence of the person he'd believed himself to be had vanished in an instant because of me, because of something I'd pushed upon him. I grasped only in that instant how hard it would have been for his parents to tell him the truth, and why they hadn't. And I hated myself for my own failure of imagination, for my own lack of tact and empathy, that I'd dropped that bombshell so lightly.

Dad reached out with his thumb and wiped a tear from my cheek. 'So yes,' he continued. 'I'm sorry it's been hard for both of you. And it has. I'm not denying that at all. But just try to, you know . . . realise. It's been really bloody hard for me too. I pretty much had a breakdown over this.'

We sat in silence for a moment, taking it all in, both Jake and Dad pretending to study their menus.

I was running through Dad's little speech in my mind, trying to remember all the adjectives he'd used. I somehow didn't want to forget any of them.

'Undeserving,' I said suddenly. 'You said undeserving. Why?'

Dad looked up at me and licked his lips. He shrugged and I saw his eyes were beginning to tear again. 'Well, they died, didn't they?' he said, so softly it was almost inaudible. 'My mother, my father, my grandparents . . . They all died. Every single one of them was murdered. But for some reason, I got away. Christophe and Genny saved me. And for what?'

'What do you mean, *for what*?' I asked.

'I mean, what have I ever done with my life?' Dad said, his voice cracking as tears started to roll down his cheeks. 'What have I ever done, other than live an ordinary, normal life?'

My own vision was blurring and my throat was too tight to speak. But then I saw Jake reach across the table and lay his hand on top of Dad's.

'Isn't that why we fought, though?' he asked. 'Isn't that the whole point?'

'I'm sorry?' Dad croaked.

'The reason people fought and resisted the Germans and saved people and died in the war . . .' Jake said. 'Wasn't it so that the Jews and the Roma and the gays and the communists and the disabled and everyone else who wasn't a perfect, blond, blue-eyed German could live an ordinary life? Wasn't it precisely so that you *could* live your ordinary life and get married, and have us, and we could grow up and not have to be Nazis? Wasn't it so that we could *all* live normal lives?'

We sat silently for a moment. Jake's eyes were shiny with tears, too, and it crossed my mind what a strange sight we must make for anyone looking on.

Dad swallowed hard and then flipped his hand over to take Jake's palm within his own.

He sniffed and nodded slowly before continuing. 'You know, maybe it was, son,' he said. 'Thanks for that. I think you may be right.'

Ruth. Part Eight.

Jake executed his part of the bargain first, tracking down Dad's Uncle Joshua within the week. Abby helped him with this, by all accounts, contacting the Red Cross Holocaust Victims Tracing Center, who had quickly found the answers we needed.

Joshua Rosenberg had been living in New Jersey until 1997, when he'd died aged eighty-two. He'd had a happy life and had been married with three children, Craig, Thomas and Cindy, two of whom Jake managed to contact via email. Following this, Craig had written Dad a rather lovely message that Jake had printed and delivered to Dad. In it he said that his father had often wondered what had happened to baby Menashe, and would have been thrilled to hear that he'd survived and was living happily in London. He also said that if Dad ever wanted to visit his cousins in New Jersey, they'd welcome him with open arms.

As for my trip with Dad, it took a little longer to organise, but in the end, we flew from Stansted on the 3rd of September. The owner being such an obnoxious sod, it honestly wouldn't have been my choice of airline, but as they offered the only direct flight on that date there really was no other option.

I felt strangely excited to be on my way to see Igor and unexpectedly ecstatic to be going away with Dad. Though we'd had plenty of foreign holidays when we were kids, essentially in Spain and Greece, travelling with him alone felt special.

Despite having cost a mere £38 each, return, the plane did not fall apart and we landed in Bordeaux just after five. The temperature was a sultry thirty-six degrees – a kind of heat that whacked you in the face like the jet of air from a hairdryer the second you stepped from the plane.

As Dad had done the trip before for Grandpa's funeral, I rather lazily let him organise the whole thing for both of us. Following him through the airport and then on to the shuttle bus, then a tram, and finally through the streets of Bordeaux to the hotel he'd booked, seemed to reinforce the child–parent nature of our relationship and, surprisingly, it felt nice. I was Dad's little girl again for a few hours, and I let myself go with the flow.

His choice of hotel – a budget Ibis – would not have been my choice either. As this was my first and probably last holiday of 2005, not to mention my first proper overseas break since becoming a mum, a pool and a jacuzzi might have been nice. But the Ibis was cheap and central – situated right on the edge of the Botanical Gardens – and as Dad reminded me, we would be there for only one night anyway. So I did my best not to notice the lack of view (my room looked out on to a brick wall) and not to ponder whether the shower was particularly narrow or if, since giving birth, my hips had become abnormally wide.

Within an hour we'd showered and changed and were strolling along the banks of the Garonne, and I felt as if my mind hadn't caught up with my body. I was struggling to believe that I was really there.

We ate in the area behind Saint-Pierre church. There were four small restaurants including ours, one on each side of a lovely little square, their tables mingling beneath the plane trees.

Once the waiter had brought us our aperitifs, drinks Dad had ordered in what sounded to my inexperienced ear like perfect French, I asked him if being in France felt relaxing, like coming 'home'.

'Home?' Dad said. 'Relaxing? No, it feels like a stressful trip to see my father's secret . . . *boyfriend*? I suppose that's the right word.'

We both laughed, and I felt relieved that Dad had managed to joke about the situation. He'd been particularly monosyllabic during the journey, and I'd been worrying he'd be unable to relax for the entire trip. But now he had a glass of wine in his hand, he seemed to have retrieved his sense of humour.

'Not sure about *boyfriend* though,' I said. '*Partner's* probably the best word, considering his age. And are you stressed? Because you have met him before, after all. We both have.'

'Sure,' Dad said, then, 'And I'm fine.' I could tell that was a lie.

'It will be fine, Dad,' I told him. 'He's just a guy. He's just an ordinary guy who loved Grandpa Chris the same way we did.'

'Not in *quite* the same way,' Dad said, smiling cheekily. 'But yes, I know that. Of course I do.'

'I was really talking more about all this,' I said, gesturing at our surroundings, and Dad followed my gaze. For a few seconds we scanned all the relaxed people chatting and drinking and eating – a perfect tableau of relaxed continental life. 'Does this feel like home to you in any way at all because of your roots? Or does it feel as foreign as it does to me?'

Dad shrugged. 'Foreign, I suppose,' he said.

I did my best to disguise a sigh. I was guessing that his three-word reply was all I was going to get. But he surprised me again by sipping his wine and continuing, 'It feels a bit . . . I don't know . . . *stolen*, perhaps? That's not the right word at all, but . . . I suppose what I mean is that there's a bit of me that feels like this was my birthright. This lifestyle, I mean. This relaxed way of living. Eating outdoors and wandering around markets in the sunshine. Instead of rushing around in the drizzle in London the way we all do. It feels like something in my genes might have enjoyed living like this, if that makes any sense.'

'Wow,' I said, surprised by the fact that Dad had said something so succinct and elaborate. It seemed that seeing a shrink had done wonders for his powers of self-expression. 'That actually makes perfect sense,' I continued. 'For what it's worth, I think something in everyone's genes would prefer living this way.'

We sat for a moment, enjoying the atmosphere, and then a question popped into my head. As Dad seemed in such a relaxed mood, I decided to take the risk of asking him. 'Did you never suspect?'

'Suspect?' he repeated.

'That Grandpa was gay? Or that Genny and Ethel were, for that matter.'

'Not really,' Dad said, then, 'Kind of. Maybe. Not Dad. Never Dad. But maybe Genny and Ethel. It was only once, really. But there was a moment . . . and then I just pushed it out of my mind, really.'

'As you would,' I said.

'I'm sorry?'

'I just mean that seems quite a reasonable reaction.'

'Perhaps,' Dad said. 'I wouldn't know.'

'Can I ask when that happened? What happened, I mean?'

Dad sighed. 'I suppose,' he said. He cleared his throat. 'Um, it was one time we dropped in unexpectedly. Genny had a thing for sunflowers, and we saw they had some in a florist's. So we bought them – it was your mother's idea – and went round there to give her the surprise. You and Jake must have been about three and five. We thought they'd be happy to see you.'

'I think you mentioned this once before. This is the last time you ever dropped in unexpectedly, right? Mum said something about it once.'

Dad nodded.

'So what happened?'

He fidgeted in his seat. Visibly, the memory still made him feel uncomfortable. 'It was nothing really specific, more an atmosphere.'

'OK . . .'

'We bumped into Dad in the stairwell. Your grandad was coming down, and he made this big, strange fuss about coming back upstairs and then knocking on their door to tell them we were visiting, but that we were going up to his for a cuppa first . . . It was all a bit false. A bit theatrical, if you know what I mean. It made no sense.'

'He warned them through the front door, you mean? He warned them you were coming?'

'Yes, looking back, I suppose that's what it was. And so we went to his and had a drink, and then when we finally got to theirs, you could tell they were all flustered. That's it, really. There was never anything concrete. Just a strange feeling.'

'But you suspected.'

'I think I must have. I felt awkward about it anyway. I mean, she was supposed to be Mum's cousin, remember. In those days, two women . . . that would have been enough to make most people feel uncomfortable. But on top of everything else, Ethel was her cousin, so that was two taboos for the price of one, really. At any rate, that's what I believed.'

'Because that's what they'd told you.'

'Exactly.'

'So you stopped calling round.'

'Yeah. I just kind of didn't want to anymore. And I always felt a bit strange about Ethel after that. It seemed liked she'd . . . I don't know . . . seduced her, I suppose. And taken her away from Dad.

He seemed like he didn't even have the balls to care, too, and that really annoyed me. We know better now, of course, but that was how it seemed.'

'And to top it all Ethel stole her away to Brighton . . .'

'Yes. I suppose that's how I felt. I tried not to analyse it too much, because, like I say, I was never very comfortable with it. I mean, now we know Ethel wasn't her cousin at all. So it's not so bad. Not bad at all, I suppose. But . . . it's hard to put into words. I never thought that clearly about all of this. But something about the two of them always made me feel a bit funny.'

'And Mum? What did she think?'

'She never really said anything specific. She said something like, "That was strange."'

'Strange?'

'Yes, as we were leaving, she said, "Well, that was strange." And one time, I think she said there was something dodgy about the two of them.'

'Sounds like Mum.'

'Yes. But anyway, enough of that. I don't want to be . . . I mean, I'm not being homophobic or whatever you call it – at least I'm trying not to be – but it still makes me feel a bit queasy, if I'm honest.'

'Sure,' I said. 'That's OK. That's probably normal too. Because it doesn't fit with what they told you the whole time you were growing up, does it?'

'No. That's what the shrink said.'

'He was good was he, the shrink?'

'She,' Dad said. Then he nodded and shrugged at the same time as he reached for the menu. 'Yes, I think so. And now I'm hungry.'

'OK,' I said, forcing a laugh. 'So what are we ordering, Monsieur Frenchman?'

The next morning we met for breakfast in the hotel restaurant before checking out and dragging our cases around the corner to Hertz, where a sexy Frenchman handed us the keys to a Clio.

Dad offered to drive and I was happy to let him do so. He seemed at ease negotiating the roads out of Bordeaux, and when I commented on this he reminded me of the many holidays when he'd driven us around Spain, so we chatted about our memories of those trips for a while.

Most of the journey was motorway and the landscape was flat and dull. I don't know quite what I was expecting – perhaps just something that looked more foreign – but I was left feeling a bit disappointed.

Dad seemed to be feeling it too because, as he accelerated away from one of the toll booths, he said, 'I hate motorways. I hate the way everywhere ends up looking the same. This could be anywhere, really, couldn't it?'

I glanced past him at the industrial estate we were passing – a collection of ugly, corrugated-iron hangars that appeared to have been dumped in a field.

'Almost true,' I said. 'Only in England all those lorries would say Eddie Stobart rather than . . . rather than however the hell you're supposed to pronounce that.'

Dad turned, glanced out of his side window and laughed. He made a valiant attempt at pronouncing Kuehne+Nagel, which was written on all the parked lorries, and then added that he didn't think it was a French name anyway.

Though Igor had invited us to stay at his house in the village of Mios, Dad had insisted we reserve a hotel in neighbouring Lanton instead. Personally, I would have preferred to stay at Igor's – or at least, I suspected I would – I didn't know him that well, after all. But as I guessed that the idea of staying in his father's home with his father's partner was just too emotionally fraught, I agreed without a fight.

The hotel having been chosen by Dad, it was yet another economical choice, but it turned out to be quite lovely all the same. The place appeared to be family-run, and consisted of a series of small, two-storey buildings set among immaculately kept gardens, less than two hundred metres from the beach.

Once we'd checked into our rooms I met Dad downstairs at the bar as arranged. It was furnished with wicker tables and armchairs and was set behind huge bay windows that had been rolled back, so that the bar area spilled out of the hotel and into the grounds. The result was most inviting and, though it wasn't even midday, Dad was already seated with a beer, so I joined him and ordered a coffee.

'Did you call Igor yet?' I asked after a moment. 'Does he know we've arrived?'

Dad shook his head and sipped at his drink. 'The beer's lovely,' he said. 'Ice cold.'

'Great,' I replied. 'It's a bit early for me. I'll stick with coffee for now. And are you going to? Call Igor, I mean? Because he might want to come over and join us.'

Once again, Dad just shook his head.

I pulled a face. 'Dad?' I said. 'You know that's why we're here, don't you?'

'Of course I do,' Dad said. 'But we've got all day tomorrow. And the day after that. So today I'm allowed to relax with my favourite daughter, aren't I?'

'I suppose,' I said, doubtfully. 'If he's not expecting us today.'

'No,' Dad replied. 'He isn't.'

'Tomorrow, then,' I said with meaning, because I was imagining Dad trying to wriggle out of meeting with Igor altogether.

As if to confirm my fears, Dad said, 'Yes. Or the day after. We'll see.'

For two days we played perfect sweaty tourists. We drove into the centre of Arcachon and wandered around the town. We stopped at oyster bars so that Dad could tip the slimy creatures down his throat, visited Mauresque Park and swam at stunning Moulleau Beach. We really were having a lovely time together, and in some ways, that was unexpected.

Yet by the time the sun had passed its zenith on day two, I was worried. The subject of when we were going to visit Igor was fast becoming taboo and when I'd repeatedly hinted that it was time we contacted him, Dad had simply ignored me. I'd tried asking him directly, too, and each time he'd either changed the subject or said something like, 'Relax! We still have all day tomorrow.' On the one occasion when I'd really insisted, he'd got annoyed and gone off for a walk.

I'd been right all along, I realised – for whatever reason, he really was nervous about meeting up with Igor. And if there was one thing I knew my father was good at it was avoiding anything emotionally challenging.

I realised too that his fear of not having the courage to do this was perhaps the reason he'd brought me along. And that realisation meant there was only one thing left to be done: I'd have to take matters into my own hands. So, telling Dad I wanted to call home to check up on Lauren again – I went to my room to phone Igor.

'Is this Ruth?' he said on answering. 'Is everything OK? I've been worried about you. I've been waiting for your call for two days! I didn't even want to leave the house in case I missed you.'

I apologised profusely and explained that my father was feeling nervous about the meeting and had been difficult to pin down.

'Nervous?' Igor said. 'What's he got to be nervous about?'

I laughed. 'I don't really know. But I suppose chatting to your father's partner isn't the most mundane situation for someone of Dad's generation. Actually, it's not that mundane for any generation, really.'

'Sure,' Igor said. 'I understand that. But we've already met. Repeatedly. I thought he liked me.'

'He does,' I said, although I really had no idea. 'He's just being weird. He does this. Which is why I wondered if you could come here instead, and sort of surprise him?'

A few hours later, Dad and I were in the bar, sipping our drinks, when Igor walked in. He had a full head of grey hair and tinted tortoiseshell glasses. He was wearing a beige linen suit over a sky-blue polo shirt. He looked younger and hipper than I'd imagined.

'Bill!' he said, when he reached us. 'And lovely baby Ruth!'

Dad looked startled and, as he turned and glanced in my direction, annoyed. But then he regained his composure and stood. 'It looks like my darling daughter has jumped the gun,' he said, embracing Igor. 'Hello, Igor. How are you?'

'Your darling daughter was worried the gun might never get fired,' I said, winking at Igor and, when my turn came, hugging him too. 'But this way we can all eat together. This is perfect, isn't it?'

'Yes,' Dad said, with a sigh, then, as an aside, 'It'll have to be, really, won't it?'

Once we'd finished our drinks we strolled down to the seafront restaurant where we'd reserved a table for two. Luckily, they had no problems accommodating Igor.

The conversation during the walk had been polite holiday chit-chat. When did you arrive? What sights have you visited so far? You know the kind of thing. But as soon as we sat down, Igor inter-linked his fingers and leaned forward, looking serious.

'So the first thing I'd like to say is that I'm incredibly relieved someone finally told you,' he said, addressing Dad. 'It's what Ethel and I wanted all along, but the others didn't agree. So I just wanted you to know that.'

Dad frowned at this and fiddled with his cutlery for a moment before saying, 'I'm sorry, but . . . When you say it's what you wanted, it sounds . . . It's just that . . . you didn't really know me, did you?'

Igor laughed at this. 'Of course I knew you!' he said. 'I saw you plenty of times, either in the shop or over at your father's place. And he talked about you all the time. I followed every step of your life, albeit from a respectable distance.'

'Really?' Dad said. 'I don't really remember seeing you much. I'm sorry.'

Igor shrugged sadly and said, 'Memory can be strange.' Once he had struggled out of his jacket, he turned to me and went on, 'I met you once, too. But you were only about this big.' He raised his hands to indicate a baby-sized package.

'We spoke at Grandma Genny's funeral, too,' I reminded him. Then, trying to lighten the tone of the conversation, I added, 'I'm afraid I don't remember that other time, though.'

'Well, your father left you both with Chris for the afternoon, and he rushed you down to the shop so that I could meet you.'

Dad nodded thoughtfully. 'I vaguely remember that,' he said. 'We generally left you with Mavaughn, but one time I had to leave you with Dad. I don't remember why, but your mother was terrified he'd drop you or lose one of you or something. You must have only been about nine months old.'

'Well, he didn't drop you,' Igor said, smiling at me warmly. 'He sprinted down to your Uncle Igor's shop, and while Jake played with a spinning top, we smothered you in kisses. You giggled every time we kissed your tummy. You loved that.'

'Still do,' I joked, to ease my embarrassment.

'He was incredibly proud of you. He was incredibly proud of all of you.'

'If you say so,' Dad said.

There was a lull in the conversation just then, and luckily the waiter came to break the silence.

Once he'd handed out drinks and left, I asked Igor if he thought the tapes gave an accurate rendition of Grandma Genny's life.

'I do, actually,' he said. 'Obviously there are some dates and things I might quibble over. After all, it was a long time ago. But yes, everything she said ties up pretty well with the bits I remember and the stories other people told me. When you read it in one go, it's quite an extraordinary oeuvre.'

'Yes,' I agreed. 'It is.'

Another silence fell upon us, during which we all sipped our drinks.

'So, Dad,' I prompted when the void got to be too much for me. 'I'm sure you've got some things you want to ask Uncle Igor, haven't you?'

'Me?' Dad said, looking like a rabbit in the headlights. 'Um, I'm not sure. Have I?'

'It's OK,' Igor said, laying his hands placidly on top of each other. 'It will come. There's no need to force anything, Ruth.'

Dad realigned his knife and fork before turning a fake smile on us both. 'It's hard,' he said, finally, 'because there's so much detail in the tapes, isn't there? So it's hard to think what to ask.'

'Yes,' Igor agreed. 'Yes, the tapes are incredibly detailed about your parents' lives, especially when they were younger. And about your origins too, of course. But not so much about Chris and me. So perhaps you have some questions about that?'

'Um, I think I'm OK,' Dad said, and I distinctly saw him blush. And then he stood and, making excuses, vanished to the loo.

'I'm sorry,' I said, once he'd gone. 'He's more uptight about this than I thought.'

'Yes,' Igor said. 'Yes, I can see that. But that's OK. I'm sure it's a lot to take in.'

'So how long did you live with Grandpa?' I asked, consciously trying to demonstrate that at least I wasn't fazed by my grandfather's sexuality.

'We were more or less a couple from '61, albeit a very discreet one. But we only really lived together once we moved here,' Igor said. 'We didn't get as long as we'd hoped, but, you know, it was lovely while it lasted.'

'That's sad,' I said. 'I'm sorry you didn't get longer.'

'It is what it is.'

'And Ethel and Genny, they were together from when they were, what, fourteen?'

'Oh God, those two, honey!' Igor said, and for the first time he sounded vaguely camp. 'They were incredible.'

Dad returned at that moment, clearing his throat as if to warn us of his arrival. I sensed he wanted to interrupt our conversation but instead I decided to forge on. 'One thing I never really understood from the tapes was the relationship between the four of you,' I said, then, to Dad, 'We were just chatting about how long they were all together.'

'Sure,' Dad said, reaching for the menu.

'Between the four of us?' Igor said. 'I'm not sure I understand.'

'I mean, how did your . . . I'm tempted to say "love triangle", but there were four of you, so . . .'

'How did our love rectangle work?' Igor offered with a grin.

'Exactly. That must have been complicated, mustn't it?'

'Sometimes it was,' he said. 'But mainly it worked quite smoothly. I've never really tried to analyse it before, but I suppose

375

you could say that there were two couples, two very lucky couples, and—'

'Lucky because?'

'Oh, because we were very much in love,' Igor said. 'That's not as common as people like to think. Ethel and Genny were . . . fusional, I suppose you'd say. I think you can sense that from the transcript. They were almost like one person. They never even argued that I can recall. And being apart simply wasn't an option.'

'Yes, you can see that from the way Genny follows Ethel to London,' I said.

'Exactly. And they were always like that. We used to joke that they were joined at the hip. Chris even used to refer to them as "Gethel". Whereas your father and I . . . Our relationship was more *soupe au lait*. I'm not sure how you say that in English. I think I've been living here too long.'

'Milk soup?' Dad offered, looking confused.

'Yes, but it means someone who boils over easily. The way milk does in a saucepan. So we'd argue and shout and fall out and make up again. But we always did make up, because we loved each other.'

'And the four of you?' I asked, doing my best to ignore the fact that my father was shuffling in his seat and trying to catch the waiter's attention. 'Did you all get on together?'

'Ha!' Igor laughed. 'Not always. But there were two very powerful friendships in there holding it all together. Genny and Chris, obviously. It's hard to explain, but they were almost like a married couple too. I mean, they lived as a married couple for years, so maybe that's why, but I suspect it was the other way around. I suspect they were able to do that *because* they loved each other so deeply. It's a chicken and egg situation, isn't it, so you never really know. But I often thought Genny understood Chris better than I did. When we argued – and we argued a lot – it was often Genny who'd calm me down. It was Genny who'd explain what Chris had meant and how I'd misunderstood.'

'So you were close friends with Genny?'

Igor nodded, albeit vaguely. 'Sure, we got on fine. But her allegiance in any argument was always to Chris. The one I really liked, other than your grandfather, obviously, was Ethel. I thought Ethel was great. She was so sharp and witty and sarcastic and I loved that about her. She really made me laugh.'

'So there were two couples in love. And two sort of diagonal friendships between you and Ethel and Genny and Chris,' I said.

'Yes. Yes, that's a very good way of putting it. And don't get me wrong, we all loved each other. We all respected each other deeply. But when we found ourselves together as a foursome, Genny would always end up talking to Chris while holding hands with Ethel. And I would invariably end up yakking away with Ethel.'

'While holding hands with Grandpa?'

Igor laughed. 'Not so much. We weren't demonstrative the way Genny and Ethel were. But we'd often end up talking diagonally, do you know what I mean? If Genny was opposite Ethel and I was opposite Chris, Genny and Chris would end up talking about one thing and Ethel and I about another. It was just the way the . . . in French they'd say, *it was the way the current flowed*.'

'The current?'

'The electricity. It was the way it flowed most easily.'

'Oh, I see. You must have been devastated when she passed away. Especially the way it happened.'

'Oh, I was. Absolutely. Not so much by *how* it happened because I suppose I understood why. After everything they'd lived through together . . . And now they were gone and she was alone, and in pain? Who could blame her? She was tired, I think. She felt she'd had enough. Plus, I knew she wasn't afraid of death.'

'She wasn't?'

'No, death was something she'd made her peace with. She'd had to, really. After everyone she'd lost. Her whole family . . . So she had this theory, and she used to say how before we were born, we were nothing. And that lasted billions of years . . . since the dawn of time. And it wasn't horrible, was it? It wasn't anything. So she thought that dying was just about going back to that state of nothingness. "Why would we be scared of that?" she used to say. "Why would anyone?" But I miss her, obviously. I miss them all, horribly.'

We were interrupted by the waiter then, and once we'd ordered, Dad started asking questions about life in Arcachon, making it impossible for me to carry on talking about Grandad and Ethel and Genny.

Igor seemed happy to go with the flow and talked about life in the region and how the seasons were defined by the ebb and flow of tourists. After that Igor started asking me about *my* life, so I told him about Dan and Lauren and our interlinked apartments and my job.

At the end of the evening, as we walked back to the hotel, Igor invited us to lunch at the house and before Dad could put up any objections I accepted on both our behalves.

'Good,' Igor said. 'Because I have something specific I need to talk to you about.'

As we watched him drive away in his little Citroën, I asked Dad what he thought that was.

'Not sure,' Dad said. 'Maybe Grandad's ashes. I'm not sure what they did with them. Or the house. Perhaps we're going to inherit it one day. I don't think Igor had any children.'

◆　◆　◆

Despite an ominous weather forecast, the next morning turned out to be sunny. As it was our last full day there, we returned to

Moulleau Beach for a swim, after which we nabbed two sunbeds next to the tiny hotel pool.

While Dad re-read his favourite novel – a Steinbeck – I alternated between roasting in the sun and cooling off in the pool, all the while trying to think what questions I wanted to ask Igor.

I struggled to come up with anything specific, though, because the things I wanted to know weren't really facts. I just wanted some kind of way in to understanding who my grandparents had actually been.

'You found it OK?' Igor said, meeting us at the front gate.

'Yes, I remembered it from last time,' Dad told him, which was an absolute lie. We'd been driving around in circles for at least fifteen minutes.

The house was a bit of a disappointment, really. I'd been hoping for something a bit exotic; if not a chateau, at least a few dry-stone walls or some pretty louvred shutters.

Instead, the house was a generic seventies-build bungalow, its only saving grace the well-tended garden surrounding it, and it was there that Igor started our tour.

Dotted among the shrubs were various cats, and one by one, Igor made loving introductions. The old one was Pedro, and that one was Patty. The big ginger tom over there was Gaspard.

After the garden, Igor led us through the house, and had it not been for the presence of three more cats, Mangui, Paloma and Titus, it wouldn't have taken long. There were two boxy bedrooms and a bathroom with original seventies wall tiles. The only room to have been renovated appeared to be the kitchen.

One nice thing was that there were photographs of Grandpa Chris everywhere – photos I'd never seen before. On top of the television was a black and white image of him in a three-piece suit, and on the bookcase another showing him rowing a boat. The fridge had more recent colour pictures clipped to the door with magnets.

'I've never seen any of these,' I told Igor, studying another image of Grandpa outside a theatre.

He crossed the room to join me and laughed. 'I'm not surprised,' he said. 'That's me.'

'Gosh, you looked alike!' I said, straightening. 'Dad, look!' But Dad was busy studying a photo of Igor and Grandpa together.

'We would have looked alike,' Igor said, 'if it hadn't been for the age gap. But as it was, I always looked the way Chris had looked five years earlier. But you're right. People often say that whenever they look at our photos.'

Lunch – a simple omelette with home-grown salad – was served beneath a little gazebo at the bottom of the garden. While we ate, Igor explained that he and Chris had bought the place together, but he now needed to write a new will in case anything happened.

'And let's face it,' he said. 'Sooner or later *something* happens. There's no escaping that one.' He and Chris had no other descendants, he explained, and so he wanted Dad's permission to leave it to him.

Dad seemed embarrassed about this, but in the end, when Igor said that it had been Christophe's explicit wish, there was nothing to do but accept gracefully, and to my relief that's what Dad did. Whether we ended up having holidays here or selling it, I could see very little downside to one day inheriting a house in France.

About three, Igor started glancing at his watch, so I asked if he had somewhere he needed to be and it turned out he had a dentist's appointment.

'I don't want to go at all,' he said, 'but I think I really need to. I've a tooth that's been playing up for months.'

'Please,' Dad said. 'Feel free. We're fine, aren't we, Ruth?'

Once coffee had been served, Igor asked if there was anything else we wanted to ask. 'If I'm honest, I was expecting more questions,' he said.

'Not really,' Dad replied, and for some reason I didn't believe him. I could almost hear some massive, unanswered question sitting on the tip of his tongue.

'And you?' Igor asked, looking at me.

I gritted my teeth and sighed. 'I don't know . . .' I said. 'I sort of wanted . . . I guess I hoped to find out who he *was*. Because I don't feel like I knew him.'

'Ask,' Igor said. 'Ask anything.'

I shook my head and tutted in frustration. 'If I'm honest, I don't know what to ask either. What was he like, maybe? How did *you* see him, perhaps?'

'You sound like you never met him,' Dad commented, sounding annoyed with me.

'No, I did. I know I did. It's just that he was . . . I don't know . . . A bit austere, maybe. A bit . . . distant? He always seemed very guarded somehow.'

Igor nodded. 'I see,' he said. 'It's a disease. A gay disease. Or it used to be in our day.'

'I'm sorry?'

'It was our circumstances, you see. It was how we had to be back then. Or how we thought we had to be, anyway.'

'I'm not sure I understand,' I said.

'No. And I'm not sure I can explain it to you,' Igor said. 'But we had to be very careful all the time. Not to laugh too loudly. Or too camply. Not to dance too enthusiastically. Never to shriek in a high voice, no matter how big the surprise. Not to dress too flamboyantly . . .'

'Of course,' I said. 'I get it.'

'Ultimately, we ended up working so hard at being ordinary that I think we became *too* guarded. A lot of us did, anyway. In the seventies, for example, there were lots of straight men wearing flowery shirts and jewellery and boots with heels and patchwork flares, but we would never have dared. So we ended up being *too* careful – being more worried about being found out than we needed to be. So we ended up, as you said, being somewhat austere.'

'That's sad,' Dad said.

'It actually sounds like really hard work,' I added.

'Oh, it was! But for a while back there our lives *depended* on it. For a long time – for most of our lives, actually. And then, by the time things began to change for the better, it had become a habit. That's what made our friendships so special.'

'Because, with each other, you could be yourselves?'

'Exactly,' Igor said.

'In fact, that's it,' I said, feeling suddenly hopeful. 'That's what I want to know. It's what I sensed was always missing. What was Grandpa Chris really like? What was he like when he was able to be himself? Because I don't think I ever saw it.'

'I don't think I did either,' Dad said. 'I think that's why.'

'Why . . . ?' I repeated.

Dad shrugged. 'Why everything, really. Why our relationship was so vague.'

Igor nodded slowly. 'He was very damaged,' he said. 'The trauma lasted his whole life. I'm not sure if you want to know this, but there were things . . . His nightmares . . . His fear of dogs. His fear of being hungry. The fact that he could never really . . . you know . . . have sex. Not properly.'

'Because of what the Nazis did to him?'

'Yes. He had terrible problems, you know . . . down below . . . Right up until the end. But we got on fine without all that. We were still very tactile and that was enough for me.'

382

Igor smiled gently and then continued. 'But he wasn't just a bundle of trauma. I wouldn't want you to think that. He was funny. He was very funny. And he was generous and kind – one of the kindest people I ever met.' He swallowed with visible difficulty and his eyes started to glisten. 'He liked to dance. He was a crazy dancer – all arms and legs. Genny used to say that he danced like a bunch of cats in a bag! And he liked to sing. He sang all the dooby-doo bits to all the pop songs.'

'The dooby-doo bits?' I repeated, grinning.

'Yes, you know. The bits the backing singers do. That would have been his dream job: a backing singer in a band, wearing flares and a flowery shirt and stepping forward to sing shooby-doo-wa.'

'The singing plumber,' Dad said. 'I never heard him sing once, so I'm struggling to imagine. But I'll take your word for it.'

Igor shrugged. 'He liked gardening, and flowers. And poetry, and music. I was always more classical, but Chris liked the Beach Boys and Bowie.'

'Bowie?' Dad said. 'Really?'

'Oh yes, he loved Bowie. I think he had a bit of a crush on him, truth be told. And Lou Reed.'

'OK,' Dad said, looking embarrassed.

'He liked to bake. He made wonderful bread. He loved to tell stories. He could make up an incredible story about just about anything . . .'

'Yes, he told us lots of tales when we were kids,' I said. 'Dad felt they were a sort of device, to avoid talking about anything important.'

'Sometimes they were,' Igor said. 'And sometimes they were the only way he knew of *to* talk about anything important. They were how he dealt with the past. Most of his stories were rooted in the war in some way. So I think making stories was a sort of device he used to rewrite things – to rewrite his memories, to ease the pain. It's actually a psychological process called sublimation.'

'That's very true, actually,' I said. 'I spotted bits of Grandad's stories in Genny's interview. Like that town La Vielle-Loye in the wolf story.'

'Like the wolves themselves,' Igor said.

'The wolves?' I repeated.

'Yes. Johann was mauled to death by dogs. So I think telling a story where they tore the Germans to pieces instead was a kind of therapy, and I think that's why he told that one so often. And all his stories were that way. They were all elements of the past, rehashed.'

From the corner of my eye I saw Dad wringing his hands together, so I turned to look at him.

'The truth is that I didn't know him at all,' he said, his voice cracking with emotion. 'That's what's so hard. Neither of them ever let me anywhere near.'

'I know,' Igor said. 'And that's why I wanted them to tell you the truth. That's why Ethel and I both did. We could see the cost of *not* telling you – the distance it created. But you know, considering what he lived through, I think he did pretty well. That's what you need to keep in mind. You have to remember where he came from – what he lived through. Bringing up a child after that . . . well, it's quite an exploit.'

'Did they even want me, though?' Dad asked, unexpectedly.

'I'm sorry?' Igor said.

'Did they want me?' he said again. 'That's the only question I really need answering. Or was I just something that happened along the way? A bundle that got dropped in their laps.'

'Oh, God,' Igor said. 'Oh, Billy, you can't possibly think that.'

'Can't I?' Dad said.

'They loved you,' Igor said, nodding slowly as he spoke. 'They loved you more than anything.'

'How can you be sure?' Dad said. 'Because I read that transcript, and it didn't sound like they had much choice.'

'They loved you so much that they stayed together until you were eighteen. Because neither of them could bear to be away from you.'

'Really?'

'Of course. It would have been far easier for them to go their separate ways. But they needed to be with you. They *both* needed to be with you. Because you were the person they loved the most. Actually, talking of those stories, did he ever tell you the one about the lonely sheepdog?'

'The lonely *patou*?' I said. 'Oh, I used to love that one.'

Dad nodded. 'It was one of my favourites, too.'

'Well, it was an allegory, wasn't it?' Igor said. 'It's about feeling different to other people, and finding love all the same. Ultimately, it's about founding a family, too. The puppy they find – because, if you remember, they can't have one of their own – so the puppy that makes their lives complete—'

'Oh God, Dad, that's you!' I interrupted, reaching for his hand across the table.

Dad closed his eyes and licked his lips. 'Maybe,' he whispered.

'Definitely,' Igor said. 'It's no accident he told you that story.'

A tear rolled down Dad's cheek. 'I wish I'd known that, though,' he said softly. 'I wish I'd *felt* it.'

Igor stood and moved around the table so that he was standing beside my father. 'This is where you stand and you let Uncle Igor give you a hug,' he said.

'Erm, I'm not really much of a hugger,' Dad said. 'Like father like son.'

'No,' Igor laughed, reaching out to pull Dad to his feet. 'Well, stand up, because I have something to tell you. Something that will set you free.'

Dad reluctantly stood but remained rigid as Igor wrapped his arms around him.

'He may not have let you see much of it,' Igor said. 'But he liked to hug. Your father loved to hug. He loved to sing, too. And he loved to dance. So if you're a real believer in *like father, like son*, you can enjoy all those things too.'

Igor started to force Dad to sway then, and I could tell that Dad was both mortified about being held in Igor's arms but was also quite moved by the experience. I wiped the tears from my eyes, and willed my father, for once in his life, to let go.

'I miss him,' I heard Dad croak. 'I never even knew him properly, but now he's gone I miss him. I miss them both so much.'

'Well, I really *did* know him,' Igor said, sending me a complicit wink. 'And for what it's worth, it doesn't help at all. Because I really miss him too.'

They swayed through 360 degrees before Dad suddenly said, 'Enough,' and pushed Igor away – taking his elbows and holding him at arm's length. I could see that, despite his tears, he was smiling.

'The good thing, as far as I'm concerned, is that you came,' Igor said. 'Because, Christ, you remind me of Chris. It's almost like he's back. Almost every mannerism is the same.'

'And I'm glad to know he had you in his life,' Dad said, with a sniff. 'I honestly am. Because you seem like a really good man.'

'Oh, I'm nothing special,' Igor said. 'We were just perfectly ordinary people. It was all we ever aspired to: normal lives, normal jobs, fitting in, not being noticed . . . Because that was how you earned the right to carry on living. It was how you earned the right to carry on *loving*. We didn't care about stuff or cars or whatever other people seem to spend their lives worrying about. We didn't want anything exceptional, really. It was just the relationships we built . . . the love your father and I shared – the love that we had for each other, all four of us – our friendship. That really was something special. And that's real. That's the stuff that makes life worthwhile.'

Epilogue.

TALL TALE #3: THE LONELY SHEEPDOG.

Did I ever tell you the story of the lonely sheepdog?

Well, once upon a time, a farmer called Jean owned a sheepdog called Butch.

He was what the French call a *patou*, and had been brought up with the sheep from when he was born. As you know, *patou* will do anything to protect their sheep families from rustlers and wolves or even other dogs.

This was a small farm and the farmer only had Butch to keep an eye on his twelve sheep and, as a result, Butch was always very busy. But he was also very lonely.

Sure, he got to spend all day with the sheep, and he loved them and cared for them as if they were his own, but he also sensed that he was different to them. Though he could understand everything the sheep said – because sheep language isn't that complex – the sheep couldn't understand Butch's barking at all.

One day a nearby farmer retired and, because he knew farmer Jean was so poor, he gave him eight sheep to add to his flock, and along with them, his own *patou*, Charlie.

It was only when Butch saw Charlie for the first time that he realised why he'd always felt so alone. Because he wasn't a sheep after all! He was a *patou*, just like Charlie.

Well, as you can imagine, Charlie and Butch were much happier together. While the sheep were grazing they'd frolic around the edges of the field, barking. They'd snap at butterflies in summer, and on cold winter nights they'd huddle together and keep warm.

But Charlie, who'd grown up with brothers and sisters, wanted something more. Charlie wanted a puppy of his own.

Now because both Butch and Charlie were boy-dogs, making a puppy together was impossible. A puppy was the one thing Charlie wanted, and it was the only thing Butch couldn't give him.

Still, they did their best to be contented, working to look after the sheep. But occasionally Butch would catch Charlie staring into the distance, and he could tell that Charlie was dreaming about the puppy he'd never have.

One summer's day – there was a gentle breeze fanning the leaves – Butch heard barking coming from a far corner of the field. Worried there might be some kind of danger to the sheep, he bounded across the field, only to discover a tiny puppy beneath a bush on the other side of the fence. The puppy looked dirty and hungry, so Butch barked loudly until Charlie and the farmer came over to see what was wrong.

'Where did you come from, little one?' farmer Jean said, reaching over the fence and scooping the muddy bundle up in his arms. The tiny puppy licked the farmer's face, making him laugh.

Butch noticed that Charlie behaved strangely. He didn't bark, and he didn't whine. He simply stared at the puppy like he wanted to eat him, and as the farmer crossed the field, taking the puppy home, Charlie followed him at heel, never letting the puppy out of his sight. When the farmer passed through the gate to the house, Charlie sat watching through the fence, and when the farmer vanished inside the house, Charlie sat and stared at the front door.

For three whole days, Charlie didn't move from that spot. He wouldn't eat or drink or help with the sheep, so Butch had to do everything alone. And because it seemed as if Charlie was more interested in the puppy than he was in his own best friend, Butch ended up feeling jealous and sad.

On the fourth day, the farmer opened the front door and crossed the garden. In his arms he was holding the little dog, tiny and still a bit thin, but now clean and fluffy after a bath.

Standing behind the gate, farmer Jean smiled down at Charlie. 'Is it this chap you're waiting for?' he asked, and Charlie wagged his tail. 'Well, is it?' he asked again, and this time Charlie rolled on to his back and kicked his legs in the air.

The farmer laughed. 'Well, let's see what sort of parent you are,' he said, and he leaned over the gate to place the puppy on the ground. 'I've called him Gooseberry,' he said. 'After all, you did find him under a bush.'

Charlie started licking him immediately, and Gooseberry barked and wagged his tail in delight.

'Don't let him bother the sheep!' the farmer said, and Charlie barked in a complex way, doing his best to convey that of course he wouldn't let him bother the sheep. After all, he was a *patou*!

Because he feared that Charlie loved Gooseberry more than he loved him, Butch felt nervous about their newly expanded family. But as time went by, he discovered something important: that love isn't like a cake. It doesn't get smaller when you give bits of it away. Love is more like a tree. The more you nurture it, the bigger it grows. So though Charlie had nothing but love to give to Gooseberry, it was a kind of love that grew so big it spilled over into his relationship with Butch, nourishing them all.

No one ever found out where Gooseberry had come from, but in the end they were all thankful he'd appeared, because he made their lives complete.

From that day on the three dogs, Butch, Charlie and Gooseberry, were inseparable. Charlie and Butch finally had everything they'd ever wanted, the love and friendship they provided to each other, a big, woolly sheep family to keep them warm on cold winter nights, and an excitable puppy they could raise as their own.

So you see, it wasn't the story of a lonely sheepdog after all. It was the story of three of the happiest dogs on the planet.

AUTHOR'S NOTE

Though this novel is a work of fiction the original concept was inspired by the brave testimony of Pierre Seel (1923–2005), the only French homosexual to have testified about his experience of deportation.

Unlike the Pierre described within the pages of this novel, Pierre Seel did not escape Alsace but was tortured and deported to Vorbruck-Schirmeck concentration camp, where he was starved and horrifically mistreated. While there he was made to witness the murder of his lover, Jo, killed by guard dogs, and on release was forcibly enlisted in the German army and sent to fight on the Russian Front. His tragic life story is told in *I, Pierre Seel, Deported Homosexual: A Memoir of Nazi Terror*, a recommended read for anyone wishing to know more. Also recommended is *Branded by the Pink Triangle* by Ken Setterington, along with the excellent documentary *Paragraph 175*, which is available from multiple streaming services.

ABOUT THE AUTHOR

Photo © 2016 Rosie Aston-Snow

Nick Alexander was born in 1964 in the UK. He has travelled widely and has lived and worked both in the UK, the USA and France, where he resides today. *Perfectly Ordinary People* is his seventeenth novel. Nick is the author of multiple international bestsellers, including *Things We Never Said*, *The Photographer's Wife* and *The Other Son*. Nick's novels have been translated into French, German, Italian, Spanish, Norwegian, Turkish, Croatian and Estonian. Nick lives in the southern French Alps with his partner, four cats and three trout.